## IN THE BELLY OF THE TERRORIST BEAST!

Cross lost the revolver and stepped back, drawing the Tanto from its sheath on his chest, the Gerber BMF from the sheath on his belt. Men charged toward him, anger and hatred having replaced reason and tactics.

There was an explosion louder than the rest now, chunks of granite falling into the tunnel, men screaming, barely audible over it.

Cross saw Hughes, the Gerber fighting knife in his left hand, the Walther P-38 in his right, a tongue of flame leaping from it in the swirling dust of the collapsing ceiling; a man down, the knife hacking outward, opening a throat.

Babcock's right hand was moving like a snake, the Bali-Song there opening and closing, slashing faces and hands, his left hand holding his Beretta inverted, using the butt like a bludgeon . . .

# SURGICAL STRIKE

## JERRY AHERN

CHARTER BOOKS, NEW YORK

SURGICAL STRIKE

A Charter Book/published by arrangement with
the author

PRINTING HISTORY
Charter edition/June 1988

ISBN: 1-55773-036-9

Charter Books are published by The Berkley Publishing Group,
200 Madison Avenue, New York, New York 10016.
The name "CHARTER" and the "C" logo
are trademarks belonging to Charter Communications, Inc.
PRINTED IN THE UNITED STATES OF AMERICA

10  9  8  7  6  5  4  3  2  1

*For Samantha and Jason, growing up in an uncertain world—here's hoping it gets a little better . . .*

# Author's Note

The victims of terrorists are usually peaceful people—teachers, businesspersons, the clergy, persons from all walks of life who bear no personal responsibility for the self-supposed injustices on account of which the self-styled "freedom fighters" torture, maim, and kill. There are peaceful means to settle redress and to achieve social progress. When peaceful means have been exhausted, and only then, do those who have just grievances have the right and obligation to seek other than peaceful solutions. And in such dire straits, civilized men—to include men and women of all races, religions and ethnic backgrounds—fight while making every possible effort to avoid the wholesale slaughter of noncombatants and the historic segments of society that are spared from combat, that is, civilian women, children, the elderly, the infirm, members of the clergy, etc.

In recent decades we have seen children employed as assassins, seen the bombings of crowded shopping areas, the submachine-gunning of schoolchildren on their buses. We have seen a return to barbarism on an unprecedented scale.

In books and in films we have seen heroes of all types and for all reasons combat this social pestilence. And, in reality, of course, there is the inspiration of the Israeli commando raid on Entebbe, the daring of the British SAS and other elite units.

But so many innocent lives go unavenged.

So many, that I wondered what would it be like if one of the victims had the chance to become the avenger?

Here is his story.

Jerry Ahern
Commerce, Georgia
January 1987

# SURGICAL STRIKE

# *Prologue*

The rain was heavier now. He sat in the car with the wind-shield wipers shut off and watched the yellow parking lot arc lights. The way the rain distorted the lights, the world outside the nine-year-old Ford almost looked pretty. Abe Cross smoked his cigarette, the window on the driver's side cracked a half inch to clear the smoke. His left arm was soaked from the rain, the left leg of his pants wet from the rain too. He left the window open and inhaled the smoke along with the rain smell and the warm smell of the night and the smell of rotting garbage. His grandfather had taught him to smell rain. But that had been a very long time ago.

The car radio was still playing, and Cross didn't want to shut it off because the radio almost never worked anymore, and when it did, all he could usually get was elevator music. But tonight, maybe because of the heaviness of the low clouds, he had been able to tune in that one station that played the jazz stuff that was so slow and easy and so alive. He could never get it on the radio in the apartment.

So he closed his eyes, smoked his cigarette down, the lighted end burning his first and second finger a little but not so badly that he felt like tossing the butt into the rain. And he listened to the bounce of timpani sticks on the vibes. . . .

If he got out of it alive, he wanted to make it so that GI's traveling aboard civilian aircraft anywhere in the Middle East would carry passports rather than military I.D.; their military I.D. could be transhipped separately to their destination.

Cross had noticed the eyes of the rat-faced one when the rat-faced man and the plain acne-faced woman had come around collecting passports and he'd given them his United States Navy ID. There had been a long pause while the man looked at it, then looked at him. The man had said nothing. Neither had Cross.

They had come back an hour later and collected all of the valuables, taking the wedding ring off the finger of the pregnant French girl—she could hardly have been twenty—who sat behind him. She couldn't get the ring off, and the rat-faced one had said in his bad English that they would cut the finger off if the ring did not come off. Cross had then spoken his first words to the rat-faced man, or to any of them. "Wait a minute. I can get it off her finger," and he'd taken the girl's finger in his hands and used shaving soap from his flight bag to ease the ring from her swollen finger.

They had taken his Rolex Sea-Dweller, his wallet, the money clip he had inherited from his grandfather.

A blond-haired woman across the aisle had protested when the acne-faced woman had started to rip a chain from her small daughter's throat. The acne-faced woman struck her in the face with the butt of her pistol, and dragged the little girl into the aisle.

He had started to get out of his seat and do something. He didn't know what. The rat-faced man had rammed the telescoped butt stock of a submachine gun into his stomach, and he doubled over to the floor, watching while the acne-faced woman slapped the little girl a few times and then ripped the chain from the little girl's neck. There was a mezuzah on the chain. The acne-faced woman spat on it. He saw the submachine gun when the muzzle of it was pressed against the tip of his nose. It was an Uzi. That an Israeli gun should be used to hold him back from helping a little girl who wore a symbol of the Jewish faith around her neck struck him almost as sharply as the butt of the submachine gun.

He let himself be thrown back into his seat. The blond woman was bleeding badly, and when she hugged the sobbing little girl to her, the little girl's dress became covered in front with blood. The dress had been white.

The flight had originated in what he'd already known to be one of the most irresponsibly managed airports in the world: Athens, Greece. There was irony here, too, in that the U.S. air base in Athens used the same runways, as did Soviet Aeroflot jets. The flight had made it as far as the Adriatic coast of Albania, as best he could judge it, when two men and two women appeared from the back of the aircraft, running along the aisles, shouting for everyone to keep their heads down, shouting that they had guns and grenades and would kill anyone who interfered.

He had seen at least one grenade, the pin out, and seen at least four guns, the women carrying the pistols and the men carrying the submachine guns. A woman, who would have been very pretty if the insane look in her black eyes could be ignored, was the one with the grenade, her pistol shoved into the waistband of a full skirt and making her look rather silly. But there were always the eyes, and there was nothing silly about her eyes.

The first-class passengers were herded into the tourist-class cabin. All except one, who was kept beside the woman with the grenade and the insane eyes.

At first he had thought this man, very Arab-looking, was one of the hijackers; until he had noticed the way the man's limbs shook, and after a while, the wet stain at the front of the man's pants.

The 727 had diverged from its original course, and instead of the short hop to Rome, had started across the Mediterranean. The fourth hijacker, who was clean-featured and almost western-looking, had announced something about everyone aboard being the prisoners of some group with an unpronounceable-sounding name, that anyone who resisted would be killed, and that anyone who was Jewish needed to be ready to report to the first-class cabin when called.

It was announced that they would land in Algeria, but that never happened, the aircraft circling for what Cross judged a half hour—he'd been robbed of his watch somewhere over the Med—and then flying on.

He began betting with himself that they would land in

Libya, but he could share his thoughts with no one because they weren't allowed to speak, except for the still bleeding blond-haired woman and the little girl who still sobbed. So, except for the little incidental noises of the aircraft, the occasional sounds of the footsteps of the hijackers as they moved about the aircraft, the rattle of a swivel on the one submachine gun that had a sling, and the crying and soft whispering between the injured girl and the injured woman, there was no sound at all.

Until the argument by the food-preparation station just aft of his seat. Cross could pick out the word "Tripoli," and he heard something that he knew was profanity in Arabic, though he didn't know exactly what the phrase meant.

The aircraft had begun banking a few minutes before, and the rat-faced man grabbed the injured woman, shoved her little girl into the seat, and dragged the woman up the aisle by her blond hair.

Cross started to get up again, but felt the prodding of the acne-faced woman's pistol beside his right ear. Then she hit him with the pistol and he slumped forward, his ear feeling warm and cold at the same time. He could see blood dribbling down onto his right thigh and to the cabin floor.

He heard the public-address announcement about a half hour later. "We will be landing at a place of safety, where we will be met by many of our comrades. Remain perfectly still."

There was a smell, and the older woman beside him began to cry. As he shifted his eyes to see what was wrong, he realized she'd urinated right there in her seat and was crying out of shame and terror.

The plane started to land, and the man who wasn't rat-faced told everyone to keep their heads down and lock their hands behind their necks in a crash position. He then walked up and down the aisle, checking to see that everyone had obeyed his instructions.

As the aircraft landed, Cross looked up and along the aisle, and saw the woman with the wild eyes and the grenade drag the Arab with the urine-stained pants out of one of the front seats and into the aisle.

She had covered her almost-black hair and most of her face

with something that looked like a small, heavy shawl. And for the first time he heard her speak. "The American Satan is evil, but not so evil as those who pretend to be our brothers and serve the Great Satan." She handed the grenade to the man who had spoken over the PA, and the rat-faced man ordered everyone to sit up but to keep their hands locked behind their necks.

Cross sat up and dizziness washed over him.

The acne-faced woman stationed herself at the back, by the stewardess station, and moved the muzzle of her submachine gun.

The good-looking man who now held the grenade ordered, "Everyone will look forward!"

Cross looked forward.

The woman with the insane eyes took the pistol from the waistband of her skirt, worked the slide, put the muzzle of it about two inches from the terrified Arab's right eye, and pulled the trigger. Blood and brains and bone fragments sprayed onto the bulkhead and all over the still-bleeding blond woman who'd been dragged forward earlier.

Then she was dragged out of her seat, and tripped over the body of the dead Arab that had fallen into the aisle. The woman with the insane eyes spoke again. "The Jew occupiers of Palestine are the enemies of all oppressed peoples."

He started to his feet because he knew what they were going to do. He tried to go for the acne-faced girl with the Uzi submachine gun, but the gun muzzle cracked him across the right cheek and the bridge of the nose and he fell. As he rolled to his knees in the aisle, the Jewish woman screamed. The one with the insane eyes shot her in the mouth, and her body flopped back into the seat as if she were exhausted and just sitting down.

The plane had been taxiing all the while.

He felt it in his stomach when the aircraft finally stopped.

And he saw a pair of women's white tennis shoes and darkly suntanned legs, and raised his eyes to the level of the hem of the pale blue skirt.

Cross heard her say, "Tell us your mission."

He didn't have a mission. "I'm going home for Christmas to my aunt's house in the States."

"Liar. American bastard liar."

"I'm going home to my aunt's house for Christmas."

"Why do you not go to your father's house?"

"He's dead. So's my mom."

"Stand up, American pig."

He stood up. She was holding his ID card. "Abraham Kelsoe Cross, United States Navy. You are an officer."

He didn't speak.

"A lieutenant."

He didn't speak. He watched her eyes. Behind her, through one of the windows—the shades never pulled down—he could see men and equipment moving up across what looked like a desert.

"What do you do in the United States Navy?" she said, and spat into his face.

He tried to think of something innocuous. "Personnel. I work in Personnel."

"Liar."

There was a hint of laughter in the muscles around her eyes, but not in the eyes themselves. Because of the head covering she wore, he could see nothing of the rest of her face. She took the still-sobbing little girl from her seat and put the pistol to the little girl's right temple. The little girl stopped crying and looked up at him.

He tried to smile at the child.

"Tell me what you do. Your skin is nearly as dark as my own. You have strong-looking arms."

He didn't speak.

She moved the pistol closer to the little girl's temple.

She was going to kill him anyway, and if he lied again, she would just murder the little girl. "I command a SEAL team."

"An American spy," she said matter-of-factly.

"No, ma'am. I'm not a spy, and all I'm doing is going home for Christmas."

"Take him into the back of the aircraft," she ordered.

The rat-faced man and the other woman put their hands on his arms and started to pull him away. Cross thought for one fleeting second that he could try for it, but the woman with the insane eyes genuinely smiled as she shifted the muzzle of the pistol she held from the little girl's temple to beneath his nose. She forced his mouth open then. The pistol was coppery tasting and very cold, the taste of his own blood, salty and mixing with this coppery taste. It felt as though she had broken some of his teeth.

They dragged him backward along the aisle. He lost his balance, and when he started to fall, the pistol was rammed deeper into his mouth and he started to gag. He was on his knees now.

The woman with the crazy eyes left the pistol in his mouth, taking the acne-faced woman's pistol, saying something that he didn't understand. Then the acne-faced woman took the pistol that was in his mouth, slipped her right first finger into the trigger guard and just held it there. The rat-faced man walked back down the aisle with the other woman.

The acne-faced woman spit in Cross's face, and he blinked his eyes against the spittle. She ordered him to put his hands on top of his head and lock his fingers together. Cross obeyed her.

He was in the small compartment that served as the kitchen; he could see the small oven where food would be heated, the refrigerator, the hatchway used for servicing the kitchen. Already he was starting to fantasize a plan—to formulate one when all that was needed to end his life was a twitch of the finger, would have been insanity. But if they took the pistol from his mouth—when, he told himself—he could—

His heart sank. Keffiyeh-clad men were boarding from the front of the aircraft. They wore mixed fatigues, rumpled sports clothes, and carried AK-47 assault rifles and Uzis.

As a half dozen of them moved along the length of the aisle, one or another would stop to strike a passenger or drag a passenger from his seat, stare at them for a moment, then throw him or her back into the seat. If the hands of the passenger didn't reclasp behind the neck immediately, punishment was dealt out.

The woman with the insane eyes, and two of the dozen or so men who had just boarded the aircraft, came to where Cross knelt.

He looked up. The woman was showing the two men his ID card, and he heard her saying something about his being a SEAL.

The good-looking man who held the grenade joined them, and so did the rat-faced man, the newcomers now holding the rest of the passengers at bay. They formed a circle around Cross.

One of the two newcomers who had come to the rear of the aircraft with the crazy-eyed woman spoke in nearly unaccented English. "So. You are one of the Navy commandoes. Why, tell me, is a Christian pig named after the Prophet Abraham? Remove the gun from his mouth so he may answer me."

The acne-faced woman took the gun from his mouth, but spit in his face once more. As he blinked the spit from his eyes, Cross saw the man with the grenade replace the pin, to lock the spoon to the body of the grenade.

"I asked you to tell me something, Lieutenant. Tell me."

Cross looked up at the man, the man's AK-47 slung beneath his right arm, the man's hands long-fingered and almost womanly graceful. His face was well-featured, his eyes gray.

"I was named after my grandfather. He was named after Abraham Lincoln."

"A great man, Abraham Lincoln, but unfortunately an unbeliever. You realize we will kill you."

"Why?" Cross asked. There was nothing to lose, he felt.

"That is a logical question, under the circumstances. You may feel the answer is less than logical, I'm afraid. But the American military must understand that there can be no hope of defeating us. One cannot defeat an idea with force."

"Then you can't defeat our ideas by killing me." It sounded logical, Cross thought, grasping.

"And what are your ideas which we cannot defeat, Lieutenant?"

"Truth. Justice."

"Do not forget the 'American way.' Perhaps if you believe in Superman, yes—but I abandoned all childish fantasy when I abandoned childhood, when my parents were killed, my home 'burned, my friends murdered. Have you ever been beaten very badly?"

Cross didn't know what to answer.

"Perhaps not." The man smiled. "Well, then I will share this with you. Let yourself sink into the pain, abandon all hope of survival. Let your consciousness ebb quickly. Become one with the pain and it will be easier. Good-bye.''

Cross licked his lips.

The well-spoken, gray-eyed man walked forward along the aisle.

The rat-faced man and the other newcomer held Cross's arms back so far that he felt they would be ripped from their sockets. The acne-faced woman took the pistol from the woman with the crazy eyes, who dropped to her knees in front of him and looked him square in the face. "I will beat you. It is more degrading for a man to be beaten to death by a woman. But resist me. Perhaps I will tire and you will live that much longer.''

She was taking his belt from his pants as she spoke. Then she doubled it and stood up. It was a wide belt, the leather heavy, the kind worn with blue jeans and a trophy buckle. She stood back from him a little, and as she started the swing, he involuntarily closed his eyes to protect them. The stinging of the belt across his face was the sharpest pain he'd ever endured.

She struck him again and again with the belt, and Cross realized he was screaming and that he couldn't keep from screaming. He tried to tuck his head down, but the blows from the belt crashed down then against the top of his head, the side of his head, his neck. He felt a hand drag his head up, back, fingers balled tightly in his hair. The belt kept hitting him—she kept hitting him. His lips felt so swollen that they had to be larger than his entire face. He thought that if he opened his eyes, he wouldn't be able to see, because his face felt so horribly swollen. He was choking, he realized, on his own blood. His head was let go. His head sagged forward to his chest. His arms were loosed and he fell forward, vomiting.

Cross felt his lower body being kicked, but didn't, couldn't open his eyes. He threw up again, knowing there wasn't anything to vomit anymore except blood, but still vomiting anyway. No one kicked him, and he was left to lie in his bloody mess, he felt a sudden clarity he had never felt before. He was going to die, and the way he was going to die would bring an infinity of pain. If he waited for them to kill him, he would have to wait until he drowned in the pain.

Abe Cross tried to open his eyes. He was able to, but only a little bit, as if squinting against a strong sun. He didn't dare move his head. But he could see the tennis shoes and the tanned legs of the woman who was beating him to death. His fingers would still flex. He inhaled, coughed, his throat and lungs burning.

Cross threw his body weight up and back, his right hand punching upward under the hem of the blue skirt, along the tanned thighs and into her crotch as his left hand grabbed for the pistol that had to be there. He remembered her putting it back into her waistband.

The pistol was an FN/Browning High Power, and his left fist closed over it as the insane-eyed woman screamed from his right fist's tight grip on her underpants, pubic hair, and flesh. Cross yanked, and she fell toward him as he tore the gun free and worked the hammer back, praying she hadn't cleared the slide. He jerked his finger against the trigger, the muzzle of the pistol almost touching her left cheek. His eyes closed involuntarily, his ears ringing with the gunshot in the confined space, the skin of his face unable to feel, but his hands and throat feeling the stickiness of the blood spray.

As his eyes opened, her body fell against him, covering him.

The acne-faced woman stabbed her pistol toward him. She fired again and again, Cross feeling the dead woman's body over him jerking with the hits. He punched the pistol upward and fired, the slide ripping the dead woman's hair out by the roots as it caught in it. The pistol flew from the acne-faced woman's right hand and she fell backward into the aisle.

Cross was to his knees, to his feet.

The newcomer was bringing his AK-47 up. Cross didn't have time to raise the pistol, so he rammed it into the terrorist's testicles and fired, the man screaming as his body rocked back against the rat-faced man.

Cross saw the good-looking one coming at him over the acne-faced woman's dead body, the grenade in his right fist, his left hand grasping for the pin, jerking it clear. Cross threw himself over the dead woman and into the man's chest, his right fist closing over the spoon of the grenade, his left fist hammering the butt of the High Power down against the man's face, smashing the bridge of the nose as the once-handsome man screamed like a woman.

Cross had the grenade, the pin lost. He swung the man toward the kitchen service door, stuffing the grenade down the front of the man's pants and letting the spoon snap away as he twisted the man around and threw his body against the door.

Cross jumped back against the starboard bulkhead. There was a lavatory there, and he swung the door open and threw himself inside as the grenade went off and chunks of human flesh and globs of blood sprayed along the aisle.

The fuselage door had blown open. Cross started for it, slipping in the blood, losing his balance. The rat-faced man, covered with blood and idefinable gore, came at him with a knife. Cross rolled into the blown-open hatchway and fired the High Power twice, then twice more.

He half fell through the opening in the fuselage.

After a moment he realized his mouth was filled with sand and that he was on his back. In the fuselage doorway he saw another of the newcomers, and Cross raised the pistol. It would be too late because the man already had his AK-47 to his hip. Cross stabbed the gun toward him and fired out the magazine, the desert sun so bright, Cross could barely see him, the bullets rippling along the chest, the body falling back as the AK discharged, chunks of insulating material sprayed outward from the cabin roof onto the desert floor.

Before he realized he was doing it, Cross was running, away from the aircraft, the empty High Power in his left fist still, the slide locked open. There was a U.S. surplus Jeep dead ahead of him, and he threw himself into the run, his lungs aching with the exertion. The man behind the wheel of the Jeep tossed back the face covering made from the tail of the keffiyeh with his left hand, his right hand dragging a pistol from a tanker-style chest holster.

Cross sprang for the Jeep, but he had misjudged the distance, his shins banging into the body work, his body jackknifing forward. The terrorist, or whatever he was, had the pistol almost clear. Cross dragged himself to his knees on the front passenger seat and rammed the pistol into the man's face, the bared barrel gouging into the man's left eye. Cross's right hand moved cross body to lock the man's gun-hand wrist back. The man shrieked with pain. Cross tore the pistol from the eye socket and hammered it down against the man's forehead again and again, the resistance from the man's gun hand suddenly gone. Cross looked back once. Men who had been surrounding the aircraft were running toward him, and men from inside the aircraft were streaming out both the front and rear fuselage doorways.

Cross threw down the empty High Power and worked loose the knife that hung from the man's pistol belt. It was an M-16 bayonet. The man was either dead or unconscious. Cross raked the knife across his throat to settle that, the knife glistening with blood. Then he used it to hack apart the straps that harnessed the tanker holster to the terrorist's chest.

Cross rolled the body back past the wheel. The keys were in the ignition, and he let the body fall away as he slipped behind the wheel and tried gunning the engine to life. It didn't turn over. "Shit," he snarled, not looking back. He held his breath and tried again. The Jeep started.

He threw it into gear, popping the brake and clutch simultaneously. The Jeep lurched ahead. Before the aircraft had landed, he'd sneaked a look through one of the uncurtained windows and guessed they were coming down near the Gulf of Sidra. He hoped they were. He glanced skyward now, his swollen eyes squinting tightly against the sun, as he tried to figure which way was north.

Gunfire from behind him. He could hear bullets ricocheting off the Jeep's body work.

Any attempt to rescue the passengers would have resulted in a bloodbath within the narrow confines of the aircraft, and if the pilot had attempted to take off, the aircraft would have been shot down, if the tires weren't shot out first and the aircraft even got off the ground.

Cross thought about that now, about the little girl whose mother had been murdered, the old woman who had peed in her clothes because she wasn't allowed to get up, and the pregnant girl with the swollen fingers.

"Damnit!" He screamed the word through his puffed lips and into the desert.

Gunfire answered him.

He kept driving.

The tanker holster. He tore the pistol the rest of the way from it and worked open the hook and pile fastener over the spare magazine pouch, freeing the magazine, tossing the holster out of the side of the Jeep.

The pistol was another High Power. He figured the number of shots to be thirteen, at least, or maybe fourteen in the pistol and thirteen rounds in the spare magazine. Twenty-six or twenty-seven rounds, and an M-16 bayonet. He glanced at the fuel gauge. It showed half full.

The Jeep's windshield was turned down and sand blown on the scorching desert wind assaulted his face—and now he could feel again, the stinging of the sand heightening sensation until the numbness of his pain from the belt lashing vanished. The pain washed over him, his stomach knotting; the pain so intense that it was a struggle to breathe, to see, to keep from passing into unconsciousness.

Cross turned his face. Beside him, almost dead even with him, was a two-and-a-half-ton truck, the tarp covering over the bed flapping wildly in the slipstream, no one in the bed. Aside from the driver, there was a bareheaded man with an Uzi hanging from the passenger-side running board. Cross jacked back the High Power's hammer and fired, then fired again and again. The big west-coast mirror to which the man clung shattered. Submachine-gun fire ripped across the hood of the Jeep, the windshield disintegrating into a shower of glass fragments. Cross averted his eyes, nearly losing control of the Jeep. More submachine-gun fire, Cross making the Jeep zig-zag across the sand now, then steadying the vehicle as he stabbed the pistol across his body and fired toward the submachine gunner. The Uzi in the man's hands went wild, and the magazine emptied into the sand in what seemed like a second as the man's body toppled from the running board. The truck lurched as the rear wheels rolled over him, cutting his scream short.

The Jeep was going as fast as Cross could make it go.

The truck was edging closer—to ram him, he knew. He

started to fire the pistol toward the truck cab, to get the driver. The truck's right front tire impacted the left side of the Jeep, and then Cross cut the wheel hard right, trying to get away. He fired the High Power, but to aim it would have been impossible. The truck swung away, then veered toward him again. He emptied the High Power, shattering the truck's windshield in two or three places, but the truck still kept coming. He cut the wheel hard right, but the truck picked up speed, the right front tire hammering into the Jeep's left rear fender. Cross tried cutting the wheel, but suddenly the steering was gone and the Jeep was starting to turn over. He grabbed the pistol tighter in his fist and jumped.

The sand slapped up toward him, and he rolled, coughing as he swallowed sand, realizing he was still alive. He couldn't breathe for a second, gasping, spitting sand. The Jeep was now a few yards ahead of him, cartwheeling across a low dune; the truck was turning a sharp left. He caught his breath, spitting more sand as the truck heeled over, crashing down as it nearly attained the height of the dune.

He got to his feet, with the pistol, the spare magazine in his pocket. He'd lost the bayonet. Cross started running in the direction the Jeep and the truck had been going, hoping it was still north. His right thumb found the Browning's magazine release and dumped the empty, his left hand ramming the spare up the magazine well. He worked the slide release down—it was stiff, and he had to tug back on the slide to get the pistol into battery. He kept running.

The ground was rising ahead and he leaned into the run, his stomach locking, his shins stiffening, his lungs feeling hollow, burning. He kept running. . . .

A tenor sax was wailing into the night, and Cross snapped the cigarette through the open door into a puddle where a Styrofoam cup floated almost lazily. Then he killed the engine, wondering if he'd ever get the song back. He stepped out of the Ford and into the rain, pocketing his keys, slamming the door shut behind him. He hadn't done anything about raising the window, but the seat was wet already and so was he. He aimed himself toward the "Now Open 24 Hours, 7 Days, for Your Convenience" supermarket about a hundred yards away and started searching his blue jeans pockets for another cigarette. . . .

There was another Jeep closing on him, and he told himself he wouldn't look back anymore, just keep running. There had been five men in the Jeep, counting the driver.

Cross kept running, the ground rising sharply now, the horizon line a bright blue, and jagged as a saw blade. If the Gulf lay beyond it—

He could hear the roar of the Jeep's engine—whoever was driving it redlining the engine compression, he thought. He kept running.

Gunfire tore into the sand near his feet, and he threw himself up over a ridge of sand and bleached white rocks and rolled onto his stomach, the High Power in both fists straight out ahead of him as the Jeep bounced over the brow of the dune. He fired, and the driver's hands went to his head, blood oozing between the splayed fingers, the whole thing happening almost in freeze frame as he watched it, the Jeep crashing down, one of the remaining four men bouncing out. Cross shot him while he was still airborne.

On his feet once more, Cross started running again, the horizon line nearing.

More gunfire, and his right leg went out from under him. He pitched into the sand, rolling onto his back, firing the High Power toward the man who held the AK-47. Cross's eyes filled with a fine spray of sand as the AK discharged again, the man's body toppling back.

Onto his knees, crawling. To his feet, his eyes burning and then starting to tear. He turned back, squinting to see, the fourth man from the Jeep diving toward him bare-handed. The man's fingers locked over Cross's throat as Cross fell back under his weight. Cross's right knee smashed up, and he punched the Browning toward the man's chest as the man rolled off, doubled up at the groin from the knee smash. Cross fired once, and the Browning's slide locked open, empty.

He got up from his knees, lurching toward the horizon line. His right leg was on fire, blood pumping from his thigh.

The voice he heard behind him—the fifth man—was the voice of the one with the gray eyes.

"You are a brave fighter."

Cross let his shoulders drop as he turned to face his pursuer. The gray-eyed man held an Uzi submachine gun. What had happened to the AK-47 that he'd carried earlier didn't concern Cross.

"Fuck you," Cross shouted, and hurled the empty High Power toward the man, throwing his body down and forward into the sand as the Uzi discharged. Uzis had a fast cyclic rate—too fast, Cross had always thought. As he hauled himself up and toward the gray-eyed man, the Uzi dumped into the sand between them. The gray-eyed man's left cheek was streaming blood where the empty pistol had hit him. Cross's hands went for the eyes as the man's hands went for a knife. Cross's left thumb pressured the gray-eyed man's right eye, but a knee smash caught him in the stomach and winded him. Cross lost his grip, both of them falling into the sand, rolling down along the ridge that led toward the sea. For an instant Cross could see it far below, and then he could only see the hatred in the gray-eyed man's face.

The knife stabbed downward. Cross felt it slice across the top of his right shoulder as his left fist hammered up and caught bone, the gray-eyed man's head snapping back.

Cross was to his feet.

Over the dune ridge he could see another Jeep coming, a Browning .50 mounted in the rear, and another two-and-a-half-ton truck—but the truck bed was loaded with men this time—humping over the ridgeline right behind it.

His gray-eyed adversary lunged for him. Cross sidestepped awkwardly, dropping, his good left leg sweeping the gray-eyed man's feet from under him. Cross threw himself on the man's back and his opponent, incredibly, rose to his knees. The gray-eyed man's right hand held the knife, but Cross's right hand pinning the man's right arm to his side. The man's left hand curled back, and before Cross could dodge his head out of the way, his hair was caught in the man's fist and his body was being flipped over his opponent's shoulder.

As he flipped, Cross's right hand swept up and caught the gray-eyed man by the right ear, half ripping it from the head, hauling the gray-eyed man over his own shoulder as he impacted the sand. Cross rolled right, coming down on his gun-shot right leg. He heard himself scream, his hands scooping sand, hurtling it into the gray-eyed man's face. Then Cross dove toward him, the man's hands held high, both fists balled over the haft of the Bowie-bladed fighting knife. Cross's hands locked over the gray-eyed man's hands.

Again Cross screamed with pain, as simultaneously he and his opponent stood, their hands still locked together on the knife that was over both their heads. Cross took a knee smash from the gray-eyed man, in the pelvic girdle rather than the testicles. His body twisted so he could snap his left elbow into the gray-eyed man's head.

Cross could see it now—the blue waters of the Gulf below them, perhaps a hundred feet down at the base of a sheer drop, the water dotted with upthrusting rocks, around which white surf lapped; the water looked deep, very blue.

Cross heard the men from the Jeep and the truck shouting in Arabic or something like it. The gray-eyed man was trying to let go of his knife.

Cross's eyes met his eyes.

"You're comin' with me, motherfucker!" And Cross threw his body weight right and over the edge, locked in combat with the gray-eyed man. . . .

Cross took a shopping cart and started into the first aisle, leaning against the cart handle a little heavily. He'd been drinking, then got rid of the feeling of drunkenness with three or four glasses of ice water, then urinated. But the feeling was starting to come back. He tried remembering what he'd done with his cigarette, the one he'd lit in the rain, in the parking lot. He remembered. It had gotten so wet that it had crumpled and fallen apart in his fingertips and he'd snapped it away. His fingers were still marked with little flecks of sticky tobacco, and he wiped it away on the thighs of his wet jeans.

Black-stenciled letters on a white box—generic cornflakes. "Not so bad with beer," he said under his breath, and an older black lady looked at him curiously. Cross looked back and made himself smile. "I said these things aren't too bad with beer. Michelob, anyway.'' He walked on, rubbing his left hand across his face—he'd forgotten to shave again today. Five days: Five or six, he thought.

He was used to odd looks from people. First it had been his face. The welts and bruises and cuts had healed well enough, but the damage to the bone structure had required four operations. Each time after the bandages came off, he would look at himself in a mirror and see himself just as ugly as he'd been before the first operation—the puffiness, the irregularities, and the dark blue and purple and black skin. He'd seen the look of disgust in people's eyes. It looked pretty disgusting to him too. They'd finally gotten the nose right—almost. It would have taken a separate operation to get rid of the bump on its bridge, and they'd told him it would probably have screwed up his sinuses, so he'd taken a pass. It wasn't much of a bump. The knife scar on the left side of his face, just above the upper lip and below the nose, could have been taken care of, too, but he'd always wanted to grow a mustache; so he'd grown one, and unless he trimmed it too short, the scar couldn't be seen. . . .

The water's surface was so hard at the angle he hit that Cross felt as if someone had slammed him into a brick wall. It knocked the wind out of him, and his head ached maddeningly. He was going down, his body twisting, and suddenly the gray-eyed man was there in the water, the knife still in his right hand. Movements were slower underwater. Cross tried to pull back, enough to save his throat, but the point of the Bowie-shaped blade caught in his flesh just below his nose, and as he turned his face away, he felt it rip. . . .

Cross was standing in front of the snacks. He grabbed a bag of pretzel sticks. He grabbed a bag of potato chips. He grabbed a second bag of pretzels, but this time the little ones in the shapes of bows. He'd taught himself, in the last five years, to eat off the outer edges of the loops without making the bow crumble.

He started to reach for a bag of sour cream and onion chips. They always made him belch. He belched now from the beer, just thinking about it. He took the bag of chips and threw it into the cart.

Macaroni-and-cheese dinners—he grabbed six packages and dropped them into the cart. Chocolate pudding, the kind that came in little cans. He took a six-pack and put it into the cart. He came to the beer. "And on the eighth day," he murmured, taking one six-pack of Michelob in bottles, then another, then another and still another, stacking them in the cart, careful not to crush the potato chips and pretzels.

Cross tried to remember if there was anything else he needed, and decided that was pretty much it. The six macaroni-and-cheese dinners were lunch and dinner for three days. He had enough beer and cornflakes, and that was all he ever had when he had breakfast at all.

"Cigarettes," he said to himself, and started toward the front of the store. He squinted up at the lights. It was too damn bright in here, he thought. He was low on whiskey, but there was enough for a few boilermakers when he got home and started watching television, enough to get to sleep on. And they didn't sell the hard stuff in the supermarket. "Hell of a store," he rasped under his breath.

Only one checkout lane was open. The old black lady was ahead of him, and she looked at him with undisguised disdain. He grinned back at her and said, "Hi!" Generic pickles—the big whole kosher dills—were on sale, and he picked up a bottle. To be healthy you needed vegetables, he told himself.

A man in jogging pants and hooded sweatshirt was nearly through unloading his cart; then it would be the old black woman's turn, then his. Cross shrugged, opened the pickle jar and plucked out a pickle. He belched again. The old black lady turned around and wrinkled her nose at him. "Wanna pickle, ma'am?"

She didn't answer him, just turned away.

The open checkout lane was flanked on the right by the service counter, high and paneled and fitted with a sign that said: SERVING YOU ALL THE WAY! Cross's eyes drifted to the girl behind the checkout counter. She wore a smaller version of the sign worked into a name tag over her left breast, where the nipple would just about be. He couldn't read her name, but he wondered what it would be like if she served him all the way. Brunette. He liked that. Good tits, he thought, liking that too. He couldn't see her eyes. The color. It was something left over from the airplane hijacking, but girls with eyes so brown they seemed black turned him off.

The guy in the jogging outfit was through unloading the cart. Little cocktail onions, yogurt, carrots, chicken. "Yuch," Cross growled under his breath. The black lady looked at him again, and he guessed she had pegged him for belching again. He took another bite of the big kosher dill. A little on the sweet side, but okay.

The in door swung open. The first guy with the ski mask had a sawed-off shotgun, and the guy right behind him drew a pistol from under his windbreaker as he jumped over the railing so he could block anybody from leaving. It had looked cool, drawing the pistol in midair like that. The other three guys, all in ski masks, weren't even all the way through the interior door when the first guy, the one with the sawed-off, shouted, "None of you motherfuckers moves or you get this!"

Cross took another bite of his pickle while the guy brandished his shotgun. The guy shouted, superfluously, Cross thought, "This is a robbery!"

"No shit, Sherlock," Cross said aloud. He finished the first pickle and started fishing another one out of the green brine.

The guy with the shotgun pushed past the healthy guy in the jogging clothes. The checker sucked in her breath so hard it sounded like a scream and made her breasts look even bigger. There was a guy in shirt-sleeves behind the service counter that Cross hadn't seen before, but he saw him now, the face going as white as the shirt and the bib of the grocer's apron.

"Open the fuckin' safe, asshole! Move!"

The other three guys had spread themselves out in a kind of fan shape, covering the girl behind the checkout counter and the healthy guy and his yogurt and carrots. Cross shrugged. He'd known guys in the last five years since he'd left the Navy who could have been done in by active cultures or vegetables.

"I can't open the safe. Ahh, I don't know the combination."

The shotgunner brandished his weapon again, rapping the

double barrels down against the service-counter desktop. "Then I blow your damn head all the way off, man!" He rapped the shotgun on the desktop again. "Open the fuckin' safe!"

Cross voiced what he felt was an intelligent, however obvious, observation. "Ahh, safe's can't fuck. Only living things can do that."

The shotgunner wheeled toward him, the little shotgun going up almost to his shoulder. "What?"

"Wanna pickle? They relieve tension. It's like watching tropical fish, man. Lighten up. Have a pickle."

"How about I blow your brains out, shithead?"

Cross shrugged. "Hey, just a suggestion, huh?" He continued eating his pickle.

The shotgunner shifted his interest back to the service desk.

He exchanged more unpleasantries with the store manager in the white shirt, white apron, and white face. The manager looked like he was going to cry or throw up, possibly both, still insisting he didn't have the combination to the safe.

"You're dead!" The shotgunner stepped back from the service desk.

"It's got—got a little slot. The money. You shove it in the slot!"

"Hey." Cross grinned, eating his pickle. "That slot stuff sounds promising. Maybe safes can make it together."

The guy with the shotgun wheeled toward him again. "One more word, asshole—" He grabbed the old black lady's purse from the little infant seat in the back of her cart. She held onto the handles, and the shotgunner raised the shotgun like it was a club and started the downswing for her head.

"Damn," Cross grunted, taking a long, striding step forward and throwing the contents of the half-empty pickle jar into the shotgunner's eyes. Cross's left hand reached up, catching the sawed-off midway along the tubes between the receiver and the raggedly cut muzzles, and ripping the muzzle up at a sharp angle. One hammer fell, and the shotgun discharged, chunks of light fixture and ceiling tiles crashing down, showering Cross with plastic, glass, and insulation.

Cross was between the old black lady and the shotgunner now, the empty pickle jar still in his fist. He slammed it against the side of the shotgunner's face, letting go of it in time before he got a handful of glass, his knee smashed up into the shotgunner's crotch. The shotgunner was down. Cross kicked him in the mouth. The shotgunner was out.

Cross inverted the shotgun and swung the muzzle. "Down, ladies—you, too, jogger," and he had the second hammer back and let the second tube go into the nearest of the three guys covering the jogger. But Cross was already moving as the man he'd just shot fell backward into the detergent display. Some of the boxes were ripped wide open by stray pellets, blue dust rising in a cloud. Cross flipped onto the checkout counter and swung the shotgun tubes into the face of the second of the three, produce guards, then dropped as Cross's left hand cupped the revolver in the man's right hand.

Cross backhanded the empty shotgun into the man's face, then the gun hand went limp and Cross had the revolver in his own fist. He dodged left as the third man fired at him. Cross pitched the shotgun and double-actioned the revolver. It was a Smith & Wesson K-Frame, and from the way it bucked in his fist, he deduced it was loaded with hot .357's. He fired again, the web of his right hand—he had shifted the gun to his right—ached.

"Needs a trigger job, a set of Pachmayrs," he noted under his breath as he threw himself into the soap powder, skidded along the floor, and did a wrist-punishing double tap into the last guy, the one by the door.

The last man's pistol—it sounded like a 9mm and looked like a Colt—discharged into a three-liter bottle of Coke, and the bottle exploded as the man's head slapped into the glass of the exit door too fast for the electric eye to open the door. The glass spiderwebbed and as the body dropped downward, Cross could see bloodstains where cranium had met safety glass. The safety glass had won.

He started to his feet, hearing the scream. He spun toward the sound, almost slipping on the linoleum-tiled floor in the brown and blue and red mixture of Coke, detergent powder, and blood. The shotgunner—the lower part of his face bloodied red, the ski mask partially pulled away, what might have been teeth protruding through under his lower lip—was holding the old black lady against him, a good-sized knife that looked like a switchblade edging into her throat.

"Let her go or you die," Cross told the erstwhile shotgunner honestly.

Cross raised the revolver to eye level, his right arm at maximum extension. He thumbed the hammer back. The man raked the knife across the right side of the old lady's throat and pushed her forward, Cross firing as her carotid artery spurted. And she died. The tomato juice can just behind where her killer's head had been exploded as the .357 hit it.

The killer ran. Toward the rear of the store.

Cross lowered the revolver, saying, "Too slow, Cross. Too many beers. You killed her just like you did it yourself."

The man he'd bludgeoned with the shotgun started to stir, and Cross looked down at him, letting the man get his hand on his pistol—it was a Smith & Wesson 39 series 9mm. As soon as the man's hand closed on the butt of the pistol, Cross shot him in the head, then threw down the empty revolver.

Cross searched his pockets for his cigarettes as he started for the back of the store. He heard a frightened-sounding woman's voice saying, "He can't get out back there, mister. The door to the alley's double locked and bolted."

He heard a man's voice, either the man from behind the service desk or the jogger. "The police are coming." Cross heard the sirens wail.

His cigarettes were sodden, and he threw the pack down to the floor. He passed the rack where the cigarette cartons were and he grabbed a carton of Pall Mall 25's with the red label. He tore open the end of the carton. He'd been meaning to pick up cigarettes anyway. He pulled out a pack and dropped the rest of the carton as he walked toward the rear of the store, down the aisle with videotapes, tampons, toilet paper, and comic books.

It looked like Batman was still hale and hearty, he noticed. No sign of Robin. He had the pack of cigarettes open, fired the Zippo and lit a cigarette, inhaled it hard and stopped walking.

He couldn't see the thing who had slit the old black lady's throat. But he could see the meat department, and unless the thing—it had ceased to be a man, as far as he was concerned—

was hiding behind the open-top meat displays, it was inside the butcher room.

Abe Cross felt the corners of his mouth upturn in a smile. "The right place," he whispered.

He was standing next to a wine display, and he picked up a bottle the size of a fifth. A Rhine wine. He held the thick end of the bottle in his fist and smashed the neck of the bottle against the edge of the meat counter, letting the wine pour out onto the floor. The jagged end of the bottle was what he wanted.

Cross clambered up into the meat counter and stood on two stacks of pork steaks as he looked right and left behind the counter. It wasn't there. He jumped down, the bottle still in his fist.

He walked to his left, toward the swinging door that led into the butcher room.

Cross kicked the door open inward and it stuck that way. "Try real hard and kill me, old lady killer. 'Cause I'm gonna kill you." Cross stepped inside slowly, but it wasn't just inside the door. No meat hung. It was too late or too early. There were butcher knives on the long table at the back of the room near the freezer door, and a hefty-looking Chinese cleaver. He threw down the broken bottle and picked up the cleaver, opening the freezer door with his other hand. It opened outward. "I'm coming for you," Cross said softly, condensation rushing at him from the colder air inside. He stepped inside and his breath made steam as he exhaled. Or was it the cigarette smoke? He remembered that he was still smoking, and the cigarette was in the left corner of his mouth. He spit it out onto the frosted floor.

Dead things hung on hooks to be carved up.

Cross began walking again.

The freezer was longer than it was wide, and the meat hung so close on both sides of him that his shoulders nudged against it as he walked.

He could feel it before he saw it—or maybe it was that his reaction time was getting really slow, he thought absently. The thing that had slit the old black lady's throat came at him with a meat hook in the right hand and a pathetic el-cheapo switchblade in the left. Cross dodged right and swung a hanging side of beef into the thing, and when the thing started to fall back, Cross turned halfway on his right foot and his left leg snapped up and out, double kicking into the thing's crotch.

The meat hook and the switchblade dropped from its hands as it fell.

Cross was standing over it.

It pleaded. "Hey, no man—it was an accident killin' the nigger woman, man."

Cross smiled. "Resorting to racial slurs denotes a want of vocabulary." Cross's foot crushed down into its chest and his hand grabbed away the ski mask just enough to knot his fingers into sweaty, greasy brown hair. Cross's arm arced downward with the Chinese cleaver, to where the neck and the shoulder joined and death would be pretty fast—but not real fast.

There was a sort of scream, but it never really made it all the way. Cross dropped the cleaver and left the freezer, wiping his hands of blood and hair tonic on a clean butcher's apron hanging by the freezer door on the outside.

He slammed the freezer door shut so the meat wouldn't spoil.

He walked out of the butcher room and around behind the meat counter.

There was a small pastry section just opposite the meat counter, and he picked up a package of chocolate cupcakes and opened it slowly. . . .

Cross and the gray-eyed terrorist had fought under the surface of the water for so long that Cross had felt that his lungs would burst. All the while, blood had streamed from the cut below his nose and over his lip. His right leg didn't want to move anymore. And the saltwater was eating at the wounds that had become his face.

The gray-eyed man made a swipe with the knife again, and Cross caught the knife hand in both of his and twisted the fingers back. He had the knife. He made for the surface, the gray-eyed clinging to him to drag him down.

Cross's head broke water, and he gasped air as he hauled his knife arm up. The gray-eyed man's head broke the surface and Cross hacked downward with the knife, the blade biting deep where the neck met the right shoulder. . . .

The police sirens were really loud now, and Cross realized the booze was hitting him now that the adrenaline rush was down and he sat with his back to the meat counter and ate one of the chocolate cupcakes.

The police were walking down the aisle toward him, their dark uniforms neatly pressed, their revolvers in their hands, their bodies crouched, one of them even carrying a riot shotgun.

"Freeze, sucker!" The voice sounded more like a pre-pubescent twelve-year-old's than a man's voice. Cross didn't do anything except start eating the second cupcake.

# Chapter One

"We gave that guy a blood test, right—see what he was high on? No drugs. Just booze. Enough alcohol in this guy Cross's bloodstream to put a whole St. Patrick's Day parade under the table."

Wendell LeBrie looked down at the computer printout in his hands and then up at Dr. Hale's brown face. "Doc, you wanna know who this fella Cross is?"

"Escaped psychopath, right? But even money he's got some kinda special military experience."

"Got that right," LeBrie replied, swung his legs down from his desk, stood up and walked toward his solitary window. It was still dark, and he could see his face in reflection on the dirty glass. His blond hair was thinner, and his face fatter than it used to be. "Abraham Kelsoe Cross. He was a lieutenant in the U.S. Navy, it says, some kinda special warfare whatever."

"A SEAL?"

"Yeah, I guess. Born in 1952."

"Jeez, he looks like he's in his forties," Hale said, sitting down on the corner of LeBrie's desk.

"He was a hostage. Airplane hijacking. The one that went down in Libya about five or six years ago—five, I guess from this."

LeBrie looked at Hale and lit the cigar that had been in the corner of his mouth. Hale said, "That was the one—aw, shit."

"One guy escaped. Killed the leader, the story goes. The damn terrorists blew up the whole airplane and killed all the rest of the passengers."

"This guy Cross—he lived with that. Mother of God," Hale murmured.

"Somebody's mother, anyway." The cigar didn't draw, and he tried lighting it again.

LeBrie had watched his image vanish from the window, and continued watching until the sun was too high and he had to go back to looking at the printout he had thrown down on the desk.

Cross had left the Navy—honorable discharge. There was a medical disability mentioned, a whole string of operations with long, technical-sounding names, and something about medical disability payments being refused.

LeBrie looked back at the beginning. Born in 1952, Chicago, Illinois. There was a list of schools, all of them public, some of them places you didn't go near now without a two-man squad car to back you up. Cross had graduated high school at the top of his class in 1970 and attended a small university whose name LeBrie instantly recognized as synonymous with academic exclusivity. There was a naval ROTC program, and Cross had participated in it and been commissioned upon graduation. There was something about Cross having missed qualifying for the '72 Olympic swimming team because of a medical problem. But no evidence of medical problems surfaced in the succeeding material. Cross had been an all-around athlete and scholar, it appeared. Once in the Navy, he had been one of the comparative few—LeBrie had been in Army ROTC—to be offered a Regular commission as opposed to the Reserves. Cross had volunteerd for special warfare training. There was a list of citations. Some years of his activity were deleted, LeBrie imagined for security reasons.

LeBrie sat back with a cigar, working the years in his head. Cross would have just been up for promotion when the thing with the hijacking had taken place.

LeBrie stepped through into the detention room. Cross was sleeping, he guessed. Or from the amount of alcohol Dr. Hale had said there was in Cross's bloodstream, maybe just passed out. LeBrie had gotten a friend at the Chicago *Tribune* to dig out the files on the hijacking, and the guy had read him the pertinent data. There had been operations to restore Cross's face after it had been turned into pulp by the terrorist hijackers.

LeBrie studied Cross's face now. There was evidence, however subtle, that the nose had been broken. But beyond that and the generally disheveled appearance, the face was actually handsome, the forehead high, the jaw firm. Cross's head turned and his eyes opened. LeBrie came closer, but not too close. The eyes were brown, like the hair.

"I'm Sergeant LeBrie. How you doin'?"

Cross sat up, apparently too quickly, cushioning his face against his open palms. The hands seemed massively large, the fingers as long as a surgeon's or—he remembered something from the stuff in the printout—those of a pianist. Cross had minored in music in college, and he might have played the piano, LeBrie. His daughter played piano, and so did his wife.

"I've done better." With his face covered by his hands, the voice was muted.

"Everybody at the supermarket said you were a hero. We're trying to figure out what the hell to do with you. You killed five men."

Cross raised his face and looked at LeBrie across his hands. "Well, when you get it all figured out, be sure to let me know, huh?"

"Whatchya been doin' with yourself since you left the Navy, Mr. Cross?"

"Taking a correspondence course so I can be a taste tester at a distillery."

LeBrie laughed. "I mean for money."

"Play piano at Rita's Nightdreams Lounge over on Elston. You ever catch me?"

"No. When was the last time you worked?"

"Couple weeks ago. Rita died. Her husband put in a rock combo."

"Gettin' unemployment?"

"No." Cross didn't say anything else.

LeBrie mentally shrugged. "What were you doin' in the supermarket at that time of night?"

"The same thing the old black lady and the guy in the jogger's clothes were doing—shopping." His face had gone back to his hands, but now he looked up. "Got a cigarette?"

"I smoke cigars." LeBrie looked out into the corridor and spotted Patrolman Mary Gersch. "Mary, hustle me some cigarettes for the guy in here, okay?"

"What kind, Sarge?" she called back.

"Just a sec," and he turned back toward Cross. "What kind of cigarettes?"

"Pall Malls—Camels, if they don't have 'em."

LeBrie relayed the brand to Mary Gersch and she flashed a smile and disappeared down the corridor. LeBrie had been conducting an experiment in psychology. Cross wasn't completely gone. He still had preferences, which meant he still had ego. He turned back to the detention room. "So, you got any suggestions what we should do with you?"

"Release me?"

"That's a thought, for sure. How about some breakfast? Almost time for it."

"Don't suppose you brought my beer and cornflakes from the supermarket."

"No, we didn't. How about some coffee?"

"Machine?"

"No, got a Mr. Coffee in my office. I'll be right back, okay? Bring your cigarettes with me," LeBrie said, stepping back through the door and let it lock. He turned to the man he'd posted outside the door, beyond Cross's field of view. "Keep an eye on him through the mirror in case he tries hurtin' himself—just like you been doin'."

"Right, Sarge," the black patrolman answered.

LeBrie started down the corridor, intercepting Mary Gersch and paying her for the cigarettes she'd gotten for Cross. In his office, on the desk, he found a note. There was still no word from the Navy. He'd been trying to contact the people at Great Lakes for the last two hours. Maybe they'd have an idea what he could do with a man who'd just killed five other men but was called a hero by the witnesses. He poured the coffee and poured one for himself—it had been a long night, and his wife would be ticked that he hadn't gotten home after they'd gotten him out of bed about the massacre at the supermarket. That's what it was called when the phone call came in and woke him up, and that was what it had looked like when he got there.

A tall guy who looked like a bum in handcuffs, and smoking a cigarette though half asleep. Five dead men and the murdered black lady.

He took the coffee cups, one in each hand, and started back to the detention room, Cross's cigarettes—Mary had found Pall Malls—in his suit-coat pocket.

LeBrie gave a nod to the cop at the door, and the door got opened fast enough. It didn't look like Cross had moved. He still sat on the edge of the cot with his face in his hands. But he said, "Get any coffee for the guy outside?"

"You're a sharp guy, considering. Here." He handed Cross a cup. Cross took it, sipped at it, and set it on the floor beside his track-shoed feet. The shoes looked funny with the laces taken out.

"Thanks," Cross muttered.

LeBrie handed him the cigarettes.

"Thanks," Cross said again. "Got fire? They took mine."

LeBrie flipped Cross his disposable lighter. Cross worked a cigarette from the package and lit up, then tossed the lighter back, LeBrie catching it, pocketing it, taking a pull on the coffee. It was better than the machine stuff, but not as good as his wife's coffee. Nothing was quite that good. "How about a shower? Could you use one?"

"You're the one smelling me—could I use one?"

"Yeah, you could. When you're ready. We got a room down the hall. Why'd you kill that last guy? The one who killed the woman? I mean, you don't have to talk without a lawyer present."

"Because he killed the woman. That was a good enough reason. What would you have done?"

LeBrie shrugged. He would have done the same thing, maybe, but that was none of this guy's business. "That's gonna be the tough one, and maybe the guy you shot in the head. But he had his hand on a gun, so you can talk your way out of that. Why'd you refuse a lawyer? You might need one."

"Why would I need a lawyer?"

"Juries these days—maybe a lot of the folks who might get on a jury won't think killing five human beings is justified under any circumstances. We got a public defender. But they told you that."

"I didn't kill human beings."

"Don't tell anybody that, fella. They'll think you're kill happy and put ya away."

"Then they're full of shit," Cross said matter-of-factly.

"I didn't tell ya they weren't—I just told ya."

Cross lit another cigarette off the butt of the first one. LeBrie started to say something, but there was a knock on the detention room door and Mary Gersch peered inside. "Sarge— that call you were lookin' for."

"Right." He turned away from her to Cross and flipped him his lighter. "I'll be back."

"Oh, boy." Cross nodded, exhaling a cloud of gray smoke.

LeBrie left, walking faster than his normal pace toward his office, the phone on his desk off the hook. He picked it up. "This is Sergeant LeBrie."

He was told to hold. After about thirty seconds a voice came on that reeked with authority, asking if Cross was in apparently satisfactory physical condition.

LeBrie said he guessed so, but he wasn't a doctor. He told the voice that hadn't yet identified itself what Dr. Hale had told him about Cross's blood alcohol level.

The voice fell silent for a moment, and LeBrie thought the connection had gone. Ever since the phone company had been deregulated, it seemed everybody was using two tin cans and a string, anyway. Then the voice came back. "You keep him there. We'll see to it that he can be released to us. Thanks." The line clicked dead.

LeBrie hung up and wondered just who was fixing what, and why.

# Chapter Two

The guy in whites with the blue raincoat over his arm and the two Shore Patrolmen flanking him was an ensign. "Lieutenant Cross?"

Cross tried to make his face turn into a sneer, and he rolled over away from the door and studied the wall.

"Sir, I've been instructed to relay Colonel Matthew Leadbetter's compliments and request that you accompany us. Charges against you have been dropped."

Cross had showered but hadn't trusted himself to shave, or trusted anyone else to shave him. And now he was tired and knew that if he got himself too wide awake, he'd start wanting a drink too badly. "Fuck off." He closed his eyes.

"Colonel Leadbetter further instructed me, sir, to tell you that he is giving you the opportunity to do what you wanted to do five years ago, but understands if you won't, ah . . . won't have the . . . have the guts to do it."

Abe Cross sat up. He swung his feet to the floor.

Sergeant LeBrie walked past the two Shore Patrolmen and extended his left hand. "Here are your shoelaces. The rest of your stuff's at the property desk. Keep the lighter. Good luck."

Cross thought LeBrie was smiling as he turned and walked away.

He'd asked about his own car when they got into the For Official Use Only Plymouth and had been told that his car and his other personal affairs were all being taken care of. He didn't quite know what that meant. The FOUO gray Plymouth drove with its little red Kojak light on all the way toward the lake and turned in by the Shedd Aquarium for Meiggs Field. The helicopter wasn't marked Navy, but wasn't marked anything else either. Cross and the ensign and the two Shore Patrolmen got aboard, the wind cutting through Cross's still damp windbreaker like a knife. The hatchway closed and the helicopter was airborne almost instantly.

He looked down over the city and watched the blue choppiness of Lake Michigan turn into mostly rectangular fields of concrete, patches of dull green grass and rooftops and highways, and the city start to all but disappear, and O'Hare Airport start to take its place.

The helicopter landed. There had been no conversation. Now the ensign said, "Sir, please come with us."

"What if I say uh-uh?"

The ensign, who had blond hair, blue eyes, and pink cheeks that looked like a razor had never touched them, didn't answer. Cross shrugged his shoulders. "Come on, sonny," he said, and started out of the chopper.

There was a very short walk between the chopper and the all-but-unmarked twin-engine business jet. Cross boarded the little business jet, and this time the ensign and the two SP's stayed behind. He sat down in a swivel chair; the swivel locked, and he strapped himself in and closed his eyes. If the flight needed a jet, it would be long enough that he could sleep, and he needed that now. A man in gray slacks, a windbreaker, and tennis shoes came out of the cockpit through the red curtain and closed the fuselage door. Cross asked him, "Where we going?" The man just turned, and walked back, and disappeared through the curtained doorway.

Abe Cross awoke. His mouth was dry and tasted bad. His hands shook a little when he tried to move them from his lap. His stomach hurt, and figuring he was about to have the runs, he got up and walked aft to find the head. There was no one else in the passenger compartment at all. He found the head, and was right about the runs.

After the hijackers had taken his watch, he'd bought another Rolex, and even when the bucks had been low, he'd never pawned or sold it. He looked at it now, wishing he'd looked at it when he'd boarded the jet. The cloud cover had all but dispersed, and beneath the aircraft he could barely detect what looked like farmer's fields and patches of desert. He leaned back in his chair with his hands over his stomach and tried to fall asleep again.

Cross woke again as the plane was starting to land, and he tightened his seat belt and stared out the window. He knew the landing field, had been there once before, six years ago or better, when he had cross-trained with some Delta Force special response teams in desert survival. It was in Nevada, he had figured then, but never really known for sure. There was no proper name for it that he had ever heard except "Site 18," and it was rumored at nights—in the few hours of rest time there had been—that the place had once been a private retreat for a multimillionare who felt that the world was going to end in a nuclear war. Ten percent of the facility was aboveground, smack in the middle of the desert, with the nearest mountains almost a hundred miles away and the nearest towns well beyond the mountains. Ninety percent of the structure was underground. Cross had been allowed access to only the three upper levels when he'd been there before.

The jet touched down, and he started to unbuckle the seat belt. The aircraft stopped taxiing, and almost as soon as it did, the man he'd seen closing the fuselage door earlier reemerged from the cockpit to open the door.

"Had a nice, smooth flight. But the food and beverage service really sucked," Cross said.

The guy—he imagined the copilot—didn't even look at him, simply got the door open and the steps down, walked back through the cockpit doorway and closed the door curtain behind him.

Cross stood up and walked toward the doorway, saw no one waiting for him outside on the field, and started down the steps. The last step was a high one, and his land legs not quite good yet; he started to trip but caught himself. There was still no one on the field, and as far as he could see, all there was in evidence was the concrete-block structure that formed the visible top level of Site 18. Cross walked toward it, turning around as he heard the fuselage door close and squinting against the sunlight as the aircraft started taxiing off toward the far end of the field. He stood there for a few minutes, watching it, his mouth still tasting bad. The aircraft made a neat turn, began its takeoff, and as it passed within a few hundred yards of him, he gave the guys in the cockpit the finger. He watched as the white aircraft got airborne, then banked and suddenly seemed to disappear against the horizon, the sun strong, only a glint of wing tips visible now.

Cross turned back toward the blockhouse and continued walking toward it. He hadn't bothered relacing his shoes, and it was awkward to walk any long distance with them. He told himself that was why he'd almost tripped when getting off the aircraft. So he sat down on the runway, fished his shoelaces out of his jeans, fished his cigarettes and the gift lighter out of his shirt pocket and lit up, then started lacing his shoes. If anybody in the blockhouse was in that much of a hurry to see him, they could come and get him.

The length of the shoelaces wound up uneven, and he said under his breath, "Fuck it," tied them anyway and stood up, snapping the butt away and continuing to walk toward the blockhouse. He remembered the door as being automatic. It still was, opening when he was about two yards from it with an audible pneumatic thwack.

He stepped through and let the door slap shut behind him. It was cool, dark except for the lights at the far end of the narrow room, and empty except for a desk also at the far end. Two men in civilian clothes stood beside the desk, both of them wearing pistol belts, one of them smoking a cigarette. Cross lit up again himself, and started walking toward the two men, the desk and the light.

"Took your sweet time," the taller of the two men announced.

Cross smiled and stopped in front of the desk.

"You look worse than I figured," the shorter of the two men said, laughing as he sat down behind an immaculate green blotter. Cross picked snot out of his nose and snapped it into the middle of the man's desk blotter. "You—"

Cross just grinned. "Somebody wanted to see me. Colonel Leadbetter, I think it was. Tell him I'm here."

The double doors behind the desk hissed open and then smacked shut. It was Leadbetter. More gray than five years ago, a little less hair overall, but just as lean, and the smile that set the pansy-blue eyes just as evil looking. "Hello, Abe."

Cross walked around the desk. "Colonel."

"Didn't think you'd have the balls to come anymore." Matt Leadbetter's voice had always sounded like a computer doing an impression of a baritone, and as emotionless as a voice-box synthesizer.

"You were serious? What you wouldn't do five years ago? You'll do it now?"

"Come into my office, Abe. Got some catching up to do."

"Yeah. Right." Cross followed Leadbetter as the doors did their thing again and then closed so fast behind them that Cross's left shoelace almost got caught.

The corridor they entered was made of something like stainless steel and gleamed dully. Banks of fluorescent lights were set into the panels of the ceiling, the corridor so bright there was no shadow.

"Funny," Leadbetter said, turning around and walking backward, like a kid would, his hands stuffed into the pockets of his cammie fatigue pants. "I was just going to look you up when the naval base right there near Chicago got this funny call from the police, and the ONI people got back to me through channels. Small world."

He turned right, down a corridor and toward a bank of elevators Cross had been expressly forbidden to go near six years before. "Still running Delta Flight things out of here?"

"Couldn't tell you if we were, but since we aren't, I can tell you that. Except, I should probably say, 'What's Delta Flight? You mean that thing the newspapers and magazines like to talk about?' Anyway, we've got a much smaller personnel organization here now. Age of specialization." Leadbetter pushed a key into the elevator bank call, and almost before he removed the key, one of the elevator doors opened. Leadbetter went inside, Cross killing his cigarette in the ashtray between the two elevators, then following him. The doors closed, Leadbetter turning another key into the floor-level call controls, then placing his left-hand palm outward over a panel that had lit up when he removed the key.

The light died and the elevator started to move. Cross felt slightly nauseated.

"Isn't science wonderful?" Leadbetter observed.

"Oh, it's just grand, yes, indeed. What would have happened if I'd put the key in and then put my palm up there on that reader panel?"

"What do you think would have happened?" Leadbetter smiled.

Cross nodded. "That's what I thought."

The elevator stopped. There was a number 11 in numerals at least eighteen inches high on the wall opposite them as the doors opened. "I thought there were only ten floors, including the upper level?"

"There are—the numbers are all wrong. The ninth level just above us has number six all over it, like that. Confusion to our enemies."

"Not to mention your coworkers," Cross said softly.

They walked along a corridor that seemed identical to the one above, taking a right at the end, where it formed a T shape, and going past doors that looked to be made of the same metal used for the corridor walls, ceiling, and floor. The upper levels, in which he had studied, slept, and eaten six years before, weren't like this at all.

They stopped before a set of double doors with the number 4 on the wall above them. "Let me guess," Cross began. "This isn't really number four at all. Right?"

"Right." Leadbetter did a palm print on a reader panel which lighted up as his hand touched it. After a second the reader panel went out, the door lock popped, and Leadbetter went inside, Cross after him.

"We wanted to get this started a year ago," Leadbetter said, walking past an empty secretarial desk in a wood-paneled outer office, through an already open doorway, and into a larger version of the same decor that made the inner office. There was a full bar on the far wall, under a bad-looking mural of the Grand Canyon. "Want a drink?"

"Yeah; and don't tell me, I flunked the test." Cross started across the shag carpetting. The effect of the office was like a basement recreation room, but with a desk on one wall. On the plus side, however, there was a pool table on the opposite flank of the bar. There was a refrigerator under the bar, and Cross opened it, taking out a Michelob. A beer was all he wanted, he told himself. He noticed again that his hands were still shaking.

"A year," Leadbetter said, continuing the remark started in the outer office. "Took that long to get the security checks done. Boy, did you almost flunk. One of the patrons of that puke-bag bar you played piano in was the homosexual lover of a guy in the Armenian consulate who's a KGB agent."

"Yeah, the guy with the brown eyes and the tight little ass—yeah, but he told me I wasn't his type." Cross grinned, killing the beer and taking another one from the still opened bar refrigerator. He closed the refrigerator and opened the second beer.

"Tell me your understanding of the concept of a surgical strike," Leadbetter almost whispered, sitting down on the edge of the pool table.

"That's bad for the legs, ya know."

"My legs? Why?"

"No—the pool table's." Cross lit a cigarette—three were left. He closed his eyes. "A surgical strike," he began, opening his eyes then, "is a lightning-fast commando raid executed with extreme precision by a small, highly trained specialist force against a known safe target."

"Explain 'safe target' in the context in which you're using it."

"Something where you just get the enemy and you don't burn off anybody else. Not safe the other way at all," Cross said, exhaling a cloud of smoke.

"Authorization has been given for a surgical strike against global terrorism."

"All at once? How many thousands of guys you got?"

Leadbetter seemed to ignore the remark. "You want in?"

"Who gave the authorization, or shouldn't I ask?"

"Ask all you want. I can't tell you."

Cross stubbed out his cigarette, looking at Leadbetter across the bar. "If it works out, nobody says thank you, and if it doesn't, nobody's heard of us, right?"

Leadbetter's smile epitomized smugness. Then he put the smile away for later, Cross guessed. "The chance for success will be minimal, but we're doing our best with what was authorized. Three men will comprise the actual penetration team, and a fourth man will be the field controller. There'll be no reactivation of your commission, your record in the SEALs will be lost—no official connections at all, and no support outside the team. Except for the best intelligence data we've got. And transportation and equipment and funding, of course.''

Cross pulled another cigarette out of the pack, sat there silently.

"Let me give you my speech," Leadbetter continued after a pause. "When the Ayatollah Khomeini decided to leave France and return to Iran, he should have been the victim of an extremely tragic accident. But the goodie-goodies don't do stuff like that—no, of course not. When they took the embassy people hostage, we should have told them that they either release everybody in twenty-four hours or use that twenty-four hours to evacuate Tehran because it won't be there anymore come morning. The same thing goes for Daffy Khadafi Land By-the-Sea.

"Five years ago," Leadbetter went on softly, "you were in the hospital and I came to see you. After you fished yourself out of the drink, it took you four weeks to exfiltrate and reach Egypt. Your face looked like something a dog wouldn't shit on. You told me you wanted to go back and get the people who blew away everybody on the plane; you blamed yourself for being alive, the only one alive. You pretty damn well begged me to get you over there so you could kill terrorists.

"Well, my speech is this: Put up now or shut up forever. If you can make it through the training—and God knows that alcohol diet of yours the last five years isn't gonna help—and you can stay alive long enough to reach the target, you'll be the tactical team leader. But you'll take orders from the field controller. Period. In or out, Abe?''

Cross lit his cigarette—he wondered if his hands were shaking because of his alcohol diet or for another reason. "Who's the field controller?"

"In or out, Abe?" Leadbetter repeated.

"In."

"Darwin Hughes," Leadbetter said, bringing out the smile again.

"Shit."

Leadbetter nodded, putting the smile away. "That's what he said you'd say."

Abe Cross closed his eyes and took a pull of his beer.

# Chapter Three

The Ayatollah Fasal Batuta seemed to cocoon himself within his black robes as he sank into the wooden chair, his voice rhythmically even as he began to speak. "According to the Law, the three grounds for killing are adultery, becoming a disbeliever after accepting Islam, and murdering a person. But in the writings of Ibn Jarir al-Tabari in *The History of Prophets and Kings*, it is revealed to us that there are other lawful killings: as of the one who spread corruption over the land, and of the one who strayed from the path of justice and prevented its execution.

"If we can speak of the world beyond this room and this Holy Nation, and indeed beyond this corner of the world in which we struggle for the pure realization of faith, then it can well be understood that our mission is quite clear. The corruption which is spread over all of the earth is that corruption which is all but the true faith in Islam. And Islam is the ultimate justice, so those who are not of the pure realization of faith are indeed strayed from justice, and thus prevent its execution. Faith, then, demands that we eradicate this corruption, this denial of justice, in order that the pure realization of the true faith may comfort all men.

"According to the treatise of Shafi'i, we are compelled to exercise reason in our understanding of *The Koran* and to act upon the fruit of our reason," Ayatollah Batuta continued. Raka leaned forward to hear him better, enrapt by the words.

"To do other than this would be to defy the will of God, 'For it is He who has made for you the stars, that you might be guided by them in the darkness of land and sea.' God tells us that we must use reason, but only within the boundaries of His will for all men: '. . . so long as men use their personal reasoning, they will not deviate from His command, glorious be His praise.' But," the Ayatollah continued, "it is also written in *The Koran*, 'Does man think that he will be left roaming at will?' Is he, then, neither commanded nor prohibited, to paraphrase Shafi'i?"

The room remained silent. Raka breathed, but shallowly.

"We must perform the will of God as is our duty. We must destroy that which is not holy in order for that which is holy to flourish. We are here at this hour to see to it that all which is according to the will of God be fulfilled."

The other ayatollahs at the conference table bowed their heads knowingly, and there were murmurs of agreement from all of them. "Glorious be His praise," Raka intoned.

Ayatollah Batuta spoke again, and Raka fixed his eyes upon him. "We have resisted the will of God long enough, and are now unclean in His eyes. The Great Satan and the Jew occupiers of Palestine grow complacent in their supposed strength, and rally those who give only lip service to the will of God from among our supposed brothers. A killing blow must be struck against the Great Satan and its whore nations.

"There has been much wrangling," Ayatollah Batuta went on, "all in the best interests of the True Faith. It has fallen to my shoulders to read the stars God has given us, and to follow their path with all the humble powers of a man's reason, to find the true path. And the answer lay before me. Ibn Umar has said, 'Islam is built upon five things: on confessing that there is no deity save Allah, performing prayers, giving the legal alms, going on pilgrimage to the House, and fasting during Ramadan. Thus did the apostle of Allah hand it on to us, but beyond that there is holy war, which is an excellent thing.'

"My answer"—and here Ayatollah Batuta smiled—"lay before me. The plan of Muhammad Ibn al Raka and International Jihad is best for three reasons: it achieves the embarrassment of the Great Satan, the embarrassment of the Jew occupiers of Palestine and, greatest of all, it is the true path of reason.''

Raka's heart beat so rapidly in his chest that for the briefest instant he thought he would surely die, but then his heart calmed, for he knew it was the will of God that he did not.

The Ayatollah Fasal Batuta began to pray.

Mehdi Hamadan was very tall and very thin, yet his hands seemed to convey a great strength, and his black eyes—Batuta thought—held fire. Batuta sat; Hamadan remained standing. ''Holy One, Muhammad Raka is gone to the Elburz Mountains to begin at once.''

''The principal feature which attracted me to the plan of Raka was the built-in publicity factor. Yet, this even more severely limits the timing, making it more critical than it would normally have been. He knows that, leading the raid personally, he will most probably die?''

''Yes, Holy One. But how better could a man die? 'We indeed created man; and we know what his soul whispers within him, and we are nearer to him than the jugular vein.' ''

''You quote *The Koran.*'' Batuta smiled. ''And you quote it well. I am to understand that there is no personal motivation for Raka and his followers to so risk their lives?''

''Holy One,'' Mehdi Hamadan continued, ''they risk what God already owns as His for His sake. But if all goes well, even should the brave Muhammad Raka and his followers perish, great damage will be accomplished against the enemies of Islam.''

''And for this accomplishment, International Jihad should be blessed, no doubt.''

''If this is God's will,'' Hamadan answered devoutly.

''Perhaps your rival, Achmed Omani, might be found to harbor counterrevolutionary tendencies, and his group—leaderless following his trial and execution—could be taken under your guidance to the greater glory of our faith.''

''If this truly would be God's will,'' Hamadan answered. ''But a question: What of our sometime friends? Will they consider what is to come so provocative as to bring them closer to the throat of the Great Satan, and it to them?''

"You see our friends, do you not? There in the Elburz Mountains? And what do they tell you?"

"They tell me nothing, Holy One. I see them not at all."

"God truly holds you in His favor. Pray that he shall continue to do so. I will pray with you."

"Yes, Holy One." Hamadan nodded, lowering his eyes.

# Chapter Four

The shorter of the two men from the front desk at Site 18 was his driver, and Cross had elected to sit in the backseat of the several-year-old Mercedes station wagon. It wasn't a rental car, and Cross had no idea where it had been acquired; and the short guy hadn't flown with him from Site 18, either, just been there waiting at the small Clarke County Airport at Athens, Georgia. The last time Cross had been at an airport in a town named Athens, it had changed his life forever. As he'd debarked the small business jet—a different one than the one that had brought him from Chicago to Site 18—he had the uncomfortable feeling that history was about to repeat itself, that his life would forever be changed, and perhaps radically shortened.

He had spent less than twenty-four hours at Site 18, eating, sleeping, being given a couple of pairs of jeans that looked comfortably used and some shirts and other necessities to get him through until his things were transhipped circuitously from Chicago to Darwin Hughes's place. It was Hughes's own place to which he was being driven, Leadbetter had told him. Hughes had all he needed for training there, except a desert, and they wouldn't require special desert training anyway. And, using Hughes's own place just lent added credence to the cover story that would be put out if they were caught or killed—Hughes had gathered a small group of guys who could be depended upon when he decided to take things into his own hands and act where the U.S. leadership would not.

For all Abe Cross knew, the story could have been more truth than fiction. The only uniforms he'd seen since the thing had begun were the ones worn by the ensign and the two SP's who had gotten him out of the hands of Sergeant LeBrie and the Chicago PD. What if Site 18 was no longer used by the government? He had seen nothing of any of the other floors, no other personnel except Leadbetter and the tall guy and the short guy from the front desk, and a pretty blond-haired woman in her forties or early fifties named Maud, who had apparently been Leadbetter's secretary but could just as easily have been Leadbetter's mistress.

The Mercedes wasn't giving the best ride in the world now, since they had left the main highway, having driven roughly north and west for almost two hours. They were still in Georgia, but he wasn't certain where or near what.

The Mercedes made another turn, and this time it seemed as though there was no road at all, but just a rutted single track, leaves everywhere, tree branches reaching out from the scooped-out sides of the roadbed and at times brushing against the windows and roofline of the car. The short guy was driving a little too fast for these conditions, Cross thought, but he guessed at the reason for the driving display—the short guy still had a hard-on for him.

The Mercedes rounded a soft hairpin bend and began climbing. Cross bent forward to look over the front seat and the short guy's shoulders to see what lay ahead. It was a massive A-frame that seemed to cling to the ground, rather than having been placed there. Beyond it he could see nothing but blue sky and sheer drop.

The Mercedes turned into what was surprisingly a driveway and skidded on gravel as it came to a stop. The short guy said nothing, had said nothing at the airport or during the drive. Cross opened the door, snatched his flight bag from the station wagon's bed and stepped out.

He moved a few paces away from the car, which started in motion, the door Cross had left open slamming itself shut from momentum as the Mercedes twisted and lurched a little, then found traction and executed a too-fast tight U-turn and started back along the route over which it had come.

"Hope this is the right place," Cross muttered to himself.

He was walking toward the A-frame's porch when the front door opened and a man of about his own height—well over six feet, but considerably older and seemingly more fit than he—stepped onto the porch. It was Darwin Hughes.

"It's the right place, lad."

The voice was deep, the speech carefully modulated, a pleasant-sounding bass. "Mind reading these days, Hughes?"

"When I was a child, I had a hearing disorder and a set of parents who weren't about to have anything like that keep me from living a full life. The hearing problem cleared up. In fact, I've got extraordinarily good hearing for a man my age. But I kept up with reading lips."

"Oh, boy!" Cross grinned.

"Welcome to your new home." Hughes ran his hands back through his salt-and-pepper gray hair—a full shock, but fairly close-cropped—then gestured for Cross to ascend the porch.

"You're the first, lad. Colonel Leadbetter and I thought you could use a week to yourself here before the others arrived. Get some of the alcohol purged from your system, start restoring muscle tone, fine tuning your keen eye and the like."

Cross stopped at the height of the steps, determined not to show even the slightest hint of being out of breath. There were twenty-three steps, the porch built high enough to qualify as a stilt-legged house in a flood plain. Cross said nothing, controlling his breathing instead. Hughes smiled, his evenly ranked teeth ridiculously white. Cross smiled back.

"You need a teeth cleaning," Hughes said, "if you don't mind my saying so—and probably a general dental checkup as well. I know a perfectly charming lady dentist whom I might be able to get to take care of that for you. If a tooth goes bad out in the field, it can cut a man's efficiency well in half. Come on inside and let's talk a bit."

"Shit," Cross hissed. Hughes took his bag, and Cross followed the older man inside. Beyond the front door lay a great room, the ceiling vaulted and at its pinnacle reaching perhaps twenty feet overhead. "How do you change the light bulbs?"

"One of those little cage affairs on the end of a long handle. The same sort of thing they used to use back in the days of elaborate theater marquees."

The short-length hallway ended, and they went down three steps into the great room. The walls everywhere were of natural wood, huge-headed nails visible at regular intervals. The floor was carpeted wall to wall in an odd shade of rose, that somehow went with the place. A massive fireplace dominated the far wall, double French doors on both sides leading out, he assumed, to what would doubtlessly be a disgustingly spectacular view of·the Smokies. Over the hearth was a solitary rifle, an old-looking, lever-action Winchester. From the receiver profile and the protruding magazine at the base of the receiver, he guessed it was a Model 1895 .30-06.

"My dad used that in Texas in the days before the First World War," Hughes commented offhandedly. Cross was beginning to wonder if the man really could read minds as well as lips. "She still shoots, but I'm quite careful to use reduced loads. Wouldn't want to damage her. Teddy Roosevelt had a rifle just like that, But of course his had a shortened butt stock."

"Of course." Cross nodded, flopping down in the center of the right-angled brown couch. It was positioned so that the fireplace, either of the double French doors, or the large-screened television, could be seen with equal ease. The television was part of a complex-looking assemblage of electronic gear in the far corner, which included two sets of stereo speakers, what looked like two video cassette recorders, a turntable, a cassette deck, and a compact disc player. Cross spotted an ashtray on the glass-topped, polished oak coffee table that bisected the angle formed by the two arms of the couch. He lit up, still using LeBrie's lighter, saving the fuel in the Zippo.

"Make that the last one you smoke for a while, lad. You'll need your wind."

"I move okay. Probably outrun you."

It was a mistake, and Cross knew it when he said it. Hughes turned toward him and cocked his left eyebrow, which seemed almost unnaturally dark when compared to the hair on his head, and smiled. "We'll see. I know it's early for a lounge pianist, but after dinner, I'd suggest making an early night of it. We'll be up at four for a run.

"You may have noticed," and Hughes smiled again, "that nothing around this place is particularly level, so I hope you like running uphill. I have spaghetti going. I made the sauce kind of on the bland side, not knowing your tastes. Pasta is excellent for giving you the carbs you'll need. And as to booze, lad, we have beer. All you want within reason—my reason. Everything else is somewhere you'll never find it."

Cross exhaled smoke through his nostrils. "You're gonna be fuckin' disappointed if I don't fall apart on you, aren't you?"

Hughes leaned against the mantel. Pistol-shooting trophies, a bowling trophy, and assorted easel-back framed photographs were ranked from end to end there. "As a matter of fact, Cross, I'm rather counting on the direct opposite. Of all three of you, you will be the most vital and least easily replaced, which is why you are here in the first place. The other two men are very good, but you and I are the only two with any extensive combat experience or any experience at all behind enemy lines. Last time I met you—when I was teaching that explosives course—you were a very polite young naval officer, very aggressive, but almost the embodiment of clean-cut Americanism. In five years of blaming yourself for the death of 118 passengers, you've become a self-styled bad-ass, it appears. And a foul-mouthed one at that. I call that overcompensation for self-pity, gotta prove how tough you are, and prove that you're so hard that those 118 souls aren't on your conscience. You aren't here for me to save in the spiritual sense or heal in the psychological sense. You are here to become good enough again to be useful at what you do best."

"You have a piano, huh?"

"As a matter of fact, I do. I had it brought in for you specially, so the four of us can wile away the evenings up here singing our old favorites together. I hope an upright will prove adequate, but it was impossible to get anything larger up the mountain."

Cross stubbed out his cigarette. "Where's the beer?"

# Chapter Five

Cross had his shoes on and was ready before four A.M. He'd gotten up at three, felt sick for a while, then done some calisthenics to prepare himself for the run. His room was like a small apartment, actually larger than the apartment he'd left behind in Chicago. A color television, a VCR, a boom box that was an AM/FM radio and cassette player, a digital alarm clock which he already knew he would come to hate, and a comfortable double bed. His hands shook badly; it was the longest he'd gone without whiskey in so long he couldn't remember. Through the windows that overlooked the drop off the side of the mountain from the second floor, he could see nothing but darkness patched with dense gray fog. The spaghetti the night before had been good, overly filling, the sauce mild enough, but it had gone through his system like water through a sieve, anyway.

There was a knock at the bedroom door precisely as the clock turned to four A.M. Cross opened the door.

Darwin Hughes filled the doorframe. He wore black sweat pants and a gray sweatshirt with the hood pulled up, his face partially lost in shadow, his appearance that of a monk who'd lost the skirts of his robe.

Cross smiled. "What if the bad guys know we're up here and come after us while we're on this run?"

"Well, so long as there aren't too many bad guys, lad, we'll do just fine."

Cross followed him out, along the balconylike hallway that overlooked the great room, and down the wide stairs to the first floor. Hughes snatched up a key ring from the table near the front door and made the keys disappear in the muff pocket of his sweatshirt. They started down the front steps together, Cross barely able to see. "You brought a flashlight?"

"I read with considerable interest that you had superb night vision. Should have eaten more of those carrots at dinner last night. You don't look too good."

"I feel fine."

"Marvelous. You can set the pace." Hughes smiled, his teeth glinting whitely in the yellow light of the front porch. "I'll try to keep up."

"Which way?"

"Up." Hughes grinned, jerked his right thumb and started into a jog.

Cross inhaled and began running, Hughes deliberately letting him pass, then Hughes catching up, Cross trying to increase the pace, Hughes matching him.

"How old are you?" Cross panted.

Hughes laughed, not sounding breathless at all. "Over twenty-one."

"Right," Cross exhaled, running.

Once they had reached something that finally looked like the top, Cross stopped running. But Hughes had disappeared over a shelf of gray rock, and Cross had started after him, only realizing then that "up" was a wholly subjective term here, because when one ran out of one mountain, one started on the next one. The sun was almost up, and Cross had lost all conception of time when he finally fell forward, sagging to his knees, holding his abdomen with both hands and vomiting.

As he looked up, he could see Hughes's track shoes at the edge of his vision. "I'll catch up to you."

"You did six miles. That's more than I figured you could do for a while. Unless you're dying to run some more, I was intending to suggest a nice walk back down the mountain."

"Six fuckin' miles?"

"A mile and a half. This is the farthest we've been from the house. Come on, walk off those cramps, lad."

"Sure, Mr. Scoutmaster, sir." He started to get up, but couldn't quite, and stayed kneeling there for a while.

He finally got his head up and saw that Hughes was doing push-ups off to his left. "How were you gonna do anything if we had company? Outrun slugs?"

"No, give some slugs back, I guess. But no one knows we're up here, except Leadbetter, and if we can't trust Leadbetter, we're out of luck anyway."

"His short friend—the creep who drove me up here."

"He works for Leadbetter. And for that matter, so do we."

"Am I earning any money doing this?"

"If you live long enough, you'll get a paycheck every month. But like me, I know you're doing this because you want to do it."

Cross closed his eyes and then opened them again. "I really do want to do this, Hughes."

Hughes didn't speak for a moment, then completed his push-ups and stood up. "I know. Why do you think I wanted you in on this? You're qualified. Or at least you were, and will be again. But you also have to get this out of your guts."

"I maybe said ten words a day to you for ten days, six years ago or so."

"Seven. How do I know so much about you?"

"Yeah."

Hughes began doing some squats. "When that thing happened five years ago, that's when I made my proposal to the government and was turned down. I'd asked for you then. I was told you were washed up. I didn't think so. For the last five years you've certainly tried proving they were right and I wasn't. Anyway, they came to me and asked me to try it. I said I would, but only if they gave me you."

Cross lit a cigarette, and started coughing so badly he thought he'd die.

"You're wondering why, aren't you lad? Why did I take so much interest in you, right?"

"Your mind-reading act impresses me. Yeah—why?"

Hughes stopped his squats and just stood there. "It's none of your business—not yet, anyway. Now start walking or I'll have to carry you, and that'd be exceedingly embarrassing for you.''

Hughes started walking off. Cross climbed to his feet, a spasm of cramps running through him. But he began walking. And soon the cramping eased.

The days passed, and the shakes got worse, but the diarrhea lessened. His appetite started to return, and the running with Hughes each morning, the rapeling off Hughes's mountainside, the weight training and martial arts exercises, were actually getting easier.

It was Saturday night, and on Monday the other two men would come. ''Do you like pizza, lad?'' Hughes asked.

Cross bit. ''Yes—why?''

There was always something on Hughes's mind, and no question was idle chatter. ''I thought you might like to have a night out in town. There's a pizza restaurant by the interstate. And honestly—and no offense lad—but I'm tired of just seeing your face and no one else's.''

So they got into Hughes's lustrous Jeep station wagon and started down the mountain. It was the first time he'd seen Hughes with a handgun, a little Chief's Special Model 60 Smith & Wesson which he slipped into the glove compartment. As they drove down the mountain, Cross laughed.

''Share the joke, lad.''

''I remember that time after the demolition classes, when a bunch of us were at the range shooting and you showed up. Somebody asked you about guns, and I remember you told us that there was nothing worse than a little .38 Special snubby. No barrel to speak of, and you put—''

''I know what I said, because I said it, Cross. But let me ask you a question, lad, Now, what would happen if in the normal course of events you and I were to be walking out of this pizza restaurant we're going to, and some guys jumped us and tried to rob us?''

''They'd have to be pretty damned good to get very far.''

''Indeed, but think about it a little more carefully. If you or I should kill somebody with our hands, and get caught, how would we explain that we easily killed an armed man or two without recourse to weapons? Or, let's say I carry this gun

inside the restaurant with me and these same unlucky gentlemen come after us and I kill them. Well, with a little ordinary
stainless steel .38 revolver, it's not going to look suspicious at
all, is it? I mean, beyond what it would look to be normally.
But there won't be any particular attention called to either of
us except as honest citizens forced by circumstance to take
human life in self-defense. Now take it a step further. Instead
of that little .38, I take an H&K MP5-K submachine gun along,
or a Walther P-5 with a slide lock and a suppressor on it, or
something else exotic. Then what?''

"Do you ever give simple answers, Hughes?"

"Do you ever ask simple questions, Cross?"

Cross lit a cigarette, the first he had smoked all day.

There had been no desperadoes outside the pizza restaurant.

Cross and Hughes had split two pitchers of beer and a large
pizza with everything imaginable on it except anchovies and
black olives. Cross had only smoked three more cigarettes.

On Sunday morning they did their run, and Hughes asked
Cross if he wanted to go to church. Cross declined, working
out when Hughes left, then showering and sitting around in
the bathrobe he'd bought along with the other clothes when
Hughes had taken him to see the dentist.

Cross needed a television fix, and it was after he'd gone
through the video tape library in the room off to the side of
the great room that housed several thousand books and several hundred VHS tapes, that he noticed the photograph on
Hughes's desk.

He recognized one face in the photograph.

He closed his eyes.

He wept.

Cross had heard the Jeep pull up a little after noon. He'd
remained seated on the tree stump a hundred yards or so off
from the house, staring down the mountainside. He could
hear some farmer's dog barking in the valley below, saw the
glint of wings from a small aircraft along the horizon. He
heard the crunch of gravel.

"You missed a boring sermon, Cross."

Cross looked around at him without standing up. "Why didn't you tell me?"

Hughes didn't answer for a moment. Cross assumed it was the mind-reading act again. Then, "You saw the picture on my desk."

"Yeah. She had a ring on her finger and she couldn't get it off, and they were gonna cut her finger off, and I took some shaving soap and got her finger greasy with it and took the ring off her finger and gave it to them."

"Did you know her name?"

"No."

"Her name was Anjanette. The baby she was carrying was also my son Bob's baby. I'd warned them to stay out of the Middle East, but people don't listen. Give me a cigarette."

Cross took out his pack of cigarettes, the same one from the previous night, and still half full. Hughes took one and produced a Zippo lighter Cross hadn't seen before, but he'd never seen Hughes smoke before either. "Bob was the kind of guy who believed all men are brothers. And that's a fine way to feel. I remember telling him once that Cain was Abel's brother. He was an English teacher, which was something I was always very proud of because I never had time to finish high school. World War Two came along and I lied about my age, and then I was out of the Army and into the OSS, and there wasn't time for anything like school after that."

"You're one of the best educated men I've ever met."

"Thank you, lad." The corners of Hughes's mouth turned down, and there were deep ridges in his cheeks, his eyes hard as he exhaled smoke. "Bob married Anjanette and they lived in Turkey, where he taught at the university. Anjanette was going home to spend the holidays with her mother, who was dying—it would be the last time they'd have together. Bob was always good about that sort of thing, understanding other people. After Anjanette . . ." Hughes exhaled so heavily it sounded almost like a death rattle. "Afterward Bob tried very hard to tell me he was going to kill himself. He'd lost his wife and his baby, and he was telling me that he'd lost his faith in humanity. I wouldn't let him tell me that, and I took the first flight I could get to Cairo. Bob had killed himself.

Opened a vein and died like the Romans used to do it, sitting in a tub of hot water. Now you know why I wanted you on this.''

Cross couldn't decide if it were revenge or poetic justice that Darwin Hughes wanted served—or maybe both. Hughes walked away. Cross looked out across the valley. He told himself he hadn't heard Hughes crying.

# Chapter Six

The Mercedes station wagon arrived, and the short guy drove it again, but Cross stood on the porch this time, beside Darwin Hughes. Two men got out, one black and one white. The Mercedes drove off, and the two men approached the porch.

The black man—tall, lean, and well-muscled under a short-sleeved blue knit shirt—said, "Mr. Hughes, I'm Lewis Babcock, sir."

The white man, who was tall like Babcock, with arms that could have made him a fortune in body building and a neck that seemed to vanish into immense shoulders, ran his left hand back through his curly blond hair and smiled, "I'm Jeff Feinberg, sir. Nice to know you."

"This is Abe Cross, gentlemen. Speaking for both of us, it's a pleasure to meet you. Come in. Let's talk a bit." And Hughes turned toward the door and went inside.

Cross went to the bar, noting with satisfaction that Hughes had filled all the empty spots at the back of the bar with various whiskeys, vodka, scotch, rum, and gin. A sign of trust, he thought. He poured himself a ginger ale. "Want a drink?"

Babcock set down his flight bag and a suitcase and approached the bar, walking with the grace of a cat, his hands thrust easily into his pockets. His hair was short, the way so many black men wore it, his forehead high, his features

58

well-defined, the color of his skin more a rich brown than anything like black. "That ginger ale looks good."

Cross nodded, filled a glass with ice, and started to pour as Hughes, then Feinberg, joined them. Hughes took a Michelob and Feinberg asked for the same.

"We'll talk in detail tonight, after dinner. I've been doing the cooking and intend to continue, but with four of us now, I can use some help with cleanup afterward. Basically, the four of us have a job that's impossible, and we're going to rehearse the elements of that job until we have them as perfectly mastered as possible. Then, you go off and try to do the job. Chances are that you'll all get killed, but one never knows. So, Cross will show you to your rooms. Anything you need, shout." Hughes took his beer and walked off, Cross watching the other two men watching him.

Dinner was spaghetti again, so Cross assumed another hard run was due in the morning. Carbohydrates. After dinner, and after cleaning up, they adjourned to the great room, the sun setting over the balcony which overlooked the valley below. Hughes stood at his "podium," the fireplace mantel. Cross sipped a beer, Feinberg doing the same, Babcock a vodka on the rocks. Cross had noticed the black man examining the bottle.

"We need to know each other. I'll start. If I leave anything out," Hughes began, "I'm sure I'll mention it later. I have the distinction," he went on, "of being the youngest man in the Office of Strategic Services during World War Two. I didn't even know I was in OSS, that's how young I was. After the war, I didn't much relish being unemployed, and the CIA wasn't much yet, so I went to Israel and fought with the Mossad Aliya Bet, which later became the Mossad. I never wore a uniform during World War Two after they pulled me out of the Army, and I never gave much thought to anything like that, actually. But I was a captain by the end of the thing, and when Korea came up, I was involved with special operations planning, execution, and training, and by the time that ended, I was a light colonel. I worked in South America a lot and some in the Middle East, and by that time Vietnam was just starting to heat up, so they asked me back, made me a colonel, and gave me a green beret to wear. I alternated my time between training and running A-teams as far north as we could get.

"My daddy was a Texas Ranger, and I hadn't been to Texas in twenty years, so after I got through with Vietnam, a long time before everybody else did, I moved my wife and son to Texas and went to work for some private security firms down there. By that time they were starting up Delta Flight, and I got involved training in explosives, some of the special weapons and tactics stuff that I'd done in Texas, like that. I wound up teaching SEALs for a while, then moved over to work with the 82nd Airborne in special counterterrorist techniques. And here I am. I'm old enough to have fathered all three of you jointly or separately."

Babcock smiled.

"I always thought black women were exceptionally pretty, so don't dismiss the possibility, Babcock."

"Yes, sir."

"I'll make you a deal. I won't call you captain if you don't call me sir. Darwin is my first name—God knows what possessed two fundamentalists to name their son Darwin. Either that or just Hughes. I prefer that, actually. Babcock, your turn."

Lewis Babcock cleared his throat, then began. "I joined the Army out of college, where I studied law, but I transferred out of Judge Advocate General's Corps into Special Forces, then trained with Delta Flight. I had you for class, sir—I mean, Mr. Hughes. I was in Grenada. That's the only combat experience I had. Happy to be aboard—at least I think so."

Hughes smiled, his left eyebrow cocked, which didn't make it much of a smile at all. "All right, Feinberg. Go for it."

Jeff Feinberg stood up. He was youngest among them, Cross judged. He had what Cross thought of as a New York accent. "I'm Jewish. I got pissed with the terrorists early on. I joined the Corps out of high school and cross-transferred out of the Marines. I wanted Special Forces training, and it was that or SEALs, and Marines don't like the Navy much. Then I got into Delta Flight. I haven't had any combat experience. But I guess I'm gonna rectify that overnight."

Cross had met Feinberg a thousand times, but never met him. He closed his eyes, just listening for a while as Hughes spoke again. Cross knew it would be his turn, and he didn't know what to say.

"Abe Cross's qualifications are extensive, and a lot of it is classified. He has a distinct advantage over all of us, which I'll preempt him on and tell you about. He was a terrorist hostage and survived."

"He's the one—"

It was Feinberg's voice, and Cross opened his eyes. "Yeah, I'm the one."

"Hey, sorry, man."

Hughes cut in. "He left the Navy five years ago, A SEAL team leader. He's the veteran of five penetrations into what used to be North Vietnam in search of MIA's. He was involved in operations in Latin America and the Middle East. He graduated from his university summa cum laude. During one of his foreign excursions, he was shot down, his pilot wounded, and he carried the guy out. It took six weeks to get to friendly lines. He's got almost as many commendations as I've got. He'll be the tactical leader."

Cross sat up in the couch. "And for the last five years I've been drinkin' a lot of beer and assorted other grain products. Amen."

Babcock laughed.

And then so did Cross.

# Chapter Seven

After the run, the weight training, the martial arts exercises, the rappeling, a quickie with knife fighting, and a big lunch—Hughes was a master with a microwave—Hughes had Feinberg help him carry out various metal cases and set them out by the tree stump a hundred or so yards from the house.

Cross was congratulating himself for not getting outdistanced in the run and holding his own with the weight training. Of the two new men, Feinberg seemed the most fit, but what Babcock perhaps lacked in brute strength, he made up in agility and speed.

Hughes opened the cases and sat facing the three men. "Feinberg. Babcock. You men were specifically ordered to come here whistle clean as far as weapons are concerned. That was for a specific reason. If we are caught or killed, nothing should directly link us to the government, to our own identities, etcetera. But, despite the wisdom of such things, I realized that each of us would have his own particular preferences with weapons. You can't have occupations like we do and take them seriously and not have preferences. So, first we'll cover team weapons, then get to your personal preferences."

Hughes produced a pistol from one of the cases that surrounded them. "This is the Beretta 92F, a gun all of you, with the possible exception of Cross, would be familiar with. It's the new service pistol; some would call it the damned Italian gun that replaced old slab sides. I wouldn't. I'll tell you, it's a very fine weapon, and since a pistol will only be used at close quarters with an operation such as ours, I opted for reliability and high volume of firepower over reliability and a cartridge which, if anything, is only marginally better. So we're all carrying the Beretta as a sidearm rather than Government Model .45's. I know some of you may be used to H&K pistols." He looked at Cross, who had used them in the SEALs. "You'll find this vastly more than adequate for the task at hand, and we have the ancillary advantage of being able to chisel spare magazines and spare parts if needed from the people who'll bring us in, if that's ever called for. It was this or the SIGARMS gun. I chose this because of service compatibility, and because so many other nations are using it that its mere presence isn't automatically identifiable to the bad guys as being American. Plus, with the .45, resupply in the field would be damned awkward. And, compatibility with our submachine guns was also a concern. Any questions or gripes so far?"

Cross watched Feinberg, who started to say something but didn't. He watched Hughes. Hughes noticed it but just went on.

"All right—more on the body stuff. Let's go to knives for a minute. Most of us have preferences in custom knives we've developed over the years. I like the work of Jack Crain from Weatherford, Texas, for example. Not just because he's a Texan like I am." Hughes made his smile. "But again, anything directly traceable was ruled out, and each of the really fine custom knifemakers' work is as individual as a signature. So it wouldn't be to any avail for us to have custom knives made and just get the makers to leave their names off. I chose from among the best factory makers available, and selected the Gerber BMF survival knife for fighting"—he held one up—"and the Victorinox Swiss Army Champion for utility." He held up one of these, most of the blades turned out for examination. He set the folding knife on the poncho beside him, where he had set the Gerber and the Beretta.

"All this will be carried on the black versions of the Bianchi-made pistol belt, and the Beretta will be carried in the Bianchi UM-84 holster, the GI designation the M-12. For the Berettas, I have available a quantity of twenty-round extension magazines for the 93R machine pistol which work perfectly with the 92F, and will give you added time between reloadings if needed."

Hughes picked up the next item, held it up as he talked. "This is the Walther PP in .22 LR. The barrel isn't factory original; it's almost an inch longer, and threaded—for this." Hughes produced a black object that looked like a cross between a power-mower muffler and a bratwurst. "This suppressor is exceedingly effective. There's no slide lock on the Walther, but the pistol is adequately silent for limited use. One of these and twenty-five rounds of subsonic Long Rifle ammo will accompany us, just in case we need this capability."

He put the pistol down, then picked up a submachine gun. "Next on the ladder is this—the H&K MP5-SD-A3, 9mm and reworked to function wholly reliably with the Federal 9mm BP 115-grain jacketed hollow points we'll be using with the Beretta pistols. As you all likely know, this has an integral suppressor. Each of the MP5-SD-A3's we'll be using is fitted with an Aimpoint red-dot sight. If you aren't familiar with the H&K, you will be. For a submachine gun, you'll never find anything more accurate. Fires from a closed bolt. And that helps."

Hughes set down the submachine gun, turning to the largest of the cases and extracting something Cross had used before. "This is the H&K G3. I elected the fixed stock rather than the collapsible version. We can find spare magazines for these all over the Middle East, or anywhere, for that matter. We'll be using the Federal Premium boat tail .308 with it." He set the rifle down, then turned to the next case, just as large.

"Each of you will be armed with the Beretta pistol, the H&K submachine gun, and the H&K rifle—basically," and he smiled. "One of you will pass up on one or the other of the two for one of these." He produced a shotgun that reminded Cross of the FIE/Franchi SPAS-12, only slimmer. "This is very new, and you'll be seeing it everywhere in the U.S. and overseas in counterterrorist operations. It's a LAW-12, semiautomatic only variation of the SPAS-12. It cannot—I repeat, cannot—be used as a pump. Just semiautomatic. We'll use this with a standard jungle mix, slugs and Double O buckshot. And we also have this.''

Hughes set down the shotgun and took a scoped bolt-action rifle from the case; the stock and even the metal were black. ''This is the Steyr-Mannlicher SSG. This is our one and only for countersniping work. It prints under a minute of angle at a hundred yards with the same ammo we're using in the assault rifles.''

''Minute of angle, sir?'' Feinberg asked the question.

''An inch at a hundred yards. Kahles scope. The best there is for this. Whichever of you three guys gets hot with this will be the official sniper.'' He smiled. ''You should be able to reliably hit a man-sized target at ranges in excess of five hundred yards and with reasonable reliability at twice that.'' Hughes looked from man to man. ''And that's it for the official toy department.''

Hughes paced in front of them now. ''All of these guns have been checked out by two of the nation's top gunsmiths, Trapper Alexiou and Ron Mahovsky. These men are also two of the nation's top pistolsmiths and metal refinishers. They were told simply that their country needed them to produce their best work as individual personal weapons for an elite force, and then told to forget they were ever told that or ever saw these guns. Babcock, Feinberg: You both may recall participating in a survey at your respective posts some time ago concerning individual personal weapons preferences. It was very detailed. Type. Manufacturer. Caliber. Finish. And knives were covered as well, a survey of commercially available edged weapons. The only purpose of the survey was to get the personal preferences of both of you.''

Hughes stopped walking, standing in front of Cross. ''And as for you, lad, well, the next best thing was done. We interviewed the surviving members of your old SEAL team and took a survey covering their own tastes and the tastes of former members of their team, the only purpose being to find out your tastes.''

There were two other cases, as yet unopened, and Hughes dropped to his knees beside the first of these. ''Feinberg, here's your stainless steel Colt Officers ACP .45. Babcock, here's your stainless steel Walther PPK .380. And Cross—we had to put two and two together a little for you. You always liked K-Frame Smiths in .38 Special, so we figured you'd like an L-Frame in .357 even better. Custom round-butted and fixed sights. Action tuned, of course.'' He closed the case, replacing the two semiautomatic pistols and the revolver. Cross wanted to try the revolver.

Hughes opened the other case. "Feinberg—Gerber MkI boot knife. Babcock—Pacific Cutlery full-sized Bali-Song folding knife. Cross—again, we had to play it by ear a little. You ended up with a Cold Steel Tanto, the Magnum length. We've got holsters for the guns and sheaths for the knives— you can pick what you want later. Any questions?"

"Where are we going, sir?" Feinberg asked.

"Iran. We're going up against the cream of the Iranian controlled terrorist commandoes. You need to know a few things," Hughes said, standing, then sitting on the tree stump as he began to speak again. "Several years ago, before the shah was deposed, there was a survey taken. About sixty percent of the middle- and upper-class Iranian population intermarried with first cousins, which I'm sure you know is not generally considered to be genetically sound. An esti- mated three million people met the Ayatollah Khomeini when he returned from France. Dying in war against nonbelievers defending their faith is close to the ultimate religious experi- ence for a Shiite. Shiites, for centuries, have been considered the extremist fundamentalists among the Moslem faith. Iranians, in particular, have been considered to be among the most peculiar of the Islamic peoples. The average Moslem is rather like you or me. Goes to church, tries to lead a good life, and hopes, when he dies, that his maker will say, 'Well done!' Moslems pray a lot, and certainly that is to be commended.

"The Moslem faith," Hughes continued, "when studied, is a revelation. Supreme logic and faith in mankind. But like any faith, it can be perverted by men who use it to their own ends. What all this is leading up to, gentlemen, is that we are going to attack a group of heavily armed, perhaps congenitally deranged, dedicated religious fanatics in the very heart of their principal training facility, which just happens to be within spitting distance of the Turkmen Soviet Socialist Republic in the Elburz Mountains. The shah used to use the area as a ski resort. And to them, we're the minions of Satan, as evil as evil can get.

"Now, are there any more questions, gentlemen?" Hughes stood up from his tree stump.

Babcock looked like his stomach had gone sour, and Feinberg looked dangerously enthused.

Cross lit a cigarette and just closed his eyes, "Oh, boy!"

# *Chapter Eight*

Cross and Babcock were running evenly. All four of them—
Feinberg and Hughes included—were carrying full gear. Instead of ammo, each man carried weight plates in his backpack,
the plates taken from the barbells used in other facets of their
training. The weight simulated the weight of the ammo they
would carry, and ten additional pounds.

Track shoes had gone by the boards halfway into the first
week, and going to combat boots had been the first change,
then running with boots and empty packs by the end of the
first week. By the middle of the second week they had been
running with two thirds of their combat load. By the end of
the second week they had gone to the full combat load plus
the additional ten pounds, and increased the run distance by
two miles.

Cross had targeted the black Army captain, Lewis Babcock,
as the man to beat. Babcock had been a runner in college, had
remained a runner for physical fitness purposes, and was into
health foods and various forms of exercise aimed at increasing both stamina and agility. Cross had told himself that if he
could keep up with Babcock, he was doing well. If he could
beat Babcock, even once, he would be unbeatable.

This morning it was unseasonably cold for the fall, and
Cross had told himself that this would be his best chance. He
had paced himself accordingly, following the pace set by
Darwin Hughes without even contemplating trying to outdis-

tance him, which he could now do almost easily. Cross had kept his pace, a fast jog interspersed with periods of brisk commando walk and then the fast jog again. They had run up the slope reaching to the level mile where Cross and Hughes had first started it and the others had soon joined in—making their ultimate kick.

Hughes had seen something in Cross's face or Cross's manner, Cross knew, and there was a smile in Hughes's eyes when they reached the summit and Hughes threw himself into the dead run for the far slope. Cross had acknowledged nothing, merely pacing himself with Babcock; ignoring Feinberg, who was a marvelous sprinter; ignoring Hughes, who could still outlast any of them in a long duration run, Cross secretly thought. But he had concentrated only on Babcock.

Cross's right thumb hooked into the G-3's sling, his left thumb into the sling for the FIE LAW-12 shotgun, the H&K submachine gun strapped to his chest. Babcock, like Cross, carried an extra weapon, the Steyr-Mannlicher SSG. But the extra weight each of them carried was compensated for by the added weight plates carried by Feinberg, who would carry the explosives, since he was the demolitions expert.

Feinberg started dropping back, his sprint gone, Hughes laying back. Cross saw Hughes's face for an instant, and the old man was laughing.

Cross stayed dead even with Babcock. The lean, well-muscled man barely showed fatigue, but Cross's lungs were already aching just keeping Babcock's pace.

Cross told himself everything he could that would boost his own confidence. He concentrated on what he knew about Babcock. Babcock's diet was lower in carbohydrates, the stuff that gave the body endurance-staying power. Babcock had less body weight to carry—Cross forced this out of his mind. Their leg length seemed all but identical—that was a good point. Babcock started his kick, and Cross forced himself ahead, to keep dead even with the man and thus demoralize him. But Babcock had still more kick, and in an instant Cross found himself outdistanced. Cross threw his shoulders back farther, to get to full lung capacity. Babcock didn't smoke—Cross told himself to forget that. He had smoked next to nothing in these past few weeks, and his lungs ached. His shins were starting to stiffen.

Cross told himself: Ignore this—run! He kept running, the level stretch that was a perfect mile almost run out, the wall of gray rock against which they would rappel almost dead ahead.

Cross was even with Babcock again, and Babcock glanced toward him. Babcock's eyes were open wide, his mouth open wide, his face contorted. Cross ran. Babcock pulled ahead. Cross pulled even, and realized he had let Babcock make it his race. Cross told himself to give more, and threw every ounce of strength and speed and stamina into the last two hundred yards, pulling ahead of Babcock, focusing his eyes on the gray granite wall. Running was all there was.

He saw a flash of something dark—Babcock in his back battle-dress utilities. They were dead even. Cross kept running, Babcock pulling ahead. Cross had no more to give. He kept running. Fifty yards remained. Babcock was back, even with him now. Twenty-five yards. Was he ahead of Babcock? He couldn't tell. Cross kept running.

The wall— Cross impacted against it, palms going out, his body twisting to prevent him from slamming into it. He started to slip, his stomach cramping, his breathing agony.

It was like a voice shouted across a great distance. It was Lewis Babcock's voice. "Damnit! You beat me, man! Congratulations!"

Abe Cross started laughing, and then he was doubled over with pain, coughing uncontrollably.


There was a mountaineering gear kit—ropes, carabiners, ascenders and descenders, pitons and the like. But the kit would be ditched when they entered the Iranian fortress, about which Hughes had told them very little. The mountaineering kit was, in fact, to be ditched immediately prior to penetration. Each man instead would wear the Pro-Pak, which consisted of a harness constructed of 7000-pound mill spec one and three-quarter-inch nylon webbing—this acted as both harness and equipment belt—and its pack. The pack could hold from forty to three hundred feet of tubular Kevlar with reinforcements, where needed. Carabiners were sewn into the line, thus eliminating knotting.

"Cross—your turn, lad," Hughes said.

Cross stepped to the line. Hughes held his stopwatch. "Ready— now!"

Cross attached his line securely to the metal hook already plunged into the rocky surface and, holding the line in his left hand as it came out of his pack—the protective sleeve drawn out to where the rock would have its most abrasive effect on the Kevlar—he started down, line feeding from the pack. He controlled his descent with his right. By changing the configuration of the descender, the user had greater control than with standard descenders. In some of the earlier training sessions, Hughes had insisted on dead stops at various stages along the sixty-foot descent. The system, aside from being faster into operation from a dead start, allowed the maximum control needed in a rescue situation, a more versatile movement for tactical situations or, as for self-evacuation, utmost speed.

Cross kicked out and let himself drop the rest of the distance.

Hughes shouted down from the height of the granite wall sixty feet above, "Eighteen seconds—not bad, but you can get better, lad!"

"Shit," Cross hissed. His rope snaked down and he started away from the wall to repack for the next time.

# Chapter Nine

It was Babcock's ridiculously perfect health that had made him the sniper, the SSG almost magical in his hands. But what Babcock possessed in long-range marksmanship, Cross more than compensated for with the handgun in terms of experience.

They stood at the twenty-five-yard marker, all four of them merely practicing for themselves, the day's formal training sessions over. Cross had found these sessions his greatest time to relax. Both handguns he would carry into combat were on the bench before him. He picked up the Beretta 92F. He'd left the service before the pistol trials had been finalized, and although he had fired Beretta pistols in the past, he hadn't fired this latest military variant until the training had begun. Now, he'd all but fallen in love with it. The trigger was military heavy in double action, the gun by design idiot proof, but he had found it as faultlessly reliable as the .45 1911A1 had ever been. He took one of the twenty-round extension magazines and placed it up the magazine well, then thumbed down the slide stop. He aimed the pistol downrange, moved the slide-mounted thumb safety, and fired.

He double actioned the first shot, the pistol in both hands, left fist over right, working the trigger single action for the subsequent shots as rapidly as possible until the action locked open, his twentieth shot counted. Then Cross bent over to the level of the bench and peered through the spotting scope. The head of the standard silhouette was ragged and empty.

Cross removed the magazine, leaving the action open, and set the pistol down on the bench.

Lewis Babcock, beside him, tapped Cross on the right earmuff, and Cross turned. "Why do you always shoot for the head?" Babcock asked.

"Smaller target, harder to hit than center of mass. Better training," Cross answered, realizing he was shouting the way he always did when he wore shooter's earmuffs. It was the hollow quality they gave incoming sound. He tended to attempt to compensate for it by shouting when he spoke.

Babcock nodded, then resumed shooting with his Beretta.

Cross picked up the customized L-Frame Smith .357 Magnum, the cylinder open. He picked up one of the three Safariland speedloaders he would carry into combat to service the weapon.

He thought about Babcock's remark, and nodded to himself.

Cross rammed the loader against the cylinder, its center hitting the ejector star, the six rounds spilling into the charging holes; the left thumb closing the cylinder as the right hand pocketed the loader, catching the grip as the left hand brought the revolver up; his right hand closing over the memory-grooved Goncalo Alves round butt stocks; his left fist sliding under the trigger guard and closing over his right, his right first finger at the trigger, double actioning the weapon—six shots, the target vibrating each time with the impacts from the 158-grain semijacketed soft points, clouds of dust exploding from the range backstop.

Cross worked the cylinder release catch as he brought the weapon down, the fingers of his left hand pushing out the cylinder, the revolver's ejector rod punching toward him under the pressure of his thumb, the empty nickel-plated cases spilling outward and downward, the revolver nearly inverted. Already his right hand was moving the second speedloader toward the rear face of the cylinder, the gun twisting upward in his left hand, the loader impacting the ejector star, the cartridges sliding into place, his left thumb closing the cylinder as he dropped the loader from his right hand, the hand closing over the grip.

Again he fired, emptying the revolver in double taps this time; again, he had the cylinder open, the empties dropped, the cylinder recharged, the cylinder closed.

Again he fired.

He held the revolver at a forty-five degree angle to the ground, his right first finger moving from inside the guard. He didn't need the spotting scope. The silhouette's center of mass showed daylight in roughly the shape and size of a half grapefruit. If he'd shot that well there in the supermarket, he realized, the old black woman's throat wouldn't have been cut. Cross closed his eyes.

Nights were now spent studying the tactics that would be employed, and a new element for their morning schedules and utilizing the obstacle course, intended to simulate movement along corridors, up and down stairwells, and one room into the next, door entries where multiple targets were engaged with CO-2 powered pistols of the type used in combat survival games. Hughes carried such a pistol. When a man was without cover, Hughes notified him by shooting him in the heart or the spine or the head, each men wearing goggles and earplugs to protect himself from a sudden paint spray.

On Saturday evening of the third week, as Cross smoked one of his by now rare cigarettes and sipped at a beer on the couch, Hughes entered from the office. Babcock and Feinberg were playing chess in the far corner of the room—Cross was better than Feinberg and too evenly matched with Babcock to have an interesting game without a chess timer or an abundance of time to implement the most methodical of strategies.

Hughes had both hands thrust into the pockets of urban gray BDU pants, his feet shoeless, a big hole in the toe of his left sock. "I think it's time we discussed the target."

Cross heard one of the chess pieces fall over and a chair being pushed back. He looked toward the chess table. Feinberg was standing. Babcock had turned around.

Cross didn't stub out his cigarette. Those few he smoked were too dear to him for that. "Let's," Cross murmured.

Cross noticed a video cassette under Hughes's left arm, near the crook of the elbow. He tossed the cassette across the great room, Cross leaning forward on the sofa to catch it. Sean

Connery's face stared back at him, a pretty girl on either side of him, his jaw flanked by Walther P-5 pistols, one a mirror image of the other.

"I loved *Never Say Never Again*; we're going after nuclear warheads? And as far as distribution of the girls, either Kim or Barbara's fine by me." Cross smiled.

"Just put the tape into the machine, lad."

Cross did as he was asked and waited in front of the machine to adjust the sound. In seconds Sean Connery was running along a road in some tropical location and Lani Hall was singing the title theme. Cross moved back to the couch, Babcock and Feinberg flanking him, Hughes standing behind them. Cross's cigarette was dying a lingering death in the ashtray, and he stubbed it out of its misery. He lit another one as Connery took out a sentry with a blowgun. Then Connery slid along a cable toward the compound that was his target. Cross had to hand it to him—he had some good moves. Another sentry.

The sound and light grenade—they had some for their mission, whatever it was—was tossed into the house where the terrorists were, and Connery swung in through the window and—

The tape flickered, and Hughes walked toward the machine, picked up the remote, and the flickering paused. "Unfortunately, if we don't do it right the first time, we can't do it better in the retake, gentlemen. You're slipping Cross—did you notice the new electrical surge protector on the VCR?"

"No."

"It's a decoder. Without it, this exceedingly well-made film—"

"A classic," Babcock interjected.

"Exactly—it would have run in its entirety. With it, the first several minutes would run as we have seen. The good guy wins in the end, by the way. At any event, with it, a special track laid in on a frequency demanding a power conversion for viewing becomes visible—just in case anyone did know we were up here and decided to play with my tape library. Let's watch."

He pushed Pause and the flickering and fuzz continued, then abruptly stopped. Snow-capped mountains were visible in the distance. Hughes said quietly, "If anyone wants to see the rest of the movie, I have another copy of it, by the way. What you are seeing now is the Elburz Mountains. Keep watching. In the interests of international cooperation, the next time you see the KGB, remember to say a kind word. This film, now transferred to tape, was originally theirs. This wasn't a loan. Suffice it to say, Dzherzhinsky Square has its security leaks too.

"Now, coming up there in the left corner of the screen, lower left—upper left—not very good photography, I'm afraid . . . there—that darker spot? That's an entrance to a network of caves. That's the back door, so to speak, to the training complex for an organization called International Jihad, which is headquartered, performs principal training exercises, even executes prisoners in a system of caverns—huge things—within the mountains themselves. No one has ever been inside the caverns and gotten out to talk about them—no one who wasn't a Shiite Moslem allied with or part of International Jihad, at any event. Now, watch carefully."

The plane that carried the lackluster photographer was climbing; Cross tried to gauge the altitude. There was a sheer rock face over the entrance to which Hughes had referred, a drop of perhaps six hundred feet, perhaps more, and beyond it a rise which dropped at perhaps a forty-five degree angle overall over what looked to be a distance of several miles, then abruptly split, Y-shaped.

Hughes continued to speak. "Where the plateau forks—to the right in relation to the screen—is the Soviet Union, to the left is Iran. You come in from the left and ascend that graduated plateau, then rope down that cliff face to the tunnel entrance."

The screen began to flicker, and the film content and quality abruptly shifted. The same mountains, apparently, but a wide, unnatural opening at what appeared to be ground level, the opening fenced, guarded, and barely visible—the quality was getting worse—what appeared to be massive, vaultlike doors leading into the mountains themselves.

"That's the main entrance. You could get inside that way if we had a division to back you up and either a low-yield tactical nuclear device or a few tons of trinitrotoluene to use on the doors. But in the meantime you'd alert the thousand or so terrorists inside in their various stages of training, and flushing them out of the tunnel network would make Vietnam tunnel-ratting look like a pleasant stroll in the park. And could take weeks. Poison gas? A lovely thought, if you got inside, but the tunnels are such, as we understand it, that the natural aeration would suck out most of the gas before it did its work. Plus, there are villages within a few miles of the complex, with innocent people, some of whom are totally unsympathetic to our old pal the Ayatollah. To endanger them needlessly would make us as bad as the terrorists. Hence, even if push really came to shove, the place couldn't be nuked. And nuking it would be tough and likely considerably less successful than we might suppose. And anyway, we're not about to risk global thermonuclear war to mop up scum like this. So—one way in. But, look there. . . ."

The tape had flickered again. The KGB film apparently, and this time another sweep of the same location, but visible in the lower right corner something that looked like— Hughes freeze-framed the tape.

"A helicopter. A pad," Feinberg said, sounding at once obvious and spontaneous.

"Very good. That is the way out. If you get that far. Which is doubtful, as you may have guessed."

Cross looked into Hughes's face. The eyes smiled.

"No shit," Babcock said. "A thousand guys, you say?"

"Give or take. I intend that you three will penetrate the terrorist base, take best advantage of the natural structure of the caves. You, Feinberg will kill as many as possible with explosives. Or, just seal them forever in granite. That's immaterial. Kill anyone else you can, destroy anything you can. If there appear to be any interesting papers, take possession of them. Anything really exciting the folks back home might like to see—like Soviet advisors, for example, or Cubans, whatever, grab a few snapshots, perhaps. Then, after the full tour of the place, steal a helicopter, if there's one there—and satellite data indicates there usually is. Steal it and sabotage anything else they could put into the air to go after you. Then fly home and tell me about your trip. More details, of course, but are there any questions so far?''

He was smiling.

Cross asked him, ''Can we see the rest of the movie?''

Hughes still smiled. ''Later, lad.''

# Chapter Ten

Since the amount of alcohol in his system had become vastly reduced, he had found that sleeping through the night was becoming very difficult. It could be called insomnia, he supposed, but it was aptly described as the absence of passing out into unconsciousness. Then he had found that a good workout in the evening helped to physically tire him enough so he could sleep soundly.

Abe Cross took the Cold Steel Magnum Tanto in his hand, its edge taped over for the sake of safety; and he began the kata he had begun improvising since the blade had first been given to him, and since he'd constantly worked to improve.

He drew the knife from its sheath in a saber hold, then rose to his full height and stepped away from the corner of the workout room where he had lain the sheath. At the middle of the beige walled room, now, he drew himself up, expanding his chest, his shoulders lowering, the knife still in a saber hold.

Cross drew his right foot back, shifting his balance rearward, his left hand extending toward his invisible enemy, palm outward as though blocking a blow or feigning one, the haft of the Tanto spinning in his fingers, the blade along the inside of his right forearm, point toward the elbow, edge outward, the brass skull-crusher pommel just protruding at the top of his balled fist.

He shifted his weight forward, striking at air with the

Tanto's pommel, then the blade edge arcing outward and slicing. The haft of the Tanto spun through his fingers again as he recovered from the strike, the left hand palm outward again, the Tanto beside his right hip in a saber hold, edge downward, ready for a close-quarters thrust. His right leg straightened, his left knee flexing as he threw his weight slightly left and back. His left palm drew back almost against his chest, his right arm snapping outward and slightly upward, the Tanto's pommel to his left, the blade to his right, edge outward, steel parallel to the floor surface.

His right leg moved back, the Tanto spinning again in his fingers, the knife in a saber hold again near his right hip, edge downward.

Cross stepped forward on his right leg, snapping the Tanto outward, edge left, the reinforced point of the blade aimed at an imaginary throat. He stepped forward with his left foot, advancing on the imagined opponent, the knife spinning again in his fingers, the Tanto point up, edge forward, ready for a downward hack or slice. His left leg snapped back, the Tanto spinning again, the blade against his raised right forearm, edge toward the imagined opponent, prepared to block a strike or make a sudden cut.

The man from whom he had learned much of his knife-fighting technique had moved with a blade as though his actions had been choreographed for the ballet stage. Cross had learned, too, from this man, that mere imitation of a style was inadequate, that to truly master the close-range use of a blade, one had to make one's own style, which became second nature in conjunction with the flow of one's own natural body movement.

Cross drew back, prepared to try the kata again.

Raka rose from his prayer rug, and neatly rolled it after reciting the specified taslim, consisting of salutations on the Prophet and His house. He especially enjoyed the sunset, evening, and dawn prayers, when audible recitals from *The Koran* were needed, as opposed to silent recitations.

This was his quiet time of day, for personal prayer, meditation, and the melding of body and spirit. He had worked once with a Japanese who had fought against his boot-licking lacky government, which was the pawn of the Great Satan. Though an infidel, Raka had learned what he felt was a valuable lesson from the Japanese. The lesson was, that the mind and body of the warrior must function together in such perfect harmony that they were as one, and the rhythm of the body then would be the divine rhythm of the human mind.

Raka cherished this lesson, and—more importantly—he used it.

He used it now.

He picked up his knife. It was unique, one of a kind. It would never be duplicated, because he had used it to cut the throat of the man who had made it for him.

Its blade was a full twenty-two centimeters in length.

The guard was heavy brass overlaying steel, the brass to catch the blade of an opponent, the steel to keep the brass from being broken. The haft was, after the Japanese fashion, wrapped in sharkskin.

He moved the knife ever so slightly in his hands, letting the blade catch the artificial light. It was a highly modified Bowie pattern, the recurving false edge very short and deeply curved, almost hooklike, the spine of the blade sharpened as a full secondary edge. He had specified D-2 tool steel in its construction.

He rolled the knife in his hands. At the butt of the haft there was a triangular spike, less than three centimeters long, made, like the blade, of tool steel.

He began to move with the knife now, as though the knife were merely an extension of his hand. This secret he had also learned from the Japanese: that when mind and body were one, whether the weapon was an empty hand or a blade or even a firearm, this, too, was one with the user.

The blade wheeled in his hands.

# Chapter Eleven

There was another trick movie tape this evening. The movie this time was *Conan the Barbarian*. And Arnold Schwarzenegger hadn't even appeared yet when the static started.

Hughes, his sandaled feet propped on the edge of the coffee table, worked the remote.

It was newsreel footage, and Cross recognized the face on the television screen. It was the face of the shah of Iran, the man who took power abdicated to him from his father, an officer in the Persian Cossack Brigade, who left Iran rather than rule under the military occupation of both the Germans and the British. The shah stifled the democratic waves his father had created in order to revolutionize the country. He failed and left his homeland in 1979.

"That's Mount Dizan. The shah and his family used to ski there, as you see. Beneath Mount Dizan is the heart of the target. Let's talk numbers," Hughes said. "At least a thousand terrorists in various stages of training for work as members of International Jihad. But it's the perfect target for us. No children inside, and no innocent bystanders. The only women are themselves terrorists."

It was different footage now, but of the same area, deep in snow, bright sunshine glistening off snowcapped mountain peaks, as ideal-looking a spot as something out of a ski resort brochure. Positively inviting-looking, Cross thought, smiling at the images it brought to mind. Sitting before a roaring fire, a glass of rum on the floor beside him, a pretty girl snuggled against him, their boots off and their feet rubbing each other.

Hughes spoke again, and it drew him from his fantasy. There was a fireplace, but no fire roared in it. No glass of rum, just a half-emptied bottle of Michelob. No pretty girl, no women at all.

"We have reason to believe that the leadership of International Jihad is in the KGB's pocket. There have been token acts against Soviet citizens, but nothing truly serious. Elements of International Jihad's leadership cadre tend to disappear occasionally and return with great suddenness. We know that the field commander for International Jihad, a man named Raka, spent three years in Moscow and graduated from Patrice Lumumba University. We know a number of other things about this guy Raka." The TV screen went to static.

Hughes stood up and walked to the middle of the open expanse between the television set and the couch where Cross, Babcock, and Feinberg sat.

"Raka doesn't give the orders. He takes them. From a man named Mehdi Hamadan, who is a Soviet sympathizer and apparently using the Islamic fundamentalist movement as a means of keeping the United States—or the Great Satan, as we're called over there—off balance. And 'off balance' is also the perfect way to describe Raka. Surrounding him, Raka has a group of twelve men he calls his 'Immortals.' Each of the twelve has, as part of his training, worked in the torture chambers at Evin Prison outside Tehran and at Gohardasht Prison and at Tabriz. I don't have to tell you what skills they refined. Each of them has had significant combat experience in commando units used in the early stages of the Iran-Iraq War. Since these twelve are handpicked by Raka, it's to be assumed their skill levels are inordinately high, because a lot of his people are very good.

"Raka himself," Hughes continued, "is devoutly religious, and psychological profiles worked up on him seem to suggest he is obsessively homicidal. And he's also brilliant. Not just as a tactician, but intellectually gifted. He's engineered and supervised several assassinations for the International Jihad leadership, and he's probably the toughest of the terrorists serving Iran. And the best. We have Raka, his twelve Immortals, and more or less a thousand others at varying skill levels, all religious fanatics prepared to die for their cause; a wide array of weapons available to them in a fortified location which is probably wired to self-destruct, in the unlikely event that an intruding force ever should seize control. Raka and his men are like homicidal demigods coming down from Olympus to do their dirty work, then returning to a hero's welcome.

"But, on the plus side," Hughes smiled, "if we get the job done, we couldn't strike a more damaging blow against Iranian-sponsored terrorism. In these last few weeks you've been training for a mission you knew very little about. So, here it is in a nutshell. You'll be inserted via Turkey, cross into Iran and travel along the border with Armenia until you reach the Caspian Sea. Once inside Iran, you'll be met by members of the People's Mujahedin, all of them experienced resistance fighters who'll serve as your guides and as additional firepower. Once you reach the sea, you'll travel along the coast to Tankabon, and then from there into the mountains and to the target. As you already know, we're banking on being able to steal a helicopter for you guys to use to get out and back into Turkey. If there is no chopper, you'll have to exfiltrate the hard way. I'll remain in Turkey, and I'll remain there until the mission is accomplished and/or I learn of your deaths. Each of you will be given what they call a 'death pill' in the spy stories. If you're captured, use it, or for however long you live, you'll regret it. Believe me. Against the slight chance of escape, you'd be gambling worse tortures than any sane person could imagine possible."

He thrust his hands into his pockets and looked at them each in turn. His eyes stopped on Cross's eyes. Hughes asked, "Any questions, then?"

Feinberg stood up, his hands locked behind him as though he were at parade rest. "Sir?"

"Yes, Feinberg."

"I mean, I'm all gung ho for this. You know that. But I just wanted to know. Do you think we have any chance at all, sir? I mean, to get back?"

Babcock didn't let Hughes answer. "Being realistic," he

said, "I don't think anyone would want us back. If we're dead, we can't talk about it. Isn't that right, Mr. Hughes?"

"I'll promise you this. I don't know official policy on this, but if anyone tries to pull your plugs, they'll have to get over me to do it. I swear that to all of you."

Feinberg sat down.

Hughes spoke again. "Cross will be the tactical team leader, as all of you know. He's the best man for the job, the best man to get you other two back alive. We've already smuggled a duplicate set of weapons and gear into Turkey for your use. And a duplicate set of my gear as well, just in case I have to do any traveling. You weren't aware of this, but the weapons and equipment you trained on will stay here. We go into Turkey clean. The weapons have been checked by myself and a team of independent experts to be identical in every respect to the ones you're using now—trigger pulls, balance, everything. We'll travel under assumed names, all using American passports. The man coordinating this for us in Turkey is a man I personally trust. So, we're all right there. Any other questions?"

Cross downed the rest of his beer. No one said a word.

Cross had always considered Russian roulette a foolish game—a six-round revolver was emptied of all cartridges but one, the muzzle pressed to the head after the cylinder was given a hearty spin and closed shut. You pulled the trigger, gambling that the hammer would fall on an empty chamber.

But this surgical strike against terrorism . . . it was like playing Russian roulette with a fully loaded gun; rather pointless in bothering to ask which pull of the trigger would kill you.

# Chapter Twelve

One of the advantages of being a lounge pianist was the opportunity it afforded of memorizing the basic melodies of all the old standards and then improvising for those times when you misplaced the one fake book you needed. An ancillary advantage was that, after a while, you could sit down and play almost anything and sound at once good and innovative, and if you put the right look on your face, the women thought it was really sexy.

There were no women around, but he liked playing the piano anyway. Cross closed his eyes, almost seeing the opening bars of "You Go to My Head."

His fingers started to move, he realized, as though his hands had a mind of their own.

When he played the piano, he focused his concentration so completely that it was almost like sex. He could see a beach, hear the roar of surf—Laurie Morris. Her auburn hair cascaded along her back, over his naked arms as he held her—

"Cross?"

Cross stopped playing. He looked behind him. It was Babcock.

"You play very well."

"Thank you. What can I do for you?"

"Keep playing—please."

"All right." He nodded, his fingers resuming the run where he had stopped it.

"What do you think our chances are?" Babcock leaned against the piano, a beer in his left hand.

"About the same as making this piano sound like a violin."

Babcock smiled. "My mother tried getting me to take the violin—"

"I know, but you were afraid the store detective would see you." Cross laughed.

"No, I'm serious." Babcock grinned. "That was before the Suzuki method—or if it wasn't, nobody in our neighborhood had heard about it. But I told her no way."

"My mother had a crush on Liberace, and her sister had a crush on Hoagy Carmichael. When my parents were gone and my aunt raised me, my style of playing sort of shifted a little," Cross told him. He broke into Carmichael's most famous song. "Stardust," while telling Babcock, "Light me a cigarette, huh?"

Babcock took the pack of Pall Malls and the Zippo from the folded-down music rack and shook one free, then lit it, coughing as he exhaled a little puff of the smoke. "How can you do this to your lungs?"

Cross reached over and took the cigarette. "It goes with my image—you know, playin' 'Set 'em Up Joe' with a drink next to the keyboard and a cigarette hanging from my lips—the women freak over it, no shit," and he started to laugh.

"No chance, huh? Well, I'm gonna work in a lot of chess games between now and time we leave, then. Try some marathon reading."

"Tolstoy?"

"No. I was thinking more of Max Allan Collins; I love detective stories. That why you're playing the piano tonight?"

"Because I like mysteries?"

"No, to catch up on things, I mean."

"Maybe. But I do think we have a chance. Otherwise, there'd be a couple tons of cigarettes and beer I'd be workin' on consuming."

"You said as much chance—"

Cross abruptly stopped playing and stood up, putting the cigarette down in the ashtray, leaning over and raising the lid of the piano. He started plucking strings.

"It sound—"

"Like a violin," Cross said, and smiled.

A detailed scale model of the target had been erected on the table that dominated the center of the room. His Immortals surrounded him now. Raka spoke, his speech carefully measured. "The training here is very nearly come to an end. All of us here know that nothing but death will be the final resolution to the action we are about to undertake."

He studied their faces, his twelve, and was reminded of the great teacher whom the benighted Christians considered the son of God. His twelve apostles. The clarity of their eyes, the resoluteness of their expression, the strength and dignity they seemed to exude.

"We will pray together that our mission will be the first phase of the death blow to the Great Satan and the Jew occupiers of Palestine and all who serve them."

"In the name of God the merciful, the compassionate," Raka intoned the takbir, declaring the greatness of God. He then recited to his followers certain sections from *The Koran*, bowing and prostrating twice after each inclination and ending the cycle of prayers with the obligatory taslim.

Abe Cross closed the letter. He'd told his aunt that the things she had worried about concerning him were no longer problems. His drinking was perfectly under control. He had found purpose in his life again. He told her that whatever happened now would be for the good. He thanked her, as he had so many times in the past, for taking him in, for raising him as she would have raised her own child, for standing by him in the difficult times, for loving him.

The letter would be mailed for him. She could not know what was to happen. He sealed the letter in its envelope, picked up the Tanto, and walked from his room and onto the balconylike hall that led to the stairs. He started down the stairs, leaving the letter on top of the bar—it had become the mailbox. He'd never used it before. Feinberg wrote home daily, it seemed. Babcock wrote, but it was never clear to whom. Cross realized the letters would be opened, read, censored if necessary, or perhaps destroyed.

The writing was the important thing anyway, cathartic. He reached the weight room, which smelled of sweat. Feinberg was just finishing up some sort of martial arts kata that looked like Tae Kwan Do.

Cross waited. There would be time for him. And his knife.

# Chapter Thirteen

"Anytime Neal James and the Neal James Band get together under one roof, you've got good entertainment," Darwin Hughes declared, killing the Jeep's ignition and pulling the key. Abe Cross sat beside him, studying the enthusiasm evident in the older man's face.

The parking lot outside Whiskey Hollow was reasonably well-filled, and the show wouldn't start—Cross checked his Rolex against the time posted on the marquee near the entrance to the parking lot—for another twenty minutes. More cars were pulling in.

"Let's go inside. I want to get us a good table, and those pizzas we ate could definitely stand some more washing down," Hughes said, opening the driver's side door and getting out. Cross climbed out as well, Babcock and Feinberg getting out from the backseat.

The four of them started across the paved ground. The night was gray and misty, and the parking lot outside Whiskey Hollow cold, damp. Cross hunched his shoulders against it, the collar on his brown bomber jacket raised. Hughes had left his little revolver in the glove compartment. Cross assumed that all four of them were clean.

Tomorrow night would be the last night. In the afternoon of the following day they would drive to Athens and board a commuter flight that would take them to Atlanta, then using their false passports and false identity papers—driver's licenses, Social Security cards, credit cards—they would fly from Rome to Istanbul, then by private aircraft to Ankara, and then on to their staging area.

The thought crossed his mind that fake credit cards might open golden opportunities to someone unscrupulous enough to use them beyond the scope of their intent. He smiled at the thought.

There was a girl playing the piano, and the place was already so packed that only a few tables were empty. Cross felt instant relief that Babcock's wasn't the only black face in the crowd. His attention drifted back to the girl at the piano. She had long, straight, chestnut-brown hair that seemed to move almost in time to the music she played. He almost tripped over the low step up, Hughes beside him, saying under his breath, "She's pretty, isn't she?"

Cross nodded as Hughes wound his way between the tables. Cross guessed the older man had been there before. His suspicions were confirmed when one of the waitresses came up to Hughes and planted a kiss on his cheek, Hughes embracing her briefly. Either that or Whiskey Hollow was an exceedingly friendly place. The girl who had kissed Hughes—a blonde, about thirty or so, and with a pretty face and a nice-looking figure, assumed leadership of the column, aiming them toward a table near the stage. The band instruments were already set up, a bass-drum head confirming the sign on the marquee—the Neal James Band.

They ordered beers all around—the blond waitress had just given a laugh, when Babcock asked for vodka—and by that time the pretty girl with the long hair had stopped playing, curtsied in her ankle-length floral print skirt, and walked off. The hum of the crowd sounded appreciably louder when the erratic but enthusiastic applause died down. Cross checked his watch. Neal James was due.

The girl came back on the stage, wrestling the microphone out of the stand and breathing into it—even her breathing sounded good. "Now here he is—who y'all been waitin' for—Neal James and the Neal James Band!" She started applauding, and so did everybody in the place, even Feinberg, who didn't like country music. Cross realized he was smiling.

The band guys had filtered out onto the stage while the girl was talking. Then a tall, burly guy with a black cowboy hat, a short curly beard, and curly hair bushed out under both sides of the natty-looking black cowboy hat, came on stage in a hurry and the band started playing. The song was "Spent Most of My Life." Cross recognized it from the album he'd heard. It started out slow and a little lazy, like New Orleans jazz with a good guitar sound backing him up. Cross watched the man's face. It was clear that Neal James enjoyed making music. Cross started to laugh—one of the lines in the song was about spending most of his life trying to treat the ladies right. It wasn't a bad way to spend one's time at all, Cross reflected.

The keyboard player cut in with an almost thirties sound. Cross mentally doffed his hat—or would have if he'd been wearing one—to the pianist. The piano hadn't sounded like that when the girl had played it. But, on the minus side, the girl was nicer to look at.

The tempo shifted up. Some people in the audience started clapping their hands in time to the music.

The tempo shifted again.

Cross's eyes shifted to Hughes's face. They flickered right, Cross following them. About a dozen guys came in the doorway Cross and the others had entered through, the guys looking like renegade bikers from a Hollywood back lot. Cross thought he heard Hughes mutter something, and he watched the corners of Hughes's mouth turn down. There were bikers in the place already, just having a good time. These guys somehow didn't look like they wanted a good time—at least not in the conventional way.

The tempo picked up, all the guys in the band and Neal James himself jamming on it, but some of the clapping going down in volume, Cross noticing others in the crowded room turning toward the twelve men in rotted-looking black leather and ragged-looking denims who'd just come in.

The apparent leader, a big guy with a wild look in his eyes and red hair, was flanked by two guys half his girth and several inches shorter. The flankers pushed their way through the crowd. Trouble, Cross thought absently.

The big guy with the red hair sat down at the table near the stage, opposite Cross, and the others. His sidekicks, more diminutive by comparison, pushed the two couples already occupying the table out of the way. Neither of the displaced men looked over twenty-five, and one of them was built like a college football player. When he started to move on one of the two sidekicks, the girl he was with pulled him away. He gave them the finger as he trotted off in tow with her, but apparently no one at the table saw the gesture. The remaining nine who had come through the front door spread themselves out around the room.

Babcock leaned toward Cross. "What the hell is going on?"

Cross shrugged and sipped at his Michelob. Neal James kept playing on the stage, but otherwise, since the arrival of the twelve guys, the place had gotten quieter. There were other bikers in the place, Cross catching two bikers and their girls watching the newcomers. The bikers already present in Whiskey Hollow were tough-looking guys, but looked like they had the real toughness that didn't need to constantly be demonstrated and proven. The twelve guys who had just come in looked just the opposite, and mean as well.

Cross sipped again at his beer.

Hughes's expression combined worry with amusement. Cross glanced toward Feinberg—the New Yorker seemed to be grooving on the music, completely unaware of the tension amplifying in waves now.

The song stopped. Everyone applauded. There were some whistles and shouts; everyone except the twelve guys. The band began another song Cross recognized from Hughes's album, but the name of it escaped him. Then the lyric told him it was "Shimmer in the Night," a very pretty love song.

Doris, the blond waitress came back to the table, asking if they wanted refills. Her hands were shaking. Cross watched her eyes as Hughes asked her, "Who are those men?"

"That's Thurmond Pettigrew—the big guy."

Cross started to laugh. "Thurmond Pettigrew?" Upon reflection, Cross decided, if he'd been stuck with a name like that, he would have acted like a bad-ass as well, simply out of self-defense.

"What exactly is a Thurmond Pettigrew?" Babcock asked, sounding sincere.

"Him and his gang was thrown in jail when Hiram and Molly testified against them after they near beat a coupla young fellas t'death out yonder in the parkin' lot."

"Hiram and Molly Walsh own Whiskey Hollow," Hughes advised. "They were in a car accident a few weeks ago, and they're both still hospitalized, I understand."

"Wasn't no accident. Was them that done it." Doris's pretty eyes hardened as she looked toward the table where Pettigrew sat, and then around the room where his associates "mingled."

"Do the police know?" Babcock was leaning very close to Doris—to be heard over the band, and not talk so loudly as to be rude to the entertainers, Cross realized.

Doris took Babcock's right hand in both of hers. "Hiram and Molly—they were afraid." And her blue eyes got saucer wide.

The voice that shouted out over the music had a rare combination of qualities in it, Cross thought—almost classic ignorance, magnificent conceit, and atrocious diction. The syntax was indescribable. "Hey, nigger! Get y'all's hands off all over that there piece a' ass!"

Cross leaned back in his chair and sipped at his beer. The music sort of trickled off and died. Cross closed his eyes and shook his head.

Babcock stood up fast and his chair fell back with a loud cracking sound against the floor.

Before Babcock could speak, Cross said in a loud stage whisper, "Thurmond Pettigrew—wonder if that's a family name he just inherited or if his parents were sadists? Hmm!"

Babcock looked around at Cross. Doris disappeared. Hughes inhaled very loudly. Feinberg asked, "Why'd the music stop?"

Cross told him. "That shithead over there said something stupid. Not to change the subject, but wasn't the music pleasant, though!"

Neal James, holding onto his guitar with massive hands that looked as though they were about to strangle the instrument, shouted down from the stage. "Pettigrew—why don't y'all join the twentieth century or get the hell outa here?"

"This's 'tween me and lover boy, theah, song man!" And then Thurmond Pettigrew turned back toward Lewis Babcock and stood up. Pettigrew was most similar in size to an upright meat locker. "Y'all got y'all a name, nigger?"

"It's Babcock, bad-ass." Cross admired Babcock's firm delivery.

"Babcock, huh? That what y'all thinks is 'tween y'all's legs for thet white woman?"

"Your turn, Lew," Cross said pleasantly.

Doris shouted from over by the stage. "He was askin' me what y'all was doin' here, Thurmond. Why don't y'all leave? Ain't y'all done enough mischief?"

Neal James's voice was low, even. "Pettigrew, people are payin' me and the band here to perform. Maybe next weekend they'll hire y'all. So, wait y'all's turn and shut up!"

Several of the bikers—the ones who hadn't come in with Pettigrew—and other patrons of Whiskey Hollow stood up. Pettigrew's two sidekicks backed off and their hands went under their coats and came back with knives, el-cheapo switchblades like the kind the guy in the supermarket had used to kill the woman.

There were some gasps from women in the place, the kind of gasps that sounded like something out of a high school play, Cross thought—a mixture of alarm and excitement.

Cross pulled at his beer. Feinberg stood up. Hughes said, his voice even, "Nothing that looks too spectacular, lads, please."

Neal James came down off the stage. "Pettigrew, I've known y'all, God help me, for a dozen years. And y'all are still the same stupid fool y'all always—" He never finished the sentence, because Pettigrew had hauled a five-pound-ham-sized right fist back. Neal James ducked, sidestepping, his left fist snapping out into Pettigrew's jawline, Pettigrew's head snapping back, his body toppling back like an axed-through tree. One of the sidekicks started to catch Pettigrew. The other came at James with his switchblade. James turned toward the man and started swinging his guitar—a nicely finished acoustic—and the guitar shattered against the side-kick's face. Babcock started to move, as one of the other nine raised a chair to crash down over the country singer's back. Babcock's left foot snapped up and out, a double Tae Kwan Do kick in the right ribcage, hurtling the man down.

Pettigrew was up. There was an ill-cared-for .45 Colt automatic in his right fist. "Cross!" Hughes snapped.

Cross threw himself out of his chair, slapping the beer bottle backhand across Pettigrew's face, Cross's left hand coming down over the .45, interposing the fleshy web between thumb and first finger, between the hammer and the slide. "Aw, shit!"

He'd have a blood blister, but the .45 wouldn't go off.

Pettigrew fell back, his face covered with blood, but his right fist didn't let go of the gun, and Cross was dragged after him.

Cross fell onto the man, the body odor and cheap cologne smell nauseating. And then, as Cross looked up, there was fighting all around him. Cross heard a sound at the door. More of Pettigrew's people were coming in. If people was the right word, he reflected.

Cross looked right and left. Pettigrew was starting to stir under him. Cross's right hand found the right arm brachial artery and applied pressure. Pettigrew started screaming louder, but his fist opened and Cross had the gun. Or it had him. He freed the web of his hand from it, raising the hammer, then upped the safety. He stuffed the .45 in his belt under his jacket.

At least a half dozen more of Pettigrew's gang had joined the brawl, chairs and bottles smashing everywhere around him. Pettigrew started to get up, and Cross's right foot snapped up, the side of his foot catching Pettigrew under the base of the chin. He could have killed Pettigrew by impacting the base of the nose instead, but remembered Hughes's advice.

Hughes.

Cross saw Hughes, locked in combat with one of the two sidekicks, the sidekick still holding onto his knife, Hughes attempting to rectify the situation. Hughes's right knee smashed up, into the sidekick's crotch, the sidekick doubling over, Hughes twisting right and back, dragging the sidekick off balance and forward. Hughes's left hand released the grip on the knife hand, then snapped down, a classic karate chop impacting behind and beneath the sidekick's right ear. He smashed his right knee up again, against the man's jaw, the body snapping to full height and flopping back. Hughes wheeled, saw another of Pettigrew's men coming at him, and caught the man's right hand and wrist in his own right. Hughes's left hand caught the man's other elbow, and Hughes's body moved almost not at all, the attacker cartwheeling forward and slamming into the floor.

"Very good, Hughes! Hey, what can I say!" Cross started forward to congratulate the older man. But one of Pettigrew's men vaulted toward him. Cross sidestepped, his left leg snapping out, tripping the guy and as he started to sprawl. Cross rabbit-punched him with a drophammer right over the spinal column.

Babcock and one of the non-Pettigrew bikers were back to back, each of them duking it out with a Pettigrew man. Neal James stepped in and tapped the Pettigrew man who fought the biker on the right shoulder. The Pettigrew man turned toward him, and James's right fist rocked up, the Pettigrew man's head snapping back, James's left fist impacting the Pettigrew man's beer belly, then his right coming up for the uppercut he'd just suckered the guy into taking. The Pettigrew man took it and dropped.

Babcock was using his Pettigrew man's face like a striking bag. James and the biker—evidently friends, the way they shook hands and smiled—watched with apparent enthusiastic amusement. The Pettigrew man's head kept rocking with the blows; Babcock's fists were flying. Babcock jumped into the air and turned 360 degrees around, then continued the striking bag exhibition. James and the biker and more of the bikers and other patrons near them applauded. The band was starting to play a loose and informal-sounding arrangement of the main theme from "Rocky."

Cross turned his attention elsewhere.

Feinberg. The blond-haired Jewish ex-Marine turned Delta Flighter had three of Pettigrew's people against the far wall, his fists and feet flying, their bodies slamming back into the wall each time he struck one of them. Cross started to laugh. But then he saw Pettigrew. His face bloody, Pettigrew had something the size of a Bowie knife in his right fist. As Feinberg drew back for a roundhouse punch, Pettigrew started the downswing with his knife.

"Feinberg! No!"

Cross shouted the words so hard his throat ached. He could see Hughes moving to his right, a blur of motion. Hughes shouted, "Don't kill the bastard!"

The knife and Feinberg's right forearm connected. Feinberg's arm was there for an instant in freeze frame, the knife's primary edge lost in flesh. Cross's left hand caught Pettigrew's right forearm, the heel of his right hand smashing up into the outside of the right elbow. The sound of the elbow breaking was like a short clap of thunder. Pettigrew screamed. Hughes— Cross could see the older man at the far left edge of his peripheral vision—decked one of the three men Feinberg had fought with a short left, slamming the body into the other two.

Cross slapped Pettigrew against the barroom wall. "Ever want children? Well, you're gonna have to adopt, asshole." And Cross's right knee smashed up. Then again. Then again. Pettigrew dropped to his knees. Cross started a left backhand, saying, "Think you could use a nose job, man?" His knuckles impacted the left side of Pettigrew's nose, and the nose spread over Pettigrew's ugly face. As Pettigrew started to sag down, Cross hooked his right thumb in the left corner of Pettigrew's mouth and let the man's massive body weight do the ripping. A short knee smash to the right side of Pettigrew's jaw took care of the dental work.

Cross dismissed Pettigrew from his thoughts, turning back toward Hughes. Babcock was there, and so was the country singer, Neal James, each of them decking one of the last two Pettigrew men while Hughes had Feinberg's head cradled against him; Hughes's pressuring Feinberg's right arm to keep him from bleeding to death, Cross guessed. Cross's eyes scanned the room as he dropped to his knees beside Feinberg. The fighting had stopped, Pettigrew men sprawled everywhere, over tables and on the floor, the patrons and members of the band crowding around Hughes and the injured Feinberg. Cross saw Neal James had crouched beside him, saying to Hughes, "Darwin, that boy bleeding to death or what?"

"Missed the artery, but severed some tendons. Look, we don't need involvement with the police. All I can say is that you and your band and the rest of the people in here can do your country a favor if you forget we were ever here. We have a doctor who can look after this lad. What about it?"

The country singer stood up, raising his voice over the murmuring of the crowd. "Look. I've known this man ever since he came up here into these mountains. He tells me we can do something good for this country of ours if we pretend we never saw him and his friends here tonight. Pettigrew's guys can say what they want, but they don't know any names. How about it, y'all?"

Somebody shouted from the back of the crowd, "Let's go for it!"

Another shouted, "All right!"

Doris was beside them now, towels in her hands, Lewis Babcock taking them from her and packing them against the several inches long, deep-looking gash in Feinberg's right arm. "Let's get him to that doctor," Hughes declared.

Cross stopped Hughes for a second, Cross's right hand going to Hughes's left shoulder. "He's out of this."

Hughes nodded. "And I'm in," he said, his eyebrows rising.

# Chapter Fourteen

Hughes made a call from a pay telephone at a gas station a few miles down the road from Whiskey Hollow, and minutes later the wail of police sirens was in the air. Babcock held the makeshift bandages in place, Cross driving the Jeep, Hughes cautioning him several times to slow down lest they all need the services of a doctor. There was a full medical emergency kit in the Jeep, but they had elected not to tamper with the packing since the bleeding had slowed dramatically. Feinberg was conscious, talking, wrapped in a blanket and Babcock's jacket to keep him warm and retard the progress of shock.

Hughes at last told Cross, "Turn in here," and Cross took a sharp left into an empty parking lot, a solitary light visible in what appeared to be a private medical clinic.

Feinberg insisted on walking under his own power, and they got him inside, Babcock going in to assist the doctor—a tweedy-looking man with no southern speech pattern at all—who looked as though he'd just been rousted from a sound sleep. Babcock, of all of them, had the most emergency medical training, from the Special Forces.

Cross and Hughes sat in the emergency waiting room, Hughes bumming the rare cigarette, Cross resisting the impulse to chain smoke. "You mean you're coming in," Cross finally said.

"You'll still be in charge of the mission, the tactical leader. You're the only man I've ever worked with that ever gave me this feeling—but I think you're better than I am. Or can be. Once we're on the ground, you'll run the show, just as it should be, lad. I can fill in for Feinberg with the explosives, and since all four of us have trained together, we should still be able to function as a team. The important thing is if Feinberg will be well enough to fill my slot in Turkey. If he can't, the mission will be scrubbed. We couldn't bring in an extra man now even if we had the authorization. This is my fault. If we hadn't gone out to celebrate . . ."

Cross didn't know what to say. The concept of self-blame wasn't new to him. As he'd sobered up, he'd realized why he had been drinking so much, let his life, his self-respect, just ebb away from him. The people aboard the hijacked flight. The ones he hadn't tried to rescue who had been murdered as punishment for his escape. He closed his eyes, inhaling the smoke from his cigarette.

He opened his eyes when he heard the door from the surgery opening. The tweedy-looking man said. "In layman's terms, he almost severed a tendon, has a couple of hairline fractures, and he's lost a decent amount of blood. The blood is being taken care of by his friend in there. The rest of the stuff won't get taken care of so easily. As far as heavy-duty physical activity, no way for your friend there for at least a few weeks. I'll have a more definite prognosis a little later."

Hughes asked, "Would he be well enough for an overseas flight and a little paperwork and the like? By Monday?"

The doctor seemed to consider. "He's a strong-appearing young man, seems in excellent overall physical condition. If he took it easy and didn't use his right arm, he could engage in limited activity safely enough. That answer your question?"

Hughes looked at Cross. Cross nodded.

# Chapter Fifteen

A black-bearded musician stood by the curbside playing a brown twelve-string guitar. Muhammad Ibn al Raka was inwardly revolted by the man, by all the people who surrounded him here. It was warm, despite the fact that it was early in the morning. Old people, men and women, moved listlessly along the sidewalks, some even smiling at him, a few saying things to him in their hated tongue. He would have taken the pistol the cab driver had had for him, used it now and killed these unclean things, but then the mission would be lost. Their day would come, he told himself. He regretted he would most likely die before then.

Raka stopped at the small doorway between the two shops, one of which sold food, the smell of which nauseated him, and one of which sold western clothing.

He let himself in through the doorway and into the small, foul-smelling hallway beyond it. It was dark here, and he closed his eyes and leaned against the wall, his fingertips against his eyes.

"Jerusalem," Raka hissed.

He opened his eyes. There were several doorbells, names scrawled beside them on the dirty wallpaper in pencil or pen. He found the one marked "Rausch" and rang it, wondering if indeed it worked. There was a buzzing sound from the height of the stairs beyond the inner door and the door seemed to vibrate slightly. He took the knob in his hand and twisted, then passed through and started up the stairs leading to the upper floors. The smell of the building was worse here.

A man appeared at the top of the stairs, tall enough, thin, with thinning blond hair that seemed raggedly cut, flabby arms and weak chest visible under a once-white athletic shirt.

"Mr. Farouk?"

"I came in response to your advertisement."

"You have experience in television repair?"

"I worked on industrial equipment for many years."

Rausch smiled, the code sequence apparently as acceptable to him as it had been to Raka.

"Come in, Mr. Farouk—we can discuss business over a glass of tea."

"That would be fine, sir," Raka told him, reaching the height of the stairs and then following Rausch down a long, narrow corridor with a threadbare carpet runner down its center. At the end of the corridor the apartment door on the left stood open and Raka followed Rausch inside, Rausch closing the door. Raka turned to face him. "So."

"It is safe to talk here. I am unknown to the Jews, and I sweep the room constantly for listening devices. It is safe here."

"Only the dead are safe, Rausch. But we will talk because we must."

The German nodded. "The tea? I have some. Fresh."

"No," Raka told him. The apartment was in disgusting disarray. There were western sex magazines on the coffee table. Raka silently prayed for guidance in dealing with this miserable person. "All is ready? That is why I am here, Rausch."

"It has proven more costly than I had supposed, my friend."

"I am not your friend. I would never choose to be. All my people are in place, the operation will soon begin, and you speak of costs."

"Jewish border guards do not take bribes—what can I say, Herr Raka? The smuggling of your weapons was very costly. There was a Greek freighter involved and there were customs personnel to pay off in Oman. And the Saudi who owned the aircraft to which your equipment was transferred was very demanding. You know my sympathies are with you. I make virtually nothing from this transaction.'' He shrugged his shoulders and raised his hands, palms outward.

Raka drew the Soviet CZ-75 pistol from beneath the jacket of his white suit. He dropped the safety and extended the pistol at full arm's length toward Rausch. ''I would kill you now.''

''But I have the weapons. All your equipment is safely warehoused here. I only meant to say . . . ah, Herr Raka. I will bear the burden of the added expense. Consider it . . . yes, consider it my contribution to your historic struggle, sir.''

Raka raised the safety, weighing the 9mm in his right hand, then shifting it to his left. ''I would see the warehouse and know for myself that all is in readiness. My cab driver is circling the block. We will go now.''

''I—ah, yes. My coat, please.''

''It is a warm day.'' Raka nodded toward the doorway. Rausch gulped from a glass of tea on the coffee table near the magazines and nodded. He took up keys and a wallet, the large kind American businessmen carried their vast sums of money in and their credit cards and the photographs of their whores.

Raka followed him to the doorway.

Black-hatted young women in the shamelessly short skirts of their Army uniforms walked along the street onto which Ephraim had turned the taxi, and for a brief instant Raka wondered if it were some sort of trap. His right hand found the butt of his gun beneath his jacket. But the women laughed and were unarmed, and then the taxi had passed them.

The warehouse was near the old city, and when the taxi stopped, Raka realized that were he to climb to the roof of one of the buildings, he might be able to view such wonders as the El Aqsa Mosque or the Dome of the Rock. He had no interest in such matters.

The warehouse was a long, low, flat-roofed affair with a raised loading dock area, and Rausch, who had been apologizing all the way over, was saying now, ''It is possible that Mr. Hassim will not be here and—''

"Hope that he is, then." Raka smiled.

They clambered up onto the loading dock, Ephraim staying with the old taxicab, Raka walking slightly behind Rausch. There was an office enclosure ahead, and Rausch turned hesitantly and looked at Raka—his blue eyes appearing frightened—then continued on toward it. There was no light, but there was a stoop-shouldered man who looked Palestinian inside the office. Raka heard Rausch sigh in relief.

Rausch knocked at the door. The stoop-shouldered man raised his eyes from his work and looked across his desk, then waved for them to enter. *"Shalom aleichem,* Hassim— this is Mr. Farouk, of whom I have spoken."

The bent Palestinian made a gesture of welcome as Raka closed the office door. "I have come to see my consignment," Raka said quietly.

"If you wish, Mr. Farouk. You do not look Egyptian."

"I spent much time away from my native land, Mr. Hassim."

"Ah," The old man nodded. "Very well." He threw a ring of keys to Rausch, Raka catching them instead. "Mr. Rausch. Show him. I am old and walking is a chore for me."

"Certainly." Rausch smiled, evidently regaining his confidence. Rausch left and Raka followed, tempted to kill the old Palestinian lest the police be called. But he did not.

There was an upward sliding door of the type used in garages, and Raka used the keys, opening it, letting Rausch raise it. Then Raka followed the German inside. Packing crates were stacked everywhere, and the place smelled of unclean things. He followed Rausch along a corridor made by wooden crates, the pistol in Raka's hand now, the safety off. Were it a trap, Rausch would die first.

Rausch stopped before a locked wire-mesh cage, inside it crates, the markings on them familiar to Raka. "You have done well. I wish to inspect their contents now."

"But here?"

"Should something be wrong, I can kill you as easily here."

Rausch licked his lips, and Raka threw him the ring of keys. Rausch began fumbling through them to open the padlock.

# Chapter Sixteen

Sunday had been spent doing little. Hughes was on the telephone much of the day, and by nightfall, with Feinberg seeming more embarrassed than injured as he sat among them in the great room, Hughes finally emerged from his office. "I've fixed it. We leave Tuesday instead of tomorrow. Give a little more time for resting up on this end and less on that end. If you can do it," and he smiled as he looked at Feinberg, "you'll be the ground man, so to speak. The controller. Do you feel up to it, Feinberg?"

"Why don't all of you say what you think—I fucked up."

Hughes's smile broadened and his eyebrows rose. "No. If anyone fucked up, it was me. But it was really the vagaries of chance against us. And that's all right. If there was bad luck waiting for us, we've been through it. You're on the mend, no one else was injured, and so far the police haven't come knocking on our door. So, can you do it, Feinberg?"

Cross lit a cigarette. Babcock sipped at a ginger ale.

"If you think I can, then yeah—I mean, yes sir."

"Good lad." Hughes gently clapped Feinberg on the left shoulder. "We have one more video presentation. Babcock, could I trouble you? I left the cassette on my desk."

"Certainly," Babcock said, and went to the office. His voice came back, *"Gunfight at the O.K. Corral?"*

"Yes, please." He grinned at Cross. "I thought it was an appropriate title."

Cross nodded. He took a beer from the refrigerator behind the bar and opened it, watching as Babcock got the television set and the VCR working. Frankie Laine had always been one of his favorite singers, and the movie had always been one of his favorite films, but Kirk Douglas as Doc hadn't even refused to help Burt Lancaster as Wyatt yet before the tape went to static.

The static was on pause, and Hughes began to speak. "This film is the only known dossier on Muhammad Ibn al Raka, our adversary, unless the KGB has something, which they very well might. If they're smart. Because Raka is a very dangerous man. Certifiably insane, I'm sure, homicidal, as we know. And excellent at what he does. Here goes." The tape flickered and there was a tall, well-built man in a rumpled gray suit with a black tie at half mast walking along a street, an ornate wrought-iron fence separating him and the sidewalk along which he moved from some sort of garden beyond the fence. The man moved with the grace of a cat. His features were very western-looking, the face almost aesthetic in appearance. A high forehead, a brow that looked somehow noble, the bearing of a man of supreme confidence, and yet somehow very casual. The tape flickered and the man was gone.

"That was Raka, four years ago. As you can see, he's fit, confident. And there's a carriage about the man that is undeniable. This isn't an inept man we're going after, nor a man who drifted into terrorism because he was looking for excitement or cheap thrills. This is a man of supreme dedication who believes he is morally in the right and that any act is excusable in behalf of his cause, which is the cause of God's will as he interprets it. He is a Holy Warrior in the truest sense of the word. He has no weaknesses we've been able to discern, no way to get to him. He doesn't drink, smoke, use drugs. He never married, as far as we can tell. He lives for one thing only—his work.

"From reports of his actions in various kidnappings and terrorist acts in the last several years, we've pieced together some idea of his skills. Explosives—he's apparently very good with them. All manner of firearms. An accomplished martial artist. He once assassinated—we believe it was Raka, although the killer was never caught—a western diplomat in Rome in the middle of a cocktail party, and fought his way past three armed security police with nothing more than his hands and a carving knife from the buffet table. So he's apparently quite good with edged weapons. And he's apparently simply quite good at everything. His twelve Immortals, it seems safe to say, were selected because they fought most like him, most complemented his skills. And Raka personally supervises the training at Mount Dizan. So, as you can readily imagine, the sooner Raka is dead, the fewer men there will be to benefit from his extraordinary skills and the philosophy behind their use. As far as we know, as of today, he's at his headquarters in the Elburz Mountains. And all we have to do is get inside and get him, gentlemen.''

# Chapter Seventeen

Warren Corliss sipped at his gin and tonic, in the quiet bar of the Jerusalem Hilton, a potted plant half obscuring the entrance from view, making him constantly lean forward over his drink as his eyes searched for the face he wanted to see. And at last he saw it. "Helen!" He stood up and called to her, and she smiled back, her short hair bouncing as she shook her head and started toward him, a deep tan looking deeper against her pale blond hair and the sleeveless, round-necked white dress she wore. She was a long-legged girl, with the look of easy athleticisim about her. He was sorry he was meeting her only for business. He realized that he was walking toward her, too, just before they met at the middle of the room.

"Hi, I'm Warren Corliss." He offered her his right hand.

She took it, her grip warm and dry.

"I didn't mean to call you by your first name, Miss Chelewski, I, ah, just felt we kind of knew each other after all those phone calls and everything."

"Warren, please call me Helen."

He realized he was staring at her. She had a lovely smile and beautiful gray-green eyes. "Thank you. Please. May I offer you a drink?" He started ushering her toward his table in the far corner beyond the potted plant.

"Yes, that'd be very nice, Warren."

He waited until she sat down—the skirt of the white dress tight but not too tight—and sat opposite her.

"What are you having?" she asked.

"Gin and tonic—read too many British novels, I guess. When I moved to England I just started drinking the things." He laughed.

She smiled. "I'll have the same, then."

He tried signaling the waiter while still focusing his attention on Helen Chelewski. She was so pretty. He caught the waiter's eye and signaled for two of the same as he had.

"So . . . making documentary films sounds very interesting."

"I was just about to say," he told her, "that working for the U.S. embassy here in Jerusalem must be fascinating, really fascinating."

"Oh, sometimes it is, I guess." She searched her handbag—it was white, like her shoes—and produced a package of Salems and a lighter. As she shook one out, he offered his lighter. She smiled as she bent her face toward his right hand, his hand shaking a little but the Bic firing. "Thank you." She exhaled smoke through her nostrils—she really was so pretty, he thought. "Everything seems all set for your filming. I'll confess, a lot of the people at the embassy"—and she laughed a little—"especially the women, we're very excited about it."

"You know, you've been so nice arranging this, I—could I, ah, ah, buy you dinner? Tonight or sometime, or anytime, really?"

She laughed, but not at him, he realized.

"I'm free tonight."

"Oh, that's just wonderful," he told her.

"About your film . . ."

"Yeah, ah, right." He laughed.

"What's so funny, Warren?"

"I'm laughing at myself. I haven't felt this nervous around a girl since I was fifteen."

She smiled. "Thank you."

He lit a cigarette for himself. "This is a hell of a way to get started with a girl, falling all over yourself, I mean."

"What do you mean, 'get started'?"

He cleared his throat, inhaling on his cigarette. "I mean—no,

I, ah, didn't mean anything. But I meant, uh— You are beautiful. You really are. I didn't know what you looked like, all those overseas calls for the last couple of months. But, God—you're beautiful.''

"Thank you—you're very sweet."

"I feel, ah—it's really . . . I can't talk."

"You're embarrassing me," she said, and laughed.

The waiter brought the drinks, and they silently toasted each other with a clink of their glasses.

"So, you scout your locations tomorrow, right? I've been reading up on film making."

"Yeah." He grinned. "We scout locations tomorrow, take light-meter readings, all that stuff. Not every day you get to film a group of international diplomats getting together for something as important as this."

Her smile faded. "Now, you understand, Warren—the documentary cannot be released until you have final word from our embassy that all the participants have cleared it during screening and that the results of the conference are to be made public."

"Oh, hell, yeah—yes. Sure. I cleared all that with my bosses and everything. And we'll provide both raw copies and first-edit copies, and we'll even provide final-edit copies before we lay in the titles and that. Yeah."

"You're Christian, aren't you?"

"Yeah—I mean, I guess so. I don't go to church anymore."

"I'm a Jew."

He inhaled his cigarette. "So?"

"I just thought you might want to know. I guess I was wondering what you looked like."

He cleared his throat.

"How did you know it was me," she asked him suddenly, "when I came through the doors, there?"

"Ah . . ." He laughed. "I have a buddy in State Department and he, ah—got me a photo!" He grinned.

She laughed. He felt as if he were falling in love, and it felt very good.

# Chapter Eighteen

Cross had been very tempted when the stewardess came around. He hadn't been out of the country since . . . since he hadn't been. But he took a ginger ale and watched the clouds that obscured the Atlantic Ocean below them. He watched them for a very long time before closing his eyes.

When he opened his eyes, he could no longer see the clouds, their whiteness. Instead, there was only darkness surrounding the aircraft. Beside him, Lewis Babcock was reading *National Geographic*. When Babcock evidently noticed he was awake, he said, "I told the cabin attendant you'd want dinner. It should be here any minute."

"Thanks, yeah," and Cross rubbed his eyes into wakefulness then lowered the tray table from the seat back in front of him. "Why are you here?"

"What do you mean? I'm flying to Turkey like you are."

"No, I don't mean that. I mean, Jeff—he's got a grudge, bad arm or not. And Darwin and I—we both have reasons. You know mine. I don't know yours, Lew."

Babcock put the *National Geographic* in the elasticized pouch on the seat back and lowered his tray table. The stewardesses were moving through the main cabin now, hustling trays, taking drink orders. Babcock started to speak when a pretty black girl leaned down toward them and asked what they wanted to drink. They both ordered coffee, Cross taking a beer as well.

She gave them the coffee. Cross took the beer, sipped at it, and Babcock began to speak. "I realized a long time ago that there was a great deal of evil in the world. I mean, that may be obvious, but to me it was a challenge. That's why I studied law. I wanted to do something important to make the world a better place. But I gradually realized that there were people who considered themselves above the law. Whether it was people who denied rights to other people because of the color of their skin or their sex or their religion, or whether it was people who committed criminal acts with almost total impunity because they were too big, too wealthy, whatever it was. Well, I realized there was something even worse that I just had to fight. The ultimate abrogation of human rights is murder. I mean," and he smiled, sipping at his coffee, "you don't call up somebody and say, 'Hey, hire me on to fight the forces of injustice.' You don't wait for Superman to come around, either, if you know what I mean. You have to do something, and you can't wait. So, I decided to fight a tangible evil. I volunteered for Special Forces. Then—well, you know. And when this was offered to me, I figured this was what I was meant for. I don't believe much in destiny and the like, but, well, it was tailormade for me."

The stewardess brought their food, Cross inspecting it. He hadn't been on a commercial flight in five years, and he wondered if the food had changed. It apparently had not.

"You know," Babcock continued, "I studied that affair you were involved with. I'm convinced that what happened afterward didn't happen because of you. It would have happened anyway. No one was going to accede to their demands. It was impossible. So, I guess what I'm saying is that you shouldn't blame yourself."

"You weren't there."

"No, and I realize you have a special experience none of us has ever had—and hopefully never will, if you don't mind my saying so. But maybe because of that I can be a bit more objective about it than you can, my friend."

Cross started buttering his roll. The main course looked like Chicken Kiev, and not very substantial. He tried it. It tasted good, at any event. Babcock spoke again. "I guess what I'm saying is that all of us had better consider the matter at hand and make its accomplishment our primary goal. Anything beyond that, fine, but not at the sacrifice of what we set out to do when we all got into this.''

Through a mouthful of food, Cross said, ''Look. The way I view 'the matter at hand,' as you called it, is this way: the fewer of them remaining after we leave . . .'' Speaking laterally, in case someone inadvertently picked up a fragment of conversation, was a practice he detested. But it was necessary at times. ''The fewer remaining, the less likelihood something like what happened to me, something like what happened to all of those people . . . that something like that will happen again. Oh, I mean, I know that what we're setting out to do isn't going to radically alter anything. But if we cut the numbers down, it's got to have some corresponding effect.''

''Has it occurred to you, Abe, that the immediate consequences will likely be just the opposite of what you want? We'll precipitate—''

Cross didn't let him finish. ''Yeah, I know that, Lew. Sometimes I wake up at night knowing that. Nobody's mentioned it before, but that was implicit in the whole thing, wasn't it? Yeah, and whatever our actions precipitate, maybe we'd be better off if we didn't make it out. Or we'll all wind up feeling like I do.''

''You just spoiled my dinner.''

Cross took a sip of his beer and stared out the window into the night.

# Chapter Nineteen

It was necessary to change planes in Rome, but even had there been time to leave the airport and play tourist, they would have foregone the opportunity. It might have been an opportunity for other things as well. The flight from Rome to Ankara, aboard what seemed an almost identical aircraft to the one that had carried them across the Atlantic, was vastly shorter. The distance involved was roughly the same as that from New York to Miami.

In Ankara the Turkish contact was waiting for them, a Greek named Patrakos, roughly the same age as Darwin Hughes, but potbellied and balding. Outside customs Hughes and Patrakos embraced each other like long-lost brothers, or at least very close friends. "These are my friends," Hughes merely said by way of introduction, and Patrakos, whose name they learned only after they were all ensconced in a black Cadillac limousine waiting for them outside, embraced them each in turn, Feinberg looking embarrassed.

As the Cadillac pulled away from the curb, Hughes's friend gave his driver instructions in Greek and then fingered a button on the console beside him, which raised the partition between front and rear compartments. Cross and Babcock sat on the jumpseats, facing rearward, Hughes's friend sitting between Hughes and Feinberg. The Greek smiled and said, "I am Spiros Patrakos, as you no doubt know. Was the flight pleasant?"

Cross shrugged. "Sure. Nice of you to meet us, sir." It wasn't really all that nice, Cross reflected. It was part of the job, and despite the friendship evident between Patrakos and Hughes, the Greek was likely being paid highly for the touching airport reunion, the ride, the whole nine yards.

Hughes spoke. "Spiros and I fought together against the Germans on Crete for a time during the war. Most Allied personnel there were British, but I got tagged for a special assignment and wound up spending four months there. We kept up with each other after the war, but this is the first time we've seen each other in, well . . . a lot of years."

"The years have done well by you, Darwin," Patrakos declared with evident sincerity. "Aside from the grey in your hair, you seem unaffected by them. But on the other hand . . ." and Patrakos patted his considerable belly and laughed. Hughes shook his head, smiling. "All is in readiness," Patrakos continued, "your aircraft for the flight to the border, the arrangements once you cross over. But I would caution you. I know certain things, and there have been rumors of a major terrorist operation taking place soon—its origins the place to which you go. I know nothing more, but have endeavored to learn more. Nothing. When this nose can learn nothing," and he tapped his right index finger against the right nostril of his apparently broken nose, "it is something very big."

Patrakos looked at Cross and Babcock, and as if by way of explanation, told them, "After the war against the Germans, it was hard to forsake old habits by which one had lived. I turned to smuggling as a means of supporting my family."

"How is your daughter, by the way?" Hughes asked.

"She made me a grandfather again two weeks ago."

Hughes laughed. "I shouldn't have asked."

Patrakos picked up the thread of his monologue. "I have remained in smuggling over the years simply as a means of . . . what is your expression?"

Babcock suggested, "Keeping your hand in?"

"Yes, exactly, my black friend! Unless one wishes to smuggle arms or drugs, the business is no longer very profitable. But . . . call it sentimentality, but this allows me to feel the pulse of things. It seems that the greater the operation, the less intelligence can be gathered about it. So," and he tapped his nose again, "it seems also that whatever is about to happen is very big indeed."

"Hopefully we'll stop it before it happens," Hughes said solemnly.

"Nip it in the bud, to coin a phrase," Cross said, then lit a cigarette and smiled.

The sun was just rising when the Cadillac reached its destination and they stepped out onto the tarmac. It was cold and a little damp, and Cross hunched his shoulders more deeply into his leather jacket.

The aircraft, the only one on the runway, was a Beechcraft King Air B100, from the distance appearing to be several years old, but well-maintained. Its engines began revving as Cross watched it.

"I know the person from whom this aircraft was acquired my friends—"

"A little old lady from Pasadena?" Cross inquired.

"You make the joke, young man!" Patrakos's belly rippled with laughter. Hughes's eyes looked daggers. Cross shrugged.

"Everything is aboard, then, Spiros?" Hughes asked.

"Yes. Everything, Darwin."

Cross watched the Cadillac lumbering off the runway toward an open hangar at the far end of the field. Hughes and Patrakos were still talking. A few moments after the Cadillac disappeared inside the hangar, the chauffeur reemerged, carrying what looked to be an attaché case in his right hand. Cross guessed it was probably one of the shoot-through variety that became popular with the MAC submachine guns. It would be the only reason for a bodyguard who was right handed to carry such a case in his right hand.

He realized he was nervous. He was on foreign soil again, unarmed, vulnerable. He'd forced himself to sleep aboard the aircraft on the transatlantic flight, but the sleep had been fitful and nightmarish, and he'd felt more tired afterward than before. Cross looked at the Beechcraft again. Aboard it already, if Spiros Patrakos were on the up and up, would be their weapons and ammo. He realized he was being paranoid, but somehow he would feel better once he was armed, al-

though a lone armed man, or even one with three friends—
what could they do? He had asked himself this from the very
inception of the mission. Was this just something that had
been planned by whoever planned it as a write-off from the
very first? Was there a chance, if not for survival, at least for
success?

Hughes, Babcock, and Feinberg were the best men he had
ever worked with. He'd found himself considering them friends,
as well. But would the best be good enough?

Hughes started toward the aircraft, Cross falling in step
with him. There was apparently only one way to find out if
they were good enough.

Aboard the plane it was Hughes who asked that the cases
containing their personal arms be broken out. Patrakos had
cheerfully agreed, and the chauffeur had gotten them from the
cargo hold. Once the cases were obtained, Patrakos gave the
order, this time in Italian, and the pilot began taxiing the
Beechcraft along the runway and into the wind. The sun was
at full rise now, a massive yellow ball that seemed to be
bleeding across the sky.

Hughes began opening the cases, Cross helping him, trying
to conceal his eagerness to be armed again. But his palms
were sweating. Feinberg took his Officer's ACP .45, Babcock
his Walther PPK American. Cross took the duplicate of his
four-inch fixed-sight L-Frame Smith. And for the first time he
saw Hughes's pistol of choice. During training Hughes had
fired only the Beretta, part of a duplicate set of battle gear
Cross presumed he kept for just such a situation as they now
had—with Hughes replacing Feinberg.

Hughes's pistol was a stock Walther P-38. He apparently
noticed Cross's interest, and looked across the case toward
him. "I got hooked on these things during the War. Never
much cared for the Lugers, really. Pretty gun. Point well,
shoot well, but jam easily. Delicate. Extremely delicate. But
the Walther is a good battle weapon. So, I know I'm dating
myself." He smiled as he began disassembling the weapon to
inspect it prior to loading.

•    •    •

Cross could see Mount Ararat to the northeast as the Beechcraft started descending. There had been expeditions that had attempted to prove that this was the high point of land on which Noah's Ark had at last come to rest when God's wrath had been satisfied and the waters of the Great Flood had begun to recede. It crossed his mind that to be traveling here, risking death, would have been more worthwhile in such a scholarly pursuit.

Cross had always distrusted the concept of Holy Warriors. To go to war and say God was on your side alone was the ultimate presumptuousness; to say God only favored your brand of theology was the ultimate conceit. To take human life in the name of God was the ultimate folly.

Mount Ararat was barely visible now. And perhaps that was just as well, Cross thought.

Had the wind been right, he could have spit into Iran. The wind was strong but not right. The aircraft had landed in as desolate a spot as Cross had ever seen. A high plateau, windswept and snow-slicked, great granite teeth cutting upward into the gray sky, snow heavy everywhere in the mountains around them. The landing itself had been one of those that inspired you to go and kiss the pilot afterward. Cross smiled. He wasn't that kind of a guy.

There was a hut here, temporary, Cross guessed, but warm enough with the kerosene heaters at full blast. Here, Cross, Hughes, and Babcock changed into their cold-weather battle gear: thermal underwear, black battle-dress utilities, black crew-necked sweaters, mountain-weight combat boots. And there was one final briefing.

"These charts are specially treated to burn to ashes almost instantly, once they are touched by flame. You might hold off on having a smoke, Cross," Hughes advised, unrolling card-table-sized maps and drawings from plastic tubes. "These were brought in by diplomatic pouch, so to speak. If someone had been tipped to them, we would all have been in deepest caca, lads."

The top chart was a topographic map of the area they were now in, Mount Ararat visible at its far corner. "We enter Iran here . . ." Hughes gestured with the little B & D Trading

Company Grande penknife he occasionally used as a pointer. "That's about two kilometers from our present position. We leave"—he checked the wristwatch he habitually wore, a Rolex identical to the one Cross wore—"in twenty-three minutes. I'm giving us an extra ten minutes for the walk because of the adverse conditions outside. Windchill is minus thirty degrees, a nice day in these parts this time of year. At any event, once we cross the border—we should see evidence of border patrols, but hopefully we won't bump into one—we link up with our guides from the People's Mujahedin. Then, unless the on-the-ground situation dictates otherwise, we move north by northeast to this point. That's almost the Armenian border." His hands played over the chart as if it were a Ouija board.

Hughes pulled the top chart off the table and let it fall to the floor. The next chart continued the first, covering northwestern Iran between the Caspian Sea and Iraq. "We'll proceed along the Armenian border until approximately here. A small town called Yazful, just inside the Iranian border. A little seaside village. And the hotel rates are cheap, I understand." He smiled. "There's a boat waiting for us there, and we take that along the coast. And we hug the coast, because if we get too far out, we'll bump into Soviet patrol vessels. Remember, we'll be smack dab between Armenia and the Turkmen Soviet Socialist Republic."

"I grew up in a bad neighborhood," Babcock said softly.

"Not like this one, Babcock. Not like this one." Hughes changed maps again. Another continuation. This one was bounded on its left side by Tehran and on its upper right by the Elburz Mountains. "We'll leave the vessel and proceed on horseback toward the target area. We could encounter Soviet patrols here as well—the kind that accidentally stray into Iran over the border. We could very easily encounter Iranian patrols. Also, the terrorists of International Jihad have their own patrols, which move through the area immediately surrounding Mount Dizan. You have duplicates of these maps in those little self-destructor bags. If death seems imminent, use the self-destructor bags and your duplicates will turn into ashes. If something does appear to go wrong—if the maps each of you will carry are destroyed, but then we're able to go on—I have these memorized. Which means if something really goes wrong, and I should apparently be unable to kill myself''—and both his eyebrows rose as he stared at Babcock and then longer at Cross—''I expect one of you to kill me. The information composited on these maps could be very damaging if it fell into enemy hands.''

Hughes threw the chart to the floor. There was one more—an interior of Mount Dizan, the tunnel networks and caverns. According to what Cross understood, no one who had ever gone in had come out alive again, at least no one who wasn't a terrorist.

Again, Hughes spoke. ''I told you that no one has ever gotten out of the terrorist stronghold at Mount Dizan to give us detailed information concerning what it looks like inside. That still holds true. If we're lucky, we'll be the first. This diagram you're looking at was generated in some marvelously interesting scientific ways that are none of our business. Satellites and computers and geologic data and hopefully not too much creativity. Don't take what you see here as specific, but rather as a general guide. Once we're inside, this will be the closest thing to a road map that we'll have. This one, and this one only, between now and the time we reach Mt. Dizan, is to be memorized in every detail. Resist retaining any details from any of the others. In the event you should be powerless to prevent be taken alive, the Russians might be able to figure out how these details were come up with, but our Iranian friends wouldn't have the technological base.''

Hughes threw the last of the charts to the floor and took from his pocket a bottle which looked like ordinary aspirin. He opened the bottle and poured out the contents. Three capsules. ''Wherever you carry these, never be without them. I'd advise close to the body, in the event you should be deprived of your other weapons. And consider this an 'other weapon,' because it is that. It's your last means of fighting back, depriving them of a valuable propaganda victory and hours of unwholesome enjoyment while they make you tell them things you didn't even remember you knew. You put it between your teeth, in the back here,'' and he gestured, ''and bite down hard. Forgive me if I don't demonstrate. If you did it right, you'll be dead in under six seconds. And, I do know these work. You'll have to trust me on how I know, but I know. These are not issue. I had them made up myself. Any questions?''

There were none.

Hughes looked at his wristwatch again. ''We have ten minutes. So comb your hair or go wee-wee or whatever. Then we're leaving.''

Hughes picked up the charts and bundled them together, not bothering with a coat as he exited. The door was open, and Cross could see him setting the charts ablaze. They seemed to vaporize.

The arctic parkas they wore were covered by snow smocks, the G-3's, the Steyr-Mannlicher SSG, and the FIE LAW-12 shotgun all in white jump cases lashed to their mountain packs, the packs themselves covered with Velcro fastener fitted white rip-stop nylon. Their individual weapons were beneath their snow smock, only the submachine guns exposed and ready if needed, the batteries removed from the Aimpoint sights with which each of the weapons was fitted and carried close to the body to preserve them until needed. The weapons themselves were wrapped with white camouflage tape to break up their outlines.

Snowshoes or cross-country skis were the only practical means of locomotion here, and skis had been chosen because they could be moved on faster.

Hughes stopped them with a silent signal, turned and looked back at them. Cross nodded back. He saw that Babcock had done the same.

They had entered Iran.

# Chapter Twenty

They were moving in single file along a snow-covered granite ridge, the wind howling out of the gray sky, the clouds heavy laden with more of the early snow that had consumed the higher elevations. Cross's face was cold despite the white toque he wore, which left exposed only mouth and nostrils, and the goggles which protected his eyes against the driving ice spicules hurtled at him on the wind. His right fist gripped the butt of the H-K submachine gun.

He had taken the lead once they entered Iran, Hughes telling him to as team leader. Cross had thought the formality rather silly, as Hughes was, if anything, better versed in the geography here. But Hughes walked ten yards or so behind him, and Cross assumed that if he started off in the wrong direction, Hughes would let him know in short order.

At the rear of the file was Babcock.

Cross trusted both men's abilities as he trusted his own, in the case of Hughes, perhaps more than he trusted his own.

They were overdue to link up with the unit of People's Mujahedin and Cross had determined that they would go on, past the coordinates that had been predetermined, to intercept them if possible. If the People's Mujahedin unit had come to a bad end, the mission would have to be scrubbed. And, logically, if any of them had been captured, it might be wholly possible that units of the Iranian army were moving to the coordinates even now. To have waited could have been suicidal, but to have turned back would have meant missing them entirely if the Mujahedin unit still existed. There had been no other logical alternative but to go on.

He'd decided that if they did not encounter the partisans within an hour's movement, thus narrowing the time between them and the Mujahedin by approximately two hours, the People's Mujahedin would not be coming. He would then find the most expeditious route out of Iran that missed Armenia. He'd also decided he would then find a bottle of whiskey and have a good one.

Cross rolled back the storm sleeve beneath his parka cuff and looked at the face of the Rolex—it had steamed with the sudden change in temperature, and he smudged the steam away with his glove. Forty-five minutes of the hour he had alloted for travel had already passed. He cursed silently under his breath, his breath turning to steam as it escaped his lips.

The ridge along which they walked rimmed a valley, the valley floor below them seeming impossibly far away as he stared into it for a moment, the rock that was not snow covered as gray as the sky. He kept moving.

As a pianist he had always prided himself on his nearly perfect pitch. More than once, in his college days, he had sat down at a recently concert-tuned piano and declared that it was ever so slightly off. And been proved right. His hearing had always been extraordinarily good, despite the amount of shooting he'd done over the years. And as he had worked assignments in the armpits of the world in his days in the SEAL, he'd taught himself to listen for the rhythm of his environment much the same as he listened for an out-of-tune piano.

And the rhythm of his environment somehow changed now.

Cross raised his left hand to signal a halt, his right fist still gripped to the submachine gun. He gave the hand and arm signal to disperse to cover, and didn't look back to see if it had been followed. They had practiced long enough together that he knew it would be. A V-notch between two snow-splotched chunks of granite was nearest to him, and he moved into it, working off the gun's safety. The H-K's great advantage over other submachine guns was that it could be carried chamber loaded when the tactical situation demanded it, action closed and ready for an instantaneous first shot without the betraying noise of opening a bolt.

He left the stock retracted, but was ready to telescope it outward.

The background sound shift was more distinguishable now. Movement of men with reasonably full battle gear. Cross glanced back along the ridge once—he could see neither Hughes nor Babcock, and that was as it should be.

The sounds were becoming more distinct now, and he thought he heard a subdued whisper. If it was a small unit, he would act as they had rehearsed and wait until the last man was past him, then open fire if that were called for. The MP5-SD system was among the most effective to be had, allowing use of standard supersonic velocity 9mm Parabellum ammunition, but the suppressor unit itself reduced velocity by bleeding off gas through vent holes in the barrel. There would be muzzle blast, but no crack, hence in the first few critical seconds of use, an enemy would be unable to instantly pinpoint the source of the gunfire, and more distant enemy personnel would be unable to hear it at all.

If these were enemy personnel moving along the ridge beyond the bend some thirty yards ahead, he sincerely hoped additional enemy personnel would be quite distant, the more distant the better.

Cross waited.

The rattle of equipment—perhaps loose carabiners or sling swivels—became louder, along with the sound of labored breathing, of boots crunching snow; sounds that told him where but not how many.

Cross's finger was just outside the trigger guard when he saw the first of them, snow-smocked, a G-3 suspended on an H-K sling beneath his armpit, his fist loosely wrapped around the pistol grip. Cross's eyes left the man and darted to the bootprints in the snow. His own, which there had been not time to remove, and the man's, the sole imprints oddly worn.

This could go very bad very quickly either way, and he made a decision.

Cross shouted the code phrase into the chill air between him and the first man. "Liberty or death!"

The man wheeled toward him, the G-3's muzzle snaking upward, but a voice from farther along the file called back, "Death before dishonor!"

Cross realized he had tucked back deeper into the V-notch of rock, had telescoped the H-K's butt stock, and had his right first finger inside the guard.

It was survival reaction, and he'd wondered if he still had it. He was relieved that he still did.

He almost took too long delivering the next code phrase response. "We have come to do what must be done."

There was silence, more of the small unit exposed from beyond the rocks in which he had taken cover. He glanced right and back along the ridge. He could see Hughes and Babcock now, their submachine guns in hard assault positions.

The smallest of the men of the Mujahedin patrol slogged through the snow toward him.

"You took considerable risk, American."

It was a woman's voice. The parka hood was pushed back by a gloved left hand, the snow goggles pushed down around her throat. The ski toque, dark blue, was also pulled back and away from her face, dark hair cascading over her shoulders. She was beautiful. Young.

"My name is Irania," she said in a throaty alto.

Cross leaned back into the rocks, his thumb working the H-K's selector tumbler to safe.

# Chapter Twenty-one

They learned that an avalanche had closed the track by which the unit of the People's Mujahedin had moved toward the rendezvous, and it had become necessary to continue on foot, hence the delay. Although none of the partisans had English quite as correct or as beautifully accented as the woman, Irania, all spoke the language with more than acceptable fluency. And now they moved along the trail in twos, to link up with the vehicles that had been left guarded just beyond where the track had become impassable.

Cross walked beside the woman, who was the group leader. After a while he asked, "Why are you called Irania?"

"My parents were very patriotic," she replied. "We lived in England, and they wanted that I should always remember my heritage. So, I am Irania. What is your name?"

"Abe Cross."

"How did you know that we were who we are?"

"Back there when I gave the code phrase?"

"Yes." She nodded.

"The bootprint of your point man. The sole didn't leave any tread marks, which meant it was well-worn."

"But the government troops wear boots that are well-worn. The war with Iraq leaves little else in the military budget but for weapons and ammunition and fuel."

"Yes, but this is as far from the front with Iraq as you can get. The G-3 he's carrying looks rather new. The best weapons don't get issued to the guys in the rear. And, getting back to the boot, there wasn't any heel on it. The types of boots worn by the Iranian army can't be reheeled, like some U.S. boots. So the heel couldn't have broken off. Lucky guess,'' he added.

"You are either very clever or very lucky indeed."

"Clever, but modest too. What's a pretty girl like you doing here fighting bad guys?"

She almost stopped walking. Cross felt her hand at his elbow, but then she quickened her pace. "Have you any conception of what it is like to be a modern woman living in Iran?''

"With those head-to-toe veils the religious leaders insist you wear, it must save a lot on fancy wardrobe."

"The chadar—but it is not just the face and body the Ayatollah Khomeini decrees must be hidden. It is also the intellect. The spirit. If I were a man, perhaps I wouldn't be fighting. As a woman, I have no choice. We should be quiet now. There are government patrols in this area. We have seen none, but that of itself means nothing."

Cross decided she was telling him to shut up because she had somehow become angry with him. Or maybe she liked him. Or maybe both.

# Chapter Twenty-two

Warren Corliss had discovered there were places within the U.S. embassy that he not only wasn't supposed to film, but he was not supposed to see. He'd discovered it when he turned down a corridor by mistake and practically rubbed noses with a United States Marine armed with a pistol and an assault rifle.

Helen Chelewski had been called by the second Marine there, and she had looked at him sternly. "You have to read the signs and do what they say. If it says 'Restricted Access Beyond this Point,' it means it, Warren."

He'd told her he was sorry, and told the Marines the same thing. But they had been watching him suspiciously when he looked back that once as she took him back along the forbidden corridor.

Because of the nature of embassy operations, he'd been unable to bring in a staff to take light-meter readings, work camera angles, and do all the things necessary to filming that were usually done. He had been allowed one assistant. Now Max Landers was off in another part of the building, and Warren hadn't seen him for the last hour. As Warren and Helen exited the corridor, he told her, "Thank you for bailing me out."

"You have to heed the warning signs—you really do."

"I was just trying to find the embassy pantry. We want a quick setup shot to go along with the dinner sequences."

"It's the other side of the building," she said, and smiled.

"Wait a minute—now look at this." Warren reached into the inside pocket of his leather sports coat and took out the map she'd given him of the embassy interior. He pointed out the pantry and kitchen area marked at the end of a corridor in the rear of the structure.

"Warren!" Helen Chelewski took the map from his hands and turned it around ninety degrees, then gestured with a pink painted fingernail. "You didn't orient the map, Warren. These two stairwells are identical. You came down here, which is in the security section. If you'd come down here, you would have been just where you wanted to be."

They were at the base of the stairwell on the map. "Right here," she added, giving him another smile.

He put his hands on her waist and drew her toward him. "I'm right where I want to be." Her eyes flickered right and left, then she leaned up and kissed him lightly on the lips.

"But if you wind up back here again, the Marines won't like it a bit. We take embassy security a lot more seriously these days, and especially in this part of the world, even in reliable allied nations like Israel. How about a cup of coffee in my office, huh?"

"Agreed." He smiled, and started up the stairwell beside her, taking off his coat. It was awfully warm.

Lewis Babcock flexed his fingers inside his gloves. It was bitterly cold here as they diagonally traversed the slope that led toward the snow-packed roadbed below. The two vehicles the Iranian girl had mentioned were already visible, but barely, camouflaged from aerial observation. Beside him walked the tall man who had left the file of three People's Mujahedin that had joined them. The man—Babcock didn't know his name— had been totally silent throughout the march, except for the sounds of his breathing and the occasional rattle of a piece of equipment.

Cross had taken a gamble back there at the rocks, but it had worked. Babcock would have done the same thing under the circumstances. As his party had gone ahead and not waited at the predesignated meeting site, the People's Mujahedin unit could have suspected a trap at every bend in the road, and without acting quickly to defuse the meeting there on the trail, a gun battle could have resulted. Clandestine work behind enemy lines, he decided, would never be to his tastes. When you encountered indigenous forces on the ground in a hostile nation, it was nice to know you could shoot at them.

He knew that working with resistance or partisan units was often the backbone of clandestine ops, but it still gave him the creeps.

He distrusted any organization that started with the word People's, because that word almost invariably denoted other people than himself. But an underground working against the Ayatollah Khomeini was to be welcomed, regardless of what it called itself.

As the Iran-Iraq war seemed to drag on with no end in sight, resistance to the Ayatollah and his theocracy of fear had grown. Turkey was laboring under a seemingly unending onslaught of Iranians fleeing their homeland to evade military service in an army that sent the newest recruits to the front, ill-trained and ill-equipped, as little more than cannon fodder. And within Iran itself, there was growing dissension, a vicious and bitter little war going on between these partisans and their dictatorial government.

Babcock reflected that sympathy for them was a little hard to muster, since it seemed likely that many of the young people who now swelled the People's Mujahedin had also been among those millions who had welcomed Khomeini back from France with open arms.

Cross had put it well one evening. Khomeini should have been assassinated before he ever got out of France. It was frequently the same story, though. Babcock remembered his parents talking about this young bearded revolutionary named Castro who was going to free Cuba, and showing him a newspaper photograph of the swashbuckling movie actor Errol Flynn, who had actually been wounded during some of the fighting to get Castro to power and oust Batista. The actor, his own parents, and millions of Americans had been fooled. The liberator had been only a dictator in disguise, the cure as bad as the illness.

Babcock drew the fingers of his left hand in from the fingers of his inner and outer gloves, curling them against his palm for warmth; the tips of his fingers were numb. His right hand still held the pistol grip of the H-K.

Hughes, Cross, and himself—they made a strange trio, he thought. Hughes really was old enough to be either's father. And in some ways Hughes reminded Babcock of his own father. Always a smile, but always stern. And always right.

He remembered his father sitting in front of the television set and watching the late news and sometimes remarking, "That Dr. King. Someday, God help us, he's gonna get himself killed."

Babcock remembered those days very well. His mother had kept him and his sister indoors even when they ran out of milk. His father had been called up in the National Guard. Babcock remembered when his mother's brother had come to the house; Uncle Joe was a policeman. And Uncle Joe had opened up his windbreaker. There were two guns in the waistband of his trousers, pressured there against his potbelly. He had taken out one of them, the first time Babcock had ever seen a handgun any closer than inside a police officer's holster. Uncle Joe had given the handgun—it was a revolver, Babcock learned later—to his mother, saying, "You might need this, Eloise. Here's some extra ammunition. Here's how you load the thing."

Uncle Joe had never come back to pick up the gun he'd loaned them. Uncle Joe had died during the rioting when, because of the color of his skin, he'd been mistaken as a rioter while coming out of a burning building. He'd gone inside because he'd heard a child crying, which turned out to be crying on someone's television set. Uncle Joe got a departmental citation. Babcock's father and mother had kept Uncle Joe's gun, finding out years later that it had been the service revolver he'd been given when he joined the police force twenty years before.

Babcock remembered his father that day at the funeral, saying to him and his sister, "Your mama's cryin' because Uncle Joe was her brother. But she's also cryin' because Uncle Joe was a good man. And every time a good man dies, the whole world's a little worse off. Remember that, Lewis, Mary Beth." He and his sister had promised that they would remember it.

Mary Beth had worked as a grammar school teacher, then realized that she could do more good elsewhere and became a police officer, like Uncle Joe. He—Lewis Babcock—had trained as a lawyer and decided that he, too, could do more for Uncle Joe's memory and the men like him by doing something more direct, going after the root causes of the problems in the world.

So here he was, he realized. And he smiled at the thought. Uncle Joe would have been proud of him. But Uncle Joe would have called him a fool, just the way Uncle Joe had described himself a few times when Babcock was supposed to be asleep but had caught snatches of adult conversation late in the evenings.

Babcock thought of turning to the silent Iranian beside him and saying, "I'm a fool—but that's all right." But he thought better of it. Either the Iranian knew that already—because he was a fool too—or the idea would be lost on him. So, either way, it wasn't worth mentioning.

# Chapter Twenty-three

Raka had finished his prayers. He stared out the window now, watching the target in the distance. He had to stand by the edge of the glass, and it was still difficult to see. But it could be seen.

A radio was playing western rock music, the height of decadence, but the radio also gave news broadcasts, and so he had turned it on again after his prayers, left it playing. At one level of his consciousness he was aware of the music. He had heard its ilk before. Something called "The Beach Boys," and some song about a safari.

Let the Jews listen to their sinful songs. Let them be lulled by these melodies. Let the Great Satan spread its gospel of perversion and decadence, because in the end it would be only those who truly believed who would survive. And this evil would only serve to further degenerate the enemies of Islam.

The Ayatollah Khomeini, blessed be his name, knew the face of evil and spat upon it.

Matthew Leadbetter had attended the performances although he despised opera. Almost as much as ballet. Both seemed to him to be preoccupations for effete pseudointellectuals. He enjoyed music, had a collection of Sinatra albums second to none. And he liked dancing at weddings or at parties. But the idea of people bellowing in a foreign language that better than ninety percent of the listeners could not understand at all yet pretended to enjoy, seemed ludicrous to him. And ballet—people dancing around to tell a story. The creation of the true nutball, he thought.

He had once decided on the perfect pastime for the snobs of the world. He had invented it, called it "Oplet." Everyone would sit in a chair on a naked stage, and when they had to move, stay seated and walk the chair around. When the story needed to be explained, they would recite all their lines backward and in Pig Latin.

He smiled even now at the thought—something for the true patrons of the arts, something the common man would never understand.

Leadbetter walked into the bathroom, found the urinals, and went over to the nearest one. He had left in the middle of the last act and, predictably, the men's room was unoccupied except for the little guy in the fancy jacket who stood by the washbasins and was waiting to be tipped when he handed you a towel.

Leadbetter unzipped and tried to make himself go. He didn't need to, so he just stood there and waited.

He heard the door open, didn't look around, heard the guy with the towels saying, "Good evening, sir."

Then a man in a tuxedo identical to Leadbetter's was standing two urinals down. Leadbetter kept trying to go. The man who had just come in said, "Exciting performance, isn't it?"

"*Aida*'s my favorite," Leadbetter responded.

"You know, it's mine too. But my wife likes *Madame Butterfly* best."

"A girl I used to know—she felt the same way about it."

"Have a nice evening."

"Enjoy the performance." Leadbetter zipped up, flushed, bypassed the little guy with the towels and left the bathroom. He supposed he had to retake his seat and listen to the rest of the thing.

He walked off quickly, taking his program from his pocket, rolling it and slapping it against the palm of his left hand. So, now he had passed it on. Hughes, Babcock, and Cross were inside Iran. If nobody in the government got cold feet at the last minute, just maybe this thing would work, Leadbetter thought. Just maybe.

He could hear the singing even before he reentered the auditorium, and he closed his eyes against it for an instant. On the plus side, there could have been worse places to pass along the information. But as the singer's volume increased, he felt hard pressed to decide where that could have been.

# *Chapter Twenty-four*

Although his breath still steamed, he actually felt warmer. Darwin Hughes opened his parka and pulled off the ski toque. Otherwise, he would just be colder when the vehicle stopped and they went outside again. He sat in the front seat of the Land Rover, Cross and the woman who led the partisan group in the backseat. One of the group left behind to guard the vehicles, a woman, was driving.

"We'll use the vehicles all the way to the Caspian Sea, then?"

"Yes, Colonel," Irania answered.

"We heard something interesting before we crossed the border, miss. Perhaps you could enlighten us further," Hughes said.

"In what regard, sir?"

"We heard that there was apparently some big operation coming up involving International Jihad. Have you gotten any indications of that on this end?"

"We have had some indications that personnel from the mountain have been filtering out, but there have been no massive movements in or out," Irania answered, her beautiful black eyes serious. "The training programs go on. Raka himself was seen as little as three days ago. There was some sort of meeting in Tehran overseen by the Ayatollah Batuta, one of Khomeini's right-hand men. Raka and his superior

Mehdi Hamadan, were both there. But that is not unusual, really. What specifically have you heard?''

Cross's eyes met his, and Hughes nodded. Cross told her: "Something involving weapons smuggling for use in some kind of big operation, maybe—it's all maybes. What made our source sit up and take notice was that whatever was going on seemed so security tight. It made him think it was something big.''

"I have been away for more than forty-eight hours, in order to come here for the rendezvous,'' she said thoughtfully. "It is possible the situation would have changed. We cannot stay in radio contact except in extreme emergencies. And even so, in these mountains transmissions might not be received. But still, I suppose we'll just have to wait and see. I know that's a terrible attitude, but under the circumstances . . .''

She let the sentence hang. Hughes said to her, "I agree. We can't know until we're closer to the situation. If there is something going down, at least it should make our job easier when we get inside. But more innocent lives are a hell of a price to pay.''

"If you wish that I should risk a transmission, we should be able to do so reliably when we near the sea.''

"No," Hughes told her. "You agree, Cross?''

Cross nodded. "If the transmission got intercepted, we could be signing our own death warrants. And the nearer we get to the sea, the greater chance of the Russians picking it up as well. We've got enough to worry about. No, let's wait.''

"Yes," she said. Hughes started to turn away and face the road along which their vehicle and the other two moved, but as his eyes left her, he noticed something and turned back. She had tucked back into the corner of the seat, her legs drawn up like a little girl's might. And in her hands was a magazine. His curiosity was piqued. "What are you reading, if you don't mind my asking?''

She held up the magazine so he could see the cover. He'd half expected something like *Cosmopolitan*. It was a six-months-old copy of *Guns & Ammo*. Hughes started to laugh.

# Chapter Twenty-five

Hugging the Armenian border had been a known risk. The Soviets, as was only logical, should patrol the border heavily. And the Soviets were never known for religious respect of boundaries. As the sun set, they spotted the unmarked aircraft as it made the pass.

"Shit," Cross snarled, shouting to the driver. "Stop the car—now!" He was already out on the passenger side, telescoping the stock of the submachine gun, his eyes peering into the cloud layers into which the aircraft had disappeared. He could still hear it.

Hughes was beside him the next instant. "If it is unmarked, it's Soviet. If it were Iranian, there'd be no sense leaving it unmarked."

"Agreed. Damn!"

The aircraft emerged from the cloud bank, circling toward them, but at an altitude too high to reach with conventional small-arms fire. "Get Irania—get her to wave. Get the woman behind the wheel."

Cross threw his gun inside the Land Rover. "Irania, tell the others to come out unarmed and wave like fools. Hurry!"

His eyes strained for markings on the single-engine aircraft. He could hear Hughes saying, "Irania—out—and you too. Back there, Babcock, get everybody out and waving! Leave your weapons out of sight."

Cross had no idea of anything else to do, and there was

always the chance that waving at the aircraft like a bunch of innocent boobs would allay suspicion—the remote chance.

Cross began waving at the aircraft. It tipped its right wing and finished the circle, then flew northeast. "Shit—Armenian. Gotta be. We're gonna have Ivan over for dinner."

Cross beat his right fist into the roof of the Land Rover, dislodging snow, his fist hurting.

Irania was beside him now. "He will have radioed. Even if he had been flying low enough and we had shot him down, it would have done no good."

"I know that," Cross whispered. "How much time do you think we have—maximum and minimum. And where would they hit us, and where could we hit them?" He realized his hands had locked over her upper arms, and knew from the tension in his hands that he was probably hurting her. But she said nothing.

Instead, she said, "We will be following along the Qareh River until it forks, and beyond it, in Armenia, the Soviets have a substantial base. Spetznas—their special forces. It is said that these soldiers are held there in the event that it became necessary to invade Iran. A substantial force could cut off the entire northeastern section of our nation quickly from there."

"Wonderful," Cross said. "Where would they cross into Iran if they hoped to intercept us and avoid detection by the Iranian Army?"

She reached under her jacket and produced a map folded several times, opening it, and rested it on the hood of the Rover after she cleared away the snow. "Here, I think, near the head of the river, for beyond it across the border there is a fine road which they could utilize easily. They would not risk an incursion by air. A single engine observation craft is one thing. Military helicopters would be something entirely different."

Cross lit a cigarette, Hughes and Babcock flanking him now. "We have two choices. Let them come to us, or we go to them," Cross announced. "Since we don't know how much strength they'll come in—and if Irania's right, they won't come by air—if we intercept them, we'll have the best chance."

Hughes nodded. "Agreed. Although I doubt anyone back home will be enthused about us fighting it out with Russian regulars. But on the other hand, if they come inside Iran, they won't be wearing uniform insignia. So how were we to know?" He smiled.

"Yes, exactly," Babcock agreed. "Now, however, there's the question of ammunition, explosives. If we expend too much in this endeavor, we could find ourselves lacking farther along the route, not to mention once we reach the objective."

"Good point," Hughes nodded.

Cross looked at Irania. The cold was starting to get to him. "How much resupply capability do you have for your own weapons once we link up with other elements of your force?"

"That will not be until we cross the Caspian Sea. But there should be sufficient. What are your thoughts?"

Cross told her, "The weapons we have with us are specialized and suited to our needs once we reach the objective. But our rifles and yours are the same. If we can utilize your ammunition on this—"

"Yes. We can resupply. But explosives are another matter."

"If we do it right," Hughes said, "we should be able to get along on minimal use of explosives. This is a perfect spot, really." He picked up a fistful of snow and let it fall through his open fingers.

Cross started to smile.

As they drove—Irania at the wheel, Cross beside her, Hughes and Babcock in the backseat—Irania verbally sketched the terrain for them. "Where the river really becomes a river, it cuts through a gorge that is very steeply walled on both sides, the peaks on either side almost always heavy with snow at this time of year. And especially so now, I should think, in light of the heavy snows we have had. The Soviet soldiers should come down from the northeast side and follow the river until it can be crossed safely about fifty miles downstream. They will come in trucks, the kind with tank treads instead of wheels in the rear."

"Half-tracks," Babcock supplied.

"Armored, lads—lest we forget. And our Soviet friends have very good armor," Hughes reminded them.

"You were thinking of an avalanche, Darwin. That shouldn't take much, if the conditions are right. And if the conditions aren't right—"

"If the conditions aren't right, we wouldn't have enough explosives to do the job properly anyway. If they're in armored vehicles, as I suspected they would be, we'll have to drop thousands of tons of snow in order to have the desired effect. Otherwise, we'll just slow them up, and if they survive, they'll get more of their people after us."

"Assuming the conditions are right, then—" Cross started.

"Assuming," Hughes said, "we can bury them."

Irania kept driving, pushing ahead as fast as she could. The road, if it could be called a road, was treacherous in the extreme, but time was literally of the essence.

Hughes pronounced the conditions right.

The northernmost summit of the two flanking the Qareh River here was like a spearpoint, thrusting up into the gray morning sky. They had driven through the night, taking turns at the wheel, and Cross had forced himself to sleep when he wasn't driving. When they reached the river, the immediate problem had been crossing it. Cross had declared a fifteen-minute break for breakfast and thought about it.

Halfway through the rehydrated scrambled eggs, Babcock said, "Where it narrows, there—if we could get a rope across, we could get across. I know that's obvious, but I've been giving it some thought. I think I could swim it."

"And freeze to death doing it," Hughes told him.

"No, it wouldn't be that bad. I'm a good swimmer. And those rapids aren't that strong-looking. I could bring warm clothes in a waterproof container, and even build a fire in the shelter of those rocks by the opposite bank. Hey, and you guys would be right behind me."

Cross stood up and walked toward the Land Rover. The riverbank was two hundred yards away, but the roar of the water was still loud here. He took his field glasses and followed the course of the river up toward the narrows Babcock had pointed out. It could be done, he thought.

He'd seen vastly worse rapids, had run rapids such as these several times in college and then in training. Never swam them. The speed of the current didn't seem all that fast.

He turned back toward Babcock, Hughes, Irania, and the others. "That's a good idea, but I'm doing it."

"I can swim it, Abe."

Cross looked at Babcock. "Lewis, I suffered a minor injury in college. If I hadn't, I would have qualified for the Olympics. Swimming. How about you?"

Babcock shrugged his shoulders, then, "It was my suggestion. I can do it."

"You're as good as I am in almost everything, and better than I am in several things. But I'm better at something like this. I'll swim it. Then, while I warm up, you guys can freeze your asses planting the explosives and I can organize the second phase of the ambush. That's the way it's gotta be, Lew, Darwin."

Hughes nodded and raised his coffee cup in a mock toast. "Health."

# Chapter Twenty-six

There had once been a bridge, and Cross had determined that the two remaining pieces of pylon—stone structures in the shapes of chimneys, but shorter—would at least be something to hold onto and to which he could anchor his ropes. With cold-weather diving gear, just a dry suit, the task would have been vastly easier. The sound of the waters rushing was so loud that it pushed thought away and he had to work to concentrate. He had stripped to his underwear, the long johns affording little protection from the cold as he stood there, dry, overlooking the crossing, and they would afford no protection at all once he entered the water.

He threw the blanket from his shoulders, Irania catching it. He saw her eyes. What had seemed forbidding to him at first now seemed warm. She had actually blushed when he had first appeared before her stripped of his outer garments, as he was now. It was a reaction to be remembered for its rarity these days.

"Once I get the ropes anchored, you guys get over there damned fast," Cross told Hughes and Babcock.

Both men nodded, Babcock saying, "Hey, good luck, Cross, huh?"

"You bet."

Cross took up the coil of climbing rope from the mountaineering gear and slung it cross body from his right shoulder to his left hip. He took the second coil and did the same.

He was already shivering with the cold, and saw no reason to delay anymore. He started for the water. Irania, behind him, called to him. "Please be careful, Mr. Cross."

"I'm planning on it," he replied, and started clambering down the embankment, his stockinged right foot touching the water and involuntarily drawing back from it. It seemed colder than it had when he'd tested the temperature before. He kept going, almost losing his footing in the gravel and sand, then moving onto slick rocks, trying to avoid thoroughly dousing himself until the last possible moment. With one hand he checked at the waterproof bag secured to his back with pieces of Velcro strapping, and meanwhile kept feeding rope off the top coil.

The water was calf deep here, and its speed seemed faster than he'd calculated. He suddenly realized he was succumbing to fear. If this had been a movie, Cross told himself, there would have been a convenient overhanging limb on the opposite embankment, and he would simply have turned one of the climbing ropes into a lariat, looped the limb, then swung over Tarzan fashion. Or perhaps just snaked the bullwhip from his belt and accomplished the same end. Instead he fed out more line behind him.

There was no overhanging limb, and he was neither Frank Buck nor Indiana Jones. He was simply wet now to the crotch and freezing half to death. He kept moving, realizing that at any moment the water would deepen and he'd be plunged into it and swimming or getting smashed to pieces against the rocks which rose along the river's surface.

He lost his footing and started to fall, hearing what might have been Irania screaming over the roar of the waters from behind him, where she, Hughes, Babcock, and the Mujahedin force waited. He threw himself out of the fall and into the water, swimming for it now. Suddenly the water level dropped, the rocks beneath him rising. He pushed himself over their surface, then into deep water again, feeling the rope feeding off. He was nearing the first of the two chimney-shaped pylons now, fighting the current working to sweep him away from the pylon, the rocks dotting the rapids here more jagged up close. Cross zigged when he should have zagged and gulped icy water, starting to choke on it, losing his momentum, the current grabbing for him. He reached out with his free hand. His nails were blue underneath, he thought. He wondered if that meant he was freezing to death; his body was shaking almost uncontrollably now.

He caught the handhold on the rock, losing some skin, but holding on. He dragged himself toward the first pylon, half walking, half swimming, his body entangling in the slacked rope. He worked free of it, pushing himself along, reaching out to the pylon, his right hand grasping for it, the rock slick with spray, ice-cold to his touch. His hand slipped. He reached again, his fingers finding a tiny niche and digging in.

He held, his arms going around the pylon embracing the icy stone like the warm body of a lover. He looked back— Babcock was stripping down, to come in after him, Cross realized. He started shaking his head, shouting, coughing, "No—I'm all right! No!"

He could see Hughes saying something to Babcock. Cross realized if he didn't start away from the pylon, two things would happen. He would never reach the second pylon before hypothermia set in, and Babcock would come after him, likely die in the attempt, and the mission would be scrubbed.

Cross took the small hammer from the sack on his improvised rope belt and put it in his teeth, trying to keep his teeth from chattering long enough to avoid losing the hammer. His right hand shook so badly he could barely reach into the sack of pitons, but he had one, almost dropping it, pulling the bag closed. He wasn't thinking clearly, should have looped himself to the pylon first. He tried holding the piton and working the rope, and almost dropped the piton. He got a coil of rope around the pylon and half-hitched it secure, holding himself to the pylon. The piton. He held it in his left hand and hammered away as it, getting it deep into the pylon. The other bag on his belt—that was where they were, he told himself. He was starting to lose it with the cold, the terrible cold. A carabiner. He opened it and secured it over the rope and into the piton's eyes.

The loop of rope. He undid the half-hitch and was instantly swept away from the pylon, his hands grasping for the rope holding to it as the current sucked at him, the rope gouging into his flesh. A rock—he wedged himself against it, the current pummeling him.

Cross pushed himself away. The water was seriously deeper here, he realized, and swimming his only means of locomotion.

He kept going, for an agonizing moment losing his orientation, unable to see the second chimney-shaped pylon which was his goal. His head was underwater, then he broke surface, turning around frantically. He finally saw the pylon and threw his body toward it, fighting the current as he reached out, his breathing labored, his lungs burning, his body freezing. He swallowed water, choking, throwing it up into the water around him. He kept going, the pylon near now—he reached for it, the current grabbing at him, and found purchase on one of the rocks beneath him, half hurtling himself toward the pylon.

He had it, hugging it to him. "Rope," he choked. He took a coil and looped it over the pylon, half-hitching it again. He told himself it was just a survival swim like they did all the time in training when he was just becoming a SEAL. It was that. It was just a scenario. He wondered if he'd make the grade on it. He had the hammer again—he didn't remember taking it from his belt, but told himself he was the only one here. He had a piton. He started hammering it into the rock. A carabiner—he closed it over the rope and then through the eye in the piton.

He released the half-hitch, aiming toward the opposite embankment now. He started telling himself the clothing in the waterproof bag would be warm and dry and he'd be all right. Cross kept swimming, uncoiling rope. If he didn't make it all the way across, he thought, all of this would have been for nothing.

Abe Cross kept going.

Fifty yards, he told himself. That was all he had to swim. He realized he was lying to himself. It was at least a hundred yards. He kept swimming, focusing his mind away from the cold. He wanted to sleep. With Irania, he told himself. That would be nice. She was pretty. She had a nice figure, what he could see of it beneath the heavy winter gear she wore and her pistol belt and everything. He hadn't slept with anyone—he tried remembering. It was a more cautious world these days.

A couple of months, he thought. And then he started laughing inside himself—a "couple" of months. A no-couple of months. No coupling, copulating, whatever you called it. Horny. His problem was that he was horny, he told himself. And he laughed at himself again. He was so cold, he doubted he could make it stand up if he tried.

He wasn't swimming anymore, and he couldn't quite figure that out. His hands were working the rope. He fell over.

Irania's face was over him and her body, pressed against him, and where her flesh touched him, he was hot. He looked at her and said, "So—I'm dead. How did you get dead, Irania?"

She didn't answer him. It was good to know that God ran a heaven that wasn't segregated into Christian sectors, Moslem sectors, and everything else. He'd have to tell God that he was proud of him for that. Good planning. He wondered, though—how had Irania died? He closed his eyes, deciding he would ask her later.

Cross opened his eyes.

Heaven was the backseat of a Land Rover. And that couldn't be right. But Irania was beside him, her arms folded around him and his head against her left breast. His lips touched her flesh. It was warm. Alive.

"Mr. Cross?"

He raised his head. "Hi."

"You were shivering so uncontrollably, one of us had to. I said that I would. I like you."

"You, ah . . ."

"Body warmth."

"I thought this only happened in movies," he told her, then began to cough. He had to sit up, and leaned on his elbow, Irania naked against him, pulling the blankets and sleeping bags tighter around them. "Thank you. Was I, ah . . ." He really didn't know what to say to her.

"You were a good boy." She smiled, then kissed him lightly on the forehead.

"I wasn't that good, was I?" He liked the way she smiled.

"I don't know—yet. You should get dressed. Stay here while I dress, and then I'll help you."

She slipped out from under the covers, and he was suddenly cold and pulled the covers tighter around him. "I don't remember much, ah . . ."

"You got the rope across and anchored it on the other side and then passed out. The black man, Mr. Babcock—he went across on the ropes after you, taking another rope with him. They made some kind of a bridge, and Colonel Hughes helped him, and Mr. Babcock carried you over to this side strapped to his back. They left." She checked the wristwatch on her left wrist. "They left about an hour ago to plant the explosives. There still isn't any sign of the Russians."

Irania was half dressed, trying to close her bra, Cross getting out from under the covers and drawing her body against his, his hands closing over her wrists, keeping her hands behind her. Her head cocked back. Cross's mouth found hers and he kissed her hard.

# Chapter Twenty-seven

Hughes got up from his knees, the last of the charges set, looking behind him. Babcock was skiing across the snow toward him, waving that the last of the charges were set. Hughes stepped into his cross-country skis and headed for the edge of the precipice. Looking down into the gorge several hundred feet below, the river hardly seemed as though it could have been any bother at all, just a narrow ribbon of bluish gray between two towers of granite.

He wondered if Cross were back among the living yet. The lad had nearly been dead from exposure. They had gotten warm fluids into him, wrapped him in blankets, but none of that had worked. Then the girl Irania had said,'' I will warm him with my body,'' and she'd begun, unashamedly, to strip off her clothes.

He envied Cross awakening beside her. She was a marvelously beautiful girl.

Hughes turned on his skis as Babcock stopped a few feet from him. "The last charges are set. You beat me, and you had more to set."

"I was doing it before you were born too. Maybe that gives me a bit of an edge." He looked around once more. Through his field glasses he could see where the Land Rovers were hidden from surface view. He scanned the glasses along the track that followed the river course. Still no sign of the Russians.

Hughes turned back to Babcock. "Let's get out of here, Lew." He dug in his poles, careful to avoid the place where he'd set the last charge, calling over his shoulder and cautioning Babcock to do the same.

There was one key charge, which would be radio detonated from the ground below. Hughes had the detonator. That charge would start the others going in series, making a fan-shaped network of charges that would bring down not only tons of snow but tons of rock, dropping it on both sides of the river and into the river itself. If he could just get the Russians to cooperate and be in exactly the right place at exactly the right time, it would be perfect.

It had not escaped him that he might be taking several dozen human lives, men whom he had never met, held no personal animosity toward. But it was always that way in war. And this was a war, no less a war than the first war in which he had fought, and the last one; all that was lacking here was a formal declaration. But wars were no longer fashionable—the declared kind. Korea had been a police action, and Vietnam—he'd never quite figured out what that had been at all, and no one was really saying.

This was against terrorists who had their own small armies and were dedicated to mayhem and murder. The Russians just happened to be in the way here.

A pity for the Russians, he thought.

It was odd to think of a few dozen Spetznas as being innocent victims. But in this case they were. Had they been allowed to live, however, they would have obliterated all hope for the attack against Mount Dizan. And that was the vital thing. To show the terrorists that the United States could strike back and beat them at their own game of violence.

They reached the far edge of the flat, plateaulike surface that crowned the precipice, and Hughes studied the track below them. It was steep, and downhilling it with skis like this would be even more hazardous. He shrugged, glanced at Babcock, and said, "It won't get any more inviting just looking at it, I suppose. Let's go."

# *Chapter Twenty-eight*

Cross, his G-3 loaded with ammunition given him by the People's Mujahedin, waited in a cluster of slablike rocks that looked to have been peeled away from the mountains which surrounded them on both sides of the gorge forming the river course. Irania knelt beside him, her G-3 in her tiny gloved fists. "We had planned to drive to within a kilometer of the rendezvous site and then climb up to the level of the ridge. Then, when the road was closed, we were forced to walk. We had brought no snowshoes or skis—we hadn't thought we would need them."

She had been chattering like this, about the mission—about everything but what had transpired between them in the back of the Land Rover—since she had joined him here in hiding, waiting for the Russian patrol. He was beginning to think she'd misjudged the insertion point the Russians would use, beginning to think that this downtime waiting would be for nothing, that perhaps the Russian observation plane—if indeed it had been Russian in the first place—had ignored them as being too small a unit to bother with, or thought them to be a terrorist patrol.

When he'd been in the Navy, he had never gone in for card games or any games of chance. On several occasions he'd been asked why and simply said that so many elements of daily life were gambling, really, he'd never seen more gambling as recreation. He was beginning to think he'd gambled badly. But Hughes had seemed to agree. Hughes had gone off with Babcock to plant the explosives. And Cross realized then that he was still relying on Hughes for leadership, although he himself was the designated leader for the tactical phase of the mission.

Now, he wondered if he still had the abilities needed to get the job done. So far he'd succeeded in taking an enormous risk with calling out the code phrase to Irania and her unit. The enormity of the risk had been diminished because it had paid off. He was violating his own philosophy—he'd gambled, despite the fact he had won. And he'd succeeded in nearly dying of exposure or drowning—he still wasn't quite sure of all the details. But in the process, he had succeeded in getting the rope across the river and allowing travel across, however awkward.

He'd heard tales of men who, because of their luck, were promoted to positions of responsibility for the lives of others. And then, suddenly, when their luck ran out, their world and the world of other lives for which they were responsible had crashed down around them.

"Why did you kiss me?"

Cross looked at Irania, for a moment having forgotten she was there. "I wanted to, very much. You seemed to want me to. Did you?"

"Yes."

He was about to speak, but then the tall, quiet man who had been at the head of Irania's group when they'd first encountered one another on the ridge called out, his voice a loud whisper: "They are coming! The Russians. I see them!"

Cross was up on his knees, peering over the rocks. He could see them as well, still a considerable distance away, their armored-personnel carriers moving slowly along the snowed-over road surface that stretched up into the mountains. There were three carriers, men seated on them, the men barely distinguishable as men at all. But he knew the profiles of the vehicles.

Cross looked at his wristwatch. No Hughes. No Babcock. No means of activating the explosives even if Hughes's and Babcock's lives wouldn't have been jeopardized by doing so. "Shit," he hissed.

Cross took up his binoculars and scanned the opposite riverbank. There was no sign of Hughes or Babcock. "Did I screw up on the time or what? They should have been back, right?"

"Yes—by now, certainly. I can send a man."

"No."

Too much booze, he told himself. He couldn't make a judgment call as quickly as he had five years ago. He shook his head, closed his eyes tight, trying to think. He had arranged the ambush counting on the landslide and avalanche, taken the higher ground to allow the elimination of any survivors while affording ample protection from the effects of the tons of falling snow and rock, from the momentary surge there would be in the level of the river.

There had never been any question of the explosion permanently damming the Qareh. The amount of snow would be vastly greater than the amount of rock, and the river moved with such force that it would merely reroute itself around any rocks that settled into the riverbed.

He tried to think, his eyes scanning the ground below their position. Irania and the other woman, the four men of the Mujahedin, and himself—seven. He smiled. Where was Yul Brynner, he thought, when you really needed him?

"All right. You and Mara and one of the men—the short guy. Stay up here. I'm going down with the three other guys. We're goin' to plan B, sweetheart."

Cross was up, moving.

They had taken the three Land Rovers well back from the riverbank to protect them from the effects of the avalanche and any possible enemy gunfire. Without the vehicles it would take days to reach their next destination. And the schedule was already running behind.

But where they had originally parked the vehicles, the ground was flat, the snow wasn't heavy, and snow had drifted deeply behind high rocks hiding the vehicles like a natural fortress.

He had gotten together the other three men, the tall silent one among them, then told Irania what to do. Now he waited. He could hear the Russian half-tracks, the rumbling of their powerful diesels, the creaking and clattering of their armor. The three vehicles were moving in single file along the riverbank, where nature had provided a surface better than the roadway a kilometer back from the bank.

His plan was a simple one. Attack the men who sat atop the armored vehicles and then take off quickly for the rock fortress. The Russians would likely use their heavy caliber machine guns mounted atop the vehicles but also dispatch men into the rocks in pursuit, since it would be clear that numbers were on their side. Then Irania would open fire from the rocks, along with Mara and the short guy. A simple crossfire ambush. After that he'd wing it, but his ultimate objective was to reach one of the half-tracks and seize it. Which was easier said than done, he realized.

But the choice had been relatively simple—either this poor excuse for a plan, or abandon Hughes and Babcock, scrub the mission, and have the Russians on their tail all the way back to the Turkish border. It had been no choice at all.

Had there been time, other arrangements could have been made. If Hughes and Babcock hadn't taken all the explosives, he could have mined the riverbank and blown the treads of the lead vehicle, or perhaps even blown it up.

He was scared to death, he realized.

But that was normal.

The Russian armored personnel cars were closing now. Six men were on top of the first one, about the same number on top of each of the other two. He judged there would be at least three or perhaps four men inside each of the vehicles, a total of twenty-seven to thirty Spetznas. Four-to-one odds in an ambush situation weren't that terrible, except for the APC's, and except for the machine guns mounted on top of them.

The APC's were approximately two hundred yards off now. Cross looked to the tall, silent Mujahedin man, then to the other two. They watched him, ready to move when he moved.

He looked across the river. "Aw, shit," he snarled. It wasn't that he was unhappy to see them, but now was the wrong time. He could see Babcock and Hughes coming down the defile on the far side of the peak from the Russians. There was no danger the Russians would see them, but the explosives could not be detonated with Hughes and Babcock on the opposite side of the river. They would be killed. Nor could the attack begin if they were already starting across, and from the way the river took its bend here, Hughes and Babcock wouldn't see the Russians until they were at mid-crossing and sitting ducks for the Russian machine guns.

"Wonderful," he hissed through his teeth.

And Abe Cross realized he had no options left. He had to start the attack now, before Hughes and Babcock reached the riverbank and started across.

Cross looked at the three Mujahedin. He nodded, got up from his knees into a crouch, and worked the safety tumbler. "Shit," he said, and rose to his full height, starting out of the rock fortress, slogging his booted feet through the thigh-high drifts here. When he looked back, the three Mujahedin were blissfully following him. The object was to walk right for the river, make the Russians think it was a chance meeting—that he and the other three men had stumbled into them—trade a few shots, and run like hell. Only the Russians were supposed to have been fifty yards away at the time, not three times that distance.

He kept walking, his fists balling on the G-3's pistol grip and fore end, his tongue darting out to lick his dry lips, his hands wet inside his gloves. He could see Hughes and Babcock on the other side of the river, but he doubted they could see him. He was almost in the line of sight of the Russians. If Hughes and Babcock got away, and he did not, there was always a chance they could tackle the job at Mount Dizan anyway, perhaps supplementing their force with some of the Mujahedin. Irania would be safe enough. They could link up downriver.

He kept walking, nearly to the river now, nearly in sight of the Russians. "What am I doing here?" Cross muttered under his breath.

Hughes had his bindings open and stepped out of his skis; Babcock did the same beside him. He picked up his skis and handed them to Babcock, who lashed them to his pack, as Hughes studied the opposite riverbank. The Land Rovers were out of sight, which was as it should be. He was confident that by now Cross would be on the job, and more confident still since he could see no evidence of Cross or any of the People's Mujahedin on the opposite riverbank. It meant they were waiting for the Russians.

"Got 'em—do mine, Mr. Hughes?"

"Sure." Hughes took Babcock's skis, and Babcock turned his back to him, Hughes still pondering the opposite side of the riverbank. The noise of the river here was so deafeningly loud that he and Babcock had to shout to hear each other.

He had Babcock's skis secured to the Gregory pack.

"You first or me?" Babcock shouted.

"Me, I guess," and Hughes started walking through the snow toward the riverbank. It had taken longer to get down the mountain than he had counted on, but his last sighting of the opposite bank, above the bend in the direction from which any Russian patrol would be coming, had shown nothing. He shrugged it off. That had been twenty minutes ago.

He was at the water's edge now, the icy spray pelting him. He thrust his hands into his parka pockets and considered the noise. It would have been impossible to speak to Babcock about it short of shouting into the man's ear, the noise so intense here from the rushing water. He wondered suddenly if he would have been able to hear gunshots from the opposite riverbank, had there been any.

Babcock tapped him on the shoulder, and when Hughes turned to look at him, Babcock was shrugging and gesturing toward the opposite bank, as though asking if anything were wrong. Hughes shook his head, walking up the embankment toward where the climbing ropes that had been turned into a Burma bridge of sorts were anchored.

Hughes held to the ropes, thinking, then let go and turned to face Babcock, pulling down the bottom of his toque and placing his lips beside Babcock's parka hood, where the man's right ear would be. He shouted, "I'm giving you the detonator, Lewis. When I'm at midstream, I should be able to tell what's happening on the other side. If I fire my pistol three times in rapid succession, then do the following: take the detonator, run like hell downriver, and when you think you're out of range of the avalanche, activate the detonator.

Then keep running. Don't leave the detonator behind for prying eyes to find."

Babcock was shaking his head. He pulled away his toque and was shouting, but Hughes couldn't hear him. Babcock leaned next to Hughes's ear and shouted again. "You'll get yourself killed, Hughes!"

"That's not a concern right now. And I'll be fine. I'll either catch up to you before you work the detonator or I'll meet you downstream from the other side," he shouted back.

Babcock still wanted to talk, and Hughes cocked his right ear toward him. Babcock shouted, "You'd never catch me in time before the avalanche started."

"You'll be able to see me, Lewis—to which side I cross. Just do as I say and everything will work out for the best, lad."

Babcock took a step back, pulled down his goggles, and his eyes seemed to bore into Hughes. But then Babcock nodded. Hughes took the detonator from a musette bag beside his left hip and handed it to Babcock, who studied the mechanism for a moment, turning it over in his hands, then nodded that he understood what to do.

Hughes shot Babcock a wave and pulled up his toque, then started across the rope bridge, his hands moving rapidly, his booted feet sliding along, his body weight to the arches of the boots, the heels acting like a brace against the rope as he progressed. He was a quarter of the way across now. The ropes were slick with a thin coating of ice from the spray of the river a foot or so below the lowest of them, and the spray had covered his goggles with a fine mist. Hughes had no choice but to stop, free his right hand, and pull down the goggles so he could see.

He'd been at an inventor's show once and seen a man who had developed a type of windshield wiper, only in miniature, to use with your glasses when it rained. He'd laughed at the idea, but some such device would have been practical now. He had to squint against the icy spray to see at all.

Hughes kept moving, halfway across now. He edged along, seeing but not seeing, blinking his eyes against the spray. Then he glimpsed tongues of fire from assault weapons in the hands of three men near a sort of natural fortress of rock slabs not far from the riverbank, and perhaps a hundred yards away from them, Soviet APC's, the men crouched beside them firing automatic weapons as machine guns atop the APC's spit fire as well.

"Damn!"

Babcock would be watching him, watching for the flashes from his pistol.

Hughes reached to his right hip for the Beretta in his holster, worked the flap open and drew the pistol, his right thumb working the safety up and off. He looked back toward the riverbank and fired the pistol into the air, then again and again.

Babcock seemed to wait in freeze frame for an instant, then drew himself as if to attention and made a sort of salute. The submachine gun in his right hand, the detonator in his left, he ran downstream.

"Good man," Hughes said to himself, working the safety of the Beretta to drop the hammer, reholstering, securing the flap so he wouldn't lose the pistol. He kept going, counting seconds internally. It would take Babcock a minute, perhaps a little longer, to get into a safe position, and activate the detonator. The response would be almost immediate, but it would take perhaps as long as another minute for the snow and rocks to really get rolling. Another minute, perhaps, and it would all come crashing down. If he didn't get off the rope bridge, he'd be killed. If he didn't get Cross and whoever else was fighting there by the small rock fortress off the riverbank, they would be killed as well.

Hughes kept moving, only faster, still counting seconds.

Cross fired out the magazine, then worked the release, moving the one clamped beside it up the well, working the bolt and continuing to fire as he turned and ran toward what little shelter the rock fortress would provide. He looked back at the river for an instant—he could see Hughes, alone, crossing. Babcock was out of sight.

Cross shouted, "Get away!" But he knew that Hughes wouldn't hear him.

The wall of rock behind which two of the Mujahedin had already taken cover was ten yards from him, and he threw himself into the run, catching a glimpse of the tall, silent man on the left edge of his peripheral vision, running like he was. The Spetznas on the APC's had responded more rapidly and more effectively than Cross had counted on, and were laying down heavier fire than he would have thought possible. He threw himself up and over the rock wall, impacting the snow, his face smothered in the high drifts for an instant.

He was up, firing out the rest of the G-3's twenty-round stick. The tall Mujahedin took it in the back or right leg, Cross couldn't be sure, collapsing in a heap in the snow just outside the rock fortress. Cross tossed his empty rifle to one of the other Mujahedin and vaulted over the rock wall, toward the man. Some of the Russians from the APC's broke cover and moved forward. Cross drew the Beretta from his hip, stabbing it toward the nearest of the Russians, just throwing lead, no hope of hitting moving targets while he himself still moved at the distance.

He skidded to his knees beside the tall Mujahedin, who looked up at him. "Don't worry, man—I gotchya," Cross told him, grabbing for the man's rifle. It was empty, and he didn't know where the guy carried his spare magazines, because none were visible on his equipment belt and there wasn't time to search the pockets of his coat. Cross slung the rifle and hauled the man into a standing position, the Mujahedin groaning in pain. Cross slung him over his left shoulder like a barracks bag, slogging back to the wall of rock, firing the Beretta toward the nearest of the Russians. They were closer now, and he was moving more slowly. He nailed one of them, the man's hands clasping his chest as his body rocked back.

Cross could hear gunfire only as a muted roar over the louder roar of the rushing water, but he heard a single crack and looked up. Irania was standing in full profile in the higher rocks, Babcock's Steyr-Mannlicher SSG sniper rifle at her shoulder. He saw one of the Russians go down.

He was near the wall now, throwing the wounded man into the snow. A chunk of rock near his right hand gave way as a burst of automatic weapons fire ripped into the rock. Cross kneeled over into the snow, the Beretta still in his right fist. But he was behind the wall. He shrugged out of the injured man's empty rifle and snatched back his own from the Mujahedin still at the wall, the second man tending the injured man.

Cross found a fresh magazine in the case slung at his side and rammed it home, opening fire again, two more of the Russians going down, the nearest of them now fifty yards, but taking what cover they could.

He could see Hughes, nearly at the end of the rope bridge. When the Russians spotted Hughes . . . Cross fired out his magazine, trying to keep their attention.

Hughes, but no Babcock. "Oh, my God," he whispered.

Cross rammed a fresh magazine up the well of the G-3 and grabbed at the Mujahedin beside him. He shouted over the roar of the water, "Get outa here—take them with you. The avalanche'll start any second. Move!"

The Mujahedin, a gray-faced man who looked very skinny despite his heavy winter gear, nodded vigorously, and ran back, Cross looking back to the river. Hughes was across, unlimbering his G-3 as he ran.

Cross looked back once. The skinny guy and the other man had made a chair seat for the wounded man, carrying him as they tried to run through the snow drifts. Cross picked up the wounded man's G-3, which had been left behind in the snow. He rammed a fresh magazine into it, one of the H-K assault rifles in each hand now. It was either Darwin Hughes or himself. There was no thinking required.

Cross clambored over the rock wall of the little fort and shouted at the top of his lungs, "Fuck you, Ivan," and ran straight toward the nearest Soviet position, both assault rifles spitting fire.

Darwin Hughes ran, the G-3 still silent in his hands.

Cross—he saw the younger man and rasped, "Damned fool," increasing his pace. Damned brave fool, he added to himself while still counting seconds. He was almost through counting.

Hughes threw himself down behind a cluster of low rocks and shouldered the G-3, opening fire on full auto. Two of the Russians, their cover vulnerable to his fire, went down. He fired again, getting another one of them, then pushed himself up to his feet, running, the snow and rocks beneath his feet churning as he looked back. The machine guns atop the APC's had tracked toward him and opened up. He fired the G-3 at the men behind cover, hoping Cross would break and run. Otherwise, Cross would be dead.

The roar of the rushing water now was somehow different. He looked back. The avalanche had started.

Abe Cross was under heavy fire, and he pitched into the snow behind the shelter of some upward-jutting slabs of gray rock. There was snow drifted behind them, the snow higher than his chest as he pushed himself up on his elbows. The two G-3's were empty. He could see Hughes, running for the higher rocks. And then Cross looked across the river. The entire side of the mountain seemed to be sliding down toward him.

Cross had one loaded magazine left, and he put it up the well of his own rifle, slinging the other one, firing two fast bursts as he got to his knees, then pushing himself to his feet, half running, half tripping from cover. He didn't look back, didn't fire toward the enemy. All he did was run.

Hughes reached the far edge of the riverbank, where the ground began rising sharply. He started climbing, looking back. Cross. He could see the younger man running now, tons of snow and rock cascading downward from the peak on the opposite riverbank. In another instant the gorge would be filled with it and anything in the gorge on either side of the river would be dead.

Hughes rammed a fresh stick up the G-3. The ground on either side of Cross was churning under heavy automatic weapons fire. Already one of the APC's was starting to try and back up, blocked by the other two ahead of it. Some of the Russians were running upstream and down, like mindless insects.

But a half dozen or so of the Spetznas were running after Cross.

Hughes opened fire, one man down, then another, Cross still coming; Hughes shifting from side to side to catch the right angle so he could get clear shots without risking hitting Cross.

A third Spetzna fell, then a fourth.

The ground was shaking and Hughes nearly lost his balance. Cross was still fifty yards from him. Hughes uselessly shouted into the roar of the avalanche, "Hurry, man!"

The fifth and sixth Spetzna men were still coming. One of them stopped and in an instant Hughes shouldered his rifle, taking aim. The ground shuddered again. Hughes sprayed the G-3 toward the man, emptying the magazine, putting the man down, his rifle discharging on full auto into the air as his body tumbled back.

Hughes fell to his knees as the ground shook, rocks and snow dislodging around him. Cross was still coming, the distance narrowed to twenty yards, one Russian still after him, ten yards farther back.

The last Russian stopped, a submachine gun swinging forward on its sling. There was no time for anything else. Hughes let the G-3 fall to his side on its sling, empty, snatching at the Beretta on his hip. The ground was trembling as he looked up, both his fists closing over the butt, the safety already worked off as he'd drawn the gun. His thumb drew the hammer back. One shot, he realized, maybe two at the most.

Hughes fired, the submachine gunner's body seeming to hesitate. Hughes fired again, the submachine gun opening up, Cross dropping to the snow, the Russian's body twisting, starting to fall. Hughes wheeled toward Cross. Behind Cross there was a tide of snow and rock about to engulf him.

Cross was up, running. Hughes worked the safety and holstered the pistol, then started to climb.

He lost his purchase, started to fall, the ground shaking so badly the very rocks to which he clung were dislodging. He kept going, looking back. Cross was just below him.

The Soviet APC's had vanished from sight, the Soviet sub gunner, still alive, trying to stand. Then suddenly his body moved crazily and was gone from sight.

Cross was climbing. Hughes turned away and continued climbing too. In what he guessed as half a second, if he wasn't dead, he would have made it.

* * *

Darwin Hughes pushed away some of the snow, trying to stand, snow that had all but buried him falling from his shoulders and back as he stood, at first shakily.

His ears rang, and he clapped his gloved hands together, but as he'd suspected, he could hear nothing. It would pass, he told himself.

There was no sign of Cross, but then the terrain had been radically altered. He'd been climbing, then suddenly something had washed over him and his body had been hammered at and . . . and he guessed he'd lost consciousness for an instant.

He reached to his hip, finding the Beretta, working the safety. He raised the pistol into the air and fired, hearing a very dull-sounding snapping sound. At least he could hear a little, he realized.

He looked about him. He could see Irania in the higher rocks, waving her right arm, Babcock's SSG in her hand. He waved back.

He felt something and wheeled toward it, almost losing his footing.

He dropped the safety and put the Beretta on safety.

Abe Cross stood a foot or so away, his goggles down around his neck, the toque in his right hand, his hair tousled like someone just raised from a sound sleep, snow on his shoulders, in his hair, two rifles slung across his back.

Although Hughes read lips, he was confident Abe Cross did not, confident also that Cross could hear no better than he did. But he said it anyway: "Thank God you're alive, son."

Hughes turned away, focusing his attention on the matter at hand. How to get from where they were, snow and rocks piled around them, to where Irania was in the higher rocks. He imagined the matter was even more of concern to Abe Cross, especially reaching Irania.

Hughes looked across the river, or where it had been. Spouts of water were already breaking through the snow, and soon the river would be flowing just about as freely as it always had, he judged. Now, if only Babcock were alive somewhere over there on the other side.

Hughes thought he spotted what might be a way up, and he began to climb.

# Chapter Twenty-nine

Babcock clambered up into a niche of snow-splotched gray granite and sagged down, catching his breath from the altitude and the cold. After the avalanche he had worked his way back as close as he could, but there had been no sign that anything on the opposite riverbank survived.

He'd started into a controlled run—he had called it that to himself. He couldn't leave his friends buried under the snow, he thought, not while there was a chance they were alive. He remembered the girl, Irania, saying that some ten kilometers downstream there was a suspension bridge, still standing the last time she'd seen it. She had also said that it would have been useless to go toward the old bridge to attempt to cross, because it was in such poor repair, it would not support the weight of a child, and that it was perilously high over the gorge through which the Qareh cut.

But now it was Babcock's only chance, he knew. He was totally cut off here, cut off from helping his friends and, if they were dead, from escape or linking up with the Mujahedin.

Irania had pointed out this region on the maps she carried, saying that it was heavily patrolled by units of the Iranian army, against Soviet incursions. Babcock seriously doubted the Iranian army's ability to stop even the smallest Soviet penetration.

He took a trail-mix bar from the pocket of his parka and opened it, debating the wisdom of consuming it all. He had the contents of his pack, of course, but these were emergency rations only, and precious little should his stay in the wilds of the mountains here become protracted. He had his G-3 and a reasonably decent supply of ammunition for it—his own plus that which they had scrounged from the Mujahedin unit. He had the H&K submachine gun, the Beretta, and his personal handgun, as well as his personal knife and the big Gerber. His skis were intact.

He realized he was assessing survival.

There was plenty of water available. He could boil snow.

"Damnit," he said under his breath. His ears still rang from the sound of the avalanche, but his hearing was returning.

Babcock uncased his binoculars to survey the terrain around him. Perhaps he would see the suspension bridge.

As he swept the riverbank, then followed along its length, he saw a dark shape in the sky.

It was a growing shape, like some huge insect from a science fiction novel. But it had no life of its own, its animation given to it by the men who flew it. It was a helicopter.

"Shit," he hissed.

He could see no markings yet. He continued the sweep with his field glasses. He saw the bridge.

Babcock had no choice but to wait. Moving for the bridge now—it looked worse than Irania had described it—would have been suicide. Because now he could see the helicopter better. It was a gunship, and its markings were Iranian.

Because of the avalanche, it was necessary to avoid the river course with the Land Rovers, but Cross had decided that their needs would best be met by splitting up. He and Hughes took the river course downstream; Irania and the five other Mujahedin, one of them wounded, kept to the Land Rovers.

Cross had reloaded the spent magazines for his G-3, but it was slung away in its white travel case now; he was carrying the LAW-12 now as well, and Hughes was carrying Babcock's SSG sniper rifle. Hughes's skis were broken, and there had been nothing to replace them, so they trudged along on foot, picking their way among the higher rocks to avoid the deeper drifts of snow.

"So. How'd I do?"

Hughes didn't turn to look at him as he spoke. "I'm confident I made the right choice putting you in charge. Considering the terrain, the lack of available explosives, you did the logical thing. It was a reckless act, but I understand the motivation lad, and I'm grateful for it."

"It was the only thing I could think of."

"Next time—now I'm not being critical, mind you—but the next time you're in an identical situation to the one back there . . ." Hughes started to laugh, Cross laughing too. Two men, shouting at one another over the roar of the water near them, laughing like madmen as they worked their way through enemy territory—that in itself was something laughable, Cross realized. He clapped the other man on the back as they started up through a niche in the rocks.

Hughes went ahead, saying, "Age before beauty."

"Beauty was a horse," Cross gibed.

"You've been watching Pee-Wee Herman again on Saturday mornings, lad. I've been meaning to mention— Watch out!"

The niche opened, and Hughes shoved Cross back, Cross following the older man's gaze skyward. A helicopter gunship with Iranian markings was circling a narrow area on the far side of the river.

Cross uncased his binoculars, focusing them. There were missile pods in place.

"I think they see our friend Mr. Babcock," Hughes told him. "Look there."

Hughes gestured farther downstream. Cross swept the binoculars toward the spot, missing it, lowering them, seeing something that looked like a string crossing the gorge perhaps a hundred feet up over the rocks of the rapids below. He raised the binoculars without shifting his gaze, and he had it, focusing them. It was a bridge.

"The one Irania spoke of," Hughes commented emotionlessly. "Looks in disrepair."

"Could have saved me a swim."

"Or given you a sudden trip to the bottom. No, you were wise to avoid it. If the ropes are in as poor condition as the board walkway, it would have killed you."

There was a crackle, like something breaking. The sound of the river waters still made accurate hearing difficult, and Cross's ears were still ringing a little with the avalanche. He saw a contrail. He started forward, Hughes catching him. A missile impacted into a depression in the rocks on the opposite side of the gorge. Cross brought his binoculars up again. He could see Lewis Babcock running for his life.

Babcock sprayed two bursts up toward the Iranian gunship, hoping it would at least draw back. Whatever equipment it had on board had spotted him almost too quickly. There was nothing to do now but to try for the bridge. There were caves visible in the distance on the far side, where he could take shelter from anything except a direct hit from one of the missiles.

He ran, the G-3 in his right hand, held almost out at his side. He lost his footing, caught himself, fell to his knees, pushed himself up and ran again along the broken rocks that led toward the suspension bridge. Machine-gun fire laced into the rocks near him, spraying dust and snow toward him, the goggles he still wore protecting his eyes. He kept running. He heard the sound of another missile being fired just barely over the roar of the Qareh, and threw himself down, hands over his head, feeling the concussion and the tremor in the ground as the missile impacted. He was still alive. He pushed himself up, grabbing the G-3, firing from the skyward hip, aiming for the command bubble.

The helicopter swayed a little, then veered back and away. He ran again, shifting the magazines held together by the jungle clip, working the bolt. The bridge was less than two hundred yards ahead now, and the closer he got to it, the worse it looked.

Cross and Hughes were running, keeping even with each other as they approached the suspension bridge. It would be Babcock's only choice, and crossing it under optimum conditions would be suicidal, but with enemy fire coming at you— Perhaps Babcock couldn't see the bridge as well from his vantage point as they could, Cross thought, or perhaps Babcock was reckless enough, desperate enough, to take the risk.

They kept running, Cross hearing Hughes shouting, "Slow down or you'll be breathing so hard it'll never work."

Cross took the advice, cutting his pace. There was also the possibility, running here among the rocks, of taking one wrong step and breaking an ankle or leg. He kept moving, but more slowly now. His eyes alternated from the helicopter—another missile had been fired, but missed Babcock—to the ground he traversed. There was a distinct advantage in going up against the Iranian military, their pilots included. Most of the real professionals had gotten out when the Ayatollah had taken charge of the government, and the ones left behind didn't have spare parts, skilled mechanics, or the experience to do anything once they got airborne. But logic dictated that the more missiles and machine-gun rounds were fired at Babcock, the greater the odds of a hit. He kept running, the bridge less than a hundred yards off now, great gaping holes visible in it, some of the ropes that tensioned it across the gorge visibly frayed.

Now that Lewis Babcock could see the bridge better, he began reconsidering his alternatives. He could look for a position from which to fight, but despite the poor marksmanship already evidenced by the crew of the helicopter, it didn't take pinpoint accuracy to kill you with a missile. Machine-gun fire churned the ground to his left and right. He had no alternatives, he realized. He would be the perfect target, and it looked as if it would take just a few hits to bring the bridge down.

They were ten yards from the bridge now, Hughes shouting, "Over here, lad! Hurry!"

Cross followed Hughes into a field of low rocks so jagged looking they seemed to have been chipped away from the granite of the mountains around them and just discarded here. He dropped to his knees beside Hughes, who was already helping him with the SSG. It should have been in Babcock's hands; Babcock was the better man with it.

Cross ripped the rifle from the case, tossing the case aside, working the bolt to chamber a round out of the five-round rotary magazine. It was the best factory-production sniper rifle in the world, he told himself, or certainly one of the best. An astigmatic could hit with it. He closed the bolt, fighting to control his breathing. Hughes had been right. Hughes was always right.

Hughes had his own and Cross's G-3's uncased. "I can't open fire with these until you make your play. And you don't have much time, lad. He's almost at the bridge."

Cross tore away his gloves, his goggles, his toque. He settled into a prone position in the rocks, his elbows down, his body weight shifting to get comfortable. The scope was zeroed for Babcock's eyesight. The trigger weight was set for what Babcock felt comfortable with.

Cross could see the helicopter through the scope now, the thing bobbing and weaving as though it were under fire already. If the pilot had been better, Babcock might already have been dead, but the aircraft would have been easier to take down.

There was only one vulnerable spot—the main rotor—the only spot vulnerable to a single, well-placed shot.

He tried settling the reticle, but each time, the helicopter jumped, jarred, and was gone.

He snapped away the rear trigger, the front trigger set now. "Come on, damn you! Learn how to fly, ya dumb shit!"

Cross had to change position. Suddenly his palms went wet. "Did you check that Irania didn't reload this with her stuff after she fired it? It's a different bullet weight."

"I checked. Shoot, lad."

Cross rubbed his right palm against the snow trousers, his fist tightening on the pistol grip.

He had it. He lost it.

"Lewis is almost to the bridge, lad."

"I know, damnit!"

Cross sighted the helicopter and fired. He had jerked the shot. The helicopter seemed unaffected.

"You missed."

"You wanna try it, man?"

"No time—do it now, Abe."

Cross worked the bolt, ejecting the spent shell casing, then worked it forward, chambering a fresh round. He snapped off the rear trigger. The front trigger was so light—the rifle had

discharged before he knew it was happening, he told himself.
But he knew that was just an excuse for his poor marksmanship.

"All right—be ready," Cross hissed, settling the reticle on
the main rotor, trying to allow for the machine's drifting.

"He's on the bridge. They're firing at the bridge."

Cross lightly touched the SSG's front trigger.

The helicopter's image blurred. Cross lowered the rifle.

Hughes shouted. "You hit it—look there!"

Black smoke was starting to rise. Hughes thrust one of the
two G-3's at Cross. Cross put the SSG down beside him,
shouldering the G-3. Hughes was already firing, the helicopter visibly in trouble now, its movements jerkier than before,
a plume of black smoke rising from the tomb of the fuselage.
Cross settled the coarser but familiar sights of the G-3 on the
helicopter's chin bubble and opened up, the G-3 in Hughes's
hand roaring beside him.

Cross changed sticks. Hughes was firing again. Cross resumed firing, too, the helicopter's fuselage licking flames
now, a burst of machine-gun fire coming at them, almost
half-heartedly, missing by a good twenty yards. The helicopter started limping off.

Then suddenly the helicopter seemed to stop moving at all.
It was all over the gorge. There was a roar louder than the
noise of the water, and the helicopter seemed to launch itself
upward for an instant, a ball of black, orange, and yellow
flame engulfing it, then whole chunks of it falling from the
sky. There was a high-pitched whining sound, and the fuselage crashed downward, hitting the water and rocks of the
gorge, leaping skyward with another explosion, then becoming only black smoke.

Cross looked toward the suspension bridge.

Lewis Babcock was standing on its far side. His rifle hung
under an arm, suspended cross body on its sling, and he was
slapping his hands together.

Cross looked with puzzlement at Hughes, Hughes shouting
to him over the noise of the rushing water, "He's applauding,
lad—that's all!"

# Chapter Thirty

They had linked up with Lewis Babcock a few kilometers farther down the river, where it could be crossed in relative safety. Together with the journey downriver after the avalanche, they'd consumed a day no one had planned on, putting them roughly two days behind schedule in their mission.

Cross elected to parallel Babcock's course from their side of the river, sending Darwin Hughes back to link up with the Land Rovers and the Mujahedin unit.

It was dusk on the second day inside Iran when Cross and Babcock, both of them cold and weary, reached the map coordinates agreed upon for the rendezvous.

Irania had come into Cross's arms and kissed him. And though he had always prided himself on his sexual drive, the hot meal waiting had tasted nearly as good.

By evening of the third day they had reached Yazful, a small village of perhaps thirty residences and what appeared to be a store. Irania had volunteered to go in alone, saying a woman would be less suspect. There had been no sign of the Iranian army, but by now they had to have missed their helicopter. Nor had there been any further signs of the Russians, but Cross doubted their luck would hold there either.

"I will go."

Cross looked at her eyes. He trusted her. He didn't know if it was the physical attraction he felt for her or something more than that. But he trusted her. Logic, however, dictated that someone from among the three of them should go with her, and one of the other Mujahedin as well.

The leg wound the tall, silent man had sustained during the battle with the Russians had become infected; Cross guessed silently that it was from contact with the man's ragged clothing. There was a doctor in Yazful whom Irania said could be trusted to provide the drugs needed to combat the infection and to care for the man until he could be picked up by other members of the People's Mujahedin. This added even greater urgency to their investigation of the village, to make certain that no Iranian army trap awaited them.

Cross decided that he himself should go, and only with Irania. Mara would drive and wait for them at the edge of the knot of human habitation.

Irania agreed, saying she needed a few minutes to get ready.

Cross, Hughes, and Babcock had made one of the Land Rovers a sort of headquarters, keeping their gear together there, sleeping there when circumstances permitted. When Cross returned to the Rover, Hughes and Babcock were playing a game of chess by the light of a candle in the backseat.

Cross climbed into the front seat. "We've settled things. I'm going with Irania."

"If that's your decision, lad," Hughes said, moving his king's knight.

"How can you see those pieces to move them? They're so small it looks like you should use tweezers and a magnifying glass," Cross said, changing the subject. It was one of those traveling sets that utilized a board about the size of one and a half playing cards, and the pieces were all little circles with the drawing of the actual piece imprinted on them.

"It only sharpens the concentration," Babcock volunteered.

"You're not going in dressed like you are, I assume," Hughes said thoughtfully.

It was warmer here by the sea, and Cross had stripped out of his parka and snow smock, down to his black BDU's, pullover sweater, and pistol belt.

"What would you suggest, oh master of disguise."

Hughes shrugged. "Unblouse the trouser legs for a start. Makes the combat boots less noticeable."

"Might leave the pistol belt behind and just stuff the Beretta in your trousers," Babcock suggested.

Hughes nodded. "A good idea, I think."

"All right, guys—what am I doin' wrong? I wasn't planning on goin' in there with my rifle slung under my arm. Why? Shouldn't I go at all?"

"Do you speak the language, Abe?"

"You know I don't speak Farsi."

"Yes, that's right. Could prove awkward," Hughes said soberly.

"Oh, very awkward," Babcock agreed.

"Your move, Lewis," Hughes reminded.

"Oh, thank you so much."

"All right, guys, damnit, I'm going! Neither one of you speaks the language either."

"If you are going to go—and in your position as tactical leader, it is your decision, lad . . ." Hughes said slowly, his eyebrows cocking upward. "Then, well, I'd advise going in almost clean. Maybe a single gun and a knife. If Irania's going in, she'll have to go in chadari, or else she'd attract more attention than you would with your rifle. Loan her one of the submachine guns to keep under her clothes. You could hide a small field-artillery piece under those robes if you were clever enough. Too bad you're six feet two instead of five feet seven—you could wear a chadar, too, and take your rifle."

"Fuck you," Cross said good-naturedly.

"No, I'm not that kind of a fellow, actually." Hughes grinned. "But thanks for thinking of me—nicest offer I've had all day." He inhaled with the sound of a sigh. "Borrow some clothes from our tall Mujahedin friend. He won't be using them until that infection's taken care of and the fever broken. They should look a little more like native dress than your things. And the Beretta will look military in case anyone spots it. Plenty of people travel armed in Iran these days. Stick to your revolver and your knife, if you like."

"Why not the Walther you've got with the silencer—that .22?" Babcock suggested.

"Too professional-looking," Cross said.

Hughes nodded. "I agree." Babcock finally moved his

queen. Hughes laughed triumphantly. "I've got you, my clever friend." Hughes moved his own queen. "Checkmate—at last!"

"Well, guys, I know you're broken up to see me go."

"Oh, indeed we are, lad," Hughes said. "Don't go starting a war unless you absolutely must."

Cross started unbuckling his gun belt.

The tall, silent, wounded Iranian wasn't quite as tall as Cross had thought, but aside from being a little on the high-water side, the pants were a decent enough fit over his own BDU trousers, the bottoms of the BDU's covering his boots well enough. The Iranian's jacket was old U.S. military surplus and, at least judging from news footage he had seen of present-day Iran, a popular item throughout the male population.

The round-butted, fixed sight, action-tuned L-Frame was in the rig by his right kidney, the Safariland speedloaders in an outside pocket of the jacket, which he had carefully checked for holes. He wore his own black knit watch cap; head lice were something he had never been fond of. Although the Mujahedin to the man or woman looked as clean as circumstances permitted, he wasn't eager to experiment.

Mara drove, Irania sitting beside her, Cross in the backseat of one of the Land Rovers. As he watched Mara, he was amazed her hands and feet could be free enough to manipulate the vehicle's controls. The clothing she had draped over her, like Irania's, seemed all-consuming.

Mara had been given one of the MP5 SD-A3 submachine guns to keep with her, Irania taking the Uzi that was the only sub gun in the armament of the unit, and something she was more familiar with. It was concealed so artfully under her black chadar that he had asked her before entering the vehicle if she was sure she had it. She had smiled and said she was, her head still uncovered, her beautiful hair toyed with by the wind coming up from the Caspian Sea. If nothing else, to force a woman like Irania to hide her beauty, Cross thought, was ample reason to hate the regime of the Ayatollah.

They had camped in the highlands overlooking the village, and the actual ride to the boundary of the village consumed almost forty-five minutes by Cross's borrowed wristwatch; the Rolex had been left behind as something that might attract undue attention. The watch was a Gruen, certainly a reliable timepiece, he had told himself.

The Land Rover slowed and Cross leaned forward to look between the two women in the front seat. "Mara, take the Rover off into those trees and then turn it around so we can get out of here fast, if we need to."

"Yes, Mr. Cross." As he looked at her, he thought she nodded, but with her attire, it was hard to tell. The Rover bumped off the edge of the road and toward the trees. Cross was about to advise her to cut the lights when she turned them off. Five points for Mara, he thought.

The Rover, stopped just inside the tree line, then started a three-point turn, Cross saying, "I'm getting out." He jumped from the vehicle and past Irania, drawing the revolver, moving deeper in the trees, enough of a moon now that it was unnecessary to use the small flashlight he'd brought.

He heard the Rover's engine die, gave one last look around, then started back at a slow run, mindful of the uneven ground. Irania and Mara were already out of the vehicle; their identical chadars made it impossible to tell which was which.

Then Irania spoke. "The house of Dr. Rahmadi is at the center of the village. He is a good man."

"I'm sure he is." Cross nodded, not sure at all.

"And the fishing boat is at the far end of the village by the small wharf. So we will see the entire village regardless," she told him.

He had inquired earlier about the fishing boat. It was powered by a diesel engine she assured him would run, and the vessel could do a good speed under full power. She had not known exactly how good. In that respect Irania reminded him of the used car salesman who had sold him the 1978 Ford he'd been driving in Chicago before all of this had begun.

"Let's get started into town, then," he said to her. "Mara— you be cool here. If anything starts going down in town, be ready to get out. Give us what you think would be ample time to reach you, then take off and warn the others. If it starts getting hot out here, we'll make it back on our own somehow. You just take care of yourself."

"Yes, Mr. Cross." This time, he was sure. Mara had nodded.

The size of the place gave new meaning to the word village, Cross thought, as they crossed into the solitary street. The houses were of wood, and poverty seemed in the air. As they walked down the unpaved street, keeping the shacklike houses close to one side, he asked Irania, "How does a town this size have a doctor?"

"Dr. Rahmadi lives here, but his practice is everywhere throughout the countryside and in the smaller villages as well."

"Smaller villages?"

"Many of our people are very poor, Abe. While the previous government made billions with oil, the people still went without. Nothing has changed, except to get harder."

"The poor always get poorer, don't they?" Cross said, not expecting an answer.

But she offered one. "When the Ayatollah Khomeini was about to return and the government of the shah was toppling around him, many thought that good times would come. But some of us thought that things would only be worse. And we were the ones who were right. And I am very sorry for that because there is no end to this in sight, I think. Times will get worse still before they will begin to get better. And more of the poor such as these people, or the man whose jacket you wear—for them there will be nothing but sorrow."

She seemed to float over the road beside him as he watched her in the moonlight, nothing of her visible except one hand, the robe covering all. He knew where the other hand was—on the butt of her Uzi.

It seemed to Cross as though they must have traversed half the length of the village now, and he'd apparently judged correctly if indeed Dr. Rahmadi's house was at the center, because Irania hesitated, then stopped, saying, "We have arrived, Abe."

She started for the door of a house no larger than any of the others, but walled with something like stucco over bricks, a wrought-iron ornamental fence above the wall extending about eighteen inches farther up. There was a single-doored wooden gate, and a cord extending from the lintel which crossed it. Her left hand peeked from beneath the chadar again as she reached for the cord.

"Wait a minute," he told her. "Don't you think that if the Iranian authorities are waiting for us, they'd wait here, expecting we might seek out a doctor?"

"Yes. I did not think—"

"Neither did I until just now," Cross admitted. "Let's keep walking." He took her elbow and started to guide her away from the gate. But they were being watched, he knew it would already be too late.

But no alarms sounded, no shots were fired. He kept walking her toward the far end of the village, the sea visible here, moonlight shimmering off the water's surface. Under other circumstances it would have been a romantic place to be with a pretty girl.

As they neared the last house on the right before the store, he told her, "I'll leave you between the store and that house, then duck around back and check out the doctor's place. You stay there and wait for me. If you hear anything, head along the shore. They'd expect us to try to make it out the way we came."

"But what—"

'What about me? I'll be fine, sweetheart," he lied. More likely he would be dead. He'd brought Darwin Hughes's little emergency capsule with him, just in case. "If everything's okay, I'll be back for you. Hang in there."

As they crossed before the open space between the last house—a decrepit wooden shack that looked as though it had never been painted—and the store, a larger version of the same thing, Cross gave Irania a squeeze and dodged between the two buildings. He heard a dog bark, but nothing else except the crunch of small stones beneath his boots.

He stopped behind the rundown shack and drew the revolver, stuffing it into the right outside pocket of the borrowed field jacket. He wanted a cigarette, but there wasn't time to smoke one. He moved along behind the building, avoiding a pile of boards and a few old buckets of the type fish might be hauled in, working his way slowly back toward the walled boundaries of the doctor's home. He could already see the rear of the wall, extending farther back than the rest of the buildings.

As he neared it, he stopped, focusing his eyes on every darker shadow, every spot where a man could safely expect to remain hidden from view but command a field of fire. There were several such places, but he saw nothing in them, no one lurking or lying in wait.

Then he left the shadows himself and started for the wall, running, his hand on the revolver in his jacket pocket. He reached it, sagging against it, hugging to the shadows there, the revolver out of his pocket now, tight in his fist. He eased his own breathing so he could listen for any sounds that should not be there. The brightness of the moon, an advantage as they had traveled, was now distinctly the opposite.

Cross started working his way along the length of the wall, so he could check out the other side. There were no sounds but ordinary night noises—the buzz of an insect, the low hum of the breeze, the distant, muted whisper of the sea beyond the edge of the village.

He kept moving, reaching the far edge of the wall and peering around it. Nothing.

Cross started back the way he had come, opening his coat, securing the four-inch .357 in the holster beside his right kidney.

On his left side, the sheath stuck down inside his pants, he carried the Cold Steel Magnum Tanto. He withdrew it now, his right hand squeezing the rubberized grip surface, feeling the checkering. His left thumb worked back across the spine of the blade and over the ridge.

The wall was only six feet high, the grating rising another foot and a half over that, and he leaned against it and peered over. It was a garden, meager but well cared for. He wondered wildly if any raving beauties lurked behind the wall, the sight of them forbidden to the outside world.

Cross clamped the Tanto in his teeth, took a few paces back from the wall, jumped and pushed himself up on his hands. He got one knee to the top of the wall, then crossed the grating with his other leg and dropped to the ground into a crouch. He took the Tanto back from his teeth. It looked great in the old pirate movies, he thought, but regardless of the quality of a knife, steel never tasted good.

Cross started through the garden, darker here. He looked up, under his breath saying, "Dumb ass." There were trees, barren with the time of year, but their limbs obscuring much of the light from the moon.

There was light ahead at the end of the garden, a yellow light, perhaps a lamp burning. The Gruen on his wrist wasn't luminous, but he knew it wasn't yet midnight, and it was conceivable somebody would be up even in a land without cable television. Maybe reading, he thought extravagantly.

He kept moving, then stopped.

He didn't duck for cover, but remained perfectly motionless, slowly putting down his right foot beside the left.

He had heard something. A voice. Perhaps the good Dr. Rahmadi talked to himself, Cross thought—or more likely, another member of the family. A patient, perhaps.

He started moving again, dropping into a crouch as he neared the window through which he had seen the light.

Irania had described Rahmadi. Short. Stocky. Thin-faced and balding. The man Cross saw through the window was balding, but that was where the resemblance ended. A very tall, fit-looking man held a pistol in his right hand. He had several days worth of beard stubble and disheveled clothes which told Cross that he wasn't in the military.

As Cross watched, a man matching Dr. Rahmadi's description came into his limited field of view. The doctor put his hands together, as though praying or begging—Cross guessed the latter. The man with the pistol—it was a worn-looking Government Model Colt auto, probably .45—pushed Rahmadi back, the older man sinking to his knees on the floor.

Women—Cross had wondered if there were any here. There were. An older woman in a western-looking housedress, and a young one in a plain-looking dress with a skirt that was full and modestly long, ending at mid-calf. A kind of gray color. Mother and daughter, from their appearance, the girl about eighteen or so.

Behind them, as they entered the room, were two more men, both of them armed with pistols, one recognizable as a Luger, the other something that was probably of Spanish origin and sufficiently old to be hard to identify. The one with the Luger, almost sandy-haired, but dark-eyed and dark-skinned, pushed the older woman along.

The women were forced to their knees beside Dr. Rahmadi.

And Abe Cross realized what he was watching. It was a home invasion, and these three armed men were thieves, if not worse.

# Chapter Thirty-one

Irania was becoming worried, her hands sweating on the Uzi slung beneath her chadar. From her hiding place she could see the street clearly, and she wished that she saw Cross walking toward her.

He was a handsome man, and a brave man, Irania thought. But he had such a careless attitude toward things. Always trying to make jokes. Was he never serious?

She judged the time as near to midnight. Abe Cross had been gone for more than twenty minutes. She licked her lips. But there had been no sounds of gunfire. And this American would not be taken easily, even if greatly outnumbered.

She resolved that she would wait another fifteen minutes and then investigate. She began counting seconds, because it was not bright enough to read the little watch on her wrist.

In films there was always some sort of convenient trellis or rail gutter to climb when one wished to get up on the roof of a building. But had there been one here, he wouldn't have trusted it, considering the general decrepitude of the structure.

But one of the trees—he had been bad at botany, and couldn't tell what kind it was in darkness—was close enough that he had thought he could make it, unless the roof caved in on him when he made the jump. As he edged out along the tree limb now, he began to consider the possibility of the roof collapsing when he jumped. It was slightly sloped, to allow rain to run off, and it seemed to be made of flat boards covered with some sort of unidentifiable substance, perhaps a thin layer of cement. He wasn't sure, and couldn't see it well enough to tell anyway. He had sheathed the Tanto when he'd begun the climb.

What attracted him to the roof was that, unlike the other houses, this one evidently had a second story. He hadn't noticed it from the outside, but when the women and their two captors had entered the small room which apparently was Rahmadi's study, he could have sworn he saw the momentary image of steps behind one of the men.

He hoped.

He was at the end of the limb. He got into a crouch, perched at its edge, then jumped, his hands going out to grab anything handy or necessary, his arms and legs splaying as he impacted the roof and started to slide down it. But he stopped himself.

Unless the men in the study were deaf or stupid, they would have detected that something had crashed into the roof. Maybe they'd think it was a really big bird, he told himself. He found purchase and started crawling along the roof line, noting a shadow grayer than the night—a window leading into a peaked roof structure on the far front of the house.

He crawled nearer, almost to the window, deciding it was some sort of attic.

He kept moving.

The window was sparkling clean. So much for the idea of an attic, he thought. It was curtained, but there was a crack in the curtains and he could see through to the inside just a little. It was a girl's room, a frilly bedspread, a teddy bear by the headboard, a small desk with an oil lamp on top of it and open books. More open books were on the floor, and papers were spilled beside them. She had been studying, it seemed, and been surprised. The dirtballs downstairs, he presumed, had been the source of her surprise.

He tried the window, which wasn't locked. "So far so good," Cross said under his breath. They had never been heavy on housebreaking skills in the SEALs or in naval ROTC before that, but he'd always prided himself on being able to improvise.

He had the window open, his right leg through, the Tanto viced in his clenched teeth, when he heard movement beyond the half-open bedroom door. Someone was coming, and he bet it wasn't the good doctor's daughter.

As he got through the window and threw himself to the floor between the bed and the window, he realized he was half wrong. Along the floor under the bed he saw two sets of feet beside the doorway. One had to be the young girl's, the other one of the three home invaders.

There was a conversation—he assumed it was in Farsi, because he couldn't understand a word of it. But the girl's voice sounded on the edge of terror. He saw the girl shoved out of the doorway, felt her body hit the bed and heard the door slam.

He heard crying, and raised up to his knees to look at her. She turned toward him and opened her mouth to scream. Cross clapped his left hand over her mouth and pulled her down to the edge of the bed beside his head. Her pretty dark eyes were tear-rimmed and her body was shaking, trembling.

Cross took the Tanto from his teeth. "Miss, I'm sure you don't understand English," he whispered. "But I'm not one of them. Honest."

He tried a smile, and the girl's eyes changed. Slowly he eased his hand away from her mouth. "I speak English," she whispered. "Those men are robbers. And maybe—"

"I know, kid," he told her, crossing around the bottom of the bed and going toward the door.

"Who are you?"

"I'm the Lone Ranger, and you just hide up here and don't come out until I come for you or your parents do, and maybe you'll get a silver bullet." He raised the first finger of his left hand to his lips in a gesture of silence and turned it into a kiss.

She looked embarrassed. And that was a good sign, he thought. He opened the bedroom door. Peering out, he saw a small landing, and sharply angled steps beyond, the steps barely visible, the only light from below the yellow wash from the oil lamp he'd seen before.

He started through the doorway, heard the click of a .45's

safety dropping, and thought something obscene as he snatched the Tanto from his teeth and wheeled toward the sound.

Guns going off would attract attention he didn't want, maybe attract the authorities, if there were any around, and definitely spook Mara into bolting with the Land Rover.

He could just see enough of the man's outline beside the doorway to make out the gun hand. Cross's right hand hacked downward toward it, the Magnum Tanto tight in his fist.

Two things dropped and hit the floor—he guessed the first one was the gun and the second the hand. The man in the shadows screamed, and Cross found his face and crashed the semipointed pommel of the Tanto into the center of it, his left knee smashing up, a rush of foul breath against Cross's face. His left hand found a mass of greasy hair in the darkness and his right hand raked the edge of the Tanto across the man's throat.

He wheeled toward the steps.

No one was coming. No one was shouting for the third guy.

He silently thanked God that some people were congenitally dense, then started down the steps, retrieving the .45 and shoving it under his jacket and into his pants.

The steps creaked a little as he moved slowly, staying as close to the wall as possible, to minimize the weight of his body on the wooden treads.

He could hear a frightened woman's voice—Rahmadi's wife, the older woman. He heard the sound of a slap. He'd known guys over the years who liked to hit women. These guys were apparently that type. It was a curious coincidence, Cross had always thought, that it was the same type he always enjoyed beating the crap out of.

He was nearly at the base of the steps.

The woman was crying. He reflected that tears sounded the same in any language, just like laughter did.

He was two treads above the base of the stairs, trying to picture the layout of the room as he'd seen it through the window, hoping the positions of the four people remaining in it—Dr. Rahmadi and his wife and the two men with guns— hadn't changed much while he'd been away.

He could have taken them easily with his revolver. It

wasn't like it was that night in the supermarket so many weeks ago. He hadn't even had a beer in three days. But the noise of gunfire would be something he couldn't gamble on.

It would have to be fast.

Cross reached under his coat and buttoned out the magazine on the dead guy's .45, the Tanto not going back into his teeth until he cleaned it, since bloodied knives tasted worse than clean ones, but under his left armpit—he hoped the tall, silent Mujahedin from whom he'd borrowed it would accept a promissory note in lieu of cash for the dry-cleaning bill. He emptied the magazine into his left hand, dropping it into his pocket, six rounds—the seventh was already stripped and chambered, he presumed—in his left palm.

Cross took a deep breath, trying to draw his energy to his center, focusing it from there into his right hand, which tightened on the haft of the Tanto as he regrasped it.

He stepped down the two treads and simultaneously hurtled the six rounds across the room and toward the window through which he had first observed.

The unshaven guy with the Luger—as opposed to the unshaven guy with the unidentifiable Spanish pistol—wheeled toward the sound of the cartridges hitting the glass. Cross stepped into the room, the guy with the Spanish pistol twisting his body at an awkward angle and ready to open fire. Cross had the Tanto swinging outward, parallel to the floor, his left fist coming up and almost smothering his right, both arms into the swing now. There was a look of amazement in the eyes of the man with the Spanish pistol, the edge of the eight-inch blade contacting flesh, an almost unnoticeable drag, then the blade moving through the neck like a hot knife through a stick of butter. The head toppled off over Spanish pistol's right shoulder, the body just standing there, spurting blood like a fire hydrant someone had backed a truck into.

Cross didn't have time to watch it fall. The doctor's wife started a scream. Cross flashed her a toothy grin. Luger was turning away from the window, had heard the sound of Spanish pistol's head falling, Cross thought in the instant.

Cross's leg went forward, the Tanto locked in both fists over his shoulder, chisel point up, his balance shifting, the blade edge out ahead of his shoulder as he started the swing.

Luger's pistol rose up in his hand in front of his face, almost like a medieval warrior might raise a shield. The Magnum Tanto's arc caught the arm midway between wrist and elbow, and Cross pulled back. It would have taken two such blows to sever the arm through, and he didn't waste the motion.

He wheeled on his heel, drew the other foot back for balance. The man with his arm half cut away was screaming. Cross held the Magnum Tanto edge down, blade tip presented toward the target, the haft of it and his right fist at approximately the level of his right ear. He started the thrust, feinted, then both his wrists snapped the Tanto in a short swing, across the Luger's carotid artery, ripping the throat half open.

Luger's body sagged back, the head at a crazy angle as he fell.

Cross heard a sound behind him and wheeled toward it, the Tanto raised. It was Dr. Rahmadi with the Spanish pistol—it was still a mystery, but definitely Spanish—in both fists like some cop on television. "If you can speak English, Dr. Rahmadi, I'd think twice about that gun versus this knife—especially since I'm the good guy, and that guy looks terribly old and ill-cared for. Whereas this knife . . ." Cross let the sentence hang.

Dr. Rahmadi lowered the pistol, and Cross lowered the Magnum Tanto. "Who are you that you speak English?"

If this had been a movie or an adventure novel, Cross thought, the girl would have crept down the stairs and announced to her startled parents, "He said he's the Lone Ranger."

It wasn't. She didn't.

He thought of a good line and said it. "Where I come from, we call it American, Doc."

# Chapter Thirty-two

Rahmadi spoke as he worked on the tall, silent Mujahedin. Cross had left Irania with them after first retrieving her. She had been on her way along the rear of the houses and coming to get him. Then he'd hiked back to Mara, told her everything was okay and to go and get the wounded man. Hughes and Babcock had brought him, and Cross, Hughes, Babcock and Irania had stood around the table as Rahmadi worked. The doctor had reopened the wound after sedating the Mujahedin man. "These three men you killed, sir—they have terrorized the villages near here, killing many people, raping many women. The authorities do nothing. They are too busy looking for those whose religious beliefs differ in the slightest from theirs."

He was probing the wound as Cross asked, "Then you don't see much of the army around here?"

Dr. Rahmadi laughed, his balding pate glistening sweat under the generator-operated lights of his operating room. "You have a particular interest in knowing, sir?"

Hughes spoke. "I would imagine, sir, that you have gathered we didn't just happen along with the young lady while on a tour of the countryside."

"I have heard of a group of commandoes who destroyed a government helicopter. It was said there were at least fifty of them."

"Reports of our success are slightly exaggerated," Babcock supplied.

"But you are these men?" Rahmadi persisted.

Cross deferred to Hughes.

Hughes answered, "We are these men—and ladies." He smiled across the table toward Irania.

"It is not often the People's Mujahedin takes down a helicopter of the army." The doctor's daughter stood beside him, wiping his forehead now and then, his wife handing him instruments. "I am a sympathizer to the movement against the Ayatollah, but I am not a sympathizer to violence. However, you—" He looked at Cross for a moment, his hands still. "You, young man, who fights like a devil—you saved the life of my daughter and my wife, perhaps in their cases saved them from something even worse. And you saved my miserable life. I am grateful for that as well. So, ask me your questions, but on one condition."

"Which is?" Hughes asked.

"Since it is nearly breakfast and, at least speaking for myself, I am too excited to sleep—join me in a modest but satisfying meal." He looked at his wife, and she nodded. She hadn't said a word.

"It would be our pleasure, sir," Babcock responded.

"Which way did the army go, Dr. Rahmadi?" Hughes asked.

"Along the coast. It was as if they somehow suspected your ultimate destination. Could that be?"

Hughes smiled, lowering his eyes. "No doubt it seemed that way, sir. But let me ask you this. Would we still be well advised to travel in that direction some other way?"

"Such as a boat?" the doctor asked wryly. "The boat in so substantial need of repair. Yes, maybe that would work. Several of the people here have been wondering about its owners over the past few days."

"Did any of them wonder to the army, would you think?" Hughes asked.

"No one here much cares for the army, or the Ayatollah, for that matter. You must remember, the mere fact that this young man," and he nodded his head toward Cross, his hands occupied with the wound, "and my daughter were alone together in the same bedroom, irregardless of the fact that he was saving her life from a criminal, might well subject them both to trial before a religious court. It is that way here. It should not be.''

Babcock started to ask a question, then Rahmadi exclaimed, ''I was right! Whoever performed the removal of the bullet did a satisfactory job for an amateur. But there was a wound channel here that had not been discovered, until now, and . . .'' He raised a pair of forceps, something about twice the size of the head of a pin between them. ''A bullet fragment. Voilà!''

Cross guessed that now he would have to consider restitution for the bloodstains on the tall, silent Mujahedin's jacket.

# Chapter Thirty-three

They hadn't stayed for breakfast, but had taken a bottle of warm coffee with them made by Dr. Rahmadi's daughter, and sandwiches made by his wife. The coffee was strong, the sandwiches were made on hard bread, and the meat was fresh. Rahmadi's daughter had kissed him on the cheek, and Rahmadi's wife had embraced him. Cross felt warm inside, and not from the food and the coffee. They had left the tall, silent Mujahedin in Rahmadi's care, taken the bodies and body parts of the three home invaders, and helped with cleaning up the bloodstains, in the event the authorities should come by. Hughes had commented, "Next time you kill three men, try to be a little neater about it, lad."

The sun was an hour short of rising over the water as the diesel-powered fishing boat—about twelve feet stem to stern, seven feet abeam, and very cramped—pulled away from its berth, Babcock, the Army man, at her helm, and Cross, the Navy man, standing watch. To Hughes fell the task of baby-sitting the engine. It sputtered, as if protesting, but had started quickly enough.

Part of the curse of the cramped conditions was relieved when they were out over deep water and the bodies of the three home invaders, weighted with anchor chain Cross and Babcock had expropriated from other vessels near where theirs had berthed, were thrown over the side.

Babcock had named the craft the *Intrepid*. Cross reflected

on the name as he stared out toward open water, the sun winking over the horizon, that he was not the only one possessed of a bizarre sense of humor. Intrepid this vessel was not.

Irania stood beside him, Mara and the four other Mujahedin huddled in the stern, the only place where there was room.

"Perhaps we will evade the Russians," Irania said to him over the keening of the wind.

Cross shrugged, saying, "Yes, perhaps," but thinking he was indulging in self-deceit. So far, since entering Iran, they had encountered almost every conceivable difficulty short of an earthquake or a personal appearance tour by the Ayatollah Khomeini.

Hughes's arrival beside them in the prow of the *Intrepid* aroused him from his reverie. "The engine's a bit of a beast, but she's running. Hopefully she'll continue."

"Why do you call the engine a she?" Irania asked Hughes.

He brought out his smile and told her, "I think, in the early days of mechanization, when the task of repairing machinery fell to the male of the species and the fact that machinery at times seemed irrational and temperamental, well—it probably seemed like the logical thing to do, to think of machines as female in nature. No offense was intended, Irania."

She grasped his arm and laughed. Cross watched her, and the way the breeze played again with her hair.

They were twelve hours out, calculated by the face of Cross's Rolex Sea-Dweller. He had returned the Gruen wristwatch along with the bloodstained jacket and the equivalent of five dollars in Iranian currency to the injured man before leaving. For him, the mission was over. In a week or so Irania's people would come and claim him, and soon he would be back to full strength, resuming the fight that Irania seemed to think hopeless but necessary. Cross agreed with her on both counts.

He had just relieved Babcock at the helm, Babcock needing sleep after the long day's vigil. Cross had slept for five hours when he awakened to find Irania nestled beside him amidships, near the shacklike wheelhouse. He didn't wake her, her sleep so peaceful seeming, but found a free square meter on the afterdeck and begun some calisthenics to get rid of the stiffness from sleeping in such cramped quarters.

Hughes had taken a break earlier in the day, Mara attending the diesel for him, but Hughes was now back at his post.

Cross calculated that another nine hours or so remained in their voyage. Taking the helm afforded some advantage. He had an entire compartment, however small—it was about the area of a decent-sized closet—to himself. He could catch up on his smoking, although he hadn't smoked more than half a pack a day in these past few weeks, usually substantially less.

He lit a cigarette now and inhaled the smoke deep into his lungs as he watched the sun set and the sky darken. In a few more days this would all be over. He would either be dead or escape, but he would never see Irania again. He doubted that in his lifetime Iran would become a tourist mecca. "Iran become a tourist mecca—wokka-wokka," Cross said aloud to the empty wheelhouse. Sometimes he empathized with stand-up comedians.

Then he noticed a light coming out of the purple grayness of the horizon, the sun behind them, washing the sea with its colors. The light grew as he watched it.

There was one of those tube-and-whistle affairs leading from the wheelhouse to the engine compartment, and Cross grabbed for it, blowing into it. "Hughes!"

The voice came back, "I'm not deaf, lad—or at least I wasn't until a moment ago. What is it?"

"I think we've got trouble off the starboard bow. Maybe."

"How much trouble?"

"I see what might be one searchlight or a big running light—I can't be certain."

"I'll see what I can do. But I don't think we can outrun anything besides a rowboat."

"I know," Cross told him, putting down the tube. The light was growing fast now. Cross held the wheel in one hand and reached to the wheelhouse door with the other, tugging it open. "Irania. Mara. Get Lew up!"

Babcock came to the wheelhouse door, and in a moment Irania joined him. Babcock was rubbing sleep from his eyes. "You mean I slept six hours?" he said, looking at his watch.

"Make it about twenty minutes. Look off to starboard."

Cross had both hands on the wheel again, Irania leaning over the side, Babcock half in, half out of the wheelhouse door. "Russian?"

Cross shrugged. He could see Irania more clearly now—she had field glasses in her hands and was peering toward the light. Then she turned toward him, coming past Babcock, who still held the wheelhouse door open, saying, "Russian. It has to be."

"Holy shit," Babcock muttered, then looked at Irania. "Forgive me, Irania."

"Can we outrun it?" was all she replied.

Cross just shook his head.

"What can we do?"

Cross didn't know what to tell her. But the light kept coming nearer.

# Chapter Thirty-four

Helen Chelewski pulled the sheet up under her chin. Warren Corliss told her, "This never happened before."

She just looked at him. "I mean—never, anytime," he told her.

She almost hissed, "Maybe you use it so much it's worn out, Warren," and she turned abruptly under the covers and faced away from him. "Turn off the light, Warren."

He sat up in bed, reached for the lamp on the nightstand, and turned off the light. He leaned back, the room very dark now. It was his room at the Jerusalem Hilton. He wondered how long it would be before she got up and got dressed and left him. "I'm sorry," he whispered. "I really am, Helen."

And then he felt her stirring beneath the sheet and felt her hand on his chest. "If you hadn't made such a big deal out of it, I wouldn't have," she whispered back.

"I, ah—"

"Warren, is all you want from me, ah—"

"No."

He turned toward her, and she pulled him down under the covers with her, her breasts against his chest, her breath against his face as she spoke. "That's not all I want you for either, Warren. I love you."

He started to speak, to tell her. But he just held her in his arms in the darkness and listened to her breathe, felt her hold him.

He couldn't speak.

Muhammad Ibn al Raka had finished with his evening prayers.

He sat at the dresser in his hotel room, watching his image in the mirror for a moment. Then he took the Czech CZ-75 9mm up from beside him and removed the magazine, removed the chambered round, and began field stripping it. The Russians favored this pistol when it was available for their special forces personnel, he knew. It was in Russia where he had first encountered it.

But the Russians were also not to be trusted. Mehdi Hamadan trusted the Russians, or at least worked for them. That much had been clear to Raka about the leader of International Jihad for many months. But the Russians could be used—their intelligence gathering was vastly superior to anything his own country could expect to be capable of for many years. It was all right to use the Russians. Raka used them indirectly through Mehdi Hamadan. And he used Mehdi Hamadan as well.

Terrorism was nothing except random violence without an organization, without forces that could be called up and were willing to die, without special equipment.

He had placed explosives in an airport terminal once, the operation solely his own and a few who believed like him. The explosion had gone perfectly, had killed eighteen Christians and Jews, but missed the one man who had been its target. The intelligence data had been wrong.

Raka had vowed then that to achieve the greater effect, some personal sacrifices must be made, even if that meant dealing with those he would normally condemn.

He had learned to suppress his sensibilities for the good of his beliefs: The destruction of the Great Satan must take precedence over all other things.

Tomorrow he would deal the Great Satan a blow from which it might never recover.

•    •    •

Jeff Feinberg sat alone in the hut on the plateau, the wind howling so loudly that it sounded like a human scream, the strength of it such that at times the walls rattled with it.

He was monitoring two radios, one tuned to the Iranian army frequency, but he expected no signals yet from Hughes, Cross, and Babcock. If all had gone perfectly as planned, they would be at the objective by now, perhaps already making the penetration. The earliest he would hear from them would be several hours from now. If something had worked to delay them, nothing might be heard for days. If they died— He tried not to consider that.

The second radio was set to the frequency shared with Spiros Patrakos. On this frequency Patrakos could contact him in the event of emergency and he could contact Patrakos to bring in the Beechcraft to retrieve just him—Feinberg—or the whole team.

He studied the clock between the two radios. It was time to go outside and take readings off the weather-monitoring equipment in place there as part of the cover. He was supposedly the meteorological researcher for a group that planned an assault on Mount Ararat in search of the ark some said had landed there when the waters of the Great Flood retreated. Cross had spoken to him about this, how he had watched Mount Ararat through his window aboard the Beechcraft. Feinberg had slept instead. The medication for his arm made him slightly sleepy, and he had no interest in history at any event, biblical or otherwise.

He'd missed the greatest opportunity of his life because of a bad move in a bar fight. He was here, alone, but safe. They were out there. Hughes had thrown him a bone by letting him be the ground man.

Feinberg stood up and picked up his parka, sliding his left arm into the sleeve, unable to zip it closed because his right arm could not comfortably be taken from its sling. He took up the thermal blanket and wrapped it around him the way a woman might, and felt disgust at all of this.

He should have been fighting, not waiting. He started outside to read his damned gauges.

•    •    •

Leadbetter had gotten up early so he could read the reports on the wire. None of the news services carried anything, and there was nothing on the intelligence wire, so he had left the office on E Street and started walking. He was always waiting to get busted when he went for one of his walks in Washington. Theoretically, not even private security personnel could legally carry a concealed weapon in the District of Columbia. But Leadbetter had long ago ascribed to the pragmatic slogan, "It's better to be judged by twelve than carried by six." So, there was an old Beretta 1934 inside the waistband of his trousers, a gun he had picked up just after World War II, a gun never registered anywhere and which he loaded, cleaned, and generally handled with gloves on. If he ever had to use it, he'd wipe it quickly with his handkerchief and throw it in the trash can. He had even sprayed the exterior metal surfaces with a type of polyurethane that would frustrate the use of the new, sophisticated laser equipment the FBI and some other organizations used for drawing out latent fingerprints.

He was nervous. He was waiting for an official mood swing that would suddenly make his little band of heroes into a little band of villains. Or some freshman congressman looking to build a reputation. What if somehow someone like that tripped over something that made him realize the United States was unofficially invading Iran for a surgical strike against International Jihad?

The bleeding hearts would love that. How dare we violate the sovereign territory of another nation for something as evil as revenge? It didn't matter that the terrorists did it. If the terrorists killed someone, there was outrage. If we planned to do the same, there would be hearings and investigations and the press would have headlines for weeks or maybe months.

There was something basically wrong today, he thought. He hadn't considered where his walk was taking him, but he did now. He was staring at the Washington Monument in the distance.

He turned his back and walked away.

# Chapter Thirty-five

To have outrun the Soviet patrol boat would have been impossible.

But they had planned for this eventuality.

Cross had never liked the plan, or at least his part of it.

He'd stripped to Jockey shorts; the Gerber BMF, suited more to the task than his Cold Steel Magnum Tanto, was lashed to his right calf with its own thongs. He stood on the portside of the *Intrepid*, behind the shelter of the wheelhouse, the Russian vessel less than a hundred yards off the starboard bow, its searchlight bathing the entire vessel in bright white light. Hughes shone his mini flashlight over the face of his Rolex, then over the face of Cross's, holding it over Cross's to heighten the luminosity. "Identical," Hughes observed.

"Within a few seconds," Cross amended.

"Keep track of the time, lad. As soon as it's time, I'm gunning the engine."

"I just hope the dilithium crystals hold out—gosh." Cross grinned. He picked up the device Hughes had prepared for the occasion. "Works just like you told me—stick it on and hit the switch and swim like hell, right?"

"Right—and you might hold your ears."

"Good point," Cross agreed. "Let me ask you a question— why aren't we doing like Gregory Peck and Anthony Quinn did in *The Guns of Navarone*? Nobody had to get wet blowing up the enemy patrol boat."

Hughes seemed to consider that, his face partly in shadow and partly in light. Then, "Because I'm not David Niven."

Cross couldn't argue with that. He shoved the device less than gently into the nearly empty musette bag suspended cross body under his left armpit, snapped the flap shut, and rolled over the side into the water. It was freezing cold, but not as bad as his last swim had been. And, on the plus side, there was always the possibility that Irania would have to warm him with her body again.

He kept the musette bag close against him as he followed along the water line toward the stern of the *Intrepid*. This particular variety was a Norwegian army engineer's bag. If a woman had carried an identically-shaped bag used for storing emergency necessities and slung from her shoulder, it would have been a purse. He shrugged mentally; he would never understand humanity.

He could see the Soviet patrol boat clearly now, its whatsit towering some twenty feet over the deck of the *Intrepid*, its length well over five times that of the fishing boat.

It seemed so huge—he wondered if the device would be adequate to the task

There was only one way to find out, and he began regulating his breathing, one eye on the Rolex, finally taking the deep breath and tucking under the surface. He started to swim, no need for a light, the floodlights from the Russian vessel making it bright enough just below the surface that he could almost have read by them as he surfaced for a quick breath just between the vessels. He tucked under the waves again, swimming deeper now, the luminous face of the Rolex showing him still on schedule.

Suddenly all the light vanished, and he realized he had crossed beneath the hull of the boat. Hughes had told him that to the best of his knowledge the Russian patrol boats had no sensing equipment that could detect a lone swimmer. He hoped Hughes was right.

The oxygen situation was starting to get a little tense, and he increased his kick slightly, breaking surface astern of the Russian vessel near the portside of the two powerful-looking screws. He looked at his watch. He was running a little behind. He inhaled and tucked under the surface again, avoiding the screws, following along beneath the hull by feel, on the Russian vessel's portside. The Rolex glowed dully but he could read the face. Time was getting critical. He swam faster, at the bow now.

He surfaced, eyeballing the right spot, glancing once more at the time. "Fuck it," he said under his breath, inhaling and going under again. He was a minute behind schedule, but it wouldn't affect his placement of the mine, simply his escape. There was always the chance someone would detect the placement of the mine against the hull in time to do something like send a diver over. That was the reason for the knife.

He heard a roar overhead.

It would be the *Intrepid*'s engine firing. He locked the mine against the hull and activated the switch magnetizing it, hoping he hadn't screwed up his watch in the process—Rolexes weren't cheap, and if he lived, he didn't relish the idea of buying a new one.

Cross hit the second switch. The roar was louder now, the *Intrepid*'s single screw starting to churn. It would be only seconds before the Soviet vessel responded.

The mine was armed, the timer going. Cross swam for his life, the Russian vessel's twin screws starting to turn in the water, the boat lurching ahead. Cross dove, his lungs burning for lack of oxygen. He kept going down. It was either that or be sliced to pieces by the screws.

He rolled in the water, the darker shape of the Russian vessel's hull disappearing rapidly in the dark of the water. He started for the surface, cramping a little, his head breaking the surface, waves from the Russian vessel's wake crashing against him. He sucked air and dove. It would take about another thirty seconds for the Russian vessel's speed to get up. He swam diagonally away from her vanishing stern to put as much distance between himself and the boat as possible.

He eyed the Rolex, then started for the surface.

His head broke the water and he turned around, orienting himself. He could just make out the Russian vessel, the *Intrepid* all but obscured by her bulk, moving at an oblique angle to her, making her maneuver. The Russian ship's bow raised—if he had placed the mine at about the right spot, it would blow a hole in the hull about the size of a gas stove, and with the bow elevated at speed, the momentum of the vessel through the water would serve to funnel thousands of gallons of sea water into her and take her to the bottom almost instantly.

Cross waited.

He saw the tongue of flame for an instant before the water extinguished it; he heard the roar, holding his ears against it.

The Russian vessel's bow seemed to pitch upward, machine-gun fire from her deck aimed at the *Intrepid,* answering bursts of automatic weapons fire from the *Intrepid*'s deck. Then suddenly the Russian vessel stopped dead in the water and her bow started to nosedive into the waves her own wake had made about her, the machine-gun fire from her deck stopping. The Russian vessel flipped forward, her stern pointing upward, then sank beneath the waves.

There was a secondary explosion.

There was nothing more.

Abe Cross reached into the musette bag for the one remaining item. It was an H&K flare pistol sealed in a watertight poly bag. He held it high over the water, chambered the starburst flare, and fired it overhead.

There was an answering flare a second later from the deck of the *Intrepid.*

As he started swimming toward the *Intrepid,* the fishing boat was already coming about to make way toward him in the water.

# Chapter Thirty-six

Near Tankabon, along the coast, other members of the People's Mujahedin waited. Cross, Hughes, Babcock, Irania, Mara, and the three others remaining from the initial Mujahedin unit waded in through the surf, barefoot despite the cold of the water. It was the best choice when the alternative was to spend the next several days in wet boots. The Mujahedin ran to the edge of the surf to meet them, taking the climbing bags, the weapons cases, the explosives. Cross stopped at the edge of the surf.

Babcock came to a sort of lazy man's attention, saying, "Gentlemen—the *Intrepid.*" And he saluted. Cross smiled, doing the same. Hughes shot the *Intrepid* one of those sloppy bent-hand Dung Hao salutes like the salutes everybody gave each other in World War II movies, then worked the radio detonator in his left hand.

There was a fireball and a subdued roar, and the *Intrepid* was aflame, then vanished beneath the waves.

"Isn't that what Cortez did when he invaded Mexico?" Babcock asked Hughes.

"Something like that—yes. Now, to horses, gentlemen."

Cross picked up his sub gun, Gregory pack, and boots and started toward the Mujahedin reunion festival going on a few yards farther in. About twenty-five yards still farther back were a group of horses, saddled and waiting.

•   •   •   •

Babcock apparently had little fondness for music. "Abe, will you knock it off, whistling the theme from *The Magnificent Seven,* already?"

Cross shrugged and fell silent, still humming the tune in his head. The horse had liked the music, he told himself.

They rode in two parallel files, traveling up again into the mountains. But there were no snows here, at least not at this elevation. His coat was across the pommel of his saddle—it had no horn—and his submachine gun hung on its sling beneath his right arm. Beside him, appropriately on the prettiest horse, rode Irania, the animal she had selected nearly as black as her hair.

He'd missed out on the part about being warmed with her body after his moonlight swim. There hadn't really been that much moonlight anyway. It had been necessary to stay on watch on deck all through the remainder of the voyage against the possibility that the Soviet vessel—it had gone down with all hands—had gotten out a radio message. Apparently, it had not.

The bay mare he rode was what they called "spirited," which meant he had to periodically fight her to keep her from bolting ahead or stopping dead still, in which case everyone behind would have crashed into him. But it kept him awake. Sleep had been something he'd had none of that night, and the few hours he'd had before the Russian patrol boat had been spotted were starting to wear thin.

With the six additional Mujahedin who had met them by the water's edge—all of them men—they had a combined force of fourteen. And more of the Mujahedin people lay ahead of them, nearer to Mount Dizan.

Irania, beside him, said, "I want to sleep with you."

Cross just looked at her, not knowing what to say. They had slept side by side, but sleeping had been all. He had kissed her in the Land Rover, his hands on her body, but . . .

"I know that you must think me shameless. But since we might die, there isn't time for modesty. Will you let me sleep with you, Abe?"

Cross told her, "Yes." She spurred her horse a little ahead of his, and he didn't try catching up.

•    •    •

Helen Chelewski handed him a duplicated copy of the guest list across her desk. Warren Corliss took it, then leaned back in his chair, not looking at the list, but instead looking at her as she read it. "The following special envoys will be at the banquet tonight. And again the list—I have to say this" —she looked at him and smiled, appearing very pretty this morning—"the names on this list are confidential. If you were to release this list to the press, you'd never be allowed in any U.S. government facility to film anything. And I'd lose my job, Warren."

"I understand, Helen. I really do. Just like we said—I won't release a frame of film without your permission, and without the participants in the conference having a final review edit."

She smiled at him. She was so pretty, he thought. Thinking about last night, he balled his fists tight.

"All right, then, Warren. We have the special envoy from the Syrian government, the special envoy from Israel, the special envoy from the Egyptian government. We have the special envoy from the government of Tunisia, and the Jordanian Government. And, of course, Mr. Elias Fairchild, the presidential envoy. Why are you looking at me that way? If it's about last night . . . I mean—"

"No."

"Why—"

"You're very beautiful. And I'll be sorry, in a way, once we have the filming done."

"Then it—"

"I don't want it over between us. But I think you will."

She looked at him strangely. "Why are you saying that, Warren?" She cleared her throat. "I mean, this whole documentary you're making is a gamble. You might never get to release it if the conference doesn't go off well. You know that. I wondered why you wanted to do it so badly."

"I told you," he told her. "I think that getting inside the diplomatic process would be an education for people. It would serve a valuable purpose in the public interest, not to mention its historical value."

"I never did ask you—or if I did, I forgot," she said, lighting a cigarette for herself, leaning across her desk, looking at him as though she were studying him as she exhaled. "How did you first learn about the conference?"

"I told you—you did forget." He smiled. "A newsman has his sources, and even though I produce documentaries, I'm still a newsman."

"All right. So you're leaving me after this is over. I mean, I knew you couldn't stay in Jerusalem forever, but I thought that—it's last night, isn't it?"

"No, it's today," he said, and he got up and walked out of her office.

# Chapter Thirty-seven

"It is called Kashin," Irania announced.

They had circled the village to be certain that no danger awaited them. The mountains here were the backyard of the International Jihad, and there was the ever-growing possibility of encountering a security patrol of the terrorist group or the army.

They rode now, four of them, down the solitary street which neatly enough bisected the mountain village, a collection of poor huts. These people were Kurds, and perhaps that had something to do with their village seeming so desolate, so poor, Cross thought. The village by the Caspian the previous evening seemed like a luxury suburb by comparison. Despite the cold, children clothed in rags played in the mudholes, their bodies so terribly thin that their bones showed, some of them with their stomachs swollen.

Cross had left the six new Mujahedin and the three men from the original force outside the village in the highlands overlooking the small, dish-shaped valley. Only Cross himself, Hughes, Babcock, Irania, and Mara had come down.

The plan called for circumventing the village entirely, but when each of them had looked down on the village through their field glasses, it had become impossible to pass around it, to ignore it.

And here, at its center, it looked worse.

Several of the huts were partially roofless, or the doors,

such as they were, hung from a single rough hinge. Women in traditional Moslem garb crouched before these open doorways and ground pitifully small amounts of meal or cooked over open fires that smelled of animal dung. Of livestock, there were only goats, and precious few of these, he imagined, kept for milk for the children.

They reined in at the center of the village, Cross swinging down from his mount, his eyes searching for some evidence of fear or curiosity among the villagers. There was none. What few men there were seemed to be either very old or prepubescent boys, looking as frail as the women and smaller children.

Cross held Irania's horse as she dismounted, Hughes saying, "I'm riding to the end of town. I'll be back." Mara and Babcock rode with him.

Irania lowered the shawl with which she had partially covered her hair and face, shaking her head to free her hair. She dropped to her knees before one of the women grinding meal, spoke to the woman in what Cross presumed was Kurdish, at first eliciting no response. Then, at last, a voice whose words he did not seem to understand to appreciate the exhaustion, the hopelessness, answered her.

Irania began to translate. "I asked the woman—she is only twenty-four"—Cross shivered—"I asked her why the village was as it is."

"What's she saying?" he asked, squinting as the sunlight momentarily broke through the heavy overcast. And then the sun was gone again.

Irania was crying as she spoke. "The men of International Jihad—sometimes they will pass through the village. A patrol. Or sometimes they just come here. They steal the food that is here and leave almost nothing. They take the young boys to turn them into terrorists like themselves, and those who will not embrace the principles of International Jihad—it is said—are killed. Some of the patrols—sometimes they will take the young women and rape them. But this happens very rarely. Some of the men in the village attempted to hide their sons and hold back on the food from the last patrol that was through here. That was nine or ten days ago, she says. The men of the patrol seemed to go wild with rage, and they began burning and killing, and this time they stole all of the food they could find and killed many of the older men. This—this—'' Irania touched the rim of the bowl in which the woman ground whatever kind of grain it was. ''This is all they have.''

Cross walked closer to the woman, running the fingers of his left hand back through his hair. He looked along the village street. In a few more days the children would be the first, he thought. And the old people.

''Tell the woman that where we go, we will not need food. And tell the woman to pray for us, and perhaps no more of her food or her children will ever be taken by these people again. Tell her that,'' and Cross tugged at the reins of his horse, drawing the animal closer to him, then started unlashing his pack from the saddle.

They had emergency rations. They would not need them. The People's Mujahedin force with which they would rendezvous would have enough extra food to spare them a meal before the penetration of Mount Dizan. And if the raid was a success, there would be rations aplenty awaiting them in Turkey.

If they did not succeed, food wouldn't matter anyway.

He had the Gregory pack down on the ground where he crouched now, and started taking out everything that was edible.

Hughes, Babcock, and the Mujahedin left their food as well, and Hughes also broke up the first-aid kits to leave behind anything useful for the villagers.

They rode on, not stopping when the sun began to set.

Babcock finally had a personal, tangible reason for being here, Cross thought, remembering the mask of rage on the black former Army officer's face when Irania had recounted what had happened in the village.

Babcock had been the only one among them who had needed additional reasons, personal reasons. He had told Cross, ''I don't want them ever to bother that village again. We have to do our best to see to that,'' and then he'd begun taking the food from his pack, even the trail-mix bars from his jacket pockets.

# Chapter Thirty-eight

His camera crew was already setting up for the banquet that evening, more equipment arriving from the warehouse. The footage already shot would have made an interesting documentary on its own, without the formal banquet and illustrious personages to be in attendance there.

But the banquet was the reason he'd come.

Warren Corliss stood in the courtyard, smoking a cigarette, listening to the birds in the trees, feeling the warmth of the fading sun.

He thought about Helen Chelewski.

She would hate him.

He would hate himself.

He heard the familiar voice behind him. "Mr. Corliss. I'm going to need your help with that last load of stuff from the warehouse. The boxes are locked like they're supposed to be, but there's some kind of mix-up or something. My key doesn't fit."

Corliss studied the young director's face. As American as apple pie, the blue eyes smiling under a shock of reddish-blond hair. He reminded Corliss of his younger brother, Martin. "Oh, Bob, I've got the key. The locks got damaged when we brought them in through customs, and I had to replace them. I'm sorry I forgot to tell you."

Bob Nash grinned. "I was gettin' worried there, boss. If we don't have those extra lights and those extra shotgun microphones, well, you wouldn't like what we get tonight.''

"Tonight is gonna work out just the way it's been planned, for good or bad, Bob.''

"I just wish we didn't have to get approval on this thing before we release it. People are gonna see this film, and for the first time maybe they're gonna understand how the whole diplomatic process works and the people who make it work. I think we'll be proud of this, Mr. Corliss. Real proud of it.''

Warren Corliss didn't think he would ever be proud again.

The back of the van was warm, despite the already declining sun. Raka realized he had become too used to the cooler climate of his mountain fortress.

Rausch was talking. Raka looked toward the front passenger seat. Ephraim, the taxi driver, was at the wheel. Rausch said, "What if we cannot trust the inside contact, Raka? What if the police or the army are told how to find us?''

"We can trust the inside contact for the finest reason— fear. The same reason I trust you as far as I do. You, for example, know that if you were to betray me, I would kill you. If my death resulted, one of my twelve Immortals would kill you. Or someone else from International Jihad would find you and kill you. There would be no place for you to turn, no place for you to hide. The inside contact knows this same fear that you know. So, I ask, Rausch—would you betray me?''

"Of—of course not, Raka. I believe in your cause. I—''

"You believe in my money. You believe in your own fear. Perhaps you still believe in your youth when you were a Nazi.''

"You promised, Raka—''

"Never to bring that up? So I did. I apologize. Sincerely. Now shut up.'' Raka was stoning his special knife, the one that was like no other.

He looked at his wristwatch.

As a young man he had suffered from the indiscipline of impatience. He had taught himself patience through fasting and other forms of self-denial. And through prayer.

He was patient now.

There was a heightened sense of reality, as well, now. He

had watched the sunrise with particular relish, prayed with particular fervor. Soon he would pray again.

He had eaten with particular delight. He had spent much of the evening reading in *The Koran*.

He was at peace with himself, and he found it strange that such inner peace had come from what he knew would be his most violent hours, and likely his last. But this was a small sacrifice to the glory of God.

He was reminded of the remarks attributed to Abu-Bakr, caliph to the Prophet, upon the occasion of the Prophet's funeral. "O ye people, if anyone worships Muhammad, Muhammad is dead. But if anyone worships God, He is alive and dies not."

A single life was but a grain of sand in the hourglass of the centuries. Raka continued to stone his knife.

# Chapter Thirty-nine

Mehdi Hamadan had ordered dinner sent up to his room. He had ordered a non-alcoholic drink that was one of his favorites.

He sat now in a rattan chair, his feet raised and rested on the balcony, sipping slowly at his drink. He had ordered an early dinner so that he could enjoy the sunset. From his balcony he could see much of Jerusalem, but he could not see the embassy of the United States. Which was just as well, because it would have ruined the sunset.

He had verbally verified with the room-service waiter that light meals would still be available until eleven that night. He anticipated that he would need added refreshment. It would be a long night of watching television.

And then, of course, in the morning there would be the newspapers. The American newspapers would not have full coverage yet, but the British papers might have good data in them.

By the next evening there would be nothing in the news that would match it. It would dominate the print and electronic media.

The United States would accuse Israel of sloppy security measures or worse, damaging the sometimes touchy alliance. Israel would insist that its own personnel would successfully penetrate the embassy. The United States would openly say that it favored a peaceful solution to the crisis, and privately tell the Israelis to do what seemed best, and hope that if it went wrong, which it would, the Israelis wouldn't object too strenuously to taking the blame for the fiasco in the press.

The Israelis would execute some punitive raid against the wrong people, further escalating the tension in the Middle East. The United States would spend millions of its taxpayers' dollars and send its warships back and forth along the Mediterranean. The American president would make harsh speeches denouncing terrorism to the press. The Israelis would probably erect a monument or something to the dead.

And so many troublesome governments would learn that there was nowhere their representatives could be safe to plot against the rising tide of Islam.

International Jihad would incorporate the resources of Achmed Omani after he was tried for treasonous activities. His—Mehdi Hamadan's—power would increase to vast proportions. The KGB would be pleased at the end result, if not actually with the method used to achieve it. And his power there would increase as well.

The sunset was full of promise and very lovely indeed.

Helen Chelewski stood in front of the full-length mirror, pleased with what she saw. She was thirty-three, her figure better than it was when she had received her undergraduate degree. The floor-length white evening gown was simple and elegant, displaying neither too little nor too much cleavage or back. And white had been her color ever since she'd been a little girl. Her hair had come out perfectly, and the cameo earrings and necklace she had inherited from her aunt were the perfection of understated elegance.

She thought about Warren Corliss. She had been stupid to fall in love with him. Thirty-three—and still alone.

She left the mirror, conscious of the reassuring rustle of her clothes as she walked across her bedroom and started filling her evening bag with the necessities. And, of course, her wristwatch. This was a working event for her, and timing would be critical. She had verified the correct time before she had showered.

It was sometimes cool at the embassy when the weather outside was unexpectedly warm, and tonight would likely be such a night. She took the crocheted shawl from the back of her dresser chair and cocooned it around her shoulders.

The aunt who had willed her the cameo set she wore had never married and had once said to her that a beautiful woman alone was like a great painting locked away in a dark room. Useless and unloved.

Helen Chelewski walked from her bedroom, along the little hallway, down the steps, and across her living room, double checking her purse that she had her keys.

The embassy chauffeur would be waiting for her outside.

# Chapter Forty

Snow had fallen here, but none fell now. And despite the snow, or because of its insulating effect, the temperature was not at all uncomfortable as they rode higher into the Elburz Mountains. By midnight they would stop, Cross had decided, to rest the horses and themselves, then by midmorning rendezvous with the People's Mujahedin force which would accompany them almost all the way to the final objective.

Irania had been silent since their departure from the stricken village, and from time to time he would take his eyes from the moonlit darkness of the trail along which they rode and try to see her face. A black shawl all but obscured her face from view, and her hair peeked out from beneath it. He would watch her hands, how small they seemed despite the heavy gloves she wore.

Abraham Kelsoe Cross realized he had fallen in love with a girl whose last name he didn't even know and who, in a little over forty-eight hours—if he lived, which he doubted—he would leave forever.

But he was not sorry.

By eleven o'clock Cross decided to call the halt. Irania was almost falling from the saddle with exhaustion, and Cross had leaned over and caught her once before she slipped to the ground. Enough was enough.

With Darwin Hughes and Lewis Babcock, Cross had seen

to establishing perimeter security. He had scheduled no watch for himself or Hughes or Babcock. What little sleep the revised schedule would permit them, they would need.

The silenced submachine gun in his right hand, Cross started for the blankets he would share with Irania. He could see she was exhausted, which meant he could not ask for the lovemaking he craved. But she was a brave girl.

He passed the fireless center of the camp, nodding to Mara, who slept with one of the men from the original group, passing them, at last seeing where Irania had set out their bedding. As he'd suspected, she was sound asleep within it.

He stood there for a while, just watching her.

Then, as quietly as he could, Cross got out of his weapons, gear, and boots and slid in beside her. It was warm here, and she moved closer to him, his right arm folding around her shoulders, her head leaning against his chest, her hair cascading over his own body. It smelled like perfume.

# Chapter Forty-one

When the door opened, dinner conversation in English, French, and Arabic could be heard as a jumbled cacophony. When the door closed, it was suddenly gone. Warren Corliss wished all of it were gone.

Bob walked over to him across the small anteroom that was theirs to use while the banquet was being filmed, and lit a cigarette. "Mr. Corliss, I wanted to check with you on something."

The director rested his right foot on top of one of the foam-padded steel cases, which were like miniature hinged lid coffins, each secured with a padlock.

"Sure, Bob," Warren Corliss said, and lit a cigarette for himself. In the anteroom with the door closed, it was impossible to tell there was anything going on outside in the main banquet room.

And the soundproofing worked two ways. At times, Helen Chelewski had told him, this room was used to hold one course while another was being removed, as some of the other anterooms that ringed the oval of the main salon were being used even now.

"What is it you want to ask?"

Bob exhaled smoke through his nostrils, tapped his foot on the top of the case on which it rested. "What's in these, Mr. Corliss?"

"I figured it'd be smart to have backup stuff if we needed it. More lighting gear—like that."

"They're heavy. More like cameras. But we've got all three cameras being operated right now. The two movies and the video for the B-Track."

"You're right." Corliss grinned. "There's an extra video camera. You know how sensitive those things can be. And I've got a great marketing idea for the B-Track once we get approval to— "

"Can I see?"

Corliss looked at Bob and then at his wristwatch. "Sure," he said, starting to search his pockets for the keys. "Sure you can. Everything goin' all right out there?"

"Yeah, great," and Bob's expression and manner seemed to ease. "Should be bringing out the dessert pretty soon. Then the president's envoy makes his after-dinner speech."

Corliss had the keys. They had been in his left-front trouser pocket, but he'd needed an extra minute.

He crouched beside the case on which Bob had rested his foot. He started working through the keys on the ring. He'd memorized each key's serial number and matched it to each lock. But he kept searching.

Another glance at his watch. He nodded.

"What?"

"Nothing, Bob. Better move your foot."

Corliss put the key into the lock and turned, the shackle popping. He took it from the hasp. A hand-held spotlight and two extension cords.

The door from the rear of the anteroom opened. A dark-haired woman in a black maid's uniform, starched white apron, and lace-trimmed white cap entered. Behind her was a balding man who was very tall and thin, dressed in formal butler's livery. Behind him was a white-jacketed busboy.

"Hey, guys, this is the wrong room," Bob said, rising from where he knelt beside Warren Corliss.

Corliss looked at Bob. "I'm sorry, man." He lifted the tray from the top of the steel case, letting the spotlight crash to the floor. The maid pushed past him and reached inside, her hands emerging with one of the submachine guns.

"Holy shit, Corliss!"

The maid worked back the bolt of the Uzi and shoved the muzzle of it under Bob's nose. "Up!"

"Mr. Corliss."

Corliss rose to his full height, inhaled deeply on his cigarette and closed his eyes. He could hear the butler and the busboy arming themselves as well, and heard a dull thudding sound. When he opened his eyes, Bob was lying on the floor, blood dripping from his left temple, his eyes wide open and glassy.

Warren Corliss closed his eyes again.

Muhammad Ibn al Raka watched the second hand of his Rolex sweep to the twelve. "Ephraim—now."

The van's motor groaned and came to life. Rausch started to open the passenger side door. Raka said, "No—now you will no longer fear me," and he reached forward, grabbing Rausch's face by the nostrils, snapping the head back. Rausch started to scream as Raka raked the primary edge of his knife across his throat. Raka stepped forward, still crouched because of the height of the van roof compared to his own, reaching past the throat-slit German, wiped the knife clean of blood over the German's white shirt. Raka worked the door handle, then pushed the dead man into the street as he slipped into the front passenger seat, Ephraim already starting the van into motion. Raka eyed his wristwatch.

The woman in the maid's uniform waited beside the door leading to the main salon, the maid's cap on the floor by her black-shoed, black-stockinged feet. One hand held the Uzi, the other reaching behind her to loosen the little white collar of the dress.

The man in butler's livery was passing out bags of spare magazines to the busboy, who slid them beneath a tablecloth-covered cart. Then two more Uzis. Then some kind of automatic pistol, the Uzis going under the cart as well, the automatic pistol disappearing under the man's white tunic. Corliss realized he was watching it as if his eyes were somehow only a camera lens.

The butler handed a bag of magazines to the maid. She slung it cross body from her left arm.

"Keys!"

Corliss threw the butler the key ring he'd used to open the first and second chests. The butler opened the third chest, distributing dark-lensed goggles to the maid and throwing a pair to Corliss. The butler did the same with small, thimble-shaped, transparent plastic containers with key-chain rings on them. Corliss slipped the goggles on over his head, leaving them to dangle beneath his chin. He opened the little plastic case, breaking it in the process. The earplugs were flesh-toned and had a strange shape.

The butler donned his own goggles, leaving them around his neck as well, pocketing the earplugs minus their case in the watch pocket of his livery vest.

The busboy was already leaving through the rear door, closing it behind him, the cart rattling less than it had when he'd entered because of the added weight.

Corliss looked at his wristwatch, admiring their efficiency. Right on time.

Raka reached under his shirt and took out the CZ-75 9mm. It was wet with perspiration from being pressed against his flesh. He worked the slide, leaving the Czech pistol cocked and locked, then placing it under his right thigh. Ephraim was turning into a narrow street. Raka looked at his watch. "Slow down before you wreck us. We are on schedule."

Raka closed his eyes. Ibrahim would be wheeling his cart along the service corridor now, then entering the kitchen through the stainless steel swinging doors. He would reach under his busboy's jacket and produce his pistol.

Hala and Riva would leave their dirty dishes, cross to the main kitchen doors, and each of the women take one of the Uzis from beneath the tablecloth. The rest of the kitchen staff would be locked in the meat freezer, to be released later as a gesture of magnanimity.

Ibrahim, Hala, and Riva—now they would be leaving the kitchen by the rear doors, the two women approaching the sides of the front entrance from each side of the embassy building, Ibrahim going with Hala as far as the end of the building, then putting his pistol beneath his busboy's tunic and walking straight for the front gates.

Raka opened his eyes.

Ephraim was making another turn. Already Raka could see the deflection barriers at the edge of the short drive that led into the embassy compound, the great iron gates beyond it still closed.

Ibrahim should be just approaching the security hut beyond the interior gates. The women, Hala and Riva, would be in position.

Jamal and the woman with him would be readying themselves with the sound and light grenades.

Raka looked to his right—along the street came a Mercedes station wagon, four of his Immortals inside. He looked to his left. Along the street came a Cadillac limousine flying the flags of Egypt.

The limousine slowed, turning into the embassy driveway.

Raka looked at his wristwatch. Now—he heard the shots through the open window of the van, from beyond the second gate.

The Cadillac limousine's four doors opened, the other eight of his Immortals exiting. He could hear the sounds of their submachine guns, the Cadillac reversing into the street, the doors still flying open.

The deflection barriers lowered, the main gates opening. There was more submachine-gun fire from inside the embassy compound.

"Hurry now, Ephraim," Raka said evenly. The van sped forward. The Mercedes station wagon cut a sharp right and turned up the driveway, going through the open compound gateways, the Cadillac into the street now. As Ephraim drove the van past it, the Cadillac turned in behind them, Raka seeing it for an instant in the sideview mirror.

The woman in the black maid's uniform and white apron said something Corliss guessed was in Farsi or Persian, the man in butler's livery nodding, taking the earplugs from his vest pocket with his left hand. The woman already had placed her earplugs. She freed her dark hair now. It fell over her shoulders.

She hitched up the front of her dress, unwinding something

that was over her slip. It was a dark shawl, which she threw over her head and wound back across her left shoulder.

The things in the butler's hands—his goggles were in place, and Corliss raised his—looked like large eggs. Corliss knew what they had to be, though he didn't recognize them. They were a special kind of grenade that released a very high-pitched sound and a burst of extremely intense light which would temporarily blind and deafen anyone unprotected by special goggles and ear protection.

The maid's goggles were already in place.

She opened the door, the butler's Uzi swinging across his back as he stepped through, and ran after him. Corliss dropped to his knees and closed his eyes beneath his goggles, putting his hands over his ears for further protection. He'd been told the earplugs only partially neutralized the effect of the sound.

The van rocked over the grid for the deflection barriers, Hala and Riva advancing from their positions on the sides of the building now, the four Immortals from the Mercedes jumping from the vehicle, assault rifles blazing. The van skidded to a stop at the main entrance to the embassy building. Raka jumped out. "Faithful Ephraim—there shall be the *rowzeh khvani* to honor your holy sacrifice wherever the sun shines on the faithful, good friend."

Raka ran back into the courtyard. The van—four-wheel drive—started to accelerate, reached the base of the low steps and began to climb.

Raka watched from the shelter of the Mercedes station wagon, the body of the Mercedes between him and the embassy front doors. The detonator was in his left hand.

As the van reached the height of the steps, uniformed United States Marines firing at it with M-16 assault rifles, Raka activated the detonator.

The explosives had been positioned throughout the vehicle's body work, inside the door panels, along the interior of the roof. The effect was that of a gigantic fragmentation grenade.

The fireball rose and rolled along the arched roof over the steps, belching outward, fragments of shrapnel punching forward as people screamed, one of the Marines tumbling down the steps, his clothing aflame.

Glass shattered everywhere along the front of the embassy structure. A chunk of shrapnel hit the hood of the Mercedes.

Raka rose from cover. Riva knelt beside Hala, the woman's body impaled by a fragment. She covered Hala's face with her apron.

Raka looked back toward the gates. They were closing, the deflection barriers rising, the Cadillac—also loaded with explosives—parked laterally, blocking the space between the main gates and the interior gates.

Already ten of his Immortals and the woman Riva and Ibrahim were storming into the embassy building through the massive blown-out window openings which ran along the front of the building.

Two of the Immortals, their AKM's in hard assault positions, were exchanging fire with the guards on the roof. Raka ducked into the Mercedes, the roof specially armored. He prayed that the shrapnel had not damaged the motor. It started and he drove forward, hearing gunfire pinging against the roof, his two Immortals in the backseat.

He reached the steps, where chunks of the destroyed van and parts of charred human bodies littered the once-polished granite. The two Immortals exited the vehicle, firing long bursts toward the roofline. Raka ducked from behind the wheel and ran under the shelter of the archway.

He drew his pistol, his Immortals joining him now.

They walked along the steps.

Corliss tore off the earplugs and dropped the goggles to the marble floor. The men and women of his crew—the servers, the embassy personnel, the foreign dignitaries—writhed on the floor, screaming senselessly, some holding their eyes, some trying to stand, stumbling over one another, falling in their blindness.

There was the sound of gunfire everywhere. Soon Raka would be here. Corliss moved about the room, looking. At last he saw her, her white dress stained with something that had spilled on her and all over the carpet near her. She was crying, screaming insanely, holding her eyes.

Corliss dropped to his knees beside her and took her head in his arms, holding her against his chest.

Her screaming quieted and she repeated his name.

He didn't speak to her.

She could not have heard him.

Warren Corliss simply held her tightly against him.

The doors leading into the salon opened loudly, as though kicked inward.

Muhammad Ibn al Raka stood in the center of the doorway, flanked by two men with assault rifles. As he entered the room, others joined him, all of them carrying guns.

Raka seemed to be searching for something.

Then Corliss saw Raka smiling. Raka walked toward him. Corliss simply knelt there, holding Helen Chelewski in his arms, rocking her like an injured child.

Raka stopped a yard or so away from him. "Warren. You have done very well."

"You promised nobody'd be killed. What was all that gunfire?"

Raka didn't answer, looking about the room, still smiling. "About releasing your brother. I released him personally before I left the Elburz Mountains. I released Martin from all earthly cares and toil."

Raka turned and walked away.

Warren Corliss wept.

# Chapter Forty-two

Matthew Leadbetter had driven across the river to his apartment in Alexandria, spent some time reading the newspapers, watching Cable News. Nothing.

He'd decided on an early lunch and walked again, settling on Maher's as a good place to seek diversion. There was always somebody playing the jukebox, and all the jukebox ever had was sixties music. And the deli sandwiches were good.

He had asked for a table by the windows, and now he sat sipping at a beer, watching people walk by. Some faces seemed happy, a few sad, most neutral or full of concentration. He saw a man who resembled Darwin Hughes—the right age, the right height, but not as erect and vigorous, his pace slower.

Leadbetter's hot pastrami sandwich arrived and he took a bite of his pickle. They had the best pickles here.

Then he saw a face in the window that he recognized. It was a worried face, and it was the same face he'd seen in the men's room at the opera.

The face disappeared from the window. Leadbetter took a larger swallow of his beer; the sandwich suddenly looked unappetizing.

He gazed across the not too crowded floor of the restaurant, young couples at tables, a Beatles song playing—he couldn't concentrate enough to care which one. He saw the man in the doorway. The man shrugged off the hostess who offered him a menu. He walked across the room, dodging the tables, stopping and sitting opposite Leadbetter.

"You have to scrub," he said. "International Jihad just seized the embassy in Jerusalem. The presidential envoy is there, couple dozen diplomats. If your boys do their thing now, we'll have a bloodbath."

"I can't stop them."

"You have an appointment in . . ." The man looked at his watch. It was expensive. "Thirty-three minutes."

"With who?"

"If you really can't pull their plug, you'd be better off if it was St. Peter."

Leadbetter swallowed the rest of his beer and almost gagged on it.

# Chapter Forty-three

A few of the Marines of the Great Satan, and some embassy personnel whom Raka strongly suspected were part of the CIA, had barricaded themselves on the top floor and on the roof, supplementing the snipers in place there.

The police, the Mossad—as well he wagered, the army's flying squad units— analogous to the British Special Air Service commandoes— and a number of men and women in civilian clothes, had gathered outside the embassy fence.

As yet, no news personnel.

Raka spoke through a bullhorn, standing just inside the great corridor running the entire width of the embassy structure at the front of the building. There were portraits here of American presidents, as well as ones of Jews such as Ben Gurion and Golda Meir. He would order the portraits removed.

"I demand that the following be accomplished. First, the Marines and security personnel barricaded on the top floor and on the roof must be evacuated by helicopter. They must leave their weapons behind on the roof. If any more than one helicopter comes toward the building at one time, all the hostages will be executed. I demand that the government of the Jew occupiers of Palestine's official representatives be brought within the sound of my voice so that we may discuss important matters. I demand that representatives of the Great Satan also be brought here for the same purpose. I demand that the press and other media be brought within the sound of my voice and that no attempt be made to block free access to this event in any way to the media, domestic and foreign. I demand that there be no interruption in the electrical or water services to this compound. I demand that no jamming procedures be inaugurated against this compound. I demand all this in the name of International Jihad, the fighters for freedom from the oppression of the Great Satan, the Jews, and the lackeys of these and other fascist dictatorships.

"Should any attempt be made to penetrate this compound or otherwise interdict this situation, the following events will transpire—and the deaths brought about by these actions will rest upon your heads and yours alone. The envoys of each of the powers present here for the formulation of a conspiracy against the Moslem world have each been fitted with harnesses. The harnesses are fitted with explosives which can be detonated in a variety of ways and might indeed detonate if any radio or television frequency jamming were to occur. In all, we control the fate of eighty-two hostages. There is a news crew here for the purposes of filming a documentary. We have ordered that filming will continue. Should your actions precipitate the deaths of those held hostage here, these actions will be recorded for all to see. My next communication to you shall be within the hour."

He opened his fist, shutting off the bullhorn.

He turned to Ibrahim, who had removed his servant's garb now. "See to it that these paintings are removed from the corridor walls and that they are destroyed."

"Yes, Muhammad."

Raka started back along the corridor toward the grand salon where he had assembled all of the prisoners. Many of the personnel who had been nearest to the sound and light grenades were still experiencing severe perceptual difficulties.

But the American envoy could hear.

Raka crossed the room, noticing Warren Corliss watching him. Jamal had changed from his butler's livery and was now aiding Corliss in operating the video camera which had been brought into the embassy in the chests along with the weapons. The sound and light grenades would have destroyed the functional characteristics of the camera in operation at the time. And Raka wanted tape that could be run instantly, not film which could be more easily controlled.

Some of the embassy workers were being used to carry in television sets from throughout the building so he could remain constantly informed of the actions of the enemy. The media, especially the American media, seemed pleasantly cooperative.

Raka stopped before the American envoy, whose harness of explosives had just been fitted. The man evidently could not yet see clearly, but Raka thought he could hear.

"You do hear me?" Raka shouted the words.

"Who are you?" The man's eyes darted from right to left.

"I am the man who holds power of life and death over you." Raka laughed and walked away.

Joseph Goldman counted himself fortunate. He had taken the late afternoon to work on the '57 Jaguar again and gotten himself filthy in the process. His wife Anita had prepared dinner, and after dinner and a drink, he'd showered. Not until then had the call come. He counted himself lucky because it would likely be the last shower he would get for some time, and what he was about to begin was sweaty work.

The car stopped, and he exited it and walked toward the knot of police and military personnel. He recognized the colonel who was usually in charge of terrorist-related activities. "Yuri," he called.

Yuri Markovski turned away from the officers he was conferring with and smiled, extending his hand. "My, my—I thought you were on holiday?"

Goldman smiled. "I was until about forty minutes ago." He shook the taller man's hand, released it and searched his pockets for his cigarettes.

"I thought you were giving up smoking?"

"Until about forty minutes ago, yes, I was," Goldman replied. He found his cigarettes and lighter. It was the first cigarette he'd had in ten days, and it tasted delicious as he inhaled. Then he coughed, and ran his left hand through his thinning hair. "So, I got a telephone call, told there was something happening I was needed for, to be ready in ten minutes and that there would be documents for me in the car."

"I know—no real information."

"Nothing hard. Does that mean you don't know more than who it is? Not even how many?"

"Let's talk," Markovski said, nodding toward the street.

Goldman fell in step beside him, the cigarette in the corner of his mouth, his eyes squinting against the rising smoke which crept between his glasses and his eyes.

Markovski sheltered a match in his cupped hands, lit the curved-stem pipe and said, "We know they had inside people. And we know that maybe as many as a dozen actually penetrated the embassy from the outside. They claim they are with International Jihad. We think they're telling the truth about that. We had a man on a rooftop with a long-range telephoto lens when the spokesman told us about the explosives."

"What explosives, Yuri?"

"Harnesses on the chests of all the hostages. I doubt that. But probably on the chests of the important ones. But we got a photo of the man, and we're running it and checking it with the CIA, the British, and the West Germans, and if any of them feels like telling us—or if we have a make on him ourselves—we'll know who he is in about an hour. Maybe sooner. We've been in touch with the American State Department. They are being very quiet, and have officially asked that we do nothing—at least not yet. Just contain the situation and humor them. He wants news coverage, and we have about forty-five minutes before he'll be talking to us again and demanding to know where it is. The Americans asked us to stall."

Goldman stubbed out his cigarette and lit another one. "Sure—we stall, and they go crazy, and the Americans blame us. No—we can have our cake and eat it too. Why not get one of your army units in there in civilian clothes with their cameras and everything—the ones who film those wild parties you have out in the desert?"

"We could. But they'll expect to see some of it on the televisions they have in there."

Goldman considered that. "What about a power blackout?"

"The spokesman said that if there were any interruption of utility services, he would execute all the hostages."

"Fucking wonderful," Goldman hissed. He was getting too old for this. "Let me think—we can't jam them. I presume they told us not to or they'd do the same thing."

"Yes," Markovski said through a cloud of pipe smoke. An errant breeze caught the smoke and lifted it. Goldman watched it drift toward the embassy as it dissipated.

"That's it, of course."

"What, Joseph?"

"We can't jam them. We can jam everyone else by simply not broadcasting, utilizing cable to get the signal up to the top of one of those buildings and then broadcasting it to the embassy. Maybe a dozen other buildings would get it, but we can evacuate those for the safety of the occupants. We can just let everyone else miss their late-evening and early-morning television programs. And the next day and the next day, I suppose. Your people can provide the tape for the real broadcasters to use in their phony news bulletins. It'll work for a while."

"How do I do this? I mean, newspeople . . ."

Goldman nodded toward the street—as if conferring with it, he thought. He realized he looked silly. He told Colonel Markovski. "Hell, promise them all exclusives if this works. Threaten them with parking tickets—I don't know. Appeal to their patriotism. Whatever. But we need it done fast. Get some of your people over there to check everything before it goes on the air to make sure nothing is given away by accident. What's the possibility of sending in some phony reporters to interview the terrorists?"

"We can ask," Markovski agreed.

"If we can do that, then we could see if they have all the hostages together. They frequently do, even though that's stupid."

"We're betting on the grand salon where the state dinner was being held. You know who's in there."

"Some important diplomats. That's all I was told," he said.

Markovski stopped walking. "Special envoys from Egypt, Syria, Jordan, our own country—and the special envoy of the

American president. A conference to deal with the threat of Moslem fundamentalism to peace in the Middle East. Even have some Moslems in on it—that's why it was hit.''

Goldman started to swear, but he'd promised Anita he would try to stop that along with his smoking. The smoking promise was lost, but the swearing he could still work on.

"All right. We need to know what these people want us to do. What our government wants us to do."

"Nobody's talking yet except the Egyptians. They offered us any assistance we might need.''

"Like that SWAT team of theirs?''

Markovski smiled. ''Their intentions are good.''

Goldman nodded in agreement. ''All right, you work on the television stuff and I'll work on the governmental end. Shit.''

He lit another cigarette from the last one and walked back toward his car. He thought of it as he neared the car, and shouted back toward Markovski: ''And warn everybody—no radio telephones. They'll pick us up. And the Lord knows what kind of stuff the Americans have in their embassy that people could use.''

A helicopter was flying overhead. Markovski shouted to him, ''It's taking Marines and other embassy staff off the roof. One of the conditions.''

"You talk to them first, but don't wear them out. We can get some good stuff from them,'' Goldman called back, climbing into his car. ''Find the nearest pay telephone,'' he told his driver.

He was already wishing for another shower.

# Chapter Forty-four

Cross awoke before sunrise, determined to let Irania sleep until the last possible moment. But when he opened his eyes, he found her propped on one elbow beside him and staring down at him.

"Good morning," he said hoarsely.

"Why didn't you waken me, Abe?"

"You were sleeping so soundly, so . . ."

"I'm wide awake now."

Cross sat up, the morning air freezing cold. She began moving her hands along his body, opening his shirt. He felt stupid saying it, but told her, "I gotta, well, hold the thought for a couple seconds? Please?"

She smiled and leaned back, pulling the covers up over her head. Cross climbed from beneath the sleeping bags and blankets and was instantly freezing. He walked stocking-footed away from the camp, one of the Mujahedin sentries nodding to him. He found an isolated spot, opened his pants, and did what he had to do, the air temperature so cold that steam rose on the ground where he did it. He closed his fly and started back.

Irania was still hidden beneath the covers, and he slid in beside her. As he reached out for her, he realized she was naked.

"Your hands are like ice!" she said.

"I'm sorry," Cross told her, putting his hands under his armpits to warm them.

"Keep your hands there until they get warm." She laughed, and he felt her hands opening his pants. She touched him. "It's cold too."

"It was just out on an excursion," he whispered.

She began warming it. He took his hands from his armpits and touched her breasts. She shivered, but whispered, "Keep them there."

He felt her nipples harden under his fingertips.

Cross rolled over on top of her, his hands moving over her nakedness now, feeling the heat from her body. His lips touched at her breasts, her neck—found her mouth.

His right hand held her left breast, her hands exploring him under his clothes.

"I love you," she whispered as he moved his mouth along her neck, kissed her ear. Her fingers pressured against his buttocks. His hands arched the small of her back, her hands helping him as he entered her. "I love you," she said again.

He knew she did.

# Chapter Forty-five

"Why can't you stop them, Colonel Leadbetter?"

Leadbetter looked up from his hands and out the lace-curtained window for inspiration. There was none. He looked back into General Fife's face. As he started to speak, Fife's wife entered the room with a small tray supporting a thermal coffeepot, two cups, and a plate of chocolate chip cookies. They smelled fantastic and fresh.

"Thanks, Marian," General Fife told her.

"Yes, thank you very much Mrs. Fife. The cookies smell delicious."

"I just baked them, Colonel." She smiled. "I'll leave you two. If you need any more coffee, just sing out." She left the room, her dress rustling. With her perfect-looking white hair and a still comfortable-looking figure, she reminded him of an ideal grandmother, the kind nobody ever had.

When the door closed, Fife stood up, walked around his desk, and started to pour coffee. They both drank it black, so she had brought no cream or sugar.

"So . . ." He handed Leadbetter a cup of coffee. "Her cookies smell fantastic. You ever try 'em?"

"No sir, I haven't had that—"

"Privilege? They taste like shit. I tried feedin' 'em to the dog, until the dog died. But you'd better eat some or I'll be stuck with the whole damned plateful."

"Yes, sir." Leadbetter stood up and took a cookie off

the plate. He bit into it. General Fife was a master of understatement.

"Why can't you stop them?"

"Remember, sir—I mean, we agreed that radio communications would be out of the question."

"We could have used something passive."

"The satellite wasn't up yet that could do that, sir."

"Damnit, if your guys make it there and do anything like they're supposed to, Matt, those assholes occupying the embassy will croak everybody in the place."

"I'm aware of that, sir."

"Yeah, but you're not aware of this. Look." He took a manila envelope off his blotter and handed it to Leadbetter, who had to shove the rest of the cookie into his mouth in order to have a hand free to take it.

He set the cup down on the tray, opened the envelope, and shook out a fuzzy looking black and white photograph. It was shot with some kind of telephoto lens under poor light conditions, he guessed. But the face was readily recognizable. "Oh, my God."

"It's little Mr. Raka, the all-purpose religious fanatic and homicidal nutball, isn't it, Matt?"

"Yeah . . . I mean—"

"And that's his group your guys are assigned to eliminate, right?"

"Yeah—well—"

"There is one way to stop them, Matt."

"Ah, what's that, General?"

Leadbetter knew what the one way was, but wasn't going to mention it, just in case General Fife didn't know yet.

"We get the KGB to do it for us."

That was the one way, all right.

"Do it, Matt."

"That's murder, sir."

"I'll accept your resignation, and you can date it the day before yesterday if you want. It'll never come back to you."

"No, sir."

"What the hell do you mean, soldier!"

Leadbetter stood up again. He was taller than General Fife, but not by much. "You can have my resignation sir, or bring me up on charges for refusing to obey a direct order. But I'm not ordering my own men killed. You wanna do it, sir, then you order somebody else to do it."

"Matt, I've heard of screw ups with people getting their pensions. . . ."

"Well, that's just fuckin' wonderful sir. And you're right, the cookies suck." Leadbetter set down his coffee cup and started for the door.

"Matt—I mean it."

Leadbetter turned around and looked at him, his hand on the door knob. "So do I, sir." He opened the door and walked out.

# Chapter Forty-six

Mehdi Hamadan had watched the screen for hours. He'd turned channels. The same thing. Nothing.

Technical difficulties.

"Damn them!" he screamed.

The sun would be rising soon.

He walked toward the balcony doors, opened them, and walked out into the air.

All that was necessary was to plug the device into the wall outlet, set the timer and leave. Ten minutes later there would be a massive power surge which would black out the entire floor and send a radio signal that would be picked up by Raka and his team. The signal, a single tone, would order the deaths of all inside the embassy.

He could do it now.

He punched his fists against the railing, staring down into the predawn traffic.

Jerusalem seemed so normal.

What was happening? What were they doing?

He stared into the street and tried to think.

Jamal was a genius at electronics. Raka stood behind him in the embassy communications center, Warren Corliss next to him.

"Jamal, is it possible they are feeding us disinformation?"

"It is very possible, Muhammad," Jamal agreed.

"Warren, my friend."

"I have no idea, Raka. And if I did—"

"You wouldn't tell me—I know." Raka watched the tiny red and green lights, the diodes with numbers that were meaningless to him.

He looked at Corliss. "The blond-haired woman who works in the USIA. She is a Jew, is she not?"

"I don't know," Corliss told him.

Raka laughed. "Warren, Warren, what am I to do with you? You think because your brother is no longer among the living that I have no power over you. But you are wrong." Raka raised his voice.

"Ibrahim! Riva!"

The door behind them opened into the control room. Raka watched as Corliss' jaw dropped.

The blond-haired Jewess named Helen Chelewski, wrists bound in front of her with adhesive tape, her mouth gagged the same way—toilet paper stuffed inside for good measure— was pushed into the room.

Riva took her knife and placed it beneath Helen Chelewski's nose. "I believe," Raka began, "that there is an American expression about cutting off one's nose to spite one's face. Well, if you spite me, Riva will cut off the Jew's nose." Raka nodded.

Riva kneed Helen Chelewski from behind and she fell to her knees. Ibrahim knotted both fists in her hair, snapped her head back against her neck, and Riva laid the knife beneath Helen Chelewski's nose. The woman sounded as though she were choking to death.

"Do I nod my head again, Warren?" Raka studied Corliss's face.

"Let her go," Corliss pleaded. "Take the gag off her so she can breathe, and put her back with the others. I'll do anything it's in my power to do."

"I don't know, Warren. Perhaps you are sincere. Perhaps not. Perhaps if we cut off part of her nose, we could be more certain. What do you think?"

Warren Corliss dropped to his knees in front of him, lowered his head. He whispered. "Please . . . please, sir."

Raka let himself smile. "Take her away. Do as Warren has suggested. Unbind her and keep her with the others."

"Yes, Muhammad," Ibrahim said. They dragged the woman to her feet and took her from the room.

Corliss still knelt before Raka.

"They have a powerful transmitter here, and, it would seem logical, a powerful satellite dish," Raka said.

"Yes," Corliss whispered, barely audible.

"I distrust the television broadcasts that have been transmitted to us. Can you arrange to pick up television or radio signals outside of this country? Will it work?"

Corliss hesitated for a moment, then answered him. "Yes, it should work."

"Then proceed immediately to alter the position of the antenna, and find me what is really being broadcast, what is really being told to the world. I must know this. Jamal will assist you. He is very competent in these matters. Stand up."

Corliss stood up.

Raka smiled at him. "Warren, you are proving to be the truly indispensable man."

"You're going to kill her anyway, aren't you? Because she's Jewish? You're going to kill all of us."

Raka clapped Corliss on the shoulders with both his hands. "There are many ways to die. For example, should I tell you how your brother died?"

Corliss didn't answer him.

# Chapter Forty-seven

There was a massive natural overhang, and Cross and Irania, in the lead of the column, rode toward it. A man was visible on the flat rock above it, the profile of an assault rifle visible even at the distance. The horses quickened their pace, perhaps smelling fresh food and water, Cross thought, or perhaps just smelling more of their own kind. He was not an expert in equine psychology.

"You are a good lover," she told him.

Cross just looked at her, never having been told that before.

"Thank you," he said at last.

"We will sleep together tonight. It will be the last night we will have, Abe."

"Yeah, I know that. And yes, we'll sleep together tonight. I love you, and I'll miss you a great deal. I know that sounds stupid."

"It does not sound stupid, as you say," Irania told him, looking at him, smiling. "It sounds beautiful. And I will always remember what you have told me, no matter how many years will separate us."

"Why did . . . why, ah—"

"Why couldn't I have been an American, or why couldn't we both have been something else?"

"Yes, something like that. 'Why' covers an awful lot, doesn't it?"

"Yes, a great deal." Then she fell silent, and they took the trail that led around a small depression and toward the cavelike overhang.

The horses quickened their pace still more.

Cross's eyes scanned beneath the overhang and over the apron of gray granite that seemed almost to have been frozen in waves here. There were People's Mujahedin fighters everywhere, more people than horses to carry them, most of them men, but some women as well. Cook fires burned beneath the shelter of the overhang, and as they neared the apron of gray granite, Cross could smell food—lamb perhaps.

Irania reined in, Cross beside her still. She swung down from the saddle easily. Cross remained mounted; he distrusted so many armed strangers all at once, and kept his right hand casually near the butt of the H-K submachine gun.

A short, swarthy-looking man with black hair streaked with gray came toward them, and Irania ran into his stubby arms, bending over to embrace him because of his girth. They spoke in what Cross by now recognized as Farsi, the man laughing, Irania looking away from him and up at Cross, the man hugging her more tightly.

"Might be her uncle, Cross—I'd watch it, lad." Hughes laughed good-naturedly.

"Something similar happened to me once," Babcock added, leaning out of his saddle and clapping Cross on the back.

Cross smiled broadly, showing plenty of teeth. "You guys are just so sweet—gee." He reined his animal away from them, swinging down off the bay mare, standing less than a yard from Irania and the man who was roughly the size of an overweight black bear.

Irania towed the man with her, embracing Cross with her left arm, still embracing the bearlike man in her right arm. "My uncle." She smiled proudly. Cross heard Hughes and Babcock chuckling behind him.

The BBC was referring to a mysterious emergency at the United States embassy in Jerusalem and what appeared to be a news blackout. No members of the press, including Israelis, were being allowed within a six-block radius of the embassy, the entire area evacuated of all civilians. The embassy was surrounded, the news reader went on to say, by a growing

number of Israeli police and military personnel. BBC corre-
spondents had attempted to question the White House regard-
ing the affair, but official Washington had remained silent. A
highly placed source, speaking under conditions of anonym-
ity, said that the U.S. sixth fleet was moving toward Haifa.
All four American news networks were apparently as much in
the dark as news agencies in the rest of the free world.

French newspapers were reporting that members of the
top-secret United States Delta Flight rapid-response group had
been flown to the island of Cyprus.

Muhammad Ibn al Raka said to Warren Corliss, "It appears we are being deceived."

He stood up and walked from the room, Corliss shouting
after him. Raka slung his Uzi forward from his back, his right
fist tight on the pistol grip. He walked up the stairs, turned
down the front long corridor, and started toward the salon. He
had trusted the immediate guarding of the hostages to six of
his twelve Immortals.

At the doors to the grand salon he stopped, closed his eyes
for a moment, then reopened them. He opened the doors and
walked inside.

The dining table had been moved aside, and the center of
the room now served as the holding area for the hostages.
They were forced to sit, the women with their hands in their
laps, the men with their hands in their pockets—all except for
the Marines and those few civilians he had decided were
embassy security personnel. They were bound, hands behind
them, and blindfolded with linen napkins taken from the
table.

Raka addressed his Immortals and the assembled hostages.

"I have been deceived. The news crews outside the embassy, the photographers, all of them—they are not who they
appear to be. The world does not yet know of circumstances
here. But I shall remedy that situation. I require two of the
Marines and two of the civilian security personnel. Bring
them to the front entrance."

There were little sounds—whimpers, cries, moans—but he
ignored them. His heels clicked against the floor as he retraced
his steps along the corridor, bare spots on the walls now, dust
outlined, where the offensive paintings had hung.

He stopped before the blown-out doorway, a cool breeze there despite the apparent intensity of the sun. Raka looked back behind him. Two of the Marines and two of the civilians, still blindfolded and bound, were being herded along the corridor by some of his Immortals.

Ibrahim supervised the guarding of the entrance, Riva with him. "Muhammad, there is difficulty?" Ibrahim asked.

"Only a momentary setback," Raka replied as he picked up the bullhorn, his fist closing over the handle. "This is Muhammad Ibn al Raka, leader of the forces of International Jihad which now control the embassy of the Great Satan here in the land of the Jew occupiers of Palestine. I have learned that news of the takeover of the embassy has not been disseminated as I have instructed. This saddens me. It will sadden you more."

He turned toward the nearest Marine and handed the bullhorn to Ibrahim. The Marine seemed barely twenty, and appeared quite fit.

The fingers of Raka's left hand edged inside the back of the Marine's collar and tightened there as he shoved the young man ahead of him, down what remained of the steps that led down from the main entrance into the compound yard.

He walked the Marine out of the shade and into the sunlight. "Feel its warmth now," Raka told him.

The Marine started to speak, hesitated.

"Yes, speak freely," Raka told him as they stopped near the center of the courtyard, where they could be seen clearly by the watchers outside the embassy fence.

"You don't understand the American people, sir. You guys can't get away with this."

"The people you speak of—they will be angered because of what I have done?"

"Damn right, sir. Give it up. America'll go to bat for ya with the Israelis. I know we will."

"You have a great deal of faith, however misdirected."

Raka took out his knife and slashed it across the young Marine's throat. He let the body fall to the surface of the driveway and returned the way he had come.

At the height of the steps he retrieved the bullhorn from Ibrahim. "Three more hostages remain by the doors here.

One will die each hour until there is global news coverage of this event. Only then will my demands be made. Once these three hostages remaining by the doors are killed, if you have not met my demands, I will begin murdering female hostages two at a time every fifteen minutes. You have one hour.''

Raka handed the bullhorn to Ibrahim and looked once into the courtyard at the dead body of the Marine, a growing pool of blood around his head.

Soon there would be enough blood in which to drown.

Phil Donnelly was operating the video camera, and Corliss thought he already looked like a dead man there. "I'll take it," Corliss told him. "Go sit down."

Donnelly looked at him, dark circles under his eyes, his skin gray with exhaustion. "You motherfucker," Donnelly whispered as Corliss slipped behind the camera.

"Get outa here and rest."

Corliss assumed Donnelly had taken his advice. He did not try to follow Donnelly with the camera, but instead, the automatic zoom buzzing, he kept shifting it about the grand salon, searching for one face.

And he saw the face. It was Helen Chelewski's.

As he watched her, he took the camera in for the closest possible shot. Her eyes were tear rimmed, and he wondered if the tears were for him.

Joseph Goldman bit into his apple.

"How can you eat?" Yuri Markovski asked him.

"I was awake all night, I didn't have any breakfast, and if I pass out and am unable to make decisions, it won't bring that young American Marine back to life, will it?"

"We have forty-five minutes."

They sat alone in a bare storefront around the corner from the embassy, on metal folding chairs before a card table. Racks of women's clothing were pushed back against the walls on either side of them, mannequins that had been taken from the display windows leaning against one another behind the sales counter, their bodies in ungainly and sometimes suggestive positions.

Goldman continued eating his apple.

"I said we have forty-five minutes. What are we doing?"

Goldman bit into the apple and held it in his teeth as he stood up and started to skin off his jacket. His armpits were soaked with sweat, even the shoulder holster for his Walther P-5 sodden with it. He draped the coat over the back of his folding chair and sat down again, taking the apple from his mouth. "Raka—it was so nice of the Americans to notify us of who he was."

"Maybe they didn't have his likeness."

"Sure, and maybe the Ayatollah Khomeini's Hebrew, huh?" Markovski laughed. "What are we doing, Joseph?"

"I'll have to clear it with the cabinet first, but I think we can start something going. He wants reporters. He'll get reporters. Call all the wire services."

"I thought—"

"I do have to clear it, but there's no alternative, so they don't have any choice but to agree. So let's save time. Call all the wire services, the American networks, the BBC, the French—everybody and his great aunt Sadie. Right? Give him the media circus he wants. It'll buy us some more time. How's the thing going with the tunneling effort?"

"Not very fast. The engineers tell me it would be at least seventy-two hours to break through into the basement of the embassy, and it might be longer. If they could use explosives or pneumatic drills or something, it'd be a different story."

"Check with the engineer if any of the universities have a working laser system that might help to cut through some of that rock," Goldman suggested. "I doubt it, but why not try? Why should anything else go right, huh? So, we've gotta stall Raka as long as possible, and hope the Americans make up their minds to tell us something before their people get killed."

Markovski was lighting up his pipe as he stood up and started for the door. "We get screwed either way, don't we?"

Goldman didn't smile.

# Chapter Forty-eight

Irania's uncle, Shapur Mariq, spoke as he ate, sometimes the food winning and making his words all but unintelligible. "The SAVAK disliked me because they said I was loyal to the Ayatollah, which was not true. The Ayatollah disliked me because I was said to be irreligious. Which was also not true. Someday, if the People's Mujahedin is successful, they will dislike me too. It is not that I am a revolutionary or a malcontent. It is that I see things that are wrong and I work to change them. I see hypocrisy, and I attempt to make the truth known to all. This is, young men—as your older friend Colonel Hughes would no doubt agree—the greatest way in which to become unpopular."

Darwin Hughes laughed.

Uncle Shapur continued his monologue. "When the shah attempted to modernize Iran, there was much opposition. When the Ayatollah attempted to return Iran to the past, there was again much opposition. It appears that I am the perfect Iranian, in that I am never content and constantly seek change, but to what I am uncertain. When I was a young man, in my dowreh there were many different political beliefs. There were communists, there were fascists. There were Nazis. There were even some who felt some sympathy toward the Hebrews. I, myself, began to believe in the diversity of man as man's salvation. All of us held strongly to diametrically opposed beliefs, but all of us respected the rights of each of the others to hold those beliefs.

"The problem," he continued, "is that we are a nation largely composed of—you Americans have a lovely word for it—wimps?"

"Wimps?" Babcock repeated.

"Yes. Women have few rights, but exercise great power. Their sons will soon have the full rights of all males, and so the women utilize their sons as tools. They make them dependent by spoiling them, and the more powerful a family, the more so this is true. And so, those men who could lead our nation, have been too concerned with themselves and their own happiness to do what is right. And so," and he shrugged his shoulders and raised his open palms toward the roof of the rock overhang, "here we are, aren't we?"

Cross, finished with his food, leaned back and lit a cigarette. As he took the Zippo away, he looked at his watch. He imagined they would be setting out soon enough for the final camp from which the two prongs of the offensive would be launched.

There were sixty-eight fighters in all, not counting Irania, but counting Mara and all the others from the first Mujahedin band, as well as those who had rendezvoused with Cross and the others by the shore of the Caspian.

The arms of the Mujahedin were mixed—everything from AK-47's to an occasional M-16 to the G-3's in evidence earlier. There seemed to be few handguns, but a preponderance of knives, and even some swords. There were no uniforms except for the ubiquitous U.S. Army field jackets; these gave an appearance of some uniformity, however accidental. He heard a rumbling in the distance beyond the cavelike overhang, and he started to rise, but Irania smiled and gently placed a hand against his chest.

Uncle Shapur said, "The vehicles that will transport us to the final camp are coming. If we traveled by horseback, it would still take us days."

Cross nodded, leaning back to finish his cigarette. Irania took it from his fingers, put it to her lips and inhaled, exhaling smoke through her nostrils as she returned it to him. As someone who had grown up in the west, it was interesting for him to note that Irania had left no impression of lipstick on his cigarette. Oh, for a piano, he thought. And for an excuse not to go and die.

# Chapter Forty-nine

Matthew Leadbetter had tried going over General Fife's head. It hadn't worked.

He'd returned to Maher's, a different crowd there now, and ordered another hot pastrami sandwich. But this time, instead of beer, whiskey.

There was only one way Fife could stop Hughes, Cross, and Babcock. It was to slip the word into the pipeline of information sellers who could be confidently relied upon to get the information into the KGB and hence into the global terrorist network, thus filtering it to Mehdi Hamadan, wherever he was now, so that he could warn the training facility and headquarters at Mount Dizan.

Fife would put out the agreed-upon cover story that was to have been used in the event of the capture or deaths of any or all of the men making the surgical strike. Darwin Hughes was an old war dog who, because of the murder of his daughter-in-law and her unborn child five years ago, had worked tirelessly to put together the capital from right-wing business elements that would allow him to finance his own private attack on terrorism. A smuggler who had fought with Hughes during World War II, now posing as a respectable businessman, had the underworld contacts to smuggle weapons and clandestinely obtain the intelligence data necessary for the raid to be carried off.

Abraham Cross had gone into it with Hughes out of guilt

for his own involvement in the fiasco five years ago, and out of a similar desire for revenge. They had enlisted Babcock, who had become disenchanted with the military because he felt he was being held back from promotion because of his race, and also because Babcock had expensive tastes and was interested in the possibility of making money. Feinberg, partially because he was Jewish to begin with and felt he had a vested interest in fighting terrorism in the Middle East, but also because he'd been in and out of trouble in the military, being obsessed with violence and the desire to prove himself in battle.

U.S. authorities had been about to close in on Hughes before he could precipitate a diplomatic incident, but using assumed names, forged passports, and other identification, Hughes and the others had escaped the country, leaving weapons and other incriminating data behind.

The cover story had been constructed so it would be just the sort of thing the Russians would eat up and the Iranians would accept as divine revelation. When you confirmed already existing suspicions with a lie, it was that much more likely to be perceived as truth.

Leadbetter's sandwich arrived.

He'd been watching the faces of passersby again. He wondered almost absently if any of them would have believed what he knew, believed what was about to be done, was probably already being arranged—would they believe that three men, possibly four, or five if you counted the Greek friend of Darwin Hughes, were about to be sold out by the very system for which they were risking their lives?

He doubted that they would. It sounded too much like something out of a spy story. Everybody knew that covert operations these days were strictly regulated. Everybody knew that.

Leadbetter drained his whiskey after muttering, "Here's to fiction!"

# Chapter Fifty

They had packed into five trucks, all sixty-eight of the People's Mujahedin, including Uncle Shapur, plus Irania, Hughes, Babcock and Cross. They had driven throughout the late day and into the early evening, stopping once to allow those so inclined to answer the call of nature, then continuing on into the darkness.

Cross, Irania, Hughes, Babcock and Uncle Shapur sat behind the cab in the bed of the first truck, Shapur reminding them at every bend in the road that military trucks were a common sight here, bringing supplies to the terrorists. And at every other bend they were reminded that the terrorists patrolled these mountains and would stop military trucks to inspect them. So perhaps they might be discovered and the battle might begin here.

But they were not stopped. Cross had peered out beneath the tarp cover as the trucks had turned off the road one by one, into a valley that seemed darker than the night around them. They had driven on for another hour before stopping.

No fires could be risked so close to Mount Dizan, and no lights either, so everyone drifted in and out of the trucks as the camp settled in for the night, eating cold food, or cleaning their weapons by feel and the dim moonlight.

Cross, Babcock, and Hughes attended to this latter task, field stripping the G-3's, the LAW-12, stripping the bolt from the Steyr-Mannlicher SSG, cleaning the issue handguns and the personal firearms, touching up the edges of their knives.

This accomplished, Cross and Babcock assisted Hughes with a final check of the explosives, mainly plastique, but some dynamite charges as well. Explosives, batteries, detonators—all seemed in order.

The explosives packed away in their carrying cases, they returned to their submachine guns, each man remounting the electronic sight, reinstalling the batteries that had been carried close to their bodies for warmth, testing the functional performance of the sight, then removing the batteries once more for warm storage until the devices would be needed the next morning.

To avoid letting the weapons out of their sight, the meeting with Uncle Shapur and a half dozen of the People's Mujahedin who would serve as field commanders for their phase of the offensive took place in the first truck.

Squatted like children at camp about to be told a ghost story, Cross watched them as he spoke. "This was all worked out in advance, so really what we're doing here is reviewing your end of the operation. All you know about our end," he told them, "is that somehow we're going to attempt to enter the tunnel network under Mount Dizan, and once inside, we're going to attempt to kill as many of the International Jihad personnel as possible and blow up their headquarters. Then we'll try to escape with our lives. That's basically all you need to know. Suffice it to say, we have rehearsed this operation until we can do it in our sleep. All phases of it separately. Tomorrow we pull all the elements together and do it.

"Tomorrow your end of the operation is of such great importance it cannot be minimized," Cross told them, noticing Hughes watching him with almost fatherly pride from the other side of the truck. "They will not expect us, specifically, although they may expect something because of the problems we had with that Russian intervention force back along the river. They definitely will not expect three men attempting to take them out."

"Take them where?" It was one of the Mujahedin field commanders, a little guy in a slouch hat who wore a sword.

Irania smiled as she translated for the man. Then he nodded. "Excuse me very much."

"No problem, friend." Cross nodded. "Actually," he went on, "if they do expect a little something, it will work to our advantage. When you guys start your diversionary attack, they'll think it's the actual assault, and that should give us an even easier time of getting inside. So, what you guys have to do is hit the main entrance very fast and very hard with everything you have, then, when the resistance starts getting just heavy enough, it'll look convincing—but not so heavy you all wind up dying. Start to withdraw. If you can sucker a lot of them out after you, all the better. But don't be heroes. Remember, your job is to make these guys look the other way while we sneak in the back door, give them something to do so the numbers we encounter during the initial phase of the penetration will be as low as possible. That's all. They have superior firepower, manpower, and may have airpower. Once you've drawn out as many of them as you can, take your people and disperse into the mountains to minimize the possibilities of your withdrawal being turned into a massacre."

"It is unimportant if we die, or even if you die. What is important is to crush International Jihad," Uncle Shapur announced enthusiastically, his lips curling back in a smile, his teeth looking yellow in the lamplight, yellower than they did without it. "Our lives mean nothing when compared to the greater good."

Abe Cross looked at Irania's uncle. "You bet," Cross told him.

Babcock and Hughes had elected to sleep in the truck with the weapons, explosives, and the rest of the gear. As Cross drew Irania closer to him, he thought—good for them.

"This is our last time."

"We could always stay up all night," he told her, "and try for a world's record."

"And you would be so sore you couldn't walk, Abe. Not to mention fight."

"During the sixties," Cross whispered, holding her tightly, "they used to say, 'Make love, not war.' "

"Why are you so flippant? Sometimes you are very serious, and then, sometimes . . . I love you very much, and we will never see each other again.''

"Maybe I'm 'flippant,' like you call it, because I know you're right.''

She seemed to hesitate for a moment, then spoke so rapidly that one word seemed to blend into the other. "We could steal one of the trucks and drive out of this valley and—and—ah—''

"Drive to Afghanistan, perhaps? Trade in one war for another? Or maybe the Turkmen Republic, and tell the Soviets we're sorry we trashed their APC's and killed all those guys? Where the hell could we go? And how could we look at each other if we did?''

She burrowed her head against his chest and whispered so faintly he could hardly hear her, "I know—just hold me, Abe.''

He held her.

After a very long time, kissing her, listening to the small sounds of her breathing, their lingering fingers began to move and touch as if making indelible imprints. Cross and Irania moved with and against one another, and when Cross finally came between her legs and her arms folded around him, they both made the moment last until it couldn't last any longer.

# Chapter Fifty-one

Muhammad Ibn al Raka sat on a high bar stool in the midst of the assembled hostages, his legs folded beneath him. He told them, "I will soon release my demands . . . that the Great Satan sever all diplomatic ties with the Jew occupiers of Palestine, and that the Jews be condemned in the United Nations for their crimes against the people of Islam, and that all aid in technology and weapons and intelligence be stopped. That the warships of the Great Satan be withdrawn to Cyprus.

"But then," and he raised the first finger of his right hand and laid it beside his nose, "the brigades of International Jihad shall cross from Lebanon into this wicked land and bring with them death like a great cloud of locusts that will devour all before it. And the Great Satan will break its promises and attack Lebanon, and be forced to invade this evil land to save the lives of the Jew lackeys. Then all of Islam will rise up." He raised his hands toward the ceiling, high above his head, his palms open, fingers splayed, "And death will settle over the land."

He drew his palms together over his head, then let his arms fall to his sides, his energy spent. His voice sounded almost lifeless to him now. "And all of you will die. All of us shall die as well, if that gives you any comfort. And the infidel dogs of the Great Satan will revile their leaders, and there will be confusion and great hatred, and infidel will turn against infidel, and every hand shall be turned against the

Jew. And the world will be forever changed. It is a wondrous thing, that such great occurrences can begin with such small events as this. But all of this shall come to pass. And those of you who will be selected to die, one every three hours, until my demands are met, will in some small way have helped to bring about all of these wonders. You are privileged.''

Raka folded his hands in his lap. He closed his eyes. He could hear gasps, tiny stifled screams and the desperation of tears. Such were the sounds of history.

# *Chapter Fifty-two*

Cross awakened, alone. But as he turned beneath the sleeping bags and blankets, his hand discovered something. It was a rope of her black hair, braided and knotted at each end. It carried the smell of her. He sat up and looked about the camp, the ground still shrouded in heavy mists, the horizon still gray, many of the Mujahedin gone or leaving.

"Irania," Cross whispered, touching his lips to her hair.

Cross stood in the truck, Babcock and Hughes gearing up as well now. Each of them had saved a fresh set of black battle dress utilities for this day. Cross buttoned the last button, then saw to his boots, securely double knotting each and pushing the loops and tails down inside the boot fronts just beside the tongues. He took a pair of elastic blousing garters from his kit, hooking one around each calf just above the boot tops, then rolling his trouser legs up and under, blousing them over his boots with the garters.

He then secured the belt he would use for rappeling into place, making a quick test of adjusting it for deployment.

Cross picked up the black battle vest, slipping his arms into it, zipping it up the front. He slipped spare magazines for the G-3 into the custom-sized pockets in the vest, and slipped magazines for the MP5-SD-A3 into the pouches beneath each arm hole.

Next he picked up the Milt Sparks Summer Special rig for

the Smith Model 681 .357 Magnum L-Frame, checked the revolver's cylinder, giving it a good-luck spin, then closing it easily. He secured the revolver in the leather, then secured the inside-the-pants holster by its double loops just beside his right kidney, locking it to his black-webbed belt.

He checked each of the three Safariland speedloaders, pressing the flat nosed semi-jacketed soft points against the hard surface of a wheel well, then testing the knob that locked them into position. Satisfied, Cross pocketed all three in a cargo pocket of his trousers.

He put on his pistol belt and took up the Beretta, working the slide several times, his fingers oily from its surface. He took the standard-length fifteen-round magazine and inserted it up the well, worked the slide again, and stripped the first round from the magazine, chambering it. He felt the edge of the protruding extractor which served as loaded chamber indicator, worked the ambidexterous safety on and off several times, left it on at last. He buttoned out the magazine, taking the loose 115-grain Federal JHP from the upended crate, inserting this beneath the feedlips then giving the spine of the magazine a hard thwack against his left palm to seat the cartridges uniformly. He inserted the magazine up the well, tugged a bit at the base plate to make certain it was firmly seated. He slipped the pistol into the holster at his right hip, tugged the flap down and secured it in the closed position.

Methodically, he checked the two double magazine pouches on the pistol belt, confirming loaded status. He did the same to the two double magazine pouches on his trouser belt. All was in order here.

Cross picked up the two twenty-round extension magazines for the Beretta machine pistol which would serve with his 92F. He inserted them in the special pouches that flanked the zipper along the front of his black battle vest.

He picked up the Gerber BMF, the version with the sawteeth running along the spine. The stainless steel blade was oil slicked. He sheathed it on the left side of his pistol belt, double checking that the cradle belt for the Pro-Pak rappeling unit would have proper clearance. It would.

He picked up the Cold Steel Magnum Tanto, turning its edge up toward the oil lamp, looking along the edge for any bright spots visible against the light. There were none, but rather the appearance of a long, thin black line. It was fully sharp.

Cross sheathed the Tanto, securing the sheath to his vest over his chest.

He picked up the fragmentation grenades one at a time, confirming the full downward bend of the cotter pin at the end of the brass ring, then securing the grenades to the massive D-rings of his vest, two on each side, with plastic retainers threaded through the rings. All that would be necessary when he needed to use a grenade was to rip it free of the D-ring, thus pulling the pin.

The lock of Irania's hair: Cross zipped down the front of his vest and placed it in a side chest pocket of his BDU, buttoning the flap closed.

He picked up his cigarettes and his lighter. A fresh pack of twenty Pall Malls. No one yet offered a waterproof plastic cigarette case for a twenty-five pack. He secured cigarettes and lighter inside the translucent plastic case and placed these in a cargo pocket. He doubted there would be much time for a smoke, but this was just in case.

He checked the mini flashlight and placed it in the belt pouch, then picked up the Swiss Army Champion, securing it in the same pocket as his cigarettes.

The gas mask bag. He draped this from left shoulder to right hip, cross body on its strap. The black musette bag with spare magazines for the G-3 and other necessities he draped from right shoulder to left hip.

Then he took up the headpiece. To fight a hateful evil these days, good men—and he counted himself as one of these—needed to hide their faces the same as evil men did.

It was a tight-fitting, expandable black hood. He pulled it on over his head. The tight fit was in the event that the gas mask needed to be employed—a seal could still be formed. He positioned it for the eye holes, nostril holes and mouth hole so it would be as comfortable as possible.

He looked at Babcock and Hughes, donning their head coverings.

"Halloween?" Babcock suggested.

Cross didn't laugh. He took up one of the packs, Hughes

helping him into it. He lashed it into position at the waist, having previously adjusted for the added bulk of his gear.

Babcock picked up the LAW-12 and the extra musette bag for its shells, then the Steyr-Mannlicher SSG, slinging all in place. Hughes started into the second pack, Cross helping him. The third pack, with some food and medical supplies, would be left behind, and the first two packs would be ditched before the actual penetration.

Cross slung his G-3 into place, awkward with all the gear now. He picked up the integral silencer H&K submachine gun, opening the battery cap on the Aimpoint sight and inserting the Duracells. He extended the sub gun at the full length of his arm and checked the electronic sight. It was at full functional level.

Cross inserted a magazine, chambered a round, set the safety, and slung it under his arm.

"I'm glad this is a short walk," Babcock said, similarly weighted down, with the exception of the pack.

Cross said nothing.

He picked up his gloves. The Pro-Pak required no special rappeling gloves. These gloves, instead, were of thin leather, fitting as tightly as a second skin to his hand.

He worked the black gloves over his fingers, closed the hook and pile fasteners, flexed his fingers.

They left the truck and started from the camp, already most of the Mujahedin gone, some of the trucks starting up to leave as well. Cross checked the Rolex on his left wrist.

For once in his life he was perfectly on schedule.

# Chapter Fifty-three

They had walked along the slick rock upgrade, snow here but mostly blown away on the wind. Halfway along he had begun to regret that he'd not worn his sweater. But as they reached the top and took the fork that led toward the drop on the far side of the mountain, he found that something, perhaps the anticipation of combat, had heated his blood, and the cold wind no longer mattered.

At the height of the rise the three of them stopped, and Hughes helped Cross remove his backpack, the one with the emergency gear in it in case they had been blocked from reaching the summit. But that was no longer a concern. Babcock was already driving in the massive eyebolts to which they would tie off, and those had been the only item of gear from the pack that would be required.

Cross took a sip from one of the canteens in the pack. He lit a cigarette, the last from his twenty-five pack, and put the empty pack and the disposable lighter—the one the Chicago policeman had given him—in the soon-to-be-abandoned pack. He had never liked litterbugs. And it was beautiful here, the view unbelievably grand—snowcapped mountain peaks thrusting into the gray of the predawn sky, a thin line of gold on the horizon where in a few moments there would be sunlight.

Hughes approached the overhang and looked down. "A marvelous day to go mountaineering."

Cross didn't say anything.

"They'll have started the diversionary attack, if they're on time," Babcock announced, looking at his watch.

Cross still didn't speak.

A helicopter had overflown them on the route to the summit, but from a good distance; it was unlikely they'd been spotted.

Hughes spoke again. "I took some added precautions you should be alerted to now. There was an easier line of approach, and there is a more remote entry method into the tunnels. According to our flight plan with Colonel Leadbetter—and as far as anyone else knows, including the People's Mujahedin—that was the route we would take this morning. Which is why I told both of you not to mention anything of our specific route. That's because I told Uncle Shapur the other route. I've learned over the years that misplaced trust can be deadly." Cross imagined Hughes's eyebrows rising beneath the skin-tight hood, only his eyes themselves and his mouth visible. "In the event we were betrayed anywhere along the line, we'll be expected, but at the wrong point of entry. In actuality, if we were betrayed, it will work to our advantage. Another valuable lesson, lads. Turn disadvantage to advantage, profit by misfortune. If we are expected," and he paused for an instant, "they will have diverted a considerable portion of their force to that rather remote tunnel entry. Couple that with the forces they'll need for the diversionary attack, and the odds will almost be acceptable at the entrance below us here. I suggest we move out. You first, lad."

Cross saw to his Pro-Pak, feeding out the sufficient amount of line to tie off, adjusting the harness at his waist, awkward with all the equipment but still satisfactorily fast. He fed out the protective sleeve to the end of the precipice and looked down.

Hughes handed him one of the sound and light grenades, Cross biting onto the pin.

Babcock was tying off.

Hughes began the process.

Cross looked at his watch, the grenade dangling from his teeth, the H-K sub gun slung at his right side, ready.

The sweep second hand of the black-faced Rolex crossed the twelve.

He started the drop.

# Chapter Fifty-four

Mehdi Hamadan walked briskly through the cold predawn air, his body ill-accustomed to the rigors of the mountain climate after the warmer temperatures of Jerusalem for the past several days.

But it had been necessary to take personal charge of this.

"Quickly!" He broke into a run as soon as he was clear of the helicopter pad on the small natural plateau near the upper-level entrance to the headquarters. The two men with him ran as well, Hamadan looking back once. Already, as the helicopter had settled into its landing, he had seen evidence of a major attack forming before the main entrance on the valley floor.

But he was not quite too late.

Raka's chief lieutenant stood just beneath the rock lintel of the open bomb doors, rubbing his hands together as though cold. There was a look of desperation in the man's eyes.

Hamadan slowed his pace. "Ashar, you have readied your defenses?"

"Yes, Mehdi, but I do not understand."

"A group of radical Americans is about to attack the base here. Through my extensive intelligence contacts, I was able to learn of this in time. Tunnel twenty-six is where they will attempt their entry. Divert as many men as possible from defense of the main entrance and take them along the tunnel. You have personal charge of this, Ashar. Do not fail. There will be few of these men, but they are extraordinarily well-armed and well-trained, and have come to murder us all. Hurry!''

Ashar nodded, turned and ran off, bellowing orders to his subordinates, Hamadan summoning a recognizable face, one of the training officers. ''You, take me to where I may observe from safety the defense of the main entrance. Hurry!''

As he walked abreast of the shorter man, he expropriated an Uzi submachine gun from a door guard.

If his pilot and the representative of Ayatollah Fasal Batuta had any sense, he thought, they would do the same.

They turned out of the cave opening that led from the helicopter pad and began descending along a smooth, tubular tunnel within the rock. There was moisture dripping from the natural ceiling, and the dampness chilled him to the bone. Electrical piping ran along the walls at shoulder height, linking the bare-bulb fixtures spaced every ten meters along the tunnel length.

Hamadan glanced back once as he turned up the collar of his sports coat against the cold. The pilot and the Ayatollah's representative were right behind him and had, indeed, armed themselves.

Even if these were Americans acting against the policy of their government who by attempting to penetrate the complex, the Americans would suffer, he told himself. The tunnel took a bend, the ceiling lower here but the walls wider apart, making the light appear more diffuse. The training officer set a brisk pace, but Hamadan kept up with him.

There had been no way to warn Muhammad Raka within the embassy that their base was to be assaulted. But he had done the next best thing. He'd set up the radio-beam signal device on its timer.

He glanced at his wristwatch. In another thirty minutes the second from the top floor of the hotel in Jerusalem would experience a power failure, sending a radio signal which would give Raka his orders.

Kill.

Hamadan kept walking.

•    •    •

Cross hitched the Kevlar line into an ear of the figure-eight descender, his teeth aching from gritting them to hold the sound and light grenade by its brass ring. He was just above the tunnel opening, which from the representation given him should have looked like a blast hole in a mountain wall.

He took out his earplugs and inserted them, awkwardly because of the head covering. He bit as hard as he could and tore the grenade free of its pin, hoping he hadn't ruined his crowns doing it. The last time he'd ventured out of the country—five years ago—he'd needed so much dental work he didn't even want to think about it.

He held the spoon tight against the body of the grenade, unhitched the line from the ear of the descender and kicked out.

Partway down he halted his descent and hurtled the grenade through the opening in the mountainside—it looked just as he'd pictured it.

Cross hitched the Kevlar line into the figure eight descender and thrust the H-K forward, his feet braced against the rock face which flanked the opening, his eyes closed against the flash of light, his head averted. The sound was ear-splittingly loud. He counted the seconds until the intensity of the flash would be gone, opened his eyes and swung, bracing his feet again. Two men were screaming so loudly he could still hear them with the earplugs in place, as though they were making harsh whispering sounds, holding their eyes, their weapons slung to their bodies.

Cross fired, the silenced submachine gun rocking in his fist. Both men went down.

Cross let the gun fall away on its sling, freeing the line from the ear of the descender and dropping as he swung inward. He jettisoned the Pro-Pak, advancing along the sloping rough gray granite toward the interior of the tunnel.

He removed the earplugs, pocketing them for possible use later on. On both walls there were bare bulbs shining every eight yards or so, and the rock around him echoed the sounds of running feet.

Though the sound of the grenade had been intense, it wouldn't have been heard over a great distance, he told himself. He tucked back into a niche of granite as three men with assault rifles entered the chamber overlooking the precipice. He let them get even with him, then stepped from the niche. "Bye-bye!" Cross hosed them with the submachine gun.

Cross backtracked along the natural rock corridor for several yards, then doubled back toward the tunnel mouth. He changed sticks from a stock he carried in the musette bag along with spare magazines for the G-3. He intended to save the actual on-body gear until there was nothing left. He pouched the partially spent magazine in case he would need it later, imagining he might.

Hughes was dropping through the opening now. Then Babcock, who ditched his rappeling gear quickly and helped Hughes, who was encumbered by the weight of the backpack containing the explosives.

"Hi, guys—not much action down here yet. Thirty seconds ago the tunnel was clear for about fifty yards. That was as far as I could see."

"Matches the diagram nicely," Hughes told them. "Time to use the disposer bags and get rid of the maps." Hughes reached beneath his battle vest, checking the seal on the bag, then setting the bag on the stone floor. He took his Gerber and inverted it, then smashed down on the bag. There was a small popping sound and the bag seemed to fill with a liquid about the color of strawberry jelly, then began to dissolve. Hughes resheathed.

Cross took out his knife, telling Babcock, "Gimme yours." Babcock flipped him the bag and Cross hammered twice, activating both capsules.

Cross resheathed his Gerber. Babcock cycled the action on the LAW-12. "Ready."

Cross looked at Hughes, the older man already positioning two of the plastique charges by the tunnel opening, one on each side of it, which would seal off this entrance. Hughes glanced at his wristwatch and looked up from his crouch. "Half hour?"

Cross nodded. "If we're not outa here by then, we're dead anyway."

"Agreed—a half hour," Babcock said, looking at his watch.

"We should be out in time for lunch," Hughes said easily, then tripped the activator switch for the timer.

They started along the corridor, Hughes bringing up the rear because he was the most vulnerable with explosives, Cross at the lead, Babcock to his left and slightly behind, the LAW-12 shotgun in a hard assault position.

They had agreed that under optimum conditions they would use the silenced H-K submachine gun, with the LAW-12 as a close range backup. But battle rarely took place under optimum conditions, Cross knew.

They passed the position where he'd killed the three men who had come to investigate the wail of the sound and light grenade. There was no point in disarming them, since they were already dead, and no time to disassemble their weapons to render them useless, since the weapons themselves would be too much additional to carry and were the wrong calibers to be of any use. None of the team weapons shared a common cartridge with the Soviet AKM. Cross, Hughes, and Babcock kept moving.

"I'll catch up, lads," Hughes said when the corridor took a sharp bend right, just as the diagram showed it would. Cross glanced over his shoulder. Hughes had slipped out of the pack and was securing a small charge to the electrical pipe that carried the wiring supplying current to the wall lights.

Cross walked on, the corridor starting to rise. This also was as it should be.

Babcock, beside him, whispered, "He's back behind us." Cross only nodded.

They should be nearing the end of the tunnel, Cross thought, if he remembered the diagram correctly.

The tunnel bent abruptly, Cross staying the others behind him with a hand motion. He'd heard a sound.

There was no way to tell where guard posts would be positioned. One was apparently ahead of them.

As Cross started to reach for the Tanto, Hughes tapped him on the shoulder from behind. Hughes's lips, all that was visible of his face, curled upward. In his right hand was the silenced Walther P-5.

Cross nodded.

Hughes edged ahead, Cross pulling back, the H-K sub gun

in his right fist, tensioned against its sling. Hughes disappeared around the bend, Babcock holding the pack Hughes had left behind.

Cross listened. It sounded as though the little Walther .22's slide had been racked twice.

Hughes reappeared at the bend. "A single guard. Marvelously effective suppressor." The older man made the silenced auto pistol disappear beneath his battle vest.

As Hughes shrugged into the pack again, Cross moved ahead, almost tripping over the dead man, who'd been shot twice in the head. Cross stepped over him and into the next corridor.

It stretched seemingly without end in both directions. He closed his eyes for an instant, remembering the diagram, then started to the left.

There should be a dormitory ahead of them. He checked his Rolex. It was not yet sunrise. It was possible that despite the diversionary attack in progress, there might still be men sleeping there.

He closed his eyes, seeing the diagram of the interior of the mountain in his head, then compared distances already covered with their representations in the diagram. He decided that it would be about the distance of a city block. He opened his eyes and continued ahead.

Cross quickened his pace, the tunnel taking another bend. Then he stopped dead. Massive double doors, steel, perhaps bomb proof, blocked the corridor. Cross cursed under his breath.

Babcock stepped past him, reached to the knob and looked back at Cross, who shrugged and looked at Hughes, who merely held his submachine gun in a hard assault position.

Cross shrugged again, then nodded to Babcock. Babcock worked the doorknob and pulled, the door opening suddenly, Cross diving through, Hughes behind him, Cross's sub gun swinging right, Cross knowing Hughes would be covering the left.

There was no one beyond the doors. Cross looked back toward Babcock, who was framed in the opening, the assault shotgun at the ready.

Cross was getting worried; it was too easy.

Hughes extended his right gloved hand, fingers splayed, shaking his fingers right and left, then regrasped his weapon. Cross wished for a cigarette.

Beyond the doors here the corridor split into a long passage and what should not have been a passageway at all. He was coming to have great faith in the diagram, and the diagram showed a cavern too small in size for anything but limited training, but ideal for a dormitory or recreation room. Since the enemy didn't seem too terribly interested in recreating, it had seemed logical that it was a dormitory. He adhered to the diagram, abandoning any idea of exploring the fork, telling himself it would be a cul de sac. He took the point again, continuing in the direction along which they had traveled.

The corridor took another bend, Cross peering around it. Another set of doors. He brought up his right hand, signaling toward the doors, resting an open palm beside his head and closing his eyes. When he opened them, Hughes and Babcock were both nodding agreement.

Cross stepped into the corridor, no one between him and the set of doors. Babcock moved ahead in a low, running crouch, Cross covering.

Babcock reached the doors, flattening himself against the wall to the left, the shotgun in his right fist tensioned on its sling.

Cross reached the doors, Hughes behind him, signaling for them to wait. Cross's fists balled on his weapon, open and closed, open and closed. Hughes set another charge to the electrical system, then slipped back into the pack and swung his sub gun forward.

Cross's eyes and Babcock's eyes met. Cross nodded, and Babcock twisted the doorknob and pulled one of the doors, Cross going through, knowing Hughes would be right behind him.

They saw men in various stages of undress beside their bunks, or entering or leaving what appeared to be a latrine at the far end of a massive, vaulted cavern, but some were armed and fully dressed. Guards for the new recruits? Cross wondered.

But there was no time to tell who was good and who wasn't, though Cross had always resented the theory that God would sort them out. If they were here and weren't in chains, they were either committed terrorists or dangerously close to it.

He opened fire, hearing Hughes's sub gun as Hughes did the same, Cross shouting, "Shotgun!" as two guards with AKM's turned toward them to open fire. Cross dodged left. Assault rifle fire tore into the wall beside him, ricocheting madly on the granite, a spray of granite dust erupting like a cloud toward him as he averted his eyes.

Babcock.

Inside the confines of the cavern the LAW-12 sounded like a small cannon used for a Fourth of July celebration. Silence and secrecy were gone. Cross threw himself into a roll, reached to one of the D-rings on his battle vest and tore one of the grenades from its pin, hurtling it underhand like a bowling ball toward the latrine.

"Grenade!" he shouted, Hughes stepping back in a long stride into the shelter of the doorway. Cross dropped flat. The grenade exploded, the concussion making clouds of dust from the overhead light fixtures, a bulb bursting, screams of dying men from the latrine.

Cross was up and moving, Hughes's sub gun fired out, shifted to his left fist, the Beretta in his right, his arm outstretched like some old west gunfighter as he methodically fired double taps, men going down.

Babcock's shotgun was empty. A half-naked man charged him, Babcock wheeling toward him, the butt of the LAW-12 snapping up and out, hitting the center of the man's face.

Cross fired out the stick in his sub gun, dropping it to the cavern floor. He had nothing to reload the magazine with. No time to change sticks, he grabbed for the Beretta at his hip, putting a double tap into the left eye and temple of a man with an Uzi submachine gun. The submachine gun discharged into a bunk, almost sawing it in half as the man went down. The bunk hadn't been empty.

Cross wheeled toward the door, shouting, "Out!" Babcock covered, the LAW-12 firing again, Hughes backed toward the door, emptying his Beretta.

Cross was the first one through the door, ramming the partially spent stick for the H-K sub gun up the well, waiting until Hughes was through, then Babcock. "Lookout!" Cross stabbed the sub gun through the still open doorway and fired it out in a series of short bursts. "Waste not want not," he said, tucking back, Babcock slamming the door. Gunfire pelted into the doors from inside the dormitory, the steel doors ringing with it.

Babcock was reloading the LAW-12's magazine tube. "You're a good shot," Hughes rasped. "These three sticks of dynamite."

"Dyno-mite!"

"Thank you, Jimmy Walker," Cross told Babcock.

Hughes laughed, ripping the tape from the roll and winding it around the three sticks of explosives. Cross extended the H-K's butt stock. "Do it," he told Babcock. "Cover me!"

"Right."

Hughes grabbed the doorknob, pulled, and Babcock sprayed the shotgun through the opening.

Hughes tossed the sticks in. Cross was on one knee, the red dot of the Aimpoint electronic settling on the flying sticks of dynamite, the H-K erupting in his hands, a burst cutting into the dynamite. Cross fell back from the concussion as Hughes slammed the doors. Babcock was flung to the corridor floor as well, clouds of acrid smelling smoke blowing up from under the steel doors.

"I think they've had enough," Cross said, getting to his feet, his ears still ringing with the explosion. He left the red dot sight on, Hughes and Babcock flanking him as they continued along the corridor.

An alarm began to sound, something like a European police siren or the wail of a banshee.

Cross picked up the pace.

If the diagram were still correct, there was a vastly larger corridor about a hundred yards ahead which branched right and left again. To the right and up along an incline was a larger cavern which could be anything from a main training area to the headquarters area.

The corridor took another bend.

They were running now, Hughes calling forward, "I'm putting some charges by the end of the corridor here—cover me!"

Cross and Babcock reached the end of the corridor, the larger corridor opening before them, the sirens wailing louder now. Cross entered the corridor. Men were coming from both sides and converging toward the smaller corridor which Cross, Babcock and Hughes were exiting. Cross tucked back. "Hurry it up with those charges!"

Cross swung the H-K subgun back, grabbing for the G-3. He had two magazines locked together for fast interchange, side by side. He moved the safety to auto.

Babcock was feeding jungle mix into the LAW-12.

"Ready," Hughes shouted.

Cross felt the older man's presence beside him, heard the sounds of Hughes's G-3 unlimbering. "How many?"

"A whole bunch—gee whiz," Cross cracked. "Oh boy, oh boy!"

"Exuberance'll be the death of you, lad," Hughes advised.

"Back up the corridor," Cross ordered. Hughes and Babcock started back the way they had just come, Cross eyeing Hughes's demolitions preparations as he followed them.

They went beyond the bend in the corridor, Cross shouting to Hughes, "Those charges—will they seal the corridor if we blow 'em?"

"I'm afraid they will. But on the plus side, at least we're trapped together."

"Gosh." Cross nodded. His mind raced.

He had it. "Grenades—will they pop those charges?"

"Shouldn't, really—just plastique. Unless you get too close."

"Don't know how many of us there are—I mean, we do, but they don't. I hope. We attack. Follow my lead. Each man one grenade. Count to ten seconds between each. I'm first."

Cross ripped another grenade from one of the D-rings, holding the spoon tight against the body in his right fist. His hands were sweating inside his leather gloves. He could hear shouted commands in Farsi. Then the anticipated bursts of automatic weapons fire came, the ricochet problem in the corridor serious, dust rising in clouds as granite was powdered beneath the impacts.

Cross snapped the first grenade into the corridor, pulling back, the concussion coming, his ears ringing with it again. He shifted the H-K assault rifle into his left hand for a moment, drawing the Beretta. There were ten shots left in the pistol. He got the Beretta into his left fist, the pistol grip of the G-3 in his right as Babcock tossed the second grenade.

Babcock held the LAW-12 in one fist, the H-K sub gun in the other. The concussion roared along the corridor, smoke and granite dust everywhere now as the gunfire from along the length of the corridor diminished. There were shouted commands in Farsi.

Hughes tossed the third grenade, and with the concussion came dust in clouds so thick that it was almost impossible to see.

Cross shouted, "Let's go! First squad—up the center. All the rest of you men! Cover us!" He was already running; Babcock and Hughes flanked him a pace or so behind, barely visible at the edges of his peripheral vision as he looked right and left.

They were around the corridor bend, and Cross opened fire, still running, almost tripping over dead bodies in the dust-clouded air, occasional bursts of automatic weapons fire hitting corridor walls and floor, the cacophony of gunfire around him from their own weapons maddening, hot brass pelting at his face, hot even through the skin-tight hood.

They reached the end of the corridor, back where they'd started. He estimated another twenty or so had been taken out in the last exchange. He reloaded, Hughes and Babcock doing the same, the Beretta in his fist still with ten rounds remaining.

"Now?"

"May as well," Hughes answered him.

"Sure." Babcock nodded.

"Wait—how about some more grenades?" Cross suggested.

"Gee, I don't know." Babcock laughed, snatching one off the D-rings of his battle vest. Hughes did the same.

"One right, one left—Babcock take the right because that's the way we're goin' and I want that cleared first."

"Yes, sir," said Babcock positioning himself by the corridor opening, Cross nodding. Babcock snapped the grenade. "A high fly ball and . . . it's outa the park—look out!" They tucked back, Hughes hurtling the second grenade down the other side of the corridor an instant before the first one exploded.

"Let's move!" Cross ducked into the corridor in a crouch, firing a burst from the G-3, shouting, "Shotgun behind us!"

He started running as the concussion of the second grenade came and went, and heard the roar of Babcock's shotgun firing into the forces to their rear.

The corridor defenders were knotted together in bunches—inexperienced, Cross guessed, as he fired into them, running still, assault rifle fire cracking past him. He ducked into a niche, since he figured he'd pushed his luck enough. Extending the Beretta into the corridor, he fired, Hughes and Babcock in a niche in the corridor wall almost directly opposite him.

"What we do now, kimo sabe?"

Cross shouted back to Babcock, "What you mean we, pale face? Didn't I ever tell you guys I was a Shiite? Mustafa slipped my mind." While he bantered he was juggling calculations, coming to a conclusion.

It was a miracle any of the three of them were alive.

He looked out of the niche. The International Jihad forces ahead of them and behind them were regrouping. He was reloading as he spoke. "Dynamite—supply holding out?"

"It isn't infinite, I hope you realize," Hughes called back. "But sufficient to the task at hand. Hang on."

He was shuffling out of the pack again. Cross suddenly thought, If we make it out of here and are ever stupid enough to do something like this again, we need a more efficient carry system for the explosives. He filed the thought away under ridiculously optimistic ideas, to be cross-referenced under masochistic tendencies.

Hughes held two sticks, and jerked one right and one left. Cross nodded.

Hughes shifted both sticks to his right hand and made a pistol of his left hand.

Cross nodded, shrugging.

Hughes jerked a thumb toward Babcock, who nodded.

Cross jerked his thumb up the corridor in the direction in which they wanted to go, then back toward himself.

He shifted the Beretta to his right fist.

Babcock had his Beretta ready.

Cross gave Hughes the nod, and Hughes flipped the sticks almost simultaneously, right and left, Babcock swinging out into the corridor, Cross doing the same a split-second afterward. His left fist wrapped over his right, the hammer thumb cocked, he began the squeeze as he tracked the stick of spinning dynamite, Cross leading it now, the Beretta bucking lightly in his fist.

The two pistol shots sounded almost as one to Cross as he threw himself back, the explosions slamming into him from both sides, his body sagging.

Cross shook his head to clear it, to his knees now, working the Beretta's safety to drop the hammer, shifting it back to his left fist, catching up the G-3.

Hughes was already shrugging into his pack, Cross waving them forward.

Bodies of International Jihad defenders were strewn everywhere about the natural corridor of rock, like the discarded toys of an angry child. They kept running, firing sporadically into still-moving terrorist bodies, past the carnage now and along the corridor.

Cross looked at his Rolex, twelve minutes remaining before Hughes's charges would detonate and bring down the mountain. He ran faster, glancing right and left, Hughes and Babcock flanking him. If he lived, Cross thought, and he attained Hughes's age, if he were half the man Hughes was, he'd be satisfied.

The corridor took another bend and began rising, just as the diagram had indicated. He kept running until they reached the point of the bend, then stopped.

"We have twelve minutes, lads."

"No shit." Cross nodded, catching his breath. "Write your will yet, Darwin, have you?"

Babcock peered around the corner, the muzzle of the LAW-12 going ahead of him. "There's some kinda big cavern entrance down there. This is a fascinating place—or would be if you were into exploring caves, anyway."

Cross ignored this comment, looked around the bend, trying to eyeball the cavern for what it might contain.

Hughes was planting charges. "Big cavern down there, just like in the diagram," Cross said to Hughes. "Think it'll be big enough?"

"You're the one with the photographic mind—will it?"

"I almost flunked explosives," Cross confessed.

"Well, we'll have to go and see, won't we?" Hughes nodded his head toward the corridor beyond the bend.

Cross stepped into the corridor, the G-3 freshly loaded, the Beretta freshly loaded as well. No one shot at him. "Let's go," he snapped, the three of them running, the wailing of the sirens more intensified now.

Hughes shouted over it, "Remember the concept of a destruct mechanism in the event the mountain were invaded? Hmm?"

Cross didn't answer, his mind chewing on something else. So far they had accounted for perhaps a hundred of the supposed thousand or so International Jihad estimated inside the mountain fortress. If another two hundred were lying in wait for them, and if one hundred were following up the spurious invasion plan Hughes had intentionally given to Leadbetter—and it appeared their plan had been blown . . . but even if another hundred or two were engaged in countering the Peoples' Mujahedin diversionary attack, that left four or five hundred of the occupants of the mountain redoubt unaccounted for.

Cross was seriously beginning to worry.

They neared the cavern mouth, Cross giving hand and arm signals for them to split, Hughes and Babcock going left, Cross going right.

The corridor was some fifty feet wide here and at least twelve feet high, some of the lights flickering, the wailing of the siren increasing.

Hugging the wall, Babcock looking behind them, covering their rear, they advanced, the G-3 tight in his right fist, the Beretta in his left.

Much of the interior of the cavern was visible now. Natural steps cascaded down like a petrified waterfall, and near their base . . . Cross edged forward, Hughes opposite him on the other side of the corridor.

The cavern was more massive than Cross had imagined it could be, about a half-dozen trucks parked in its center, another half-dozen Jeeps, a Land Rover, and two snowplow-fitted pickup trucks. From the way the vehicles were parked, it was clear there had once been dozens of other vehicles like these parked here. Where were they now?

"What's that look like on the far wall?" Cross asked.

Hughes answered, "Weapons racks—from their size—"

"Assault rifles and submachine guns in the smaller ones, right?"

"Yes. But most of the rack space—"

"Empty," Cross supplied.

Cross edged farther forward. There were training areas on each corner of the roughly rectangular cavern floor, some few folding chairs, but mostly, he assumed, designed for trainees to sit on the cold stone. One wall of the cavern was blocked off with a man-made wall; behind it, through windows that looked down over the training areas, there appeared to be offices.

"Will this place do?" Cross waited for a response. After a moment he got it.

Hughes said, "Despite a poor formal education, I've always been fascinated by some aspects of geology. Those walls support the dome, the center of the dome itself supporting the mountain. If two walls went out—simultaneously would be best—we could bring it down. Maybe."

Cross looked at his watch. Ten minutes at the outside. They weren't going to make it out alive, he guessed. Can't win 'em all, he told himself.

"They should have an explosives magazine located nearby," Hughes said. "That might be interesting to work with too." He tapped Babcock on the shoulder. "See if you can find it. Check the outside perimeter of the cavern. Probably a natural room with a steel bomb-proof door."

Cross called to Babcock, "You cool doin' it alone?"

"Black people are always cool—didn't you know that?"

Babcock turned into the side corridor to the left, Cross and Hughes starting ahead, into the cavern, entering from the extreme sides of the cavern mouth. Now there was a tunnel visible. It was at the far wall beyond the offices, and led toward the upper portion of the mountain. From the diagram . . . Cross closed his eyes, tried picturing it.

"I think that's the way to the helipad. I can't be sure."

Hughes was starting out of his pack. "Well, if we have the time, perhaps we can stroll up there and see."

Cross started down the steplike formation that led toward the floor of the cave, Hughes crossing along the perimeter of the cavern toward the wall near the offices. At any second, Cross realized, the rest of International Jihad might show up and yell "Surprise!"

He broke into a run, holstering the Beretta, shifting the G-3 to a hard assault position as he ran. There was a wooden stairway rising sharply up the constructed wall. He made for that staircase now, glancing back once to Hughes. The older man was already setting charges by the base of the wall, stringing ropes of plastique.

Cross stopped at the base of the stairs.

Babcock entered the cavern. "Bomb-proof doors and a small, naturally formed room." He jerked his thumb to his right. "About twenty yards that way."

Cross started up the stairs leading toward the offices, lights visible from inside through the picture-window-like glass apertures looking down on the cavern floor. But there had been no evidence of habitation.

Hughes was already sprinting across the cavern floor to reach Babcock, shouting to him, "Show me, lad!"

Cross stopped at the landing along the midpoint of the rise of the stairs, his fists balling on the G-3. At any second, he realized, someone would enter the cavern.

Hughes and Babcock disappeared. Cross looked at his wristwatch. Eight minutes or less.

Hughes had told them that photographs or documents might be useful. Babcock had the camera. Cross started up the stairs again, looking back once. Babcock and Hughes had not returned, and Babcock had taken the pack with the rest of his explosives. Maybe something could be done with the bomb-proof door to the explosives magazine. It was designed to protect the contents from explosive action, not restrict entrance, he guessed.

He reached the height of the stairs, flattening himself against the unpainted wooden railing beside the cheap-looking door leading into the area behind the false wall.

The door was partially open. Cross kicked it in, and gunfire ripped through the wall beside him. Cross flipped the railing and jumped to the cavern floor, going into a crouch and a roll to save his ankles, hitting against his right shoulder, rolling, spraying the G-3 up along the length of the stairs.

He dove beneath the raised structure for cover. He could see Hughes in the cavern mouth, Babcock with him, both their arms laden with packing crates.

His two friends tucked back as more automatic weapons fire came from the height of the stairs. Babcock started a dodging run along the perimeter of the cavern floor, Hughes behind him, Babcock firing his G-3 toward the stairs.

Cross slung his rifle across his back and moved closer to the stairwell, appraising its structure. Supports the size of standard building studs framed the stairs. He started to climb beneath the stairs, working his way through the grid the two-by-fours made as Babcock continued firing.

Cross looked at his watch. He hoped Hughes was somehow able to continue his work. Cross kept moving, clambering along the studs. His weight made them creak, but he was nearing the height of the stairs.

He heard more gunfire from the landing above him, and more returning fire from Babcock or Hughes. Cross couldn't see them now, couldn't be sure which.

Finally he was at the height of the stairs, and moved toward the edge of the platformlike structure, his hands over the side of it, his body swinging free from the supports. Chinning himself to eye level with the platform, he pushed up, his right knee on the edge of the platform, then his upper body sliding slightly forward, his right knee firmly purchased, his left leg dangling over the side. Babcock was covering Hughes, who was stringing more ropes of plastique now, trailing them to the crates Hughes and Babcock had returned with.

Cross tore a grenade from one of the D-rings on his battle vest, counted, then snapped it with his left hand across the platform and through the open doorway, dropping from the platform to the cavern floor beneath as the concussion came. Glass shattered and a fireball belched through the open doorway.

Cross was up, eyeballing the structure of the stairs as he ran toward the base. The supports looked unaffected by the explosion. He took the stairs two at a time, the G-3 at his hip in a hard assault position, running.

At the height of the stairs he framed himself beside the doorway and sprayed the G-3 into the enclosure, doing the magazine shift, throwing himself through the doorway and left, flattening himself behind an overturned desk. It was a steel office desk, one pedestal mangled from the force of the explosion, but would offer little protection from a steady stream of rifle-caliber automatic weapons fire.

He edged around the side of the desk, the muzzle of the G-3 going first. To his knees now, the rifle returned to a hard assault position as he stood.

A dead man and two dead women were on the other side of the vestibulelike room, two assault rifles between the three of them.

He approached the bodies cautiously. Death seemed so obvious here that he didn't fully trust it. But they were indeed dead.

Quickly he moved along a central hallway with small offices branching off on either side and a solitary door at the end. He checked each office quickly, grabbing up anything that looked like a map or official document.

One of the offices held a three-drawer steel file cabinet. Cross stepped back and sprayed the G-3 into the lock, part of the cabinet top can-openering away. He wrenched the top drawer open. There were documents he couldn't read, but they had some sort of official stamp. This was the good stuff, he hoped. He grabbed up a representative sampling, throwing it out into the hallway, opening another drawer, doing the same, having no idea if he were bypassing some secret terrorist code in favor of somebody's laundry list. He did the same with the third drawer, then ran into the hallway now. There was no time. He almost slipped on one of the file folders. At the last office he buzzed the lock plate with the G-3, rammed a fresh magazine up the well, then kicked the door in.

He framed himself beside the doorframe. Nothing happened. He stabbed the G-3 through and fired a burst. Nothing. He entered the office.

There was a small safe beside the desk and an Iranian flag on the wall.

Big time, he thought.

Cross raced back down the hallway, reaching the platform, shouting, "I need the backpack and enough plastique to crack a safe. A small safe. Hurry!"

Babcock, installing charges on the opposite wall, looked up, but Hughes was already running toward him, the pack and a rope of plastique in his hands, the length about four feet.

From beneath the platform Hughes tossed up the pack first, empty: Cross caught it, then the rope of explosives. "Figure where the hinges are. Wall or floor model?"

"Floor."

"How high and wide, lad?"

"Three feet high, maybe a little less. Two feet wide. Maybe three feet deep."

"A third of this along the hinge side, then split the remainder into three parts, one on each of the other door edges. Detonator in the bag—we're all but out of time."

Cross didn't waste time answering. He was already running, entering the office at the end of the hallway, tearing the plastique rope, positioning it as Hughes had told him. From the backpack he extracted a battery, wire, and detonation cord, working the detcord into the plastique, which he molded with his hands to frame the safe door, the lead wires already attached to the battery terminals. He set the lead wire into the detcord, then ran out the electrical wire from the battery until he was halfway back down the hall. The plastique rope had come in two diameters; this was the narrower diameter. It was unlikely it would launch the safe into orbit, he told himself, or down the hallway toward him.

He began stuffing as many of the documents as he could from the floor, where he'd thrown them into the pack. He refused to look at his watch.

He drew back into a doorframe for shelter, activated the battery switch and held his ears. He was hurtled to the floor, chunks of the ceiling tiles pelting down on him, a cloud of smoke and dust engulfing him, making him gag.

"Shit," he snarled. There was a fire burning in the office at the end of the hallway. He ran toward the office anyway, jumping a burning piece of ceiling tile. The safe door was blown across the room, part of the top of the safe ripped away, the interior smoldering.

Carefully avoiding the fiery hot metal, he removed the contents of the safe. A sack of coins—curiosity got him. Krugerrands. "Big time," he hissed. An address book. Two file folders and a CZ-75 pistol. He left the pistol and the Krugerrands, put the file folders and the address book under his left arm.

In the hallway now, he stuffed the files into the backpack, the address book inside his BDU blouse. Then he ran, reaching the doorway and the platform, throwing the backpack down, flipping the railing again, landing in a crouch, almost twisting an ankle.

"We're ready—come on," Hughes shouted, running toward him, catching up the pack as Babcock backed across the cavern floor, the LAW-12 in his hands covering the cavern mouth.

The up-angling chamber on the far side was their only possibility, since the massive garage doors on the opposite cavern wall presumably led to the main entrance. There could be hundreds of the International Jihad defenders there.

Cross and Hughes reached the up-angling tunnel, Cross shouting back to Babcock, "Come on, man!"

Babcock broke into a dead run, Cross already starting up the tunnel. He heard movement ahead, but there was no time to do anything or worry about it—he just kept running, Hughes beside him. He glanced back once, Babcock keeping up the rear.

Cross tried to remember the diagram, his mind racing—if the plan had been blown and they were anticipated, a significant force would have gone up along the more remote emergency tunnel, and it fed from— He shouted to Hughes. "You know what's coming?"

"Either that or stay here and get blown up."

Cross kept running, hearing a low roar from the bowels of

the mountain. He looked at his watch. The explosions were starting. "Gave us an extra two minutes on the stuff in the cavern!" Hughes shouted.

The tunnel took a bend, Cross slowing, the roaring sounds behind them increasing, Babcock catching up.

Cross unlimbered the MP5-SD-A3 submachine gun, the G-3 in one hand, the sub gun in the other. Hughes took Babcock's sub gun, one in each fist. Hughes had the police-assault shotgun.

"Well, guys," Cross said, out of breath. "Been fun. Let's go—just like we thought we were going to make it."

Hughes let both sub guns fall to his sides on their slings, his hands going to Cross's and Babcock's shoulders. "Gentlemen—it has been a pleasure."

Cross threw himself around the bend. "Shit!" But he started running forward anyway, at least a dozen men visible twenty feet away, more coming. He opened fire, Hughes and Babcock flanking him, the three of them running, firing out their weapons into the wall of human targets ahead of them; running, jumping fallen bodies.

The G-3 was out. Cross let it fall to his side, his other fist still pumping the sub gun as he grasped the Beretta and began firing it too.

Something tore at the outside of his left thigh. He kept running. Hughes stumbled, caught himself. Cross thought he saw blood. Babcock's shotgun was silent for a moment, then started up again. The roaring of explosions behind them was steadily increasing, the rock of the tunnel through which they fought vibrating with it, chunks of granite pelting down.

The H-K was out, so was the Beretta, and a dozen of the International Jihad fighters were closing in on them. Cross assumed he was going to die, so there wasn't any sense in being cautious. He rammed the Beretta into the belt of his BDU's, grabbing for the L-Frame Smith, firing point-blank into a man's face, then twice more into another man's chest. A bayonet-fitted AKM was hacking toward Babcock. Cross fired two more rounds, hammering the man's body against the tunnel wall.

A burst of automatic weapons fire numbed Cross's left arm for an instant. He found the source and emptied the revolver.

One of the terrorists, his rifle empty or jammed, threw his weapon down and dove toward Cross. Cross bludgeoned the man across the face and neck with the revolver, lost the revolver and stepped back, drawing the Magnum Tanto from its sheath on his chest, the Gerber BMF from the sheath on his belt. Men charged toward him, anger and hatred having replaced reason and tactics.

And suddenly, as he fought there, his back to the tunnel wall, the knives in his hands flicking, finding flesh, killing, returning to guard, Cross started to laugh.

There was an explosion louder than the rest now, chunks of granite falling into the tunnel, men screaming, barely audible over it.

Cross saw Hughes, a Gerber fighting knife in his left hand, the Walther in his right, a tongue of flame leaping from it in the swirling dust of the collapsing tunnel ceiling; a man down, the knife hacking outward, opening a throat.

Babcock's right hand was moving like a snake, the Bali-Song there opening and closing, slashing faces and hands, his left hand holding his Beretta inverted, using the butt like a bludgeon.

The terrorists started falling back.

Cross sagged to his knee, a dying terrorist reaching up for his throat. Cross rammed both knives into the man's chest. He got to his feet, both knives retrieved. The sharp crack of the Steyr-Mannlicher SSG, the rifle in Babcock's hands, was firing at the fleeing terrorists.

Cross looked back down the tunnel—it was collapsing. Hughes, part of his left sleeve cut away, his bloodied arm limp at his side, shouted, "As the phone company puts it, your two minutes are up!"

Cross started to run, Babcock and Hugh flanking him again as they chased the fleeing terrorists.

He'd lost the G-3, but there was no time to look for it. He rammed a fresh magazine up the well of the H-K sub gun, then did the same with the Beretta, using one of the two twenties from his vest front. Babcock was reloading the LAW-12 on the run, Hughes reloading his Walther and Beretta, then the two sub guns he had—his and Babcock's. He tossed one of other submachine guns to Babcock, who caught it and shouted, "Thanks!"

The shout was barely audible because the roaring was louder now. The tunnel floor was shaking so violently Cross lost his balance and spread-eagled forward. He waved Hughes and Babcock on, and was on his feet again, running.

His left leg screamed at him, but he kept running. Part of his right glove had been sliced away by a bayonet, the back of his right hand bleeding. His right shoulder and neck were stiffening, and he didn't know if he'd been shot, cut, or just pulled a muscle. And there wasn't time to look.

Sunlight—

The helipad. There were two helicopters, one of them already starting airborne, terrorists clinging to its skids, the machine heaving and lurching.

Cross passed Hughes as the older man flung two plastique pipe bombs toward the helipads.

Cross started to shout to him. "What—" But Hughes was already running toward the helipad where the second chopper was still not yet airborne.

The pipe bomb exploded, the terrorists running from it— but aside from a loud bang and plenty of smoke rising, there was nothing. Babcock sprinted toward the helicopter, firing out his LAW-12, hurtling his body through the open fuselage door, the chopper taking off.

Cross ran too.

The plateau on which the helipads were constructed was beginning to collapse now, and as Cross looked back once, the top of the mountain behind them looked as though it were peeling off.

The helicopter with Babcock aboard was lurching violently fifty feet overhead now, Cross and Hughes back to back, their weapons in their hands, firing as the scattered terrorists started to advance, men going down.

A rush of wind—Cross looked up, the helicopter hovering just over them, setting down. Cross elbowed Hughes, then followed him. Hughes jumped aboard, Cross jumping for the open fuselage door, missing it. The helicopter started airborne again, Cross clinging to the skids.

One of the terrorists clung there with him.

Cross looked up. Hughes stood in the doorway, his Walther in his hand. The pistol discharged twice, Cross averting his eyes. Then he looked beneath him and saw the terrorist's body falling away.

Cross looked up, saw Hughes hands reaching for him. He grasped Hughes's hands, the older man pulling back as Cross pushed, then collapsed inside.

Babcock shouted from where he was working the controls of the helicopter, "Look what I've got."

Cross got shakily to his feet, holding to the fuselage overhead with his left hand. He looked at a man on the floor of the violently lurching machine, blood streaming down the man's face.

The helicopter was still climbing, but more evenly now. Cross dropped to his knees beside the man. He heard Hughes shout over the wind, "That's Mehdi Hamadan, Raka's boss."

"Where was Raka?" Cross shouted back.

Cross and Hughes hauled Hamadan to his feet, Cross slapping him into consciousness. "Raka—where is he?"

Hamadan shrieked, "Let me go!"

"Over the side to your death?" Hughes shouted, backhanding the terrorist leader.

"It is too late," Hamadan said, dropping to his knees, begging. "You must understand. I had nothing to do with it. I would never order the deaths of innocent people. I merely fight for freedom for my—"

Cross hauled Hamadan to his feet. "What deaths?" The Magnum Tanto, still bloodstained, was in his right fist, its primary edge at the level of Hamadan's eyes.

"What did you order Raka to do?" Hughes rasped.

"I did not order him to take the embassy. It was his idea— I went to Jerusalem to try to mediate the affair, but saw that it was hopeless and that he was obsessed with death. I had returned here to plot a strategy to somehow keep Raka's insane followers from—"

Cross slammed the man against the fuselage wall. "Jerusalem. The American embassy?"

"Yes."

"Hostages?"

"Yes."

"He'll kill them when he learns of this," Hughes said.

"How many men does he have?" Cross slammed the man into the fuselage again, blood trickling from between his lips.

"His twelve Immortals. Two other men. Two women."

"Where are the rest of the terrorists who should have been here—in Israel?" Cross shouted. "Where, damnit!"

"They—they await in Lebanon. They will cross into Israel—but there are too many of them for you to stop. When—when Raka's demands are met—"

Hughes held his face inches from Hamadan's. "Guns. Explosives. What does he have? Quick!"

"Uzi submachine guns, 9mm pistols, plastique, detonators. That is—"

"Think man," Hughes snapped. "Anything else. Think!"

"It—it—it is said he has a radio signal. That if it—I do not know for sure—"

"Radio signal! What?" Hughes shouted.

"That if the thing is about to go bad he—it will tell him to—"

"Kill the hostages," Cross almost whispered.

"Yes," Hamadan shrieked.

Cross looked at Hughes. Their eyes met.

Hughes blinked. Nodded.

Cross dragged Hamadan from the bulkhead toward the open fuselage doorway, the wind tearing at him there, Hamadan screaming in fear.

Cross raked the Tanto across Hamadan's throat and pushed him out into emptiness, his blood like tiny drops of mist on the slipstream.

# Chapter Fifty-five

The mountain was collapsing as the People's Mujahedin fought hand to hand below them with International Jihad. The first helicopter was nowhere to be seen, perhaps downed by the overload of fleeing terrorists clinging to it, perhaps escaped to safety.

With Lewis Babcock still at the chopper's controls, Cross settled in beside the still-open fuselage door, Hughes opposite him. Babcock started the pass, Cross and Hughes opening fire into the ranks of International Jihad, Hughes tossing down a grenade. Babcock banked the helicopter sharply, Cross almost rolling back along the fuselage, spreading his legs wider for purchase. Then the chopper leveled off as it swept back across the battlefield, Hughes hurtling another grenade down on the International Jihad, Cross firing his submachine gun.

At the center of the battlefield he could see Irania.

He started to shout to Babcock, but Babcock was already shouting back to him, "I see her! Cover us!" The helicopter banked sharply, Cross bracing himself again, the machine starting to slip downward, Cross feeling the change in rotor pitch.

He opened fire, Irania, her uncle, and five others of the People's Mujahedin—Mara among them—encircled. Cross kept firing, Hughes firing, too, the chopper passing over them, banking sharply, coming back for another pass. Cross rammed a fresh magazine into the gun, and as the chopper hovered a few feet over the ground, he jumped clear. Hughes was beside him, their sub guns firing point-blank into the remaining International Jihad fighters surrounding Irania and the others.

The helicopter rose, then slipped forward and down, ramming its skids toward some of the International Jihad.

Hughes tossed another pipe bomb—Cross hoped it was fake, like the last ones. He grabbed Irania as the helicopter landed and dragged her from the fighting, forcing her aboard. He ran back for Mara, Uncle Shapur, and the others. Shapur was already coming, and Mara dragged a wounded man. Cross hauled the man up, flung him over his shoulder and limped back to the chopper, his left leg feeling as if it were afire.

Hughes was backing toward them—the clouds of sparks and smoke from the fake pipe bomb had fizzled, and the Jihad fighters were starting to close in again. Cross pushed the wounded man inside and turned back to the fighting. Hughes ran for the machine, throwing himself aboard. Cross half fell inside and began firing through the fuselage door as more of the People's Mujahedin clambered aboard, others holding tight to the fuselage and balancing on the skids.

"Can we get airborne?" Hughes shouted forward.

"I'm trying! Hold on!" The helicopter rose painfully slowly, almost skating over the ground but starting to gain altitude amid a rain of harassing fire.

There was a radical change in pitch, the machine dropping then suddenly rising over the battlefield. More fire came from below them, and one of the Mujahedin fighters fell away from the skids, shot.

Babcock was aiming the chopper toward a nearly flat rise a quarter mile across the valley. Cross checked over Babcock's shoulder. The fuel gauge read full.

They were nearing the rise, Babcock saying, "I can't trust a landing with this weight. When I'm close enough to the ground, get the ones on the skids to jump clear and get outa there!"

"Right," Cross replied, and fought his way back through the overloaded fuselage, toward the open door. "Irania—you tell them so they're sure to understand—when we give them the signal, they should jump clear and disperse so Babcock can land. Got it?''

"Yes. You are wounded. You—"

"I'm all right. Tell them! Do it now!'' He ripped away his face mask.

Irania shouted over the roar of the slipstream, over the hum of frightened Mujahedin voices.

The helicopter was nearing the rise now, Cross watching Babcock for a signal. The chopper drifted toward the flat surface there, then hovered, and Babcock signaled with his left arm.

"Now!"

Irania shouted orders in Farsi, Hughes covering from the doorway. The Mujahedin were jumping clear, running or crawling away from beneath the chopper, the skids clear now.

Cross shouted forward, "You're clear. Are you still too heavy?"

"Brace yourselves!'' Irania repeated the command in Farsi, Cross holding her tight against him, shielding her with his body.

The helicopter lurched violently, slipped to one side and touched down.

Hurriedly, Hughes began evacuation of the chopper, Cross climbing out, Irania beside him. The wind of the rotor blades beat down on them; Cross held her in his arms as the rest of the Mujahedin evacuated. "You have wounds—let me care for them.''

"You have people on the field. If I can come back, I will. But if I can't—I love you and I always will.'' Cross drew her close to him, his arms folding around her, his mouth crushing down on hers.

He turned away and jumped aboard the chopper, looking out the open door as Babcock took the helicopter airborne. He could see that she was calling something to him as she stood there, waving. Cross told himself she was repeating what he'd said to her.

He looked away as her image on the hilltop became so small in the distance that he could no longer see her.

There was a cold feeling inside him, like fear, but worse than any fear he had ever felt.

Then Hughes was beside him, handing him one of the submachine guns. "If our mission was betrayed—and I think it was—then I know why. I can't blame them for doing it. Once Raka learns what we've done here, if he hasn't killed all the hostages and blown up the embassy already, he will now."

Cross looked through the open doorway toward the hillside, feeling it as Babcock began to bank, setting up for another run over the battlefield. "We've got something to do, haven't we? If we can."

Hughes nodded, taking up a position on the opposite side of the doorway from Cross. "I know the embassy in Jerusalem," he said. "We know Raka has few people there; even if he didn't lose a single one during his takeover, he can't have more than two or three people on the roof. Patrakas is keeping some reserve supplies for us. More ammo. Medical supplies. He also has parachutes. High altitude, low opening—we could do it—look out!"

Hughes opened fire as the helicopter swept over the battlefield, Cross opening fire as well, burning out one magazine, replacing it with a fresh one, still firing, Hughes doing the same.

The greatest concentration of International Jihad fighters was starting to disperse. Hughes was firing one of the G-3's now, Cross using the last of his G-3 magazines with the second of the two remaining assault rifles. The Mujahedin fighters below were closing with the enemy.

Babcock finished the pass, shouting back as he banked, "Another pass?"

Hughes, his face mask gone now, looked at Cross. "Well, lad? It's your decision. Do we stay or go?"

Cross told him, "We go."

"Lewis. We're heading for Turkey—as fast as you can!"

Cross looked forward, saw Babcock make a thumbs-up signal. Then he looked through the open doorway. But he could no longer see the hilltop where Irania would still be standing.

He slid the door closed and stayed beside it in the darkness, thinking about Irania and her people. They were the same race as Raka, the same religion, observed the same customs.

But somewhere, somehow, the ways in which they expressed their humanity went in two vastly divergent directions—one group trying to preserve their world by letting it grow, the other group, dragging their people into an age of darkness, bent on destroying the rest of humanity.

# Chapter Fifty-six

When the radio signal had come, Raka paused and prayed for guidance as he was taught to do five times daily.

He stood alone now in the blasted through entryway to the corridor that traversed the front of the embassy.

He would kill them all, but hold out until the very last, in the event of somehow making his demands felt.

He had heightened security on the roof of the embassy, four of his Immortals there, and he'd ordered all of the hostages bound and gagged; only Ibrahim and Riva were watching them now.

Jamal was in the embassy communications center, and the remaining eight Immortals had positioned themselves at strategic windows around the building, and by the main entrance. He had dismissed the two men here to find themselves food and beverage.

Raka held the Uzi in his fist, tensioned against its sling. He would soon know death. He had never feared it.

In Paradise all would be as it should be. Raka had long thought that man's destiny here on earth was to mold earth into an imperfect replica of Paradise, imperfect because man could not attain the perfection of God.

When he reached Paradise, Raka knew, he would at last see a world where the unbelievers had been vanquished, where evil had forever been destroyed. But he was a realist—

much hard fighting lay ahead until there would be triumph, and many of the faithful would sacrifice their lives.

But, as he always had since his youth, he held firm in his resolve that no sacrifice was too great.

The wisdom of the Koran filled him:

> O Prophet, God suffices thee, and the believers
>              who follow thee.
> O Prophet, urge on the believers to fight.
>      If there be twenty of you, patient men,
> they will overcome two hundred; if there be
>      a hundred of you, they will overcome
> a thousand unbelievers, for they are a people
>              who understand not.

Muhammad Ibn al Raka understood.

# Chapter Fifty-seven

Patrakos's chauffeur sat quietly in the corner as Patrakos smoked a cigarette.

Jeff Feinberg stood peering through the plexiglass window, periodically smudging steam away from it. The cold had served to intensify the discomfort of his arm, so that it was too painful for him to stay outside.

Patrakos said, "The men who exposed your operation—it is apparent there was good reason. You should not be filled with bitterness."

"How the hell are we supposed to do what has to be done, Mr. Patrakos?" And Feinberg turned away from the window and looked at the old man. "Those Moslems don't know anything but kill and—"

The chauffeur spoke. It was the first time Feinberg had heard him. "I am a Sunni Moslem. I am not fond of Jews. But I do not kill them. Sometimes I care little for what the Americans do. But neither do I kill them. You are not fighting a Holy War. Among the Shiites there are those who feel that they fight a Holy War. Would you be like them?"

The chauffeur looked away and fell silent.

Feinberg licked his lips.

Patrakos smiled. "I can still get you and your friends out of Turkey and to safety—despite the fact the Turkish government has been ordered to place them under arrest, confiscate all weapons and documents. So do not be afraid, Mr. Feinberg.''

Feinberg wanted to tell him that it wasn't fear that made him tremble, but anger.

"Darwin Hughes is a very clever man, as are Mr. Cross and Mr. Babcock. We use this base because of the cleverness of Darwin Hughes. The Turkish military will be waiting seventy-five kilometers to the north. So, if our friends have survived, they will return to safety here, and there will be ample time for them to flee before the Turkish army can arrive and place them under arrest. There are many places in the world where such men as yourselves can seek refuge. Why not pray that they live, and save your bitterness until there is reason for it?''

Feinberg looked away from him.

The chauffeur had preached to him. The smuggler had preached to him. He was tired of it all. If they were such wonderful men, why hadn't they gone with Hughes, Cross, and Babcock? He wanted to ask them that. If they knew so much—

The radio crackled, the one tuned to the preagreed frequency. "This is Romeo, calling Juliet. Over.''

Feinberg tripped over the chair as he reached for the microphone, saying into it as he depressed the button, "Romeo, this is Juliet reading you loud and clear. Over.''

"Juliet, this is Romeo. Is Daddy home? I say again, Is Daddy home? Over.''

"Romeo, this is Juliet,'' Feinberg said, realizing he was breathing so hard it was affecting his voice. "Daddy is not home. I say again, Daddy is not home.'' He felt his cheeks flush as he recited the code phrase, then, "Come and give me a big kiss, over.''

The radio crackled, then, "Juliet. Can't wait. Romeo out.''

Feinberg put down the microphone and started to laugh so hard that tears welled up in his eyes.

Lewis Babcock's face looked gray under the black.

"You all right?'' Cross asked him, sitting at the copilot's controls. They had, all three of them, taken turns treating each other's wounds. Babcock had been laced twice across the right ribcage with flesh wounds, and there was a possibility of cracked ribs, but he didn't complain of pain.

"I'm fine, just tired, that's all," Babcock said, and fell silent again.

Hughes's left arm had several deep cuts along the outside of the forearm, Hughes saying only that he had zigged when he should have zagged. There was a cut that looked as though it were made by a bullet along the right side of his neck below his ear, but Hughes had simply labeled it an accident. It wasn't deep, but the cuts on the left forearm were. At the moment, however, they seemed to impair the older man little.

Cross had taken a pistol bullet in his left thigh, and Hughes had dug it out, commenting only that it was a 9mm and apparently had deflected off some hard object before striking him, judging from the deformation of the full-metal slug and the fact that it hadn't had sufficient steam remaining to penetrate and exit the other side of his leg. Cross's right shoulder, just where it met the base of his neck, had been heavily gouged by something, although Hughes couldn't tell what from the wound. Cross honestly could not remember.

Babcock changed rotor pitch and broke through the low cloudbank, Cross seeing the plateau on which the Beechcraft had landed—how many days ago? he asked himself, too tired to bother counting. It was nearly dark here, but he could make out the hut and the Beechcraft waiting for them.

He thought about Feinberg. The kid would forever think he had missed the adventure of a lifetime.

The thought chilled him. He'd realized years before that there were some men who lived for the moments they spent on the edge between life and death. Perhaps heroes were like that, he had once thought. But as the years had gone by, he discovered that the heroes were perhaps the men who hated violence, the men who didn't choose to look for glory at all, who just did what they had to do. And Abe Cross had also realized that he was neither of these. But he hadn't yet decided where that left him.

"I'm takin' her down," Babcock announced. Cross had considered that obvious, but this was Babcock's moment. He studied Babcock's face. There was a strength in it. Humor. Intelligence enough for two men.

Sitting against the bulkhead with his head back was Darwin Hughes. Cross studied the older man's face as well. There was something in Hughes that he'd never seen in any other man, and sometimes it reassured him, sometimes it almost frightened him.

If it weren't for Hughes, he would have sunk deeper into his alcoholism, into his death wish. He owed the man his life.

And when this was all over, he wondered, would he be able to keep the strength this man had given him?

The helicopter came in for the landing.

Hughes had taken a lump of plastique out of the reserve explosives and gone back into the hut; Cross, Babcock and Patrakos's chauffeur were packing out the last of the gear—radios, weapons, ammunition, medical and food supplies—to the aircraft.

Patrakos had joined Hughes, Feinberg remaining in the hut.

"What do you think Feinberg's talking about?" Babcock said. "He's got to have his chance?"

Cross threw the duffel bag full of medical supplies into the cargo hold. "I don't know. He wants to come with us. I guess."

"To do what? Die? With that arm," Babcock said, "he couldn't bail out with us. And I don't think he could fly a plane too well either. He's better off staying here with Patrakos, and his chauffeur, and the pilot."

Cross shrugged, lighting a cigarette. This had been the last of the stuff, and he stayed beside the fuselage to stay out of the wind that gusted along the plateau from the mountains above. "That was interesting. Patrakos volunteering—and his chauffeur. A Moslem. Fascinating. He was going to risk his life to help us."

Babcock stuffed his hands into the pockets of his jacket—jackets had been waiting for them when they had arrived, as well as warm coffee and warm food. They had eaten quickly, discarding all that was of no future use and leaving it in the hut which Hughes was about to explode.

Babcock said, "From the start—I don't mean of this, but with the flare-up of terrorism in the Middle East—the one thing that has always worried me most is that people are going to think of the word Moslem as being synonymous with terrorist. Maybe it helps to be black to see it that way—when you start labeling people as one thing or another, it's scary stuff.''

Cross nodded. ''Amen to that,'' he said, exhaling.

Hughes, Feinberg, and Patrakos exited the hut, the pilot with them.

Hughes was looking at his watch. As he neared them, pulling up the hood of his parka against the wind, he announced, ''The building goes up in ten minutes. The Turkish army shouldn't be here for at least twenty minutes. Wouldn't want anyone getting injured.''

Cross didn't say anything. Neither did Babcock.

''Feinberg's flying the plane. Spiros will tell the authorities that he picked up a distress signal from a landed helicopter and set down here. Then his Beechcraft was hijacked and he and his two men were left here. They drained the gas tank on the helicopter, so Spiros was stuck here. What the hijackers wanted or where they went—God only knows.'' Hughes smiled.

''They won't believe that,'' Babcock said, stating the obvious.

Cross smiled. ''Won't be able to prove it's a lie, either, though. What about Muli's trick attaché case?'' Cross jerked his thumb toward the Moslem chauffeur.

''The hijackers overpowered us too quickly, and my chauffeur and bodyguard,'' Patrakos smiled, ''decided that since our lives were not apparently endangered, that shooting might be more harmful than good.''

''Gosh.'' Cross laughed. ''Sounds convincing as hell to me.''

Feinberg started for the plane, Cross noticing that his injured arm was out of its sling. Cross just closed his eyes.

Babcock and Feinberg had copilot's and pilot's controls; Cross and Hughes were sitting toward the center of the aircraft, loading magazines for the submachine guns from the supply of spare ammo. The rifles had been left behind in the hut, to be destroyed along with the supply of reserve ammo for them; they were useless for the embassy assault because of problems with overpenetration of the 7.62mm projectiles through walls and their size-hampering maneuverability. But the LAW-12 shotgun, despite its size, had come along. The pistols were already reloaded, Cross having to rely solely on the Beretta since losing his revolver.

Patrakos had cleared an air corridor for them through Syria and into Jordan, and they had crossed out of Turkish air space some fifteen minutes ago.

Cross lit a cigarette.

Hughes said, "You think I did the wrong thing taking Feinberg?"

"Yeah. But you're in charge again. He's a flake. A nice guy, but a flake."

The corners of Hughes's mouth turned down as he finished one of the magazines and started working on another. They had only lost one of the originals taken with them and replaced that from the reserve supplies. "Every man needs his chance, lad. You did." Hughes's eyebrows cocked and he smiled. "Give me a cigarette."

Cross gave him one and said nothing else.

# Chapter Fifty-eight

He had executed seven prisoners, and at last the Great Satan seemed to be acceding to his demands. There was a certain relief, a lightening of spirit. Then one of the Immortals had called him to the television sets that had been brought into the grand salon where Ibrahim and Riva kept watch over the bound and gagged hostages. The room smelled of human waste and fear.

Raka sat squat-legged on the floor before the eighteen television sets, instructed that Riva tune them all to the same station and turn the volume to full capacity.

"What western diplomatic sources in Tehran are labeling a natural disaster of incredible magnitude has been reported in the Elburz Mountain region of northeastern Iran today. While Iranian officials refused comment, anonymous diplomatic sources confirmed that Iranian civil defense officials attribute the explosions that rocked Mount Dizan at dawn today, Tehran time, as caused by pockets of volatile natural volcanic gases. A representative of the American Society of Geophysical Chemists denounced the possibility that an explosion of such apparent magnitude would be the result of natural causes.

"Medical personnel from throughout Iran are being airlifted into the area near the disaster by army helicop-

ters, informed sources indicate, but there is some specu-
lation that secondary explosions may still occur.

"We repeat. At dawn Tehran time today—"

Raka stood up and walked away from the television set,
picked up his Uzi and turned toward the bound and gagged
hostages. He ordered that Riva lower the volume of the
television sets.

"That is my home, which your minions of the Great Satan
have destroyed. The best hope of Islam lies dead."

He handed his submachine gun to the woman, Riva. He
drew his knife.

Raka grabbed the face of a Marine, the last remaining. His
left hand like a claw, Raka's fingers gouging into the Marine's eyes, his right hand drawing the knife from its sheath at
his hip. He slashed open the throat. "The best and brightest
of Islam are dead." A woman near him was choking as vomit
oozed from the corners of her mouth, around the gag she
wore. Raka flicked his wrist and the primary edge of his knife
opened her throat. Her body spasmed, then fell back.

To one of the Syrian delegates Raka said, "You, a Moslem—
you deserve death." He grabbed a handful of the man's hair,
raking the blade across the exposed throat, letting the body
fall away.

He approached one of the Jews. "You defile the world."
He slapped the man backhand across the nose, the nose
breaking, blood spouting from the nostrils. Raka slashed open
the throat.

The body fell.

Raka stood beside it. "You will all die. This building, this
temple to the Great Satan will be vaporized."

He turned and started from the grand salon, shouting to
Ibrahim, "Prepare, brother!"

# Chapter Fifty-nine

"I buried the documents. Your notebook too. If all goes well, the documents will be retrieved and smuggled out of Turkey," Hughes said, zipping into his battle vest.

Cross's shoulder was stiff, his leg as well. He'd worry over all of that later, if there was a later.

"I intend to find three things when I get back—if I get back." Babcock laughed. "A pretty lady, a good chess partner, and a nice quiet place to relax. Four things—I've got the funniest taste for a pizza. Almost a craving."

"Maybe you're pregnant," Cross suggested, zipping his battle vest, then proceeding to check the Beretta at his hip.

"I doubt it, really," Babcock said seriously, then laughed.

Hughes walked forward along the main cabin, picking up the parachute harness, starting into it. "We play this by ear. I've done more jumps than either of you, so try to keep an eye on me, and when I pull the ripcord, you do it too."

"Gee—that's sounds neat," Cross told him.

"Hmm." Hughes nodded.

Feinberg's voice came over the intercom. "We just had a radio message from the Israeli air force. They aren't happy to see us. I even told them I was Jewish. I think we got trouble, guys."

Cross looked to the nearest window—about a quarter mile off he could see three fighter aircraft. "Wonderful."

Babcock was beside him. "Well, we could always tell

them I'm aboard, and if they shoot us down, they'll have the ACLU on their tails," he suggested.

"Why don't you go forward and ask Jeff if you can borrow the radio a second and tell them that—I betchya they'd really be interested."

Babcock grinned. "I just might."

Cross lit a cigarette.

Feinberg's voice came back. "They say that we have exactly sixty seconds before they open fire."

Hughes, his parachute already in place, started forward.

"I've gotta hear this," Babcock said. Cross clapped him on the shoulder, and they both followed Hughes forward.

Hughes took the radio mike. "Squadron of Israel—this is Brigadier General Martin Fife of the United States Army. I am entering your air space on a top-secret mission that is a joint project of the United States government and the government of Israel. This is cabinet level. You must consult with the prime minister. We will continue our same flight path and take no offensive or defensive action until you have done so. But please hurry. The security of the State of Israel may hang in the balance. Brigadier General Fife out."

"You've got a lot of crust, Mr. Hughes."

"Thank you, Mr. Babcock." Hughes put down the microphone. "Jeff—how far to go? In terms of time."

"About five minutes until we hit the edge of Jerusalem."

"Who's General Fife?" Cross asked.

"The SOB that sold out the operation, I'm betting. He could use the publicity," Hughes answered offhandedly.

Babcock was already starting into his parachute, Cross doing the same, Hughes leaving the cockpit as well, securing his submachine gun. "Teach you lads a trick. In a landing like this you want your weapon instantly ready but you don't want some unexpected impact to put you out of business with your own gun. Now, what I do—it's probably unnecessary—is carry the weapons I jump with safety on and chamber empty. It won't take more than a couple tenths of a second to correct that condition on the ground. Just a suggestion."

Cross shrugged, buckling on his pistol belt, unholstering the Beretta and clearing the chamber, pocketing the loose round. He hadn't yet loaded a round into the H-K's chamber.

There was no drop case for the LAW-12, but earlier Cross had assisted Babcock in making one out of pieces of seat cushion.

The sixty seconds were up and then some, but so far they hadn't been shot out of the sky. Cross announced, "Three minutes to the edge of the city and then we jump on my command—I'm playing this by ear."

Feinberg's voice came over the speakers. "I'm in radio contact with the leader of the Israeli pursuit squadron. He wants to talk with General Fife again."

Hughes, about to don his hood, smiled broadly. "Excuse me gentlemen—my public calls." He started forward, Cross following him. Babcock was still tending his gear.

Hughes took the microphone, leaning over the empty copilot's seat. "This is Brigadier General Martin Fife. Come in, squadron commander. Over."

The voice of the Israeli commander was not audible except as a series of rasping, unintelligible whispers through the headset Hughes held beside his left ear.

Hughes spoke again. "This is General Fife. We'll be most happy to accompany you to the airport, squadron leader. Relay instructions to my pilot. General Fife out." He dropped the headset into the empty seat as Feinberg identified himself. Hughes waited between the two seats, Cross looking past him, watching the Israeli fighters as they changed formation, flanking the Beechcraft now.

Feinberg switched off, Cross working over a map. "Jeff—when they reach this point, tell them you're having trouble with your starboard engine and start banking to port. Drop to thirty thousand feet and keep feathering the prop. As you bank to port, you should see the lights of the city. Then give me the controls. I've flown over Jerusalem on a few occasions and I can recognize the terrain features I want. There'll be lights all around the embassy, like a Christmas tree, almost. I'll set the course, and you have to keep it until we bail out. Then fall back into formation, telling them your engine trouble has resolved itself. We'll need about forty-five seconds. Cross—tell Babcock we're killing the cabin lights. That's so they don't see us opening the door for the jump."

Cross turned back into the main cabin and relayed Hughes's instructions, Babcock nodding back.

Hughes, uncomfortable-looking in full gear behind the co-pilot's yoke, was studying the map.

Cross looked at his wristwatch.

"Now, Jeff," Hughes announced.

Feinberg cut the fuel supply to the starboard engine and the aircraft suddenly dropped. Cross felt a sinking sensation in the pit of his stomach.

Feinberg was saying into the headset, "Squadron leader, this is the pilot of General Fife's aircraft, Beechcraft King Air-N-Four-Two-K-Four-Niner. Experiencing starboard engine fuel-line problem and shutting down. Dropping to thirty thousand feet and changing heading to avoid wind shear we are experiencing. I will keep you informed. Out."

He released the yoke, Hughes changing course slightly. The Israeli squadron leader's voice could be heard over the earphones, the words not intelligible now. Hughes wore no headset. "Tell Lewis to get ready—both of you lads start working on the door. Hurry!"

Cross started back through the darkened cabin, peering through one of the windows, seeing the Israeli fighters closing in, Babcock on the portside saying, "They're changing formation. They could be ready to shoot us down."

"That's it—think positive," Cross agreed, joining Babcock, starting to work on the door. Cross pulled on his face mask and then pulled down the oxygen mask from the overhead, prepared for depressurization.

They were ready to open the door.

Hughes' voice came over the speakers. "Depressurizing on five: one—two—three—four—five!"

The aircraft had been steadily dropping altitude. Cross felt the rush of air in his mask, holding it before his face, then regulating his breathing. Hughes's voice came again. "Now the door, lads."

Cross let the mask swing away, took a deep breath. Babcock was beside him, working the door open, the rush of icy wind buffeting them, Cross grabbing for the mask, inhaling. And then there was a screeching whistle, high-pitched, like nothing he'd ever heard before, yet terrifyingly familiar.

The Beechcraft rocked. The cabin began filling with smoke. Babcock dropped his mask for an instant. "Machine guns! Shit!"

Hughes's voice came again, but this time the speakers filled with static. "They opened fire. Be ready to bail out."

Cross started a final, quick equipment check.

Hughes climbed from the copilot's seat. There was another burst of machine-gun fire, the instrument panel starting to spark, but no hits this time. "Jeff, there's an extra chute back there—come on. I'll help you!"

"What the fuck's wrong with that pilot, Mr. Hughes? That's a city below us." Feinberg shouted into the radio headset, "Squadron leader—what the hell are you doing?"

There was no answer, Hughes pushing back the curtain, smoke thick now as he held the oxygen mask to his face. He threw down his headset. The squadron leader had screwed up, he realized.

Then he heard the leader's voice: "This is fighter squadron leader. An error in a targeting computer has resulted in what were intended as warning shots hitting the starboard engine of your aircraft. Please report your situation. Over."

Feinberg shouted at him. "You asshole, I'm crashing over a populated area. Over."

The squadron leader's voice came back after a split-second's hesitation. "Beechcraft, we can escort you down. Are you capable of maneuvering? Over."

Feinberg looked up from the controls, his headset pulled off. "I'm losing fuel. They hit more than the starboard engine."

Hughes looked over his shoulder. What instruments were still reading weren't looking good. The aircraft was losing altitude at an alarming rate. In less than a minute, Hughes judged, they would be unable to do the controlled drop. Ahead he saw the lights he'd been looking for. Hughes closed his eyes and leaned against the seat back. "Jeff, the embassy is there, straight ahead. But there's no place to land."

Feinberg looked at him, sweat glistening on his forehead in the yellow wash of the cockpit dome light. "You're saying—"

"I'm saying I'll take it in. You bail out with Abe and Lewis. I've done it all, anyway."

"Ride it down?"

They were running out of time.

"I can ride it down into the desert beyond the city. It'll be all right."

Feinberg glanced forward. "You're running out of time, Mr. Hughes. Look, ah, I can't do shit down there with my arm. It's killin' me to work the controls on the aircraft."

Hughes had noticed.

"Look, ah, my mom—she always said that to be buried in Israel would be—"

"I'll ride it down."

"You taught me something while I was waiting for you guys—I didn't realize it until now. But the important thing isn't how we feel, but getting the job done—ya know, Mr. Hughes? This is somethin' I can do. And you got somethin' you can do. You're running outa time, Mr. Hughes."

"I've been doing this shit all of my life. And I've never met a braver man." Darwin Hughes leaned over the boy and embraced him.

Cross stood beside the door, Babcock flanking it on the other side. There was no need for oxygen now. Hughes was coming toward them. Cross could see him in the light of his little flashlight. "Where's Feinberg?" Cross asked.

"Somebody has to stay with the plane. There are people down there, houses, hospitals— Shut the hell up," Hughes barely whispered, his voice sounding hard-edged and tight.

Then Hughes stepped into the doorway. "Ready! Now!" he shouted, and jumped.

Babcock waited a few seconds, then jumped.

Cross looked forward along the cabin toward the cockpit. The smoke had dissipated, but the cabin wiring was sparking and bright yellow flames were visible on the starboard wing, the aircraft shuddering around him. He had wondered before about heroes. "God bless you, Jeff," Cross whispered toward the cockpit, then dove into the night. He'd wondered about heroes—now he could say he had known one.

The rush of air around him was like a howl, Cross twisting

his body into an aerodynamically stable position, arms and legs spread-eagled, his eyes searching the night for some sign of Hughes or Babcock, his mind racing, panic gripping him. Trying to correct his descent path, he alternated his concentration between the altimeter on his chest pack and the ring of searchlights surrounding what he hoped was the American embassy.

Feinberg—he would be alone now, trying to keep as much altitude as he could as he searched the night for the desert. He'd try to bring it in low if he had enough fuel to keep control. If he ran out of fuel, he'd try to glide it in. The richer the oxygen, the lower he flew, the worse the fire.

The ring of lights was nearing now. He watched the altimeter, no sign of Babcock or Hughes yet. His hand tightened on the rip-cord handle. The altimeter hit the magic number and Cross ripped, the sudden shock of the opening shroud snapping his body into an upright position, his injured right shoulder aching with it.

He started working his risers, manipulating the cells to drag him closer to the embassy. The glare of the searchlights surrounding the compound was blindingly bright below him and to the north. He reached over the slider, tugging now at the guidelines themselves, his body jerking, lurching, his drift increasing slightly.

The roof Hughes had spoken of—Cross could see it, men in defensive positions there, one at each corner of the rectangle.

Thanks to Hughes's safety tip, though it was only standard practice, neither of his weapons had a round chambered. He was almost gliding in now, the man at the near end of the roof line not noticing him yet.

Fifteen feet from the roof line now . . . ten, and his height over the roof perhaps twelve feet. If this had been a movie, he thought fleetingly, he could have worked the quick release and fallen on the guy, then grabbed his weapon and sprayed the other three.

It wasn't.

Five feet—Cross tucked his legs up, readying for impact, the roof rushing up to meet him as he crossed over its edge. He hit the quick release, his body twisting violently as he hit the roof and rolled, the chute billowing along the roof.

To his knees. His only option was the Beretta. He tore it from the Bianchi holster at his hip, his other hand slapping back the slide as the man at the corner of the roof raised his Uzi to fire. Cross fired first, emptying the Beretta into the man's chest and abdomen, the Uzi spraying into the night sky.

Cross was up, ramming the empty Beretta into his belt, unlimbering the H-K submachine gun, racking the action as he dove for cover beside the body of the dead man, the only thing to take cover behind. Submachine-gun fire hit all around him from the three other corners of the roof. He saw a small hutlike affair perhaps fifteen yards away. It matched Hughes's description of the entryway down into the building. Tucked down behind the dead man, Cross rolled onto his back, submachine-gun fire ripping chunks out of the cinderlike material that comprised the roof.

Cross tore away his goggles. He dumped the empty magazine for the Beretta and took one of the two loaded twenties, ramming it up the well, the extension magazine hanging well below the butt. The Beretta in one hand, the H-K sub gun in the other, Cross opened fire, hosing the weapons back and forth along the roof from side to side. He got to his feet and ran, the enemy fire stilled for an instant, then opening up again as he neared the little hut that had been his target. Something hammered into him and he fell forward, skidding along the roof surface, the back of his hand starting to bleed again. The wind knocked out of him, he pulled himself up and lurched into cover behind the little hut, his breathing coming in gasps now. He stood up, leaning against the gray surface of the hut's south exterior wall. He edged along it, looking back. The wall was bloodstreaked where he'd rubbed against it.

It felt as though a sharp knife had slashed across his shoulder blades. He twisted his left arm behind him, his left glove coming back bloodied. "Fuckin' wonderful," he hissed.

He reloaded the Beretta and did the same for the partially spent H-K, stuffing three still useful H-K magazines into his belt.

Cross edged forward, hoping the door would be unlocked and that he could reach it. Sub-gun fire came at him again, chunks ripping out of the wall surface. He threw himself around the corner, reaching for the door handle, wrenching it toward him—it didn't open. "Damn!" Then he thought to push, and half fell through the opening and inside, where he found himself on his knees and in shadow.

Raka would be killing hostages.

Cross got to his feet, the mini flashlight in his left hand, the Beretta in his belt. He held the flashlight high, his arm at maximum extension as he started down the stairs immediately before him. He moved as fast as he could, because the three men on the roof would be coming after him.

Darwin Hughes had landed by the far wall in what judgment and past experience told him was a dead zone for any guards at the front or rear of the building. A moment after he'd gotten out of the parachute harness and started toward the near wall of the embassy structure, he had started hearing submachine-gun fire from the roof.

He kept low, the H-K submachine gun in both fists as he moved beneath the window line, pencil-thin lines of light visible between the drape halves. He kept moving, nearing the front of the embassy. There would have to be a man here, perhaps two. Raka's Immortals.

Hughes peered over a low railing at a small patio. French doors were visible at its far end, the doors flanked by windows. He crossed the patio and flattened himself against the wall nearest the window on his left. He dropped to knees and elbows and crawled beneath it, then rose to his full height as he came beside the French doors.

There was no rock handy. He reached to his battle vest, and rather than ripping a grenade free, took the Swiss army knife from his pocket, folding out the primary blade and using it to cut the plastic that anchored the grenade to the D-ring.

Leaving the pin in, he reclosed the small knife, dropped it in his BDU pants, then flicked the grenade through the window beside him, glass shattering like a series of shrieks in the night. Hughes took a step back, kicked the juncture of the two glass doors, then hurtled through in a roll.

Submachine-gun fire ripped into the wall beside Hughes's

head, and he fired toward the flash, rolled, fired again. There was no answering fire in the darkness, which was punctuated only by streaks of gray light from the searchlights beyond the walls.

He was to his feet, running.

Lewis Babcock had entered by a window at the rear of the building, counting himself lucky that as yet he was undetected. It had been a small conference room in total darkness; he'd been afraid to use his flashlight lest he betray his presence, but had worked his way around a small round table and toward the door. Opening the door onto a dimly lit back hall, he'd detected no one, then started along the hall.

At the end of the hall now, he stopped. Another hall split right and left. To the left, toward the front of the building, there were several oak-paneled swinging doors. He thought back to Hughes's description of the embassy. These could be the anterooms surrounding the grand salon, where most certainly the hostages were being held.

He started into the hallway, then froze as a scream—a woman's scream—came from the direction of the anterooms. His sub gun at high port, hugging the corridor wall, he ran toward the now-muffled sound.

Cross reached the base of the steps, light visible here between the door and the doorframe. There was no time; he could hear running feet on the steps behind him.

He threw open the door, backing off from it, gunfire coming down the stairwell toward him now. Cross fired up into the dark toward the muzzle flashes, then dove through the open doorway.

A man was running along the hallway. Cross fired the H-K toward him, the man's body rocking with the hits, slamming against the corridor wall.

After firing up the stairwell again, Cross ran to the man he'd just shot, grabbed the Uzi from his limp hands, and ran on. Nearing the end of the corridor, he paused to orient himself, then veered to the right. A small corridor lined with offices opened before him. He skidded on his boot heels, stopped and listened, hearing running feet behind him.

Cross twisted the knob of the dark office door nearest him, slipping through and closing it, the Uzi in one hand, the H-K in the other, his ear to the door.

He could hear the running feet getting louder, crescendoing, dropping. Cross stepped through the doorway and into the light of the corridor, the three men from the roof starting to turn toward him, to fire. But Cross fired first, emptying the Uzi into them.

He grabbed up their weapons, slinging two of the Uzis behind his shoulder, dropping the shot out one from his left hand, taking the third one from the other dead man. He started running again, the corridor ending at what had to be the main hallway.

He could hear gunfire now, and he started running toward the sound. He could see Hughes at the opposite end of the corridor, running, a man and a woman from near the main entrance dodging into the hallway and firing, Hughes throwing himself into a doorway.

Cross slowed his pace, at least two good bursts left in the H-K, the Uzi partially loaded as well.

Hughes returned fire toward the entryway. It looked as though a truck had slammed into the entrance and exploded. It probably wasn't far from the truth.

Two good bursts weren't enough. He changed sticks for the H-K, ramming the partially spent magazine into his belt beside the Beretta and the other partial magazine.

He kept walking, loading a fresh magazine into the H-K, then letting it fall to his side on its sling. He took one of the other Uzis, which felt half loaded, like the one in his other hand.

He would pass the grand salon before reaching the entrance.

And the hostages would be there. There was no sign of Babcock yet, but he'd worry over his friend later.

He stopped to the side of the grand salon, the doors closed, gunfire from inside. There was a scream, then a gruesome silence.

The man and woman by the entrance stepped out to spray along the hallway toward Hughes's position. Cross leveled both Uzis in his fists and sprayed, both bodies seeming to dance as they took the slugs, sprawling onto the hallway floor.

There was no time now. Cross wheeled toward the double doors, throwing the fired-out Uzis right and left, grabbing up the last Uzi from behind his shoulder, his other fist fingering the butt of the H-K submachine gun. He fired the Uzi into the locking mechanism of the doors, threw the gun down and kicked his combat-booted foot against the joint of the doors, then threw himself right. Submachine-gun fire ripped through the doors as they burst inward.

Cross hugged the wall beside the doors, gunfire pouring into the hallway now. He could see Hughes turning off down a side corridor on the far side of the salon.

Joseph Goldman gave the order. "Yuri, tell your men to attack. Something's going on in there."

Markovski looked at him, Goldman's face part in shadow and part in light behind the ring of searchlights. "When we lose our jobs, we can play cards together."

"A wonderful idea." Goldman nodded, drawing the Walther P-5 9mm from beneath his jacket.

Markovski took up his field telephone, saying into it, "This is Joshua. I repeat, this is Joshua. The trumpets have sounded. I repeat. Trumpets have sounded. Go! Go!"

Markovski started for the car, Goldman climbing in after him, the Mercedes starting for the main gates. A helicopter was lifting off from the street behind the row of shops; it had been driven into the area partially disassembled so it would not have to be flown in, then was reassembled. Flak-vested men bristling with weapons hung from its skids. The helicopter came in low over the embassy wall, rappeling lines snaking out and as it was over the roof, men skidding down along the lines, submachine guns at the ready.

The Mercedes was following a special armored vehicle designed for barricade penetration. It rammed through the wall, avoiding the driveway that had been blocked by an American Cadillac. Goldman had theorized, Markovski agreeing, that it would be booby-trapped.

Goldman ducked down, chunks of brick and metal raining

down on the Mercedes in the wake of the armored car's progress.

Abe Cross stood by the doorway, waiting. He didn't know for what.

Then he heard a voice, the English beautifully spoken, slightly accented.

"Come in—see your handiwork, minion of the Great Satan!"

Cross licked his lips. His face was pouring sweat beneath the mask.

It would buy time for whatever Hughes was doing along the hallway on the opposite side of the grand salon. And maybe for Babcock, if he'd ever gotten in.

Cross shouted back, "I'm coming in."

The earplugs. He slipped them into his ears beneath the head covering.

He had a sudden urge to urinate, but didn't. He stepped into the open doorway.

Bodies lay everywhere. Blood spattered the salon floor.

A knot of men and women, hands bound, gags in their mouths, were clustered at the center of the room.

Seven men with Uzi submachine guns ringed the hostages, but the guns were pointed at Cross. An eighth man, his Uzi slung casually at his side, stood between Cross and the hostages. It was Muhammad Ibn al Raka. "I invited all of you to watch."

Cross saw harnesses with explosives attached to them secured to some of the hostages. "Well, the other guys were busy, ya know. You know how that is. So, what's happening?"

Raka laughed, howled with laughter, doubling forward with it.

And then suddenly the laughter stopped.

Cross said to him, "Wait'll I tell ya the one about why the chicken crossed the road— you'll eat it up, man."

There was the sound of a helicopter somewhere near the building. Cross thought he heard the screech of brakes.

Raka's voice was low. He said, "All of these people will die, because of you."

"So long as you're the first," Cross told him.

The thing was played out. If Hughes were coming with the cavalry—

Cross heard the sound of a door being kicked open and he threw himself toward Raka. Raka's sub gun rose as Cross's shoulder hit his chest. There was a screech, loud even with the earplugs in place, a light blindingly bright, even with his eyes shut as their bodies hit the floor together.

Meanwhile Cross counted seconds, then opened his eyes and rolled away. Babcock—he saw him at the edge of his peripheral vision, coming through on the opposite side of the salon, the shotgun in his fists. Cross thought he heard submachine-gun fire, and saw a flash of light from the muzzle of the shotgun.

Raka was up, evidently still able to see, throwing down his submachine gun, leaping toward Cross, a knife in both hands, the blade seemingly almost a foot long. Cross dodged.

One of Raka's Immortals was spraying his submachine gun into the hostages, a man who wasn't bound and gagged throwing himself in front of a blond-haired woman in a stained white evening dress, his body laced with a burst from the Uzi.

Cross rammed the submachine gun toward Raka, firing the H-K as Raka dove into the hallway. Cross ran after him, slamming into another of the terrorists coming out of the hall, the man shouting, "Muhammad—we are under attack."

Cross emptied the K-K into the man's abdomen, the body springing back and sprawling onto the floor, skidding on a trail of blood.

Raka was running along the hallway. Cross let the H-K fall to his side on its sling and ran after him.

More submachine-gun fire.

Raka disappeared down a side corridor, and Cross followed, his left leg in agony now from the earlier wound. He kept running. As Cross ducked down the side corridor into which Raka had disappeared, he saw running men coming, apparently down from the roof. He looked behind him. Men in flak jackets were filling the main hall from the front entrance, two men in civilian clothes bringing up the rear.

Cross didn't wait to say hello—they would be Israeli commandoes, he knew.

He wanted Raka.

The corridor ended abruptly at a set of double doors. Cross slowed, edging along the wall, reloading the H-K with a fresh stick. He took the Beretta into his left hand.

The doors were partially ajar.

He stabbed the muzzle of the H-K against one of the doors and it swung inward.

"Raka!"

If it was an office, there would be windows and Raka would have gotten out through them and onto the grounds, taking his chances outside. "Shit," Cross snarled, bursting through the doorway, lights suddenly coming on, blindingly bright for an instant. Raka—he charged toward him. Cross went to his knees to swat Raka's knife away with the suppressor on the H-K, then got to his feet.

"I cannot hear. But nod if you agree. This!" And Raka brandished the knife.

Cross studied Raka's eyes and slowly crouched, setting the H-K down. He stood again, starting to holster the Beretta, remembering the long magazine, shoving it under his pistol belt instead.

Raka's eyes gleamed. Cross made to draw the Magnum Tanto from its sheath on his chest. Then he remembered that ten out of every eleven people in the world were right-handed, and Raka was holding his knife in his left hand.

Raka's right hand was moving under his jacket.

Cross sidestepped left, his right hand moving for the Beretta, Raka's right hand appearing with a military-sized autoloader. Cross's right fist closed over the Beretta, his left thumb finding the safety, wiping it upward as his body twisted toward Raka, Raka's pistol discharging. Cross felt the hit across his right ribcage, his body stumbling back as he extended the Beretta in his right fist and snapped the trigger double action. Raka's body rocked. Cross backed against a desk. He fired again, then again, Raka's body doubling over, his knees buckling. Cross fired again, and the pistol fell from Raka's hand as it discharged once more into the floor. Cross fired again, Raka's face upturned, both Raka's hands clasped over his chest. Cross pushed himself away from the desk, staggered, and fired again. Raka fell to his knees.

Cross put the Beretta onto the desktop, then gripped the haft of the Magnum Tanto, ripping it from the leather, his arm arcing outward, both fists coming together on the Tanto now, a swing.

Raka's head was severed from his neck, the neck spurting blood, the torso rocking back, the head slamming against the far wall.

Abe Cross sank to his knees and closed his eyes, the Tanto still in his fists.

## *Epilogue*

Abe Cross sat at the piano, his eyes drifting over the scars on the back of his right hand as he began playing Hoagy Carmichael's "Stardust." It was a request from the blonde at the bar with the gin and tonic.

She'd been sitting beside the piano for the longest time, a little drunk, telling him that she'd been one of the hostages at the U.S. embassy takeover six months before. He'd pretended to be shocked, but had recognized her when she'd come into the room. She told him, sniffing back tears and doing a poor job of it, that a man she'd loved, a man she thought had betrayed everything that was decent, had thrown his body between her and a machine gun and saved her life. Cross hadn't corrected her that it was a submachine gun, nor said that he'd seen Warren Corliss die.

He'd just kept playing, pretending he was listening as he thought about the past.

Hughes and one of the Israeli commando team had defused the explosives strapped to the chests of some of the hostages. A man named Joseph Goldman, who Cross thought was probably with the Mossad, had spirited them past the reporters who had descended on the embassy like a swarm of insects. Babcock had taken a bad one in the gut and was carried off to a hospital before Cross had even been found, still kneeling beside the dead body of Muhammad Ibn al Raka.

Cross had been too weary to move, the wound across his shoulder blades opened up again, the wound along the right side of his upper body deeper than he'd thought, and a couple of ribs cracked. He'd almost punctured a lung.

Cross had seen Babcock a couple of times in the Tel-Aviv hospital where they were both taken, but Cross was discharged a few days before Babcock. He hadn't seen Darwin Hughes again.

Joseph Goldman told him the wreckage of the Beechcraft had been found. It appeared that Jeff Feinberg had perished instantly. His family requested that his remains be buried in the Holy Land, and the Israeli government honored their request.

The State Department had sent a man the day before Cross was let out of the hospital. "Nobody knows your faces," the man told him. "We've been able to keep your identities a secret from the press. Except for Feinberg, of course, and we made up a cock-and-bull story about that. You'd be well advised to take an extended vacation before returning to the United States. I told Babcock the same thing a few minutes ago. I'll tell Hughes the same thing," the man said flatly.

"Where is Hughes?"

"If I knew that, he'd have been told already."

Cross had laughed. The man threw a large manila envelope on the bed and left. It contained an airline ticket dated for the following day, prepaid, the destination open; an up-to-date passport with all the necessary stamps and visas to go anywhere he might like to go; a blue leatherette wallet for travelers checks, and inside, travelers checks totaling twenty thousand dollars.

He'd flown to London, taken two weeks to catch up on sleep, eating—the little things like that. All the while he'd looked for an American bar that needed a piano player. Getting a work permit arranged had been surprisingly easy. He guessed they really didn't want him coming home. He'd written to his aunt and told her everything was fine. He'd decided to read *The Koran* to see if it would help him understand why there were good people like the Mujahedin fighters and evil ones like Raka. It had alternately enlightened and confused him.

The blonde—it was the kind of coincidence that made his skin crawl—came back from the bar with her gin and tonic balanced in one hand and his glass in the other. "How come you don't drink?" she asked him, laughing a little.

His hands were starting to play "As Time Goes By," his mind elsewhere. "I still drink—not very much, though," he replied, and forced a smile.

He drew out a run a little longer than it had to be and grabbed for his glass of ginger ale.

Cross had read something that made sense to him: "Perchance your Lord will destroy your enemy, and will make you successors in the land, that He may see how you will act." Raka and the men like him who killed the innocent flunked the test.

"Need a cigarette?" The blonde looked at him questioningly.

Abe Cross told her that wasn't what he needed and kept on playing the piano.

They fight the world's dirtiest wars

# THE HARD CORPS

## by CHUCK BAINBRIDGE

The Hard Corps—Five military misfits whose fighting
skills were forged in the steaming jungles of Vietnam. Now
they are the world's most lethal combat force—and
they're for hire. Using the world as their battlefield, it's
'Nam all over again...and they couldn't be happier.